Graham Lancaster

Graham Lancaster spent seven years with the CBI
before co-founding Biss Lancaster plc, one of the
UK's leading PR consultancies. He is also chairman
of the largest PR group in Europe, with extensive
experience of international business. His previous
books have been widely published and translated
around the world.

Graham Lancaster's latest novel, GRAVE SONG, is
also available from Coronet Books.

Payback

Graham Lancaster

CORONET BOOKS
Hodder and Stoughton

First published in 1997 by Hodder and Stoughton
A division of Hodder Headline PLC
A Coronet paperback

10 9 8 7 6 5 4 3 2 1

A CIP catalogue record for this title
is available from the British Library

ISBN 0 340 66713 3

Typeset by Hewer Text Ltd, Edinburgh
Printed and bound in Great Britain by
Mackays of Chatham, PLC, Chatham, Kent

Hodder and Stoughton Ltd
A division of Hodder Headline PLC
338 Euston Road
London NW1 3BH

To William and Lynda, always . . .

Acknowledgements

The author is grateful for permission to reproduce the DNA 'recipe', from page 3 of *The Thread of Life*, by Susan Aldridge, published by Cambridge University Press, 1996.

Prologue

Allan Calder put down the file and looked inquisitively at the younger man. 'A seemingly stateless black male. North African. Or possibly Angolan. Washed up on the banks of the Tagus,' he said in his soft Highlands burr. 'It's a matter for the Lisbon police. Possibly Europol. But not us.' As chief of MI6, the UK's Secret Intelligence Service, he spent much of his time keeping well out of other people's messes. There was more than enough to do on his dwindling budget.

Neil Gaylord looked uncomfortable, but he was there at the suggestion of his director, Calder's own number two. Despite this he knew he was telling his chief something he did not want to hear. 'Since that report, I've had details of the post-mortem. Technically, the cause of death was drowning. With concussion from the fall a contributory factor. Forensic evidence from his clothes, shoes and hands has identified paint and rust from the Lisbon Almada suspension bridge. That and the drift of the body point to him jumping. Or being pushed.'

The Scot's attention span was notoriously short. 'Drowning. Suicide. Whatever. If you've got something to say, spit it out, man.'

'Yes, chief.' But even now he paused a few moments longer before attempting to make his case. 'He jumped in a state of near delirium – hours, maybe just minutes before he would have died anyway. By choking. You see, sir, he'd been subjected to a mild dosage of some new genetic strain of botulinum toxin.'

Now at last he definitely had Calder's full attention. 'So. It's true. It's bloody true! Those supplies *were* for weapons development.' One of the Service's best sources of intelligence came from banks and certain materials suppliers, companies briefed to report any unusual or suspicious orders or transfers. In this instance a chemical firm had informed them some months earlier of an order from Lisbon for a highly specialised biological agent: a catalyst growth medium. Its only uses were in the manufacture of a type of fertiliser – or for biological weapons. They had informed the Portuguese, whose inspectors had twice made unannounced visits to the plant buying the stuff. Each time, however, they had found evidence only of the perfectly legitimate production of experimental fertilisers.

'And I'm afraid that *this* most certainly makes it our business.' Gaylord passed over the order for another supply of the biological agent.

'Same as before?'

He nodded. 'Sir James Barton, and his genetics company, Temple Bio-Laboratories Inc.'

Calder sighed. 'I knew Barton semi-socially a little. Before his fall from grace. When he was still a junior Foreign Office Minister.'

'What was he like?' The chief almost seemed to be confessing, clearing his conscience of his acquaintance with the controversial man.

'It was difficult to know what to make of him. He was always the loud man at the party. You know the type. Women loved him. He drew them like a magnet. Amazing to watch, actually. But there so obviously had to be another side to him. He's very bright, and you just knew all that hail-fellow-well-met stuff was a front. You sensed he was keeping a large part of himself hidden behind it. When he went bust – that's what, some four years ago now? – I figured that he'd finally revealed all there was to him. A pushy, minor aristocrat trying to bolster depleted family coffers. Sailing close to the wind in high-risk deals. Brilliant businessman. Eye for the main chance. But no worse. It seems I was wrong. Perhaps all this Lisbon business is letting the mask slip for the first time.'

'What should we do?'

'Given who he is, or was . . . I'll have a word myself with DGSS, and see what new they may have on him. There are still probably some political sensitivities around. Ex-Minister and all that. You alert Lisbon Station and get an agent inside Barton's Oeiras operation. That shouldn't be too hard, it's full of ex-pats out there around Cascais. And let's recruit someone very close to Barton. Someone who should really know what's going on. His Finance Director, or someone like that.'

'The Recruiter?'

Calder was always amused by his old friend's new Service nickname. 'Absolutely. It's a perfect job for the Recruiter. Drag old Perry Mitchell away from his cocoa and slippers, and task him to find someone. And this time – tell him from me, not to get this one shot!'

Gaylord laughed. 'I'll quote you on that, chief.'

'Do that.' Calder smiled fleetingly back, but it was clear his mind was already on other things.

Chapter One

The Château Mouton-Rothschild from the legendary year 1945 showed a little brown with age in his uncut, paper-thin crystal glass. As if to draw a line under six years of butchery, the soils, sun and rains of Bordeaux that year had conspired to produce its finest vintage ever.

Sir James Barton, Bt.; first nosed, then tasted it reverentially, finding leather, caramel, earthworm and still enough tannin left to keep the great wine great for a further half-century. But given what he had paid at Christie's auction – £6,000 a bottle, £1,000 a glass – it damn well should be special, he thought to himself. And that was the entire point. This dinner had to be the most memorable, most conspicuously expensive event in the lives of these four extraordinarily powerful men. Men whose own wealth and influence was the match of any medieval despot. Men whose drugs cartels supplied or controlled two-thirds of the world's cocaine trade.

The vast dining hall of the castle was decked with Germanic heraldic flags and bunting, and two huge open fires blazed at each end, billowing smoke periodically across the torch-lit room. Eight embarrassed-looking young men, four on each side, dressed in pantaloons and striped tunics, were holding colourful standards copied from those used at the Palio in Sienna. Seemingly identical-looking, gorgeous serving wenches – each wearing a flaxen wig with plaited tails, flowing waisted dresses and displaying acres of suck-me, wet-nurse cleavage – waited on table. Two were allocated to each guest, there to attend to their every need. Now, and in mock *droit de seigneur*, later . . .

This heraldic bouillabaisse was exactly the effect that Barton wanted. He had paid a film-set designer to dress and light the mock Spanish castle, built in the 1930s by an American media mogul, and re-create the baronial Europe of Ruritania up there in the hills behind Acapulco. Style and Old World money were, he knew, his strongest cards with these world-weary men. His own hereditary baronetcy, his Eton, Oxford and Guards background, along with his handsome, tall, aristocratic bearing, his accent and rich, deep voice added up to the one thing they each lacked. Class. But if their money could not themselves buy class, it sure as hell had enabled them to buy him.

Standing up to his full height, he gently tapped the table with the Masonic ring on the little finger of his left hand, calling for their attention. At six foot two and sixteen stone, he cut a powerful figure. His baronet's badge hung from miniature-wide ribbon under the collar, close up below the black tie to his dinner jacket. Under his thick fair hair, his piercing blue eyes shone with enthusiasm. The small, up-turned nose and the way his upper teeth always seemed to show gave him an Irish look, and there was a distinctive dimple cut deeply in his chin.

'Gentlemen,' he boomed. 'This has been your fourth meeting together, since Aruba. And only my second with you as a group since being appointed your – what may I call myself? – your chief operating officer. I think the figures I presented to you earlier covering our first six months trading fully demonstrate the wisdom of your decision to form the Aruba Alliance, formalising the existing trading relationships between your great organisations, and developing them further, for greater profit and mutual protection.' He spoke slowly, using even clearer diction than usual, knowing the Burmese Warlord had only basic English. 'Building on the foresight of our Colombian brothers in calling your first ever joint meeting in Aruba, you now have a highly sophisticated international trading company, and an exciting business plan to drive us forward to even greater success. With me as your first – and I hope long-serving! – CEO.

'Our annualised combined sales turnover is running at some $300 billion a year. That's bigger than the national income of many countries. And the treasury management of your huge cash flow is now as efficient as that of any major corporate, as my figures showed.

'But no less important is combining our strength to fight the biggest threat any of you have yet faced, from the new US-sponsored anti-drugs taskforce. From the trade sanctions imposed on your governments. And from new sequestration and deportation powers. You have charged me to develop a plan to counter this. Fast. We need to send a shock wave that will be felt across the world. The US President, especially, must learn that you are not mere local criminals or gangsters, but a significant and highly organised world force. I will not fail you. You have my pledge . . .

'All that's for the near future. But for now, tonight, gentlemen, please join me in a toast. Your glasses have been filled with the finest wine any man has ever drunk.'

On cue, the serving wenches came forward to hold back the chairs of their charges, indicating that they should stand. Getting up uncertainly, the four men cut an odd sight. Each was wearing a dinner suit, although the young Mexican – the one extrovert amongst them – had already taken off the white bow tie to his white tux. He contrasted with the quiet, suspicious-eyed, bearded Colombian, the baby-faced Burmese and, the oldest amongst them, the balding, Medici-nosed Italian-American. Whereas these three could have been a group of powerful bankers meeting together, the Mexican looked and behaved more like a playboy night-club entertainer. He even liked to be known as Dino, jointly named after his favourite star and his favourite Ferrari.

'The toast is: the Aruba Alliance!' Barton called, thrusting out his arm.

The first to drink, Dino spat out the precious wine, spraying it across the table. 'This is panther piss!' he yelled, laughing. 'I wouldn't put it on my zits, man!' He then grabbed one of his girls and tried to force her to try it, the glass at her lips, and wine pouring down her chin and into her cleavage.

The others looked at him coldly, each wishing they could have found somebody else equally dominant in the vital Mexican market. 'To the Aruba Alliance,' they said in unison, the importance of what they were agreeing lost on none. As a group they did indeed already have the economic power of a medium-sized nation. Now, in responding to the threat from the US President's taskforce, they had just voted Barton a foreign policy and defence budget to match.

Lydia Barton was having a good day.

One of her team of TV buyers had succeeded in booking cheap test-market rates for a campaign the TV contractor knew was no more a test-market than he was the King of Siam. This was a dream start for their relationship with the new client. But what had made her most happy was the advance sight of the independent media audit on the agency's biggest client, Eastern Foods. It showed how well the media department had bought for them over the recent months. Most of the budget, over £35 million, had been spent on TV through her team. No audit would be complete, however, without one or two niggles, and this was no exception. There was the usual criticism about not enough centre breaks, which minimise channel zapping. And a crack about too much going to Channel 6. This last point was all the more irritating for being true. But, all in all, a great report for a tough and demanding client to see.

As TV Buying Group Head in the media department of Fielding Katz Toombes – FKT – Lydia, aged twenty-seven, headed a team of six responsible for buying almost £150 million of TV slots a year at this, the London office of the middle-ranking advertising agency. 'Philip!' she called out.

Philip Kerr's workstation was just outside the ever-open door of her small office and he shuffled in immediately, his hesitant yet unhurried movements and body language faintly irritating, as ever. Lydia did not like people who walked slowly. 'How do we come out?' he asked nervously, nodding at the open media audit on her desk. As usual the untidy outer perimeters of her office were lost in a dark gloom at this time of a winter's afternoon. She never switched on the overhead lights, and used instead an old-fashioned anglepoise lamp, throwing a stark pool of yellow on her messy desk.

'It's good stuff. Pretty damn good,' she replied.

'But . . . With you, there's always a but,' he said, quite bravely.

'Just a little one. About your friends at Channel 6. And I've decided now is as good a time as any to wrap up our next year's deal with them.' There was a note of mischievous steel in her voice.

'Don't squeeze them too hard,' he warned. 'We did well out of them last year. They waived the penalty charges in October, remember? When we had to change that detergent campaign at the last minute.'

But he could see that she was barely listening as she called up BARB data on her DDS screen. 'Yes. But in turn, Philip, *I* did *not* appreciate getting that call at one o'clock on the nail a couple of weeks ago. With a pre-emption on the *News at Ten* centre break.' All TV advertising has to be confirmed by agencies at least two months in advance of the screening, by the Advance Booking Deadline – the AB Deadline. Despite this, media space – like any other valuable, tradable commodity – operates in a moving market, and media owners reserve the right to take advantage of this by gazumping advertisers if it suits them. A TV contractor can tell an agency as late as one o'clock on the day of transmission that their client's ad will not be showing on the slot promised.

Reaching for the phone, she tapped the pad to automatic-dial the station's Sales Director. It was the week between Christmas and New Year, and she was late agreeing the next year's agency deal with him. Some contracts were done client by client. Others, as now, agency by agency. They had held three meetings already, the last with her boss, the Media Director.

'Lydia. Hi. Enjoy the little party?' The Sales Director had a phone system that flashed on his screen the name and customer details of incoming calls.

This kind of telecom wizardry was, Lydia felt, efficient, but definitely iffy. 'The little party was fun.' Of course there had been nothing remotely 'little' about the station's Christmas bash for its largest customers. First-class air tickets and an overnight in Los Angeles, taking in being filmed as extras in a bar scene for an episode of the latest cult half-hour sit-com, followed by dinner with the to-die-for cast members. Channel 6, the *Daily Mail* and *Reader's Digest* were all famed for laying on great client entertainment. But for the lucky recipients, understatement went with the territory. Unshockable was cool. Been there, done that was *de rigueur*.

'And just wait 'til you get the TVRs for Christmas Eve and

Day. It's going to be terrific. Just like I said.' The analysis of viewing figure for programmes was produced by media analysts BARB nine days after screening, and formed an essential part of the negotiating armoury for both sides.

Lydia had the latest available data up on her DDS, its green glow making her look spooky in the gloomy office. The system enabled her to analyse the viewing audiences for virtually any commercial TV programming, terrestrial or satellite, broken down by area and any one of fourteen standard audiences. 'So what happened to the new sci-fi programme earlier this month, then? It bombed.'

'It'll build. A slower burner than we thought. But remember how *The X Files* grew.'

'Sure. And I also remember when RAC men used to salute my grandfather. That was a long time ago too. Anyway, that's not why I called. We need to finalise our discussions on next year's deal.' Her tone had now perceptibly changed, and the hint of estuary English she used when negotiating hard crept in. Despite all the computers and sophisticated media evaluation techniques, this was still, above all, a trader's world. A good media buyer would feel completely at home as a bond trader, or in an open-cry commodity's pit. 'We've had our arguments already about ratings. And we *still* say you're not investing in the youth market. Cheap imports and a nightly hour of poor man's MTV isn't cutting it. And you know it.'

'But I've shown you the new schedule . . .' He had also toughened up his attitude, knowing what was coming.

'Like you showed me the youth schedule in October. And it didn't deliver! Did it?' Time to press home her advantage. 'Time's tight now, and the bottom line is this. Thirty million pounds. Which, after media inflation, is up twelve per cent in real terms on last year, and raises your share of our spend to nineteen per cent. For twenty per cent discount against market price. And promised slots. With more first in breaks. That's it.'

'Twenty per cent! When you *know* what we're going to deliver on the ratings?' The shock in his voice sounded real enough. 'Can't do it. It'd kill me out here.'

'It's a tough New Year we're staring at too. Clients expect us to make every penny sweat. And a lot – a *lot* – are pulling out of TV completely. Throwing serious money now at integrated marketing. Direct mail, loyalty cards, big sponsorships, customer magazines, tailor-mades with big retailers . . . It's a whole New Millennium, in case you hadn't heard. *I* don't like it. *You* don't like it. But our delicate sensitivities, and our bonus pots, don't figure too high on clients' priorities just now. Curious, that . . .'

He knew her well enough to know this was long past the stage of being a first negotiating gambit. It seriously was the deal on offer. 'You're putting a real bite on us with this, Lydia,' he said, fighting to keep the weary air of resignation out of his voice. He had expected to go to fifteen per cent, at worst. 'I'll get back later today.'

Philip had been standing beside her, listening nervously. When she hung up he said, 'You'll need him one day. There's such a thing as being too aggressive out there, you know.' He was an old hand. At forty-nine he had seen everything, but was now burnt out and afraid of losing his job in the teeth of the bewildering explosion of media around him. New digital TV channels along with new satellite stations and magazines seemed to be springing up every day. Narrowcasting, not broadcasting was the flavour of the day. And as for the 'new media', and Web sites . . . He just hoped he could make it to early retirement by cringing below the parapets.

'No there isn't. That wasn't me killing him out there, it was the market. He knows that. So should you, Philip.'

'What I do know is that for a vegan, you don't mind blood

baths in business,' he went on mournfully, not accepting what she had said.

Lydia knew that he should have got out, or been kicked out, years ago, for his own good as much as the agency's. He always boasted over twenty years' experience under his belt, but in reality it amounted to one year's experience repeated twenty times over. It had taken Lydia just a month to learn even that as a trainee. But it was not just his age. The nature of the business had changed. Fifteen billion dollars' worth of advertising was now placed by media buyers like Lydia each year in Britain alone; $130 billion across Europe as a whole. With billions more in the USA – far the largest market of all. It was now a big, big business and much more aggressive than in the past. Especially in the print media. And people moved around so much more. Apart from a handful of real mates, relationships mattered far less. In fact they could get in the way. But she had seen Philip's hand shaking and the sweat sticking to his shirt so often that she had carried him recently. Each knew it, but for their different reasons neither openly acknowledged what was going on. It did not fit her tough-bitch image, and he in turn would not be able to cope with being helped by a 'slip of a girl'.

She was in no mood to start some shallow debate on ve-getarianism. 'I need a coffee,' she said, to change the subject. 'I'll fetch you one. Never say I'm an uncaring boss.'

Standing by the machine, she kicked it gently in impa-tience as it served up what passed for espressos. Around her, the floor housed the forty-strong media department. There were a few small offices around the perimeter like her own, but mostly the media buyers, planners and researchers had work areas in an open-plan layout. Each was fairly standard, with a PC, phone, calculator and desk lamp, and like all media units, was inherently untidy – littered with newspapers, magazines, tapes and mountainous in-trays groaning under thick media reports and media owners' sales blurb. Everyone had a pinboard, and this gave them the chance for a little self-expression. Media remains a heavily male preserve, still somehow cocooned from feminism and other now mainstream social mores. As a result there were enough advertising stills and calendars of pneumatic women to shame any garage workshop, along with sporting heroes, girlfriends and ancient media schedules. Philip's was the exception, and summarised the man. Family photographs of his wife and three children, along with one of his sailing boat – pathetically for a man of his age, an old Mirror dinghy he had built in the garage. As for Lydia's pinboard, she had a token picture of an oiled-up Arnold Schwarzenegger from his Mr Universe days, to make a statement about all the silicon babes *she* had to endure around the place. But the rest were magazine tear-outs of animals – especially pigs – along with a couple of photographs of Oliver, her dog, as ever looking cross about something.

When she got back with the coffees, Philip handed her a Post-it. 'Can you call this number? The man wouldn't give his name, or say what it was about. Sounded like a Midlander. A Brummie.'

Lydia took it and sat down heavily. 'Thanks.'

'You OK?' Philip asked, concerned about her. She had suddenly gone pale.

'I'm fine.'

'Is that call bad news? Do you know who it is?'

Turning away, she made to go back to her office. 'Oh yes,' she said grimly. 'I know exactly who it is.'

She also knew the bombings were about to begin again.

*　　　*　　　*

'So. You will come? Port Moresby is exciting. A big village. You will like it.' Chancey tried to look relaxed, but like all natives he found it impossible to lie directly without displaying some tell-tale sign. For him that was scratching his head. He did not know he was doing it, but Banto certainly noticed.

'Will go. *Kepala* and elders agree to it,' Banto said, speaking slowly, his limited English very rusty. He did not like Chancey, a man about the same age as him, early twenties. The stranger was wise in the ways of the outside world, however, and his arrival two months earlier at the main Chenga tribal village had caused a sensation. Isolated in the foothills of the Madang highlands of Papua New Guinea, PNG, the Chenga were still a Stone-Age society. A short, almost pygmy race, like the Simbai tribe, they had not discovered the wheel, had no beast of burden and no knowledge of metallurgy. Chancey's bag of magic, therefore, had excited and overawed most of Banto's fellow villagers: mirrors, mouth organs, cassette players, a Polaroid camera, shiny steel axes, fishing hooks, a pistol . . .

This was Chancey's third, and he hoped, final visit. The 25,000 square miles of unexplored valleys and mountains, home to around a million tribespeople, were discovered as recently as 1933 by four young Australian gold prospectors. But while white men remained fascinated by the mystery or profit potential of the wilderness, most Papua New Guineans of the cities, like Chancey, wanted nothing to do with it. To them it was simply a degrading reminder of their own recent primitive ancestry. Their aspirations were now to be found in the movies and magazines from Australia, the USA, Britain and Japan. 'Good. We leave tomorrow. Early. Good!' He offered Banto a cigarette, but was refused.

'No more take?' Banto asked with fear in his eyes, protectively holding his badly bruised arm.

'No more take.' Again Chancey scratched his head.

Banto nodded, not convinced, and left him. He was in some ways pleased to be going on the journey, as he still felt like an outsider amongst his own people. When just fifteen, he had been singled out by a white Christian missionary and his wife, evangelist Americans, who had one day trekked into the village and stayed over a month. As their first contact ever with the outside, the polite village elders had tolerated their eccentricities, and many – still out of politeness – had allowed themselves to be baptised, including the intelligent and inquisitive young Banto. During this time the Americans had taught him some English to act as their main interpreter, but when suddenly they left to 'convert' other tribes, the *kepala* – the chief – had refused their request to take him with them on their mission. Despite this, his association with the outsiders had left Banto a misfit, ostracised by his peers. It had also, of course, made him the obvious go-between when Chancey turned up.

That night, Banto slept in the creaking atap wood *longhaus*, in animal closeness with the other men. Females were strictly forbidden from entering: the Chenga only spend time with their women to mate – and then never at night. The elders, their beds by tradition closest to the door, spoke at length of the importance they attached to him making the brief visit to the outside. They knew from other tribes with greater exposure to the outsiders that their own world was soon to change. There had been frightening stories of great creations cutting down the forests, and others carving wounds into the mountainside. And they themselves had often seen the noisy, shiny birds – the *balas* – above them, an unwelcome sight and sound of tomorrow. Banto had been told to accept this crude man's invitation to visit his big village, Port Moresby, and become the tribe's spy. To learn about things, and then return and warn them of what to expect, and how to prepare for the battles ahead.

Much later, as the other men slept, and the smoky fireboxes hanging below the stilted floor died out, Banto lay awake, listening to the sounds of the forest: monkeys, birds and frogs. In the darkness of the fetid interior, staring at the blackened rafters, hung with jawbones of the countless pigs eaten there at feasts, he wished his father, mother and sisters were still alive to help him. But they had been massacred, along with six others, in a ritual 'Payback' clan skirmish two years earlier. He had been out hunting all day and found them on his return. Found what was left of them, that is. The aggressor clan took heads as trophies, and, like the Chenga themselves, were cannibals. The inevitable Payback revenge attack, a month later, had butchered eight of the old enemy, with Banto himself despatching two. He had also, for the first time, eaten the flesh of one of the warriors he killed, as a symbol of total victory. The forest echoed with these and other memories, and filled him with foreboding about the trip. Something was telling him he might never return. This could be his last night amongst his own people. His warrior's heart was heavy.

Chancey meantime was in the visitors' bark-walled bush house on the edge of the village. Beside him was the latest young girl he had attracted with his Western magic. As he taught his eager student different kinds of tricks – perversions he had picked up from porn videos – he thought wildly about all the money he was about to make. When he delivered Banto to the American, Bolitho, and once the tests were checked, he would at last be able to leave PNG. For Australia. Life as a street criminal – a 'rascal' as PNG slang over-innocently calls such gangsters and murderers – was no longer for him. He wanted out. A new life. The excitement of it all rushed through his body, and he pulled her head down fiercely by the hair until she gagged, panting for air.

*   *   *

The fire roared in the Adam fireplace, but Sir James Barton none the less rooted at it aggressively with the poker before throwing on yet another log. Outside the study window snow continued to fall on the parkland that stretched to the misty horizon. It was even beginning to settle now on the frozen lake beyond the ha-ha.

Cognac before lunch had become the norm at Temple Manor, and Barton helped himself to his second XO Hine of the morning. Lady Barton, his American wife, Madeleine, came in and frowned at him.

'Yes, Maddie. I know. It's not even noon.' His big, heavy-set frame made its presence felt in even the grandest of rooms.

'Well. At least you're not attacking the humidor yet. That's something,' she scolded half-heartedly.

He looked at her sharply. At thirty-two, and his second wife, she was some twenty years his junior. Despite everything she had been one of his better ideas, he thought to himself. Her family, top-drawer Philadelphia, had put Maddie, an only child, through all the upper middle-class rites of passage: Swiss finishing school – to perfect her French and Italian – before reading literature at Harvard, followed by a short spell as a classy photographic model. It was whilst over in London on a *Harpers'* shoot that she had met Barton – then a Member of Parliament and junior Treasury Minister – at a dinner party thrown by her godfather. Having monopolised her attention, at the end of the evening he had hurriedly invited her to join a weekend house party in the country before she flew back home.

Whereas her affection for him took time to grow, it had been love at first sight for his eighteenth-century ancestral home, Temple Manor. Immediately drawn to its patina of neglect, to her surprise she found herself longing to respond to its desperate plea for tender loving care and, of course, money. At the time, ten years earlier, Barton had faced monumental debts – from his divorce, the costs of upkeep, and the Lloyd's débâcle. But then he, like scores of British aristocrats before him, suddenly found salvation staring him in the face. In the shape of a beautiful young American, and her family's old money.

The elevation from headstrong American heiress to Lady Barton, mistress of the 1,200-acre Temple Estate had, after their St Margaret's wedding and House of Commons reception, appeared seamless to the outside world. *Le style anglais* was so right on her and, like the young Grace Kelly whom she so much resembled, she had always looked regal. The photogenic golden couple were seen at all the right places, did the Season, and were never out of the society and lifestyle magazines. Barton's political career was racing ahead, his charm and good looks making him a regular TV face, and with Madeleine's energy, design skills and capital, the Manor was inching nearer its former splendour. Life had become near perfect. Perfect, that was, until the twins arrived – both girls – and until the scandal . . .

A software business had gone belly-up on him, forcing his company into receivership, and – thanks to his personal guarantees and open-ended Lloyd's 'name' commitment – Barton into bankruptcy. One more statistic from the twenty thousand cases a year. A suspended jail sentence for false accounting also followed. His ministerial career ended in a blaze of publicity as he was viciously hounded from office – by then at the FCO. Soon after, he resigned his Parliamentary seat. That had been four years earlier, and until his formal discharge, he had endured the humiliation heaped on all bankrupts: denied a bank account or credit card; prevented from retaining more than basic living costs from any earnings; and disbarred from taking a directorial role in any business. But despite all this, driving himself furiously and working closely with *wunderkind* consultant, the American Tom Bates, he had in just eighteen months generated enough cash to discharge the debts to his creditors through a reverse take-over – fronted by Bates – of a struggling, quoted biotech company. James Barton had lost none of his legendary ability to spot a rising sector early. Rumours of exciting new research soon had the shares rocketing and he had – through Bates – capitalised. Still bitter and angry, he bought his commercial freedom. Now he was back. And out for revenge.

'What time's cook doing lunch?' he asked, suddenly craving the first cigar of the day that she had just skilfully tried to deny him. 'Tom's running late with the weather.'

'It's pretty bad on the M40, according to the radio,' she replied. 'Lots of accidents. Hope he's OK. Lunch'll be fine. Cook's got some of her game soup simmering, and it's just beef to follow. Nothing to spoil. Do you want me to make myself scarce once we've eaten?' She was well used to semi-social, semi-business meals, and knew that she had little to contribute when he talked shop. It was not that she was just some vacuous, pretty-pretty wife, it was simply that what he did, his endless business ventures, bored her silly. It was all detail: spreadsheets, cash-flow forecasts and trial balances – and you either completely immersed yourself in it, or you didn't.

At first, she had badly missed all the pre-scandal social life, when London's literary, arty types and politicians had joined the local county set to fill the Manor over dreamy, mischievous weekends. And of course the Season. But now she had learned to settle for less. Their usual guests now were pleasant enough scientific boffins, entrepreneurs and money men. Or of late the occasional South Americans,

Europeans and Nigerians he sometimes lavishly entertained. The Arubans, as she had heard him call them in off-guard moments. These were from that secret and she assumed Masonic side to his life of which he never talked. But if there was now more talk of Mammon than Molière, whatever he was doing, along with the allowance from her own trust money, had kept the Grade One listed Georgian roof-tiles over their heads.

The sound of a car drew them to the window, and they saw Tom Bates's maroon Jeep Cherokee tearing up the long avenue of limes to the house. Barton's mood immediately lightened and he went out to greet the American, his closest adviser and nearest thing to a friend he still had left. 'Look at you in that thing. The Fulham farmer! I bet that's the first time you've ever engaged four-wheel drive in your life.'

Tom grinned from under his floppy felt hat. 'Not true,' he objected. 'I distinctly remember engaging it once when mounting the kerb. To park near Harrods.'

'Sure,' Barton laughed, running in with him out of the snow. 'But I keep telling you to dump that American heap. Buy a real car, like a Range Rover. A better car. An *English* car.'

'English? Rover's about as English now as Prince Albert and your precious Windsors, *mein Freund!*'

They continued their usual sparring as Tom took off his coat and they made their way to the study. Maddie was standing by the fire, arm resting on the mantel. If she was honest with herself, she would have admitted to striking a pose for him, Lady Hamilton-like. And to dressing for him that day, as she had so many others. She had never been unfaithful, and never expected to be, but the handsome, cultivated, Ivy League fellow American was so much nearer her ideal than Jim could ever be.

Tom had more than an inkling of all this, but had the

manners – and the good business-sense – not to take advantage of it. 'Maddie. You look a picture. As ever,' he smiled, and walked over to her.

His social kiss left the old-fashioned, masculine scent of him around her. It always made her blush slightly at the thought that he might somehow read her mind. She liked her men to smell of shaving cream. Jim, in contrast, used an electric razor, to save precious time. 'Goodness. Your face is as cold as ice,' she said, holding his eyes. 'Let me fix you a drink. The usual?'

Having mixed his Jack Daniel's, she left them talking to fuss over lunch and check that Nanny had the twins ready. Tom watched her go. 'You know, it's like Robert Adam also designed Maddie to blend right in here, alongside all his architecture, finishings, carpets and the rest. Absolute class.'

'And I *don't* blend? She's the cuckoo here, not me.'

Tom laughed at him. He was one of the very few people who could, and the only person able to speak his mind to the bully, and still escape his legendary rages. 'Well, *there* you are again. Mr Paranoid! How are *we* today? You English bankrupts are too damn sensitive. In the States, surviving Chapter Eleven is admired. Guys put it on their CVs.'

Barton spat out an expletive. The scandal was still a festering open wound with him, and a taboo subject within his earshot. 'Why is it I take this from you? If anyone else spoke to me like that—'

'It's my boyish charm. And because you pay too much to ignore me. You chose me as a big ticket superstar advisor. So if you don't listen to me, ergo, you're criticising your own judgement. And you're never wrong. Right?'

'There's such a thing as being too damned bright,' Barton said, with an edge.

'Negative. I don't buy that. And nor do you. There *is* such a thing as being a pain in the smart ass, though. That's one of *my* faults. But someone has to knock that chip off your shoulder. It's no big deal to have gone under financially. Happens every day. Get over it. Get out of denial. All I meant was that Maddie has a timeless beauty. Like this desk, or that vase. I've called you many things in my day, but beautiful isn't one of them.'

Somewhat mollified, Barton waved to him to sit down.

Tom, now thirty, had been the youngest ever partner with World Management Consulting Inc., the firm which, alongside McInsey, ranked as undisputed leaders in international business counselling. When, as the New York-based consultancy's brightest star, he had been seconded to the European head office in London six years earlier, Barton had negotiated the equivalent of a day a week of his time on an on-going basis. The two had first met two years before this in France when Barton, climbing the political ladder as a PPS to the Chancellor, had given a guest lecture on entrepreneurship at INSEAD. Tom, on a post-grad course there, made it his business to get to know him that night over dinner. Afterwards back in the States he had opportunistically kept in touch as part of his relentless networking and, on coming to London, soon won a series of assignments from the man's portfolio of businesses interests.

When Barton later become a Foreign Office Minister, he had to distance himself from day-to-day control of his companies. To circumvent this, he made Tom a director, still pulling the strings as the major shareholder, having also moved his assets – including the Manor – safely offshore. At the time of the bankruptcy, WMC had itself been an unsecured creditor and, owed £100,000 in fees and costs, unsurprisingly refused to have any more to do with him. Tom, however, agreed to continue in a personal capacity and at his own risk, for two days a week, negotiating his contract down accordingly with WMC. They had acquiesced to this only after Tom described Barton's determination to clear his debts and prove himself again. If Tom was right, it seemed the only way they would ever see their money again.

The arrangement had suited everyone well. Retaining Tom as a consultant and trustee meant that despite the bankruptcy restrictions, he could still act as a director by proxy. As for Tom, he had share options appreciating nicely, and still enjoyed the challenges Jim's eclectic businesses threw up. Most recently this had included their take-over of a small investment house, and poaching a crack treasury management team to handle the huge funds now flowing through their new Curaçao company.

For him, Barton had meant consistent excitement, challenge, real operational influence – something normally denied consultants – as well as the chance of earning serious capital for himself. Despite the bullying side of Barton's nature, the unique experience and influence to which he was exposed through the man's businesses had spoiled him for anything else.

'But on to business . . .' Tom said seriously, sitting opposite Barton by the fire. 'The word from the City isn't good.' There was never a good time to bring Barton news he did not want to hear. Get it over quickly, that was always the best approach. 'Phillips & Drew and Merrill Lynch now also want out of the stock. They were our last two "holds". Come tomorrow, when their circulars hit the screens, we'll have a clean sweep of "sell" recommendations.'

Barton looked surprisingly relaxed at the news. Phillips & Drew were Temple Bio-Laboratories's own broker. For them to rank the stock a 'sell' was doubly disastrous. 'So, I take it another rights issue would be out of the question?' he joked.

'They were left picking up over fifty per cent of the last one they underwrote,' Tom reminded him needlessly. He was worried at Barton's jocular reaction to a scenario which could very easily escalate the business into receivership, with all the now familiar nightmares which went with it. The bank held a £40 million debenture in the massively geared UK and US quoted biotech company, with no sign of how it would ever be repaid. But now he could hear Maddie and the twins coming down the staircase. 'We'll pick up on this after lunch, shall we? It's real serious this time.'

Barton stood up, a twinkle in his eye. 'Don't worry about it. The cavalry is just over the hill. Arriving any moment,' he said, enigmatically.

'What do you mean?'

'I mean we're almost ready to tell the world about starting clinical trials on the biggest medical breakthrough since . . . since Mrs Pasteur burned the milk.' He barked a laugh.

'What breakthrough? The transgenic pigs? They already know about all that—'

Serious now, Barton looked directly at him. 'No. Not our genetically engineered porker friends. No, Tom. There are some things so secret I don't even tell you about. But we're close. So close to it now.'

Tom was furious to discover that as a director he had been excluded. Given his punishing workload on his WMC clients, on top of Barton's businesses – still in theory only two days a week of his billable hours – it was an increasing struggle to keep up with everything the man was doing. Warning bells were most definitely clattering. 'Close to what?' he asked sharply.

'To the ultimate cure-all vaccine. For some cancers, certain heart conditions, AIDS and hep. B. More things than even I can guess. We both know that Temple Bio-Labs needs a real market boost if it's to survive. If we ever needed a big financial push, it's now. And here I am, about to pull off a launch that will stand the medical world on its head, and force the whining brokers, analysts and journalists to eat their words.

'I've found it, Tom. I really have. Snake oil. The medicine man's dream. The medical Holy Grail. Don't even think of asking me how, but I've done it. And now I need your help to explain the product to all the cynics in the City. Once they realise what we've got, they'll be clamouring for stock.'

And, he thought to himself, given the free hand he had been granted by the Aruba Alliance to fight the US President's anti-drugs initiative, he would now be able to raise the £2 million of his own money he needed to deliver. A £2 million investment that would earn him billions more as part of the astronomic success fee he would extract from the drugs cartel. With it he would finally bury the tarnished image of titled, criminal bankrupt, of disgraced Foreign Office Minister and media joke . . . to become quite conceivably the richest man in Europe.

And it all hinged entirely on the next crucial four weeks.

Chapter Two

'**A**re you up for it, *Lady* Lydia? Yes or no?'

It was the direct question that she had been dreading for months. She had joined the Animal Freedom Warriors, the AFW, over a year earlier, having become impatient with the other animal rights groups with which she had been involved from her university days. Since then, her commitment and courage had never once been questioned, a veteran of numerous hunt sabotages and raids on farms, laboratories and meat-product factories. But this was different.

'Are you really sure of the facts?' she parried, feeling exposed before the small action unit.

Sam Thrower, their commander, snorted. An out-of-work college lecturer, he was no less a class warrior than an animal rights militant. He disliked Lydia and people like her. Privileged rich bitches who wore their fashionable social consciences like their tiaras and designer labels. He had engineered this showdown and intended to enjoy himself. 'Of course we are. They're using mice, rats *and* macaque monkeys in there. And, of course, the stars of his show – the transgenic, not to say *photo*genic little piggies. You've seen the colour supplement article on the "reformed bankrupt".' He tossed over the magazine, but she had no need to look at it again. The image of the two young pigs jostling for the cameraman's attention, and smiling cheekily at him, would never leave her. 'And we had a lab assistant temping in the place last month. She's seen it all. Now come on, your ladyship. If you haven't got the bottle for this one, just say so, and make room for someone who has.' His Midlands accent sneered the words.

They were asking her to raid and fire-bomb one of her own father's biotech plants.

'Stop making speeches. Just tell us when we go in,' she responded, her voice sounding more confident than she actually felt.

'You'll be told when we're ready,' he replied smugly. 'I'm tightening security. MI5 will be throwing a lot more resources at us again, thanks to the new cease-fire in Ireland. Just like the old Rimington days, trying to justify their poxy existence. So sharpen up and shut up. Got it?'

The small group muttered assent. All except Lydia. She stood up, breathed in deeply and pushed her tight polo-neck sweater into her jeans, knowing exactly the effect she was having on him. 'We're right behind you, commander,' she said with mock deference. Freeing her long blonde hair from the combs holding it up, she let it cascade, shaking her head forward. Behind his aggressive attitude towards her, she well knew that the overweight man nursed serious hots for her. 'Dream on, loser,' she said to herself, blew him a sarcastic kiss and left to face the freezing London night.

She found a cab mercifully quickly, and took it to Euston where, ever mindful of security – and without the need of Sam Thrower's reminders – she lost herself in the Underground to complete her journey to Pimlico and the small, stuccoed terraced house she shared with Oliver, her Airedale terrier. Some of her fellow activists were strongly opposed to the keeping of pets, to pet shops, breeders and the whole pet industry; Lydia, however, loved the bad-tempered dog more than anyone she knew with just two legs right then.

Meetings of the AFW in dingy, student flats always called for an immediate bath on her return home, and long baths called for a cavernous glass of chilled chardonnay. Having first walked and fed Oliver, she was soon soaking in the six-foot Duker, trying to relax – something she found difficult. Work as a media buyer was stressful: all shouting, bargaining, and bluffing on the phone. But it suited her high energy nature, soaking up some of her hyper-activity, as well as paying well. Outside its consuming maelstrom she really lived for her many causes: The Anti-Slavery League, Tourism Concern, Greenpeace and Shelter. Her involvement, however, in direct action with the AFW was not something she ever talked about. To anyone. Although all her friends well knew her passion for animal rights.

It was a life that left little room for long-standing relationships, but then that was not something she presently wanted in her busy world. In any case, her looks did not naturally invite flirtatious attention. She was always just a few pounds overweight and shortish, at five feet four inches. As a teenager, unlike her two best friends, her picture had never made it as one of *Country Life*'s weekly debby 'girls in pearls': something considered a great county accolade at the time. With her strong facial resemblance to her father – blue eyes, ski-jump button nose and dimpled chin – she was what even her own mother called striking, rather than classically pretty. Except, that was, for the thick mane of natural, honey-blonde hair which, along with those blue eyes and wide mouth, she had learned as a small girl to use to imitate real beauty whenever it suited her. She knew how to conjure up its fickle mask at will, like an actress playing a part. She enjoyed the power of surprise it gave her. It worked well in her career too, where the trick was to be popular, but tough. There was a freedom in plainness – freedom from all the bimbo stereotyping and macho hassle.

Freedom to be accepted as one of the boys. And yet, with just a few facial tricks and gestures, she could make any man she wanted look twice.

Drying herself later in a towelling robe, she poured another glass of wine and thought again about the unpleasant meeting of the unit earlier. She had no qualms about fire-bombing one of her father's plants. It was something that had somehow always seemed inevitable, the irony lost on no one. But it certainly called for renewed contact with him. Not to warn him, of course. Just to touch base, and push him to talk about what he was doing, and why. Besides, she was long overdue a visit to the old rogue. She would call him tomorrow.

Chancey was relieved to find his way back to the small plane, still safely where he had parked it. They had just completed a seven-hour trek from the Chenga village to reach the clearing by the early afternoon. It had rained incessantly most of the time, and now it had finally stopped the humidity was almost unbearable. Added to this, he was suffering bad gastric problems from the barely edible native diet of *kaukau* sweet potatoes, dried river fish, wild rice and the warm, wine-red root brew that passed for beer. There was bottled water in the plane's storage bay, and he ran the last fifty yards to get to it.

In contrast, Banto felt fine physically: a lifetime of dawn-to-dusk hunting meant he never even raised a sweat on the trek. But emotionally he was a wreck. As they confronted the plane, the reality of what he was about to do had suddenly struck him. What the night before had seemed like a big adventure, was now overwhelmingly threatening. The man had made no attempt to converse with him on the journey, and his attitude to Banto had changed dramatically now that he had got his way. Gone was the encouraging smile and friendly manner; in its place was an aggressive, dismissive attitude that made Banto feel like a trapped animal.

Having used the radio for a while, Chancey gestured for Banto to climb in the Twin Otter beside him. Banto, however, now had different ideas. Going with this man in the machine suddenly seemed a very bad move after all. Going to the big village he had described also seemed bad. He no longer trusted the man. His hunter's instincts warned him of danger everywhere. 'No go! *Tidak, tidak pergi!*' he shouted, eyes wide. 'I stay.' He slapped himself hard on the thigh in agitation.

Chancey had been expecting something like this. Jumping down, he stood beside Banto smiling his friendly smile again. 'Don't panic. Let's talk,' he said.

'No talk. I no go!' Banto was resting his hand menacingly on the hard-wood knife hanging at the side of the tanget covering his buttocks. His bow, long arrows and quiver of arrow-point holders were strung across his chest, and Chancey had seen for himself the lethal speed and accuracy with which the warriors could use them.

Chancey was watching Banto very carefully, knowing that the native would have no compunction in killing him if the mood took him. 'OK. Fine. You stay. Think about it some more, and I *kam beck* again soon. You my *bikpela nambawan* you know. Maybe you change your mind later. OK?' Chancey held his arms open wide in a gesture of reasonableness. The pidgin English he used – *tok pisin*, talk pidgin – was common in PNG. It mimicked phonetically the language of the old colonial masters – *mastas*. So *bikpela nambawan* was his number one big fellow.

'No go,' Banto repeated, seemingly placated. He understood less than half of what was said to him, but with that, and his highly developed skill in reading non-verbal signs – of men and beasts – he followed well enough.

'OK. But I'm in big trouble now with my *masta*. The big man. He'll beat me *planti* for *bagarap*. If you no go, I have to take just one more. It's Payback.' He tapped his arm.

'No more take! No more!'

'Payback. Yes!'

Banto went quiet for a while. His own tribal culture was steeped in this concept of Payback: a kind of bargaining to atone for causing almost any kind of pain or loss in others. This trade was simple. In return for him not going, he had to make Payback by letting Chancey take from his arm again. Then this man also had Payback to escape the beating from his master for not doing as he had promised. 'You take,' he agreed at last.

Moving quickly, Chancey gestured for Banto to sit in the passenger plane seat. 'I take your *banaras*. OK? They stay here, close. Yes?' Very reluctantly Banto permitted the man to put his bow and arrows on the ground, keeping them in his sight-line. A warrior was never separated from his weapons. Then Chancey clicked on the seat-belt very loosely without him even noticing. Banto's eyes widened in fear as he saw the hated wooden box containing the man's small spear. But this time, instead of using the hypodermic to extract blood, Chancey was drawing into it the comatosic Bolitho had given him for exactly this purpose. 'One last take. OK?'

Before Banto had even nodded his final consent, Chancey plunged the needle deep into his arm muscle and pressed the plunger to pump in the fast-acting knock-out drug. Satisfied, he suddenly yanked hard at the harness, binding Banto tightly to the seat. The tiny native, only five feet two inches tall, struggled with superhuman strength, both physical and mental – but within a minute his battle was over.

Wasting no time, Chancey jumped in beside him, started both engines and taxied to give himself every available metre for the very tight take-off. Only an Otter, with its reverse thrust, could have got in there in the first place. Revving up, he looked over at the lolling head of the once proud native warrior, hoping there was enough of the drug to keep him sedated for all of the fifty-minute hop over the mountains. There was still just enough compassion in him, however, to feel bad about what he was doing. He did not know why they wanted such a specimen, but he knew – not least from the big money they were paying him – that the future would be bleak for the likeable young man.

Gunning the engines, and hurtling towards the prehistoric wollemi pines, he said out loud, '*Sori*, but you *planti* big *gol main* for me. *Planti* big.' It was with this 'gold mine' that he planned to get out of PNG and start that new life in Sydney. He had relations there and his room was full of the photographs they sent him. His dream was to open a restaurant – nothing too big – then find a wife and start a family. Maybe buy a boat . . .

Suddenly, a sickening bang interrupted his reveries as the undercarriage firmly clipped a tall tree-top. No damage seemed to have been done, however, and Chancey reached for the radio to tell Bolitho the good news. They were on the way. 'Get ready to break out some cold SPs, man. Some *bias*. You hear?'

'I hear you good, *kauboi*. Get that *balus* down here safely and you can afford champagne instead of beer.'

The sound of Bolitho cheered Chancey up. Looking again at the native, he panicked briefly, afraid that he had died on him. But then he saw the chest gently rising and he relaxed, turning his mind to all those photos of Bondi Beach, the good life . . . and the women.

*   *   *

Tom Bates was having the time of his life. A little out of his depth, but as ever with Barton's businesses, he was learning fast. And *doing*, not just consulting.

'These are the day's trades,' Bill Platt said, handing him the computer print-out. 'The three-month LIFFE Eurodollar contract did well for us. We bought forward Deutschmarks and shorted the Yen as an interest play. The US Treasury bond yields, of course, are still underpinning us nicely. So are the bond futures contracts. But we're moving out of equities. Everywhere. Overheated. We think the markets are well due a correction.'

'Averaging what, overall?' Tom had a prickly relationship with the older man, the Chief Executive of the small investment bank that Barton now effectively controlled.

'Better than you want. It looks like today's yield was 3.25 per cent above LIBOR.'

Tom frowned. 'And the derivatives?' His new team had put over ten per cent of the portfolio into complicated bear-spread put equity options, backing their pessimism. They had sold the right to 'put' into the market at today's price 10,000 options as cover if the market started the bear trend they were expecting. As derivatives went, this was a fairly cautious play. But derivatives still frightened the hell out of him.

'Looking fine. Don't worry. And yes – before you ask, we *are* marking to market in everything you see. No nasty shocks.'

'Fine,' he said, satisfied that the man seemed finally to have got the message. The message that all Barton wanted was a modest turn on the huge capital flows he had brought in for them to manage. Emphatically not treasury speculation. Something the gung-ho security traders had real difficulty coming to terms with.

Despite only officially doing two days a week with Barton's businesses, Tom still had to check all end-of-day trades with Bill Platt, whatever else he may be doing for his on-going WMC client assignments. He knew, and Platt knew to his cost, that Barton could call either of them at any time, day or night, for an update on his $15 billion Curaçao-based funds. If this was designed to keep them both on their toes, it certainly worked. Whereas Platt recognised that Tom was still feeling his way in his world, he well knew Barton was completely on top of everything, asking the most probing questions like the wiliest, most experienced PLC corporate treasury management chief. And the way he had handled an initially difficult Bank of England during the sale had also shown the big man's shrewdness and toughness.

Relaxing, Tom waved Platt to sit down. 'How's it going now out there?' he asked, nodding towards the small twenty-four-hour trading floor outside, where everyone was focusing on their screens in total concentration.

'Your people? They're good. But getting frustrated,' he replied, barely perching down. 'You recruited the best in the City, the hottest kids in town to join us old donkeys. And now they're here, you don't let them show you what they can do.'

'They're still earning big bucks. What's it matter to them if we have a conservative investment strategy? They know their real challenge is finding homes for funds on this scale without moving the market.'

The old head shook. 'They need the buzz, the adrenaline – every bit as much as the big cheques. You'll lose them.'

Tom looked pensive. Poaching the team of five top traders *en masse* from the American trading house had cost a not so small fortune, and caused big waves in the City. 'I'll talk to Sir James about what you say,' he said at last. 'Perhaps we can give them a slightly bigger share of the portfolio to play with a *little* more speculatively. They need incentivising. I see that. I'll talk to him.'

Standing, Platt turned to leave. 'You can try and convince him, but . . .' He left the sentence in the air, still baffled why, with all the talent he had drafted in, Barton would not permit them to take even prudent risks to grow the portfolio. But then, he still did not understand what Barton was doing effectively taking over his firm. The Curaçao portfolio now made up over two-thirds of the funds handled by the bank.

Tom watched him go and spent the next fifteen minutes digesting the figures he had left behind, occasionally going into the Reuters option pages and Telerate screens to check out some detail. Then, once satisfied, he put the paperwork in his case, and pulled on his jacket to leave. Despite Platt's warnings, he was over all very happy with everything. And so, he knew, was Barton. It was, after all, less than five months since Barton had called him in and sprung the news that through his US contacts he had won the treasury management contract for a consortium of international companies. He explained that they were involved in a travel-voucher scheme, a payment instrument which major business houses worldwide were using for much of their corporate travel and entertaining. The companies enjoyed heavily discounted airfare, hotel and car rental rates by cutting out the travel agent and user frequent-traveller benefits. The travel company principals avoided agents' over-ride and credit card charges. And the consortium made its turn by treasury managing the huge cash flow generated, and through clever tax avoidance arrangements through the Dutch West Indies island of Curaçao. To meet the contract, Tom had been tasked with finding a London bank or securities house to handle things. Fast. There had been no time to attempt to set up a new bank, given the licensing and Bank of England hoops they would have had to jump through. And Barton, of course, a recent bankrupt.

Instead, Tom had quickly identified the small but exclusive American house, already SFA/SIB and Bank licensed, and tee-ed up what was effectively a reverse take-over by Barton. Then came the open cheque to find and poach a crack team to put in exclusively to handle the new portfolio . . .

Brilliant, exciting work for Tom. Wheeling and dealing, right at the centre of things – but always with the comfort factor that in the end, Barton would make the final decision. It had been the same two years earlier in the biotech business, when Barton had spotted the niche early. Tom had not only done all the routine consultancy business-modelling, but gone out and found the boffins and property to make it all happen. He had even amazed Barton by winning some EU funding, as new start-ups.

As he flagged down a cab by Eastcheap, Tom reflected on his luck all those years ago in cultivating Barton after INSEAD. And by hanging on in there when Barton was in the wilderness – a calculated risk that – he had certainly reaped rich rewards. Financially, but just as importantly professionally, in terms of sheer, pulsating work satisfaction. Also, by keeping his three days with WMC, he enjoyed the best of all worlds: career stability and continuity through the consultancy, and the thrilling big dipper ride and extraordinary hands-on experience of working with the piratical James Barton.

The ninety-hour weeks were beginning to grind him down, and he knew that soon he really should slow down and get a life. But not yet. Definitely not yet . . .

Lydia examined the old man's feet and shook her head. 'When was the last time you had these looked at?'

The man's rheumy eyes stared back with the incomprehension of dementia. 'Bluebottles. Bluebottles everywhere!' he said for the fourth time, deeply agitated.

'Come on. Can't have you hobbling around like this. You'll get blood poisoning. Let's have the doctor look at them, shall we?'

She helped him down the corridor to sit in the waiting area with three other much younger vagrants. They were in the Day Centre charity near Waterloo where she helped out a couple of nights a week. The down-and-outs mostly slept rough in the area, and came to the centre mornings and early evenings for hot drinks and food donated each day by supermarkets and sandwich bars. While in the place, they could get cleaned up and have basic medical attention. Feet, dental and bronchial troubles were the most common. Tuberculosis had even made a worrying return to the streets of London. But no less serious, and much harder to treat, were the mental and related illnesses – alcoholism, depression, schizophrenia and dementia.

'What's he need?' The tired-looking old doctor had come out for the next case to treat.

'Feet. I've bathed them, but there's infection in some of his toes, I think.'

The doctor looked at the man. 'Hello again, Charlie.'

'You know him?'

'Sure. He comes and goes. Like his mind.'

'What's his story?'

The doctor smiled weakly. 'Believe it or not, he was a doctor. A very well-off Harley Street practitioner. Treated royals. The type of doctor who wouldn't have passed the time of day with the likes of me in the NHS. As close as *that* to a knighthood.' He clicked his fingers. 'But then – disaster. He was suspected of poisoning his wife, but it was never proved. Big case in its day.'

'And did he? Did he poison her?' Lydia looked over at the old man with fresh eyes.

'Oh yes,' the doctor replied, cheerfully. 'None of us

doubted that. But he was very good with poisons. It was impossible to make it stick.'

'And what's wrong with him now? Dementia?'

'That, and a good few other mental problems. Shouldn't be on the streets, of course. He's got a serious persecution complex. Keeps thinking they're going to arrest him again.'

'Strange. All he says to me is the word "bluebottles".'

The doctor laughed. 'That's it. When he and I were young, "bluebottle" was the nickname for a policeman. He thinks they're still after him.'

Lydia stared down again at the husk of the man. How easy it was to fall from grace. A success one day; on the streets, shouting, the next. Perhaps this was one reason she helped out here. There but for the Grace of God and all that. After the doctor had gone into his surgery with one of the other patients, Lydia took out her purse and slipped a twenty-pound note in old Charlie's pocket. 'Good luck, "Sir" Charles,' she said gently to the haunted, frightened face.

Then, after a glance at her accusingly expensive watch, it was time to go and see another 'Sir', her father. To discover just how secure *his* grip would prove to be on the seemingly fickle Grace of God . . .

Chancey was worried. They were ten minutes off landing and Banto had started to wake up, moving his head back and forth and moaning. Despite his skill as a pilot, Chancey did not relish the thought of putting down with a violent passenger flailing beside him.

He radioed Bolitho. 'What to do, man? He's *kam bek* awake! I'm mebbe ten minute to down.'

'He's strapped in good?'

'Sure.'

'Hit him if you have to. But not too hard. You hear?'

'Sure,' Chancey replied, uncertainly, feeling down for the wrench by his right side.

Banto was now fully conscious and had opened his eyes to the most frightening experience of his life. More terrifying than facing up to a wild boar. Or than the time he startled a cassowary, the fiercesome five foot tall, 130-pound flightless bird, PNG's biggest animal. More harrowing even than battle, and the taking of his first trophy head. There below him was green. His mind had no framework to recognise it as his beloved forests. He was like a person looking for the first time at a 3D image, unable to assimilate the patterns into anything recognisable. One thing he could comprehend, however, was the sky. And this now seemed to be above *and* below him! Then, directly ahead, they were approaching a place where the green ended, and a great empty space of blue-green began. A wilderness of nothingness all the way to the horizon: his first sight of an ocean. Worse than even all this was the noise. Angry, deafening and alien to his senses, creating harmonics in his head he had never before experienced. His first instinct was to flee, and he tried to get up and run. But the harness kept him pinned to the seat, and after a brief struggle, terror washed over him and he bent double with fear, staring at his feet, shaking uncontrollably and chanting. Chancey observed all this, and finally put the wrench down, greatly relieved: not because he no longer had to beat him senseless – violence was his stock-in-trade – but because he could avoid the risk of damaging him and facing the anger of Bolitho.

The private, unlicensed runway was 400 yards long. Tight, but a breeze after the 250-yard forest clearing. After all the drama he had expected, the landing was an anti-climax for Chancey, with Banto stiff beside him, still shaking, his teeth chattering.

Bolitho ran over to the Otter and yanked open the door

to inspect the native. 'He OK?' he demanded impatiently. 'Did you hit him?'

Chancey killed the engines and freed his seat-harness. 'He's fine, *kiap*. No need to quiet him, he's *planti* afraid.'

Bolitho – in his late fifties, a shaven bullet-head crowning a once-fit body – was a 1960s Vietnam war veteran who had never been able to adjust back to the soft, domestic world he had left in Ohio. A life since as a mercenary, cargo pilot, drugs runner and general muscle-for-hire had finally washed him up in PNG, dying of cirrhosis. It was a question of months, maybe a year. That was if he, or one of his many enemies, did not blow his brains out first. 'Great work, *kauboi*,' he said. 'You done good.'

Chancey beamed, genuinely proud. He was in awe of the American, as well in fear. 'You pay me, and tonight we *pati*! Together. We *pati* with *bilas misis*. OK?' *Bilas misis* – flashy European women.

Bolitho was holding Banto's head in his huge hands, moving it back and forth as if inspecting a melon. 'Sure, *kauboi*. Tonight we can party. Once I've checked your test results on him. Then I'll find you some young white tail. How's that sound? Meet me back here at nine tonight and, if the tests are good, I'll have your money.'

Excited, Chancey ran over to his motorcycle and roared off, leaving the quaking Banto alone with the intimidating stranger.

Chapter Three

J im Barton's London house in Chester Street, off Belgravia, was lit, as usual, like a Christmas tree: the lights blazing from every room, whether in use or not. It was one of his eccentricities, a hate – fear perhaps – of darkness. The live-in Filipina maid opened the door to Tom and, as a regular visitor, let him find his own way to the first-floor sitting room.

Cigar smoke drifted down the stairs and, as expected, he saw that the cognac decanter had already seen action. 'Jim,' he said, in greeting. 'Got here as soon as I could. You said it was urgent. What's up?'

In front of Barton on a side table was some sort of computer-screen print-out. Without speaking, he pushed it towards Tom, gesturing for him to help himself to a drink, then sit down and read the thing. Passing on the alcohol, Tom took the paper, speed-read it and then read it carefully line by line. Only then did he take a seat and venture his first good look at Barton. He did not like what he saw. The booze, cigars and the kind of stress that things like this created were a sure ticket to a heart condition. It was a view, however, that he kept to himself. The news was bad enough for the man without a lecture on his health.

'Reuters put that out two hours ago from New York,' Barton said angrily. 'Great, eh?'

The newswire piece read:

*The government of Papua New Guinea has attacked
US-quoted biotech group, Temple Bio-Laboratories
Inc – led by controversial former bankrupt British
financier Sir James Barton – for patenting the cell
lines of remote tribes. Accusing Temple Bio-Labs of
the crime of 'bio-piracy', the Health Minister at a press
conference today in Port Moresby claimed the company had paid untrained local criminals to intrude
on villages and coerce blood and tissue samples from
gullible natives. The rare cell lines of these Stone-Age
peoples are believed to offer the possibility of new cures
for diseases ranging from HIV, hepatitis, leukaemia
and lymphoma. Researchers have discovered that
although these infections are common in such tribes,
they rarely lead to the diseases themselves, demonstrating remarkable powers of immunity. Scientists
hope that studies of the cell lines may lead eventually
to vaccines capable of commercial development. The
PNG government, however, is to explore legal action
against Barton's company to negate the patents. It
has also called on the World Health Organisation and
the United Nations to condemn such exploitation. The
corporation's stock fell almost forty per cent on Wall
Street on the news. Ends.*

Tom put the paper down, a look of distaste on his face.
'Is it true?'

'Is what true?'

'That we've been getting blood and tissue samples in this
way. Using untrained criminals, coercing native people?'

'Of course not! Our man down there has been using
experienced local guides and professional nurses. To take
blood samples safely. And far from coercing them, the
tribes have been falling over themselves to be donors –

for metal tools and general supplies. What do you take me for?'

Barton made a good fist of seeming genuinely indignant at the question. He badly needed to keep Tom focused and motivated, especially on the Aruban treasury management. If the American ever got to know the travel-voucher funds were really laundered from the drugs industry, he would, Barton knew, walk – and talk. Equally, Barton had to keep him in the dark about what he was *really* doing in PNG – and why . . . How long he could keep these things secret was proving a worry. But if the next few weeks went to plan, it soon would not matter. Tom Bates was very nearly dispensable.

'So what's their beef? Something's seriously upset the government.'

'They're pissed they didn't get there first. That's all. As soon as they realised I had the patents, it dawned on them that they could have taken them out first – and that now they've lost them for ever. Dozy bastards. Let *me* do all the exploratory work. Let *me* have the idea. Let *me* expose the potential . . . and then they'd have breezed in and stolen it out from under. "In the national interest" no doubt. Well, tough! They blew it. And that's all there is to it.' He got up to pace around, agitated, trying to relight his cigar.

Tom put on his professional face. He was not at all sure he believed him. Those warning bells were still sounding. 'And what do you expect me to do?' he asked.

'I need to know those patents really are buttoned down in the States. And I want to protect them and my intellectual property rights worldwide. Talk to our lawyers and patent agents. Then get me a second opinion on how secure I am on this. On whether the PNG government has any grounds at all to negate the patents. I need to know. And fast.'

Tom already knew there was no consensus on patent laws

around the world in the field of biotechnology. The USA and Japan permitted the patenting of transgenic animals; in Europe it was much less clear. A European Directive remained bogged down in drafting, with lobby groups invoking a 'public order' clause. The whole area was messy, and Barton was right to worry about piracy.

'And all this is tied up, I assume, with the new launch you've been keeping from me?'

Barton sat down again and took a deep draught of his cognac. 'Yes.'

'But I don't understand. I mean, it seems you've only been taking these samples from the various tribes for a couple of months. It'll take years to analyse them. You first have to isolate the various viruses and then crack the genetic immune system before you can even *think* about developing an effective vaccine for clinical trial. I'm no biologist, no immunologist – but that much I do know.'

'Then perhaps you think you know too bloody much!' Barton suddenly raged. 'Perhaps you should just do what you're told for once, instead of double-guessing everything I do. You've just been my puppet. My stand-in until I was free from all the bankruptcy restrictions. Don't *ever* forget that. And in return you're sitting on a fat pile of stock options that cost you nothing. You may be a director but this is *my* business, and it's not a team game. My businesses run on a need-to-know basis. And all *you* need to know right now is that I want advice on the patents and IPRs. Got it? You're being very well rewarded. Let's see you earn it!' His eyes blazed and he stood over Tom, physically intimidating him with his size, and jabbing the cigar at him aggressively.

Tom stood up, fighting to control his temper. He had encountered this side of Barton before, but only when directed at others. To find himself on the receiving end now was unpleasant and humiliating. It also for the first time called into serious question the special relationship he always felt he had enjoyed with the tyrant. Was he, after all, just like any other hired hand in Barton's eyes? Despite everything he had done for him?

'I've stood by you, Jim. Remember that. The only one . . . But if that's really all you want, a lap-dog, I'll buy you one,' he said evenly, making to leave. 'Call me tomorrow when you're more yourself.' He stormed out, slamming the door behind him.

As he pulled on his top coat downstairs in the hall, the bell rang and the maid opened the door to Lydia.

Tom was always pleased to see her, Barton's daughter from his first marriage, having spent countless weekends with the family at the Manor. They had even dated briefly and secretly after she had left university, but – partly out of mutual fear of what her father would make of it – they had not really given things a chance to develop. They still flirted though, each sensing unfinished business in that department. 'Hi,' he said, struggling to hide his anger from her. 'How's the world of advertising?'

'Fine,' she replied. She was a little thrown at stumbling into him unexpectedly, but the buzz at seeing him was very much still there.

'Well *I* don't get enough OTS you these days,' he said, using her industry jargon.

'That's easily fixed,' she said, snapping on one of her attractive-me looks. 'You can have an Opportunity To See as much of me as you like.'

He smiled, mistaking her provocative *double entendre* for Mae West-style parody. 'Is he expecting you?'

'Nope.' She took this as a tiny coded rejection, and it depressed her slightly.

'Well, a word of warning. He's like a bear with a sore

head. A bit drunk. And some bad company news just came in.'

'What news?'

'Best see if he wants to talk about it himself.' They had often sparred good-naturedly over her liberal views, but he was always careful of what he told her about Barton's businesses.

'Thanks for the warning,' she said casually, and ran up the stairs. 'By-ee!'

He watched her go, admiring her shapely, comfortable-looking figure and the long, flowing hair. She really was very attractive – a woman now, not the coltish student – even if she still had something of her powerful father's face. Perhaps he would try and start over with Lydia. He was tiring of his lonely life of casual relationships. And the hell this time with what Barton might think. The bully's attack was now festering. If, in spite of everything they had been through, he and Barton did not after all enjoy a special relationship, friendship even, then he in turn owed him nothing back. Lydia was now firmly deleted from his hands-off list, he thought to himself, leaving to face the ice cold wind outside.

'Dad! It's me!' she called up in warning.

Barton's mood immediately lightened. ''Here! In the sitting room!'

'I know. I can follow the stinking smoke,' she smiled, coming in and hugging him. 'How are you? I bumped into Tom and he said you were grumpy.'

Good old blunt, to-the-point Lydia, he thought. If everyone thought something, Lydia had always been the one to blurt it out loud. He found it impossible to be angry when she was around. 'First off, that's not stinking smoke. It's a twenty-pound Cohiba. And secondly, yes, I'm *bloody* grumpy. I just yelled at him.'

'Well don't yell at me. I bite!' She snarled theatrically. 'What's wrong anyway? Run out of nice fresh mice to poison? No monkeys to torture?'

His face clouded a little. Sometimes, however, she could be too in your face. There was seemingly nothing she would not do or say. 'Let's not get on to all that,' he said. 'Seen your mother lately? How is she?'

'She's like she's become, that's all. No change.' She looked away. This was the one subject she still could not face head on, having still to come to terms with it. Since her parents had split for the divorce, her mother had gone into a deep and seemingly never-ending depression. She had gone into some 'other room', as she herself called it. It was the nearest thing to an explanation she had ever tried to offer anyone. 'Nothing new in that, of course. But don't try and change the subject. You're looking pretty depressed yourself. What *is* wrong?'

He relented, reluctantly. 'You might as well see this tonight. It'll be in the press here tomorrow anyway.'

She took the Reuters piece and read it silently. Sighing loudly, she sat down and looked at him. 'Why this? Why can't you try and make your money some way else?'

'Why what? Why am I in biotech? Because I have to be, that's why. You make money how and when you can, not when you need it. Because when you need it, you can't make it. Believe me. That's a great and profound truth. Biotech research today is what computer software was a decade ago. And I'm a real pioneer. This is how I *can* make serious money again, how I was able to pay off my debts in just eighteen months.'

'But stealing cell lines. It's wrong. Wrong, wrong, wrong! Can't you see that? Look at what you're doing to these poor natives.'

'Those "poor natives" are cannibal savages. When they're

not butchering each *other*, they're butchering pigs and forest animals. Their entire lives revolve around hunting and being hunted. All I've done is collect blood samples to develop vaccines which might, just might, prevent misery for millions. And I've *paid* for them. Stolen nothing. So don't start quoting Rousseau's noble bloody savage at me. Because I'm very comfortable with what I do. *And*, incidentally, you and your mother used to live very comfortably on the proceeds.'

Her temper, every ounce as fierce as his, flared at the attack. 'As it happens, she doesn't need your money. Not since Grandpa died,' she fumed. 'And as for me, I make a pretty good living of my own, thank you very much. With no help from anyone. Even if you *did* give me any of your blood money, I'd donate it straight to my causes. You'd be funding your own destruction. Croak and leave me squillions, and that's *exactly* where it'll go. To all those campaigning organisations you hate.'

Barton had to laugh. 'Your father's daughter,' he smiled, stung none the less. 'In your own way you're just as determined as me, you know.'

Politically and in terms of social conscience, they could hardly be further apart. He High Tory nationalist; she soft left politically, but hard militant just on animal rights. Yet still they shared so many character traits. Determination, single-mindedness, *bloody*-mindedness. Yin and yang off the same stock. Symbiotic.

She looked at him seriously. 'I love you. But I'll do all I can to stop you on this kind of thing.'

'If anyone's going to ruin me a second time, I'd rather it was you.'

'I mean it. I *will* stop you if I can.'

'I know,' he said, serious now too. 'I can't help that. And neither it seems can you. So don't let's dwell on it. Have you eaten? How about dinner somewhere?'

'Deal,' she smiled. Relieved – as she saw it – to have cleared the forthcoming terms of engagement; her conscience salved a little in advance of what she knew she must do. 'This time it's on me. Not on your ill-gotten gains. But, you old carnivore, I know this smashing little vegan bistro. They serve nothing with a face.'

He grimaced comically, and briefly became her handsome, funny father from the happy days. 'All right. *Touché*,' he said. 'But if I really do have to turn vegetarian for a night, we'll go to a proper restaurant. The Neal Street. I can survive there perfectly well on roast porcini and a bottle of Brunello. Or their black truffle and pasta. I've never yet seen fungi with a face, have you?'

Peregrine Mitchell looked at the list of names again. It included Sir James Barton's doctor, dentist, private accountant, his personal lawyer, all his directors, a recent mistress, and a couple of semi-friends. But it was to Tom Bates's that he kept returning. The thin file lay open on his desk.

It told the old security hand little, but Mitchell had a nose, an intuition he rarely ignored. Perhaps it had to do with Tom being a high-flying management consultant. He felt he knew that particular animal well. Precociously bright, vain, few convictions, able to argue a case either way – like a barrister. As the Service's top recruiter, he had always had great success with these types. The flattery of being approached by Her Majesty's Secret Service was all but irresistible, their thirst for intellectual challenges and new experiences inexorably compelling them to become involved. A small complication this time was his US citizenship, but that could be fixed with Grosvenor Square easily enough. Yes. Tom Bates it was. He was, in any case, the man closest to Barton's affairs. The chase was on, and suddenly his mood lightened as he recaptured something of the old excitement of a new field case beginning.

The office door opened and his assistant came in. 'The partners' meeting starts in an hour and they want to brief you beforehand.'

He groaned inwardly, but his poker face showed nothing. 'Fine. I'm ready whenever they are,' he said, his tombstone teeth revealing themselves in a show of politeness. Over thirty years with the Secret Intelligence Service had ended six months ago in early retirement, following his last field operation, code-named *Grave Song*, in South Korea. The public expenditure cuts, market testing and the so-called peace dividend had seen an unprecedented exodus of middle and senior ranking staff in both MI6 and its domestic opposite number, MI5. The depth of cuts, however, had alarmed a great many wise heads in the Foreign and Home Offices, as well as a minority in the increasingly meddlesome watchdog, the Intelligence and Security Committee. As a result, a number of pivotal people, like Perry Mitchell, had been found private sector front jobs, effectively keeping them on call for a few years yet. Mitchell's 'second career' was with one of the world's leading executive search agencies, Management International. He had in fact often before posed as a headhunter using the firm as cover. It was an effective means of approaching business targets who got to see people, or countries, of interest to the Service.

His area of responsibility there was international head-hunting assignments, with particular emphasis on the old Soviet bloc countries – especially Russia, Poland and the Czech Republic where business was booming. These were also countries he knew well from his many terms of opera-tional embassy secondment. The job in return gave him cover for overseas visits, to international conferences, trade fairs and clients. But, more importantly, it also gave him access to priceless databases listing a wide range of businessmen and women, exporters and others, who regularly travelled the world, or were stationed abroad. The business community remained a hugely important resource for MI6, providing much of its non-electronic quality intelligence-gathering. Either as routine de-brief reports, or – as he hoped soon with Tom Bates – in response to a specific, short-term spying assignment on someone or someplace to which their job gave them special access.

'A word before we start, Perry.' The UK's managing partner had stuck his head around the door.

'Fine. I need you to mark my card. Get me up to speed.' Mitchell had been playing the 'new boy' game since he arrived and knew it was now wearing a bit thin. He was rapidly approaching the time when he would have to start taking the job more seriously and actually contribute something. 'I've read the papers. What do we need from today?'

The man was followed in by two more worried-looking UK partners. 'Well. Given that the last Chairman chose you, as a newcomer, to review the way we work cross-border, only one thing matters to me. London *must* remain the base for all the international work.'

The internal politics here were almost as bad as in MI6, Mitchell thought miserably. The chairmanship of the global network of thirty offices rotated every two years, and an arrogant, bullying Swiss had succeeded the urbane Englishman. Far from neutral, he had made it absolutely clear from the outset that he wanted Zurich to replace London as the centre from which to drive all the lucrative international assignments. The man would shortly be chairing the managing partners' meeting, and Mitchell was due to present his preliminary recommendations.

As if any of all this really mattered, in the order of things.

Mitchell knew, however, he was now staring at a rambling four-hour committee meeting before he could pick up the phone to Tom Bates and start spinning his latest web. 'Tell me what you need,' he said.

'The bottom line is that we have to keep all that income and the ancillary work here. In London, where it's always been done. Not Switzerland. Which of course is exactly what the Chairman wants,' the managing partner continued, wringing his hands in agitation. He was not looking forward to the prospect of having to confront the tyrant himself.

'Oh, I think I'll be able to manage the Chairman all right. Don't you, chaps?' Mitchell's tombstone teeth showed themselves again, and suddenly no one in the room doubted for an instant that this disconcerting, strangely frightening man could handle just about anyone he wanted.

'I have the consignment.'

Bolitho's voice was unmistakable, even over the bad line. Jim Barton was in his Hill Street, Mayfair office with Tom and the lawyers, working on the patents issue. Brusquely he told them all to leave as he took the highly sensitive call – something Tom always hated and resented. 'Is it in good condition?'

'A1.'

'You've tested it? For quality?' Barton could hear the tension in his own voice. So much depended on the Bolitho's reply.

'The tests are good.'

The relief was palpable at the other end of the phone. 'You're sure? Really sure?'

'Sure I'm sure. And now what? I go ahead and make the delivery as planned?'

'Yes. Leave now, as soon as you can. I'll fly out there to see it in a few days.'

'Good.' Bolitho allowed a pause before going on. 'And the delivery guy. You want I pay him off, as agreed?'

Barton closed his eyes. And his mind. 'Exactly as agreed.'

'You got it, boss. See you in Belize. I'm out of here.'

Hanging up, Bolitho sucked noisily on a can of beer and looked over to Banto, chained to the wall of the hangar. The tiny native's head was slumped forward, and he was squatting on his haunches, seemingly asleep or in a kind of trance. Swaggering over, Bolitho kicked viciously at his feet, knocking Banto sideways. Still the native avoided looking at him.

'Hey! Ape man! You hear all of that? You're going to be flying halfway around the world. You understand me?' There was no response, so he lashed at him with his foot again. 'You look at me, you piece of crap!'

Eyes wide now, Banto finally looked up at his tormentor. Then he lifted his head further back and began chanting quietly his monotone *sing-sing* tribal call. The sound annoyed Bolitho even more, and he hit him hard across the mouth, drawing blood. 'Shut the hell up!' he screamed, his face inches from Banto's. He was about to strike again, when the door opened and Chancey looked in.

'What's happening?' he demanded. 'You should not beat the *kanaka.*' Despite everything, the native was still a brother of sorts, and the American a foreigner. There was no cause to abuse him.

Bolitho stood up, forcing himself to relax. 'Hey. You're right, little *kauboi.*' Banto had now stopped the chanting, and his hunter's eyes were watching the two men intently, reading the situation as clearly as a Westerner could read a book. 'Get over here. I've got your money. Take it. Then we can have a few beers, and go and beat up on that white tail I promised.'

Chancey grinned and walked across. He had changed into his party clothes: clean denims, red jacket and loud Hawaiian shirt. 'Yeah. *Bias*. Then we *pati* good.'

Bolitho turned his back as he approached, drawing his knife. Banto watched impassively, knowing exactly what was going to happen. It did not occur to him to warn Chancey. This was a battle between two tribes. Neither of them his own, and so none of his business. Not yet . . .

Bolitho was swift and clinical, despatching Chancey silently in front of Banto, severing the windpipe to prevent any screams. Satisfied with his work, Bolitho looked down again at Banto. 'You people are just like the Vietcong gooks to me,' he spat, as if in some perverse attempt at justification.

But he saw that Banto was already back on his haunches, rocking himself in his trance. Banto was somewhere else. His own battle with the big man was not yet. For the moment he was safe. This he knew. But that battle would certainly come. It must. He would have Payback. Soon the big man would have to face a real warrior. Then Payback.

Chapter Four

This time the Animal Freedom Warriors met at a dingy bed-sit in Clerkenwell. Lydia had never been there before and had some difficulty finding the place.

Having been buzzed in on the entryphone, she climbed the poorly lit staircase to the third floor of the pre-war conversion. The once elegant Georgian townhouse had long since been broken up into as many flats as some greedy absentee landlord could create. The hall had been cluttered with bikes and prams, and reeked of a cocktail of garlic, cabbage and the unwashed. Now as she ran up, holding her breath against the stink, she imagined cockroaches being crushed under the rush matting with her every step. Outside each paint-chipped door were bags of festering rubbish. Some even had unwashed tall milk bottles waiting to be collected by a milkman who had stopped calling a decade earlier.

As she passed one flat, the door opened at the sound of her footfall, and she glimpsed the frightened eyes of a black man. Frightened of what? she wondered. The immigration authorities? DHSS inspectors? This certainly had the air of a place steeped in social security fraud. Or in milking local authority accommodation payments for asylum-seekers and homeless families. A used condom lying on a stair in front of her pointed to yet more murky possibilities.

At last she reached flat six, knocked, and was let in by Sam Thrower. 'I see we've dressed down for tonight,' he sneered at her, nodding to her denims. 'Wise move.'

Lydia did not rise to the bait. She pushed past him, nodded to the rest of the group, and sat at the kitchen table. A woman offered her a can of beer, but she refused. 'Am I late, or were you all early?' she asked, immediately suspicious that Thrower had been holding a pre-meeting without her. There were several empty cans on the table, and a full ashtray.

'We started half an hour ago,' Thrower said, unabashed. 'Some of us were still worried about your commitment on this one. Seeing as how it's your father's place and all.'

Lydia could feel her short temper rising as she looked accusingly at the four others. All avoided eye contact, except Thrower. 'And?' she demanded.

'And . . . we *trust* you. We really do. On a majority vote . . . But then you know how democratic we are.' He made it clear that he was the dissenter.

'Look, I don't need all this!' she exploded. 'If you want to go ahead without me, that's just fine with me.'

The others squirmed in embarrassment, all social non-confrontationists. All except Thrower. 'Don't get your Janet Regers in a twist, your ladyship. Like I said, we trust you. In fact, we've even decided to show it, by letting you actually plant the bomb. Your very own torching,' he sneered. 'Think of it as a coming-out ball. You've posed around holding my coat often enough. Now it's your turn. Time to cross the line.' He watched, goading her into bottling out in front of the others. 'If we get caught, you'll make real nice jail bait for all the sisters in Holloway.'

'That's enough of that!' snapped Chrissie, who was also a zero-tolerance gay rights activist. 'I don't need to hear any sexist, homophobic crap. The only person I have a problem with right now is you.' Emboldened, the two others – Tony, a mid-twenties student-drop-out, and Joan an odd, intense woman in her late fifties – murmured their agreement with Chrissie and turned their eyes as one on Thrower.

Lydia nodded a thank you to her, and then stood up, pulling back on her coat.

'Where the hell are you going?' Thrower asked, a hint of panic now in his voice.

'I don't do anything on a majority vote. I'm out of here,' she replied, making for the door. Her volatile temper had got the better of her again.

'No. Wait. We can work this thing out.'

'Work it out? Like, you apologising?'

All eyes were still fixed on Thrower. It was a showdown that everyone knew had been inevitable. He consistently taunted her and she was on a short fuse. One of the two had to back down or leave the group. That had been clear for months.

Thrower shifted in his chair, sweating. Then he laughed nervously. 'Sure. I want you in. But this is serious stuff. I needed to be sure. That's my job.'

'Not good enough.' She was now at the door.

The older woman, Joan, knew that Lydia had just gone too far. She had already won, but with her last salvo had foolishly called for Thrower to humiliate himself. Bad manners. And bad politics. She tried to defuse the situation. 'I think we're forgetting the mice, rats and monkeys in all this. I think we need to put them before our own petty squabbles, don't you?'

But Lydia, still fired up, was now in no mood for anything less than a crushing victory. 'I simply need to hear Sam say he, personally, wants me on this raid. That's all.' She held his eyes, and waited for him to break.

After an agonising silence, he finally blinked and broke off eye contact. 'Lydia. I want – you – on – the – raid,' he said, enunciating his words slowly, as if talking to a child.

Suddenly Lydia felt foolish. She had won, she had avenged his class-ridden carping. But at what price? 'Apology accepted,' she responded, relief in her voice.

'Let's forget about all of that now, and get on with the planning.' Joan again tried to help defuse things. 'All right, you two?'

Thrower looked up, cold, controlled anger welling inside. 'Sure,' he said, sniffing, fighting to regain his dignity. 'Why not? Let's run through the plan. We'll do it once. Twice. And then ten times more.' Reaching into his bag he took out copies of a large-scale Ordnance Survey map, a selection of long-range photographs he had taken, an aerial shot, and a video made of the inside of the plant by the temp he had got in there a month earlier. As ever, a militarily thorough approach, reflecting the many weeks of surveillance and intelligence gathering that he had co-ordinated. It made Lydia feel sheepish over her attack on him. 'How many people work there?' she asked, trying to normalise the situation.

'Fifty-three. And a few temps.'

'And what animals do they use?' Chrissie probed, also trying to clear the air.

'Rats, mice,' Thrower replied. Then, looking again at Lydia, he added, 'And pigs.'

'What *exactly* are the pigs being used for?' Joan asked.

'Human transplant research. Xenotransplants,' Thrower said. 'They're having some "success" with porcine organ donors, animals specially bred for hypochondriac millionaires. A breed of genetically modified pigs is created specifically to match their personal DNA profile. So, any time they need a xenograft – new liver, heart or kidney – well, Hey Piggo! Look no further. There's a little herd of porkers just *dying* to oblige. Cute, eh?'

Lydia felt sick. Until she had seen the magazine article a few weeks earlier, she had no idea her father was involved in this side of genetic engineering. 'How long has this research been going on?'

'Two years. He was one of the first into it.'

All the faces turned to Lydia. But if they expected some dewy-eyed apologist they were greatly mistaken. They still did not really know her.

'What kind of bomb do I get to plant,' she asked, trying now to impress. 'Five pounds of Semtex H? Like we used at Bristol University? Or incendiaries? Like those used on McDonald's in Birmingham? Car bombs like Salisbury? Or letter bombs like last year's Christmas campaign?'

Her outward calm belied the tearing rage inside she felt at her father. How could he? How could he do these things? Any doubts she may have felt after their bonding dinner were now gone. It was war on his business. Open war.

'Mr Bates. Tom Bates?'

'Yes.'

'Can you talk? Something personal . . .'

'Who is this?'

'My name's Perry Mitchell. From Management International.'

Tom immediately recognised the name of the executive search agency. Suddenly the man's conspiratorial telephone approach made sense. 'That's OK. I can talk.'

'Good. I wondered if you might be able to help me with an assignment I've just taken on. It's a senior position with a quoted international conglomerate. VP level. Consumer goods. Some retail. Own manufacturing. Big ambitions in Asia. China. Acquisitions. JVs. All that.

They want someone youngish, with a strategic consulting background. And investor relations' experience. Someone used to board-level counselling with major PLCs. Someone ready for a first move into senior general management. Reading between the lines, they're looking for their next CEO a year or so down the line.'

Tom was regularly headhunted, but rarely felt tempted. 'What's it paying?' Between his days with WMC and work with Barton, he was already earning over £140,000 a year, plus his maturing share options, and this question generally cut short the time wasters.

'For the right person, I've been told it's virtually open cheque book. Not less than £200,000. But make the right case and that could quickly double. Plus options, of course. The stock has been seriously under-performing the sector.' Mitchell let the juicy bait dangle for a few seconds before continuing. 'I won't go through the usual pretence of asking if you know anyone you'd recommend. It's you we're interested in. You're first on a very short list. Worth a meet?'

Bates did not hesitate. He always kept his options open, and he was still fuming at Barton's attack on him. 'When and where?'

'My club? You know the Travellers – Pall Mall? Breakfast or lunch tomorrow. I'd like to move quickly.'

'Lunch is better. How will I know you?'

'I'll meet you in the entrance hall. And don't worry. I'll know you.'

Mitchell hung up and smiled. Arranging the first meeting with his targets under the guise of headhunting almost always worked. His victims arrived feeling insecure, and under a self-imposed veil of secrecy. Being headhunted sets up one of the few times when perfectly respectable executives lie to their secretaries, their peers and very probably their wives or husbands as well. For the first look-see meeting, most kept it all very secret, not wanting to worry their partners needlessly about possible domestic upheaval – moving house, changing schools and all the other distractions that could go with a new career. So they had phantom dental appointments and the like, and effectively for an hour or two disappeared from the face of their familiar worlds. It was the perfect cover for the Service's senior recruiter.

Perry Mitchell put down Bates's file and went through to his outer office where his secretary was binding some document or other. 'Book me a table at the club tomorrow, will you? For two. One o'clock,' he said.

'But you're down to lunch with the Malaysians,' she reminded him. They were looking to recruit a full management team of European nationals to run their new car assembly plant being built in South Wales.

'Something's come up. I'll have to skip off at noon.' He avoided her eyes, knowing they would be registering major disapproval. She had been at Management International for over twenty years. In her judgement, nothing 'came up' that could ever be more important than major clients.

Feeling thoroughly in the dog house, he went back to his office, closed the door again, and opened the bottom drawer of his desk. Taking out the Lamb's Navy dark rum, he poured two fingers, added a splash of water, and sipped thoughtfully. A delegation of Malaysian tin-bashers may be very important in its own right, but was as nothing when put alongside Sir James Barton's terrifyingly dangerous game.

The man had to be stopped.

Maddie rarely drank, other than taking wine with a meal. She had never been able to handle alcohol very well, and drinking on an empty stomach was ten times worse.

Asking Tom out to dinner had seemed like a good idea at the time. Her husband had left suddenly the day before for his plant in Belize, without even noticing that it meant him missing their wedding anniversary. Dinner at the Savoy, followed by a romantic night upstairs, had been something of a tradition for them, and she had hoped that booking the usual suite might have been the key to rekindling their love life. But then she had got the call – from his *secretary* . . . Furious at Jim for standing her up, she badly needed not to be alone again that night, and to talk with somebody sympathetic. Someone who really knew Jim, and would understand. That had quickly thrown up just one name. Tom. Tom would listen. Tom would be able to help her come to terms with Jim's violent mood swings and his vicious temper.

She also needed to feel attractive again. To be treated properly.

'Well, here we are,' she said self-consciously, sipping the champagne flute. Her mouth left a thick impression of pink lipstick on the rim. 'Thanks for coming.'

'Being seen out with the boss's wife . . . You'll ruin my reputation,' he smiled.

She laughed. 'Dinner for two here, at the very public Savoy, is hardly a walk on the wild side, you know. But I need a good old gossip. Consider yourself an honorary "one of the girls" for the evening. Let's order, shall we?'

Tom Bates had hesitated before accepting Maddie's unexpected invitation to dinner, but he had sensed how badly she needed to unburden herself. And so it soon proved, as she became emotional, spilling out her most private feelings and worries to him. About being seen as a dowry American in a loveless marriage; about Jim, his business ethics and erratic temperament since his disgrace; about her relationship with Lydia – still her father's favourite;

about the girls . . . The twins had arrived seven years earlier, difficult births which had left her infertile. But he had so badly wanted a son, an heir for the baronetcy. The title passed only down the male line and, after three hundred years, would die with him if he had no male issue. His reaction to the news that she had been carrying twin girls was to show complete lack of interest. He had not been at the births, and stayed barely half an hour on a first visit the next morning. They had only infrequently shared a bed since, Jim having moved to his old rooms in the west wing. Initially this had been so he could get some sleep, away from the babies. But somehow he had never moved back.

'And now look at me,' she pleaded with Tom, eyes filling. 'Saggy breasts. Stretch marks . . . and my hair, nails, my skin have never been the same. I'm thirty-two, but feel fifty. I'm thirty-two, and married to a Philistine bully who never loved me.'

He took her hand to calm her. They had now finished their main courses and, having started on champagne, had almost got through their second bottle of Krug. Her emotional state, made worse by too much alcohol, was swinging wildly between clumsily flirting with him, and sudden, self-pitying anxiety attacks. 'Maddie. Look at me,' he said. 'You're the most beautiful woman in the restaurant. The most beautiful in the whole of London from where I'm sitting. You're witty, sophisticated, well read. A brilliant hostess. A great mother to two beautiful girls. You're just terrific.'

Leaning forward, she kissed him, lightly cupping his chin in her hand. Closing her eyes, she lingered over the moment before breaking off, embarrassed that others may be watching. Smiling shyly, she whispered, 'I needed that.'

'You also need an early night and gallons of Evian, ma'am,'

he replied, taking a chair and a whip to his own self-control, and gesturing for the bill.

Smiling back, Maddie pulled herself together, relieved now, and a little surprised that neither of them had made an embarrassing drunken pass. 'You're right. As ever. Thanks for just listening. I guess I'm kind of vulnerable right now. You're not taking advantage of that . . .' Her eyes held his, curiously, silently asking why.

He looked away, his mind racing to find an answer that would neither depress nor encourage her. 'Someone – Maugham I think – said that morality was the last refuge of the coward.'

She clucked and corrected him, slightly shaking her head and pulling a face. 'Patriotism. Patriotism is the last refuge . . . And it was Johnson.'

Minutes later, in the cab back to his Chelsea Wharf apartment, Tom reflected on the evening: on Maddie and her worries, but mostly on the private picture she had painted of her husband, the restless, brooding commercial genius who had dominated both their lives for so long. A man each had loved in their way – and feared, in equal measure. A man who, like most tyrants, had somehow attracted wholly undeserved, irrational loyalty from those closest to him.

But for how much longer? The ranks of the praetorian guard, he mused, were beginning to murmur.

There was no moon, so Manuel Ferez had little difficulty in keeping out of sight of the two men. It was also a windy night, and the breakers of the Atlantic crashing just a few hundred yards away, helped further to conceal his surveillance.

It was his fifth night, watching, waiting, hoping for some kind of night-time delivery to the laboratory at

Oeiras, just down the coast from Lisbon. The son of an English wine shipper and a Portuguese mother, he had been educated in England, and recruited by MI6 at Cambridge. After five months at the Lisbon Station, operating out of the embassy as an assistant to the commercial attaché, this was only his second modest field assignment. Like most things in the Service, however, it too was proving boring and routine, and he was pleased when at last the two Temple Lab security guards had emerged. He noted the time: 03.08. Looking through his heavy infra-red night-sights, they just seemed to be wheeling some bagged-up waste out the back. But at least it would give him something to report in his log.

Silently he shadowed the men, keeping well back. There was no need to get close. They were not going far with the tall factory trolley, its wheels squeaking and crunching across the rubble towards the land site a hundred metres away from the lab which Barton was developing for a new light industrial factory.

Ferez doubled the chew rate on his gum as he remained hidden behind a digger. '03.09. Target takes out black bag rubbish and returns,' he dictated to himself, cynically: 'Notify Vauxhall Cross without delay! Man the COBRA centre. Alert the PM!'

They manhandled the trash, throwing it into a foundation trench, then one jumped down, seemingly taking some trouble to cover it over with soil and rubble being tipped in by his partner. Each was smoking throughout, and as they returned, he noticed the one who had been in the pit had a cold, his handkerchief at his nose. 'Perceptive, or what? So this is why they recruit double firsts,' Ferez continued, bantering to himself.

Suddenly the powerful flashlight carried by one of the men lit the digger, and he ducked down quickly, cursing his sloppiness. The taller of the two guards nodded in his direction, clearly thinking he had seen some movement over there, and both men changed direction to march quickly towards him.

All Ferez's bored cockiness quickly evaporated, as in a panic he tried to calm himself and remember his tradecraft training from the Ashford centre. Damn. Damn! It was all going wrong. His career was surely now humiliatingly over, falling at the very first, very low hurdle. And these men were, he knew, armed and usually drunk by now. His career was not the only thing on the line . . .

They were now less than thirty metres away, their flashlight still on the digger. He had unforgivably marooned himself there, with no covert line of escape. In desperation, he took a stone and lobbed it high to the men's right. In the few seconds it bought as they turned to look, he shimmied up into the digger bucket, suspended six metres in the air. But the men barely paused, and continued on towards him. They looked around the machine, checking it over carefully, the light flooding and picking it out from every angle.

'Climb up and look in the bucket,' the shorter, more senior man ordered the other in guttural Portuguese.

There came sounds of someone getting on to the body of the machine, then pausing as he figured how best to mount the digger arm that thrust Ferez skyward, like a sacrificial offering. Ferez himself was not armed. Not just for routine surveillance. Not in a friendly EU neighbour state.

Then the arm began to sway, as the man started to climb up to check out the bucket. Young Ferez was by now shaking too, in fear of what he would have to do. He had no doubt that he could easily take out the climbing man, making the most of the element of surprise, and using the lethal unarmed combat head blows he had been taught. If, *if* he had the stomach to deliver them. Under pressure, he was certainly finding out about himself, as they warned he would. But even if he did now act out a text-book attack on the first one, the man below would be a very different proposition . . .

Then there was a shudder and a loud expletive rang out, as the man lost his footing and fell, crashing down on to the engine cover. Unhurt but still cursing, he jumped to the ground next to his partner. 'There's a better way,' he said.

He picked up a heavy piece of concrete and threw it two-handed high in the air above the bucket. Ferez saw it frozen in the light above him for a millisecond, before it began hurtling down at him. As it did he smashed the night-sight hard, two-handed into the bucket-base beneath him, creating a loud metallic bang, just as the lump of angular concrete plunged silently into his chest. Somehow he stifled the groan in his throat as his ribs broke. Dizzy with agony, close to passing out, his ears oddly became doubly sensitive, and at last he heard them laughing, and pushing the empty trolley back to the lab.

He waited a quarter of an hour before gingerly easing himself down, an excruciating pain in his side. But he had to check out what the men had been doing. Why had they needed to be so secretive about dumping trash in a site their company owned?

Climbing down the foundation pit proved harder than anticipated, given his injury. It was over three metres deep, and he worried about being able to climb back out. Once in, though, his task was easy. The man had made only a half-hearted job of covering the sack over – but he soon realised why they had both been smoking. The stench of rotting flesh was over-powering. The two men had just been behaving like the burial men working the plague pits of seventeenth-century London, with their aromatic clay pipes, scented 'kerchiefs and pockets full of posies. It was obviously the remains of a butchered lab animal. Something large. A big ape. Or a pig.

Taking out a pencil torch he tore open the sack.

The eyes of the dismembered head were still open, and the ivory white teeth reflected back from the young black man's hanging jaw.

Ferez dropped the thing in horror. Later he had little memory of how he got out of the pit and back to his car.

The native had been sick for most of the seemingly endless series of flights, but to Bolitho's relief they had not otherwise encountered any major problems. The journey had gone better than he dared hope.

They had flown with Continental first to Los Angeles, via Guam. Bolitho would have liked to stop over for a few days on the Pacific island. Guam was still a major US naval and air base, where he had been stationed for several months thirty years earlier during the Vietnam War. Having left a local girl pregnant, he now had an idle curiosity before he died to try and find the woman, and his son. He knew it would have been a son. But thanks to the damned native, Banto, this proved impossible. As the pain grew worse, he knew time was running out for him to tie up the many loose ends in his life.

From Guam, they had flown to Los Angeles, where Bolitho had his greatest concerns over Banto's paperwork. LA's immigration is notoriously tight. Securing a PNG passport for him had not been a problem, speeded along with payment of a couple of hundred dollars to a rascal group with leverage on a consular official. The US entry visa had potentially been more difficult. In the end Bolitho had simply taken an English-speaking rascal who looked tolerably like Banto up to the embassy at Paga Hill. There they had waited patiently in line. Purpose of visit; 'religious tourism', supposedly to visit a Bible-belt Christian centre. It had taken just half a day to obtain, and suddenly the Stone-Age Banto was a citizen of the world.

Bolitho kept Banto subdued on the flights, partly with dental Mogadon pills, but mostly with fear. Over the days before leaving, he had beaten the little man into submission, like a dog. He had hit him systematically on his legs, arms and back: nowhere that showed. Bolitho was an artist of fear, capable of both subtle and brutal displays of his age-old profession; a profession that had reached its zenith in the West in medieval times; but one still unknown to the primitive world of Banto. His tribespeople may butcher enemies, they may sever heads, and eat their flesh to show conquest, but, exactly like the Peruvians facing the sixteenth-century conquistadors, Banto had been shocked and horrified by the outsider's strategic use of cruelty. When holding an enemy for execution, primitive people honour, befriend and respect him before the speedy death. But when the Incas witnessed the torture, the atrocities visited on them by 'civilised' and 'Christian' men, they were bewildered, believing the uniformed horse-soldiers devils. Banto now also believed Bolitho to be a devil: one to be feared and obeyed for now; one to be destroyed later. For himself. Payback. And to protect his tribe.

The long journey then took them on to New Orleans, for the final hop down to Belize. Banto, who had never before been more than thirty miles from his village, had now travelled half the world, and it had nearly killed him. His incessant fear of Bolitho, too many drugs, lack of sleep, the unnatural air, deafening, strange noises and rich food:

it all left him weak and utterly disoriented. The shirt, jeans and sandals Bolitho had made him wear left him too hot, constricted and itchy. Added to which he was suffering an illness he had never faced before: the common cold, an alien virus to which he had no natural immunity, and which, when added to his acute diarrhoea, could yet prove life-threatening.

Bolitho had seen enough men die on him not to recognise this, and he certainly did not want to face Barton with a corpse. The native was badly dehydrated and running a temperature of over a hundred. He also stank like a polecat for want of his natural toilet, and lack of twentieth-century lavatory training. But now at long last, they had made their touchdown at Philip S.W. Goldson International Airport, ten miles north-west of Belize City. Mightily relieved at the prospect of getting the native away from people and having him fixed up by Barton's doctors, Bolitho also hoped to get for himself a more powerful painkiller. The gnawing from whatever a lifetime's heavy drinking had left of his liver was becoming unbearable.

There were no problems at immigration, and as Bolitho cleared customs with Banto he immediately saw a young man holding up a card bearing the name 'Temple Bio-Belize', Barton's local research plant outside San Ignacio. For the first time in his life, he could have kissed a man, so welcome was the sight of someone to share the burden.

As at last Bolitho and his prisoner fell exhausted into the big Shogun, the Carib driver looked back suspiciously at the two strangers. They both looked real sick. And there was already too much illness around at the lab for his liking. There had been too many sickies who did not get better. That was the gossip. Something strange was going on in there, and people who asked too much got into big trouble. This was a job he did not like. Maybe he would quit. Maybe soon.

Too many sickies. And now two more. They made him nervous.

Chapter Five

'**M**r Bates, isn't it? Hallo. Perry Mitchell. Good to meet you.' He offered his hand in greeting. They were in the hall of the Travellers Club, snow falling heavily outside. Having showed Tom where to hang his wet coat and hat, he asked, 'A quick snifter, or shall we go straight up and eat?'

Tom shook his head. The champagne from the night before at the Savoy had left him headachy. 'I don't normally drink at lunchtimes,' he said.

'I understand. A bit the same myself. Better none than one, eh? We'll eat straight away then. I'll lead on.'

As they climbed the staircase to the dining room, still known for reasons of distant club history as the Coffee Room, the chief steward came forward to greet them. 'Good afternoon, Mr Mitchell. We've kept your usual table,' he said, and led them to the far end of the long room, by a window.

It was Mitchell's favourite recruiting ground, the table distance good and wide. The standard Service procedure of booking all the surrounding tables in normal restaurants, leaving them empty to ensure privacy, had to him always seemed actually to invite attention and therefore to be counter-productive. He talked trivial small talk while they chose what they wanted, and he filled out the slip of paper with their order. Once the waiter had collected it, and brought them over a bottle of water, Mitchell got to the point.

'You must be approached rather a lot by executive-search people,' he remarked cheerfully, splashing water into Tom's glass. Seeing him nod, he added, 'Because the truth is, I have to tell you that I'm a bit of a fraud. Got you here under false pretences. Not really a headhunter at all.'

Tom looked carefully at the other man for the first time. Sixtyish. Bald, with a circle of black hair. Narrow, black-rimmed, what Tom called 'Buddy Holly' spectacles. Medium height, and a stocky, strong-looking body. Charcoal-grey flannel suit, well cut; a white shirt and dark blue military-looking tie. His handshake had been dry and vice-like. But the lasting impression was one of a malevolent intelligence at work. All in all a disconcerting, sinister man. 'Let me guess. You're really a financial advisor, with *just* the right investment opportunities for a man in my position. Am I right?' He knew he was not, but Tom could think of nothing else to bat back.

'And I've got you here to sell you a pension? Or investment bonds? Very good!' Mitchell laughed, but only with his mouth, showing a set of large, even teeth.

'I don't have time for quiz games,' Tom replied sharply, looking at his watch. 'I want to know why you set this up. Now. Or I'm out of here.'

'Of course you do,' Mitchell replied, not put out. Nobody was ever allowed to hurry him. 'And I'll tell you. All in good time. But first, let me introduce myself properly. As you've learned I'm not a headhunter. At least not in the conventional sense.'

'Well, what exactly *are* you?'

'I have a nickname in my old firm. They call me "The Recruiter". But that's running ahead of things. I *can* promise you that I'm not a time-waster. Your time or mine. Can we at least take that as read?' The tombstone teeth flashed briefly again.

Tom was by now feeling uncomfortable: cornered and disoriented by the man. Mitchell's whole demeanour was one of innate authority and gravitas. Whatever he wanted from him, it would be nothing trivial. 'You've got me for an hour. Go ahead.'

'Good. Thank you.' Mitchell looked pleased. He had scored his first points against Tom, and each knew it. 'Now – not that I want to put you off the excellent potted shrimps you've ordered – how much do you know about biological weapons?'

Tom was taken aback. 'No more than the next man who reads the news,' he replied. 'There was talk that Saddam had an arsenal throughout the Gulf War. But I don't know it was ever proved. And some people claim mutant killer diseases like AIDS are caused by experiments going wrong. But that seems like conspiracy theory bull to me. I don't know that biologicals so far have ever been used in war.'

'Oh it's happened. And it's nothing new,' Mitchell replied, nursing the wine list. 'The first recorded case was in 1347, at the siege of Caffa in the Crimea. The attackers, Mongols, threw dead and dying plague victims over the city walls at the Genoese. Later, Genoese traders and sailors took the bacillus with them all over Europe. It became a massive epidemic.'

'The Black Death?'

Mitchell nodded. 'Three hundred years later, Pepys also describes how plague victims flicked their scabs at rich people escaping London. And earlier this century, during World War One, the Germans infected horses in America being shipped out to the Allies. They used glanders, a very nasty bacteria which caused debilitating lesions in the animals.'

'But surely, modern-day biological warfare has been banned. Closed down years ago. The same in the States.'

'There was a 1972 treaty signed banning the stuff. But believe me, it's still with us.'

The starters arrived and they ate in silence for a while. Tom, however, could resist no longer. 'And what's all this got to do with me?'

Mitchell smiled again. 'There are any number of horrible biological cocktails that mad, ambitious or desperate men can use. And they're relatively easy to deliver. Certainly compared with nuclear devices.' He shovelled a spoonful of egg mayonnaise into his mouth. 'The real nasties include anthrax. This causes malignant pustules – blisters – on the head or arm. The skin becomes like raw liver before at last you die – perhaps of fever, septicaemia or haemorrhagic meningitis.

'Another treat is known as aphlotoxin. That causes cancer. Or haemorrhagic conjunctivitis, which causes the eyes to bleed . . . And then there's tularaemia. How're the prawns, by the way?'

Tom looked at him and did not answer.

'Well. The poison I *really* want to talk about today is a little beauty called botulinum toxin,' Mitchell went on. 'A millionth of an ounce of the stuff will kill you. Choke you to death. It works like this. First you suffer from headaches and dizziness, with blurred vision. Probably seeing double. Soon after the mucous membranes of the throat become very dry and constricted, and you'll feel unable to speak. A tracheotomy might help – cutting an air passage in your windpipe.' He made a theatrical cut at his throat with his table knife. 'But most likely you just die from a paralysis of the respiratory muscles. A horrible, noisy, slow way to go.'

Tom was becoming annoyed. Putting his cutlery down he rounded on Mitchell. 'I said you had an hour. Make that two minutes now to get to the point.'

'Haven't you guessed? Come now. I'm surprised,' Mitchell

replied expansively. 'The *point* is Sir James Barton. The *point* is we think he may be developing this stuff at your labs near Lisbon. And the *point* is that you're his closest adviser and business confidant. A fellow director of his biotech businesses.' He picked up the wine list again to choose a half-bottle to have with his lamb.

Tom was speechless with shock. This accusation, if true . . . made what Barton was doing completely unconscionable. He fought to get a grip on himself. 'So who exactly *are* you, making such fantastic, actionable allegations?' he responded sharply, showing more bravado than he actually felt.

But Mitchell was now laughing to himself. Something had genuinely amused him. Looking up from the wine list he grinned at Tom. 'You know, I've been coming here for over thirty years,' he said. 'I wonder if it's always been there, or whether someone on the Wine Committee has suddenly developed a sense of humour. Take a look at the number alongside the club claret here – the Borie-Manoux.'

Tom took it and read it out. 'Double O seven.'

'Indeed!' Mitchell chuckled on. 'This Bond business is getting out of hand again. A restaurant's even opened right by our Vauxhall Bridge headquarters called "Moneypenny"! Dear old Ian must be turning in his grave . . .

'But, sorry, to answer your question at last, Mr Bates. Who *am* I? I'm a pensioned-off spy, and now chief business recruiter for MI6. And we very much hope you're going to agree to help us stop Barton. Be our man on the inside. That kind of thing. I've already discussed it with the CIA people here in your embassy and they're right behind it. You will help? Won't you?'

For once, Tom looked and felt bewildered. Could this really be true? Was it really possible that Barton had been systematically duping him over all these years? Had he been too preoccupied enjoying himself to ask questions – the classic busy fool? Because yes, perhaps there *had* been things in his peripheral vision, things he had preferred not to see. Those phone calls Barton took in private . . . and the new product line Barton had just admitted keeping from him.

Before he replied, this all needed serious thought. Very serious thought indeed.

Jim Barton had flown to Houston, preferring it to Miami, and picked up the Continental flight for the hop over the Gulf of Mexico and down to Belize. It was a wet early evening when he touched down.

He liked his visits to the tiny, sub-tropical country, where because of the inward investment he had brought, he had become something of a celebrity in political circles. The size of Wales, and a population that of Bournemouth, it was known as Honduras when it was a British colony, becoming the independent nation of Belize in 1981. Despite this the British had remained to ward off neighbouring Guatemala from swallowing up Belize. But ten years later, the Guats formally recognised Belize as a sovereign state for the first time, and called the dogs off. Links with Britain remain strong, however, and the government looks to London still to bolster its relations with both the European Union and the USA.

It had in fact been EU money, under the European Development Fund, that had finally selected Belize as the base for Temple's biotech development lab. Tom Bates had helped secure a further two million ECU grant, which had bankrolled over half the start-up costs. And of course supplies of labour and lab animals were plentiful and cheap, and out of sight of the animal rights guerrillas which such work inevitably attracts in the developed world.

The Carib driver and young American Dr Noel Penny, the lab chief, were waiting at the airport to meet him. As the driver took the bags and led them to the Shogun, Penny shook Barton's hand. 'Welcome back,' he said. 'Good flight?'

'One steel tube's much like another,' Barton replied.

'I'm afraid we have to go by road. The helicopter's down, waiting for some spares to arrive.'

Barton snorted his annoyance and frowned at the man. He was a world-class biochemist, but seen as something of an eccentric by his peers. His impatience to bring potential breakthrough drugs forward from animal to human testing had badly alienated him from the Federal Drugs Agency. In frustration at them, he had several times experimented on himself as a one-man clinical trial, the results of which he then published on the Internet. This is how he had come to the attention of Barton. A genius in a hurry was exactly what he had needed. And, in turn, a millionaire prepared to build him the world's biggest chemistry set with which to play was Penny's idea of heaven.

'How's the native tribesman?' Barton asked.

'Physically fine.'

'Physically fine? Meaning what exactly?' he demanded, snapping on his seat-belt in preparation for Belize's notoriously pot-holed roads.

'He was underweight and dehydrated from a bout of gastroenteritis. But mostly he's over that. Psychologically though he's in deep trauma.'

'And how's that showing itself?'

'I'm no social anthropologist, but from the little I know about these things, I'd say he's suffering from acculturation. Trying to make sense of the Western world from his limited native terms of reference. He spends most of his time in some kind of trance. Self-induced. Or chanting some mantra over and over – like caged zoo animals which show repetitive behaviour, pacing or pawing the same spot.'

'Is he talking? Bolitho told me he spoke some English.'

'I suspect his English is quite good. He's said only a few words to us – but I can tell that he understands much of what's said to him. And more . . .'

They were now motoring aggressively away from the airport for the fifteen-kilometre drive towards Belize City, before heading south-west through Hattieville, the capital Belmopan and down the western highway to San Ignacio. Heavy rain over the last two days had once more flooded the river alongside the four-lane road, making conditions treacherous. 'What's that mean: "and more"?'

Penny shuffled in his seat, regretting mentioning it. But there was no way out now. 'I get the feeling sometimes that he's able to communicate non-verbally. Bolitho feels the same.'

Barton turned to look at him with a mixture of disgust and disbelief, suddenly alarmed at the kind of man Penny might prove to be. He knew that professionally the academic was controversial, but was he also some kind of New Age weirdo? There was too much riding on this for Penny to turn out flaky. 'Are you seriously suggesting that this native's got some kind of extra-sensory perception?'

'It's not so strange,' Penny replied defensively. 'There have been well-documented tests on Australian aborigines.'

Barton glowered. 'Well, don't waste time and my money experimenting on that here!' he snapped. 'We need him for one thing. And one thing only. Got it?'

Penny looked out of the window. They were just passing a long concrete building on their left. The famous brothel. It seemed a highly appropriate coincidence. Never before had he felt so acutely that he was prostituting himself and his profession. But he had no choice other than to honour his Faustian pact with the man, as the only way to fund his own genuine research. 'Got it,' he said, clenching his fist in hidden anger.

From the front seat the Carib caught his eye and grinned maliciously.

Lydia was feeling a little lost. She was now on her fifth coffee of the morning and not really tackling the paperwork accusingly covering her desk or the unopened e-mails stacking up on her screen.

The phone rang but she just stared at the thing. She got three types of calls. From clients, with whom she had to be bouncy, pleasant and keen-sounding. From mates in the industry – some of them competitors at other agencies or media independents. Trade gossip and off-the-record note-swapping was an important source of market intelligence for her. And then there were endless 'Hi Lydias' from media-owner juniors trying to flog space, or meet the weekly target of calls. These she regarded as mere box tickers. Higher up the pecking order were the slightly more targeted callers crowing about the latest BARB and how they were delivering in buckets. The better ones tailored the approach: 'I've got an interesting proposal for your car client.' Or more cunning still: 'I was chatting with your big cosmetics client yesterday, and she thought this would be a *really* great idea . . .'

Finally she did take the call: some minion in Topmags trying to tell her about a new weekly magazine targeting the over-fifties. With a small scream, she slammed the receiver down, burying her head in her hands.

Philip had noticed her mood and eventually made an excuse to come in to her office. 'What's wrong?' he asked. 'You're huffing and puffing and you've just been fidgeting around all morning.'

He was trying to help, but what could she say to him? That she had perversely chosen to make her living out of encouraging indiscriminate mass consumption, by supporting an economic system that was trashing the world, and all that lived in it. That – as usual – there was no man in her life. That her head had been crammed full since childhood with nightmare images of animal slaughter and cruelty. That even at her age, her parents' broken marriage still made *her* feel guilty. Or that any day now she would be called on to fire-bomb one of her father's labs?

Instead she simply shrugged her shoulders, knowing full well that these were things she barely understood herself.

The AFW call had not yet come, but she had since met again with the team selected by Sam Thrower, going over the detail of the raid time and time again. No one could take away the maps, building plans or photographs. Everything had to be committed to memory. It had all left her edgy and afraid. She had never been as brave as she seemed to the outside world, even as a headstrong child.

Her screen beeped as a new urgent e-mail message added itself to her list of twenty or more still unread. Casually she moved the mouse and clicked on it. The mail was simply a reminder of an office function that evening. One of the popular agency suits was having a leaving party and the serious drinking was to begin around eight at the local pub. Was she going?

She certainly needed to relax, and knew that Thrower would give them at least twelve hours' notice for the raid. A booze-up sounded good. Tapping in an 'accept' and sending it, she forced herself into a more positive mood and launched into her work. She had a client, Philip's only major client and his career meal-ticket, threatening to consolidate all his group media buying into one of the media independents. This was a growing trend in the market. The independents did not offer advertising services – creative work and production – just media buying. And by specialising and using the muscle of handling huge budgets, they could obtain amazing deals. They did have counter-balancing weaknesses, however, which could negate any financial savings: because there was only an arm's-length relationship with the creatives and account handlers – the suits – their media planning could be weaker, and some clever buying ideas lost. But when hard-pressed clients looked at price alone, and retailers generally did, the independents were hard to beat.

As a result she now faced a simple test. To better the leading media independent on a £5 million DIY store TV campaign planned over spring and into early summer. March to June is the heaviest period for TV advertising after the pre-Christmas run September to November, and retail the second biggest spending sector, after food. A very tough, competitive market.

No time like the present, she pluckily told herself. Stabbing at the key pad, she called Metropolis, the new sales contractor for the recently combined London, south, south-east and Channel Island regions. This territory accounted for almost a third of the homes in the country. They were powerful. And they knew it.

'Mike, hi. Lydia. How's the new baby? Getting any sleep?'

'I sleep at my desk. We're booked solid so far ahead, I barely have a job here.' Like a feral cat, he had already in just those fleeting seconds scented that she was in trouble.

'So if I was looking for 1,500 ratings over sixteen weeks . . .?'

He was surprised. This was a serious budget after all, and firmly put her, not him, in the negotiating driver's seat. 'Oh, I'd prop a couple of matchsticks under the old eyelids for that kind of money,' he replied, his tone signalling his willingness to deal.

When she had finished with him, with a brilliant fifteen per cent discount under her belt, she got up to grab another coffee and stood chatting for ten minutes with a girlfriend in the department, one of the media researchers. The other woman had a boyfriend problem, whilst – as Lydia ironically remarked – *hers* was a *no* boyfriend problem. Feeling a little better, she got back to her desk to find a frightened-looking Philip hovering.

'I just took a call for you from Mike at Metropolis,' he blurted. 'He was just clarifying something on our DIY spring campaign you'd just been agreeing with him. He's got the idea that we've got £5 million to spend with him.'

She blanched. 'And what did you say?'

'I just said that I'd get you to call him.'

Closing her eyes, the colour slowly drained back. 'Good man.'

Her relief told him all he needed to know, and he was appalled. 'Lydia, what are you doing? You know the budget's for a national campaign. No more than £2 million should go to Metropolis, even if we weight up London.'

'Never mind. Leave this one to me. All right?'

He snorted. 'I know what you're going to try, and it's suicide. You won't get away with it!' All this could mean was that she was agreeing the phoney inflated spend with him, on the AB Deadline, to get the kind of discount she would never otherwise have got near to with a piddling £2 million campaign. Then, very late in the day, just before Easter, she planned to spring the news on them that the client had been forced to slash the budget for some impeccable reason – a warehouse fire, or some such lie. Then she would use all her own, and all FKT's goodwill and future spending potential and lard them with 'jam tomorrow' arguments in an attempt to cling on to the same level of discount. 'What will you say to him?'

'I don't know what I'll say. All right? All I do know is that I've just done the impossible. And it might be enough to keep this balls-aching, whining client happy. *Your* client. And you in a job, Philip,' she snapped. Retail was always a pain. 'Now get out of my face on this. It's a risk, I agree, but one I had to take.'

Philip disappeared, looking hurt, leaving Lydia herself now afraid of what she had done without any further prompting from him. Damn it, she had only done it to save his ungrateful neck. It was all so unfair. As ever, Lydia was proving herself nothing like as tough as she seemed to others. She had inherited her father's chutzpah and temper, but not his thick skin.

This time she got up and went to the women's room. Not because she needed to, but to get some space. The place was empty, and she stood looking at herself in the mirror, under the bright, harsh lights. She looked terrible. Pale, tired and waspish. What was the point in worrying, she tried gamely to ask herself. After all, she could any day now incinerate herself accidentally, arming the incendiary device. Or find herself behind bars as a common criminal. That at least made the thought of a rocketing over her Metropolis bluff a little more bearable.

It also made that evening's office booze-up suddenly more appealing. What the hell. Who knows? She just might forget all her good intentions and, for once, succumb to the groping, closing-time advances of one of the less obnoxious agency Lotharios. Everybody else around her seemed to be screwing someone or other in the place. 'The agency that lays together, stays together', was the company's 1980s motto, and that at least had not changed much. Better yet, there was that new creative whom she definitely fancied, and who had smiled at her on the stairs earlier. And it had been such a long time. *Too* bloody long.

As he waited for his colleague to arrive, Perry Mitchell sipped his tea, lost in thought, watching the grey Thames through the green-tinted, bomb-proof glass of the terrace at MI6's headquarters. So much had changed since his days in Queen Anne's Gate, and later Century House. In summer, sharp-suited staff now sat outside sipping cool drinks, like embarrassed extras in some glossy American TV soap opera. He had even seen tourists taking photographs of them, as guides on open-topped buses crossing Vauxhall Bridge pointed out the two spy centres. MI6 and MI5 now glower at each other across the Thames. In Service vernacular, 'the other side', has always referred to north or south of the river.

'It must be fun being retired, Perry.' The young officer's voice startled Mitchell out of his reveries. Neil Gaylord was a liaison man with the boffins in the Defence Intelligence Staff's Scientific and Technical Directorate, and one of the few officers in MI6 with a science degree. He had obtained it while serving with the Royal Marines, the same place he obtained his broken nose as unit boxing champion. With a name like Gaylord, he always joked, there had been no choice but to learn how to fight. Here at Vauxhall Cross he reported in through the Director of Requirements and Production, number two to the chief, Allan Calder. His remit was Counter-Proliferation, and liaison with the Cabinet Office's Proliferation Counter-Intelligence Group.

'Retirement's a wonderful thing. Time to catch up on all those night classes and all that gardening I always missed.'

Gaylord smiled weakly at the thought of Mitchell any-where near a potting shed. 'So. Get here with your bus pass, did you?'

'What else? Life in the fast lane to life in the bus lane in six months.' Mitchell did not stand but waved Gaylord to sit down – subtly making clear his retained senior status. 'How's Mary and the baby?'

'Asleep mostly, when I leave – and get home.'

'You should go to GCHQ and join a trade union, with all the other Bolsheviks.'

'Handy for the Cheltenham Gold Cup. Perhaps I will!'

They joked and gossiped for a few minutes longer before Mitchell hauled them back to why he was there. He thought he had detected a patronising trace element of kindness from the younger man, as if he were talking to some retired buffer as a favour to make him still feel important. 'Now. We private sector wealth creators can't waste time jawing with junior civil servants, you know. After all, your time is taxpayers' money,' he said in mock protest. 'I mean, just think how many more hip replacements could have been paid for if you types had stayed in your perfectly serviceable Waterloo slum tower, eh?'

The smile in return was a little more watery than before, knowing that Mitchell had meant something of what he had just said. 'As you say. Let's get down to work. Shall we stay here, or go up to my office?'

'I really am, in fact, in a hurry. This executive-search front does keep me pretty busy. Let's perch here. All I need to know is the latest on the botulinum toxin.'

'Well, our lab people studied fluids from all the bodies we had dug up. They confirm the presence of varying amounts of the stuff in each. And it matches up with that found in the African suicide from the bridge. All died from paralysis of the respiratory muscles. Some quicker than others. It looks as though they've been trying different dosages, to test the most efficient way to kill with it. These were human experiments, of a kind not seen since the War.' Gaylord's mouth turned down in distaste.

That's all you know, laddie, Mitchell thought, but did not say. The bodies to which he referred had been found near the one discovered by young Ferez, in the foundation trenches alongside Barton's labs near Lisbon. Once again he had got an EU grant for the labs and even the building development, but that had only been one of his reasons for choosing Portugal's capital. The city was also Europe's capital for false EU passports, sold for big money to illegal immigrants. Initially they came mainly from Portugal's old African colonies, like Angola. But now the Justiciaro area had become a worldwide magnet for and a ready supply of nameless illegals, whose disappearance would never be noticed or reported. 'How many were in the pit?'

'Nine. All there for less than a couple of months. Apparently Barton owns the land, and work is expected to start soon building some industrial unit. He obviously expected to bury them all any day now under the foundations.'

'And his contacts with possible customers for the stuff – any more to report?' That Barton would sell and do anything for serious money they now had little doubt. Who the key customer was remained a mystery. That was why they needed someone on the inside, close to him.

'As you know, we have our agent in, working as a lab assistant. She's agreed to hang on in there. But there's nothing new from her on this point. And you? Have you found us anyone on the inside with Barton we can brief?'

Mitchell got up to go. 'You have to sign me out, don't forget. They made me hand over my swipe card when I "retired". Bloody stupid.'

'I'll come down with you. But have you found anyone yet? It's getting urgent. We think he'll be ready to ship the stuff within two to three weeks. We've got the SBS working on a raid plan for when – if – we brief the Portuguese government. And if we have to resort to that kind of raid, then the trail to whoever he intends supplying will vaporise right along with his plant, leaving whoever it was free to source something just as deadly from someplace else.'

'I've got someone nibbling at the bait. I should be able to reel him in over the next couple of days.' They walked across the atrium and took the lift back to the security desk at reception.

'What's he like? Excited about playing spies?'

'Not this one. Too much sense. But I'll get him.'

'I don't doubt that, sir.'

Mitchell did not remark on the 'sir', but took it as it was intended – a sign of the respect in which he, as the best of the old guard, was universally regarded. Eccentric, stuck in his ways – but formidable, and with more experience of the field than most of the new management hierarchy put together. And Gaylord knew that Mitchell saying he would reel in his target was enough for him to put the Lisbon Station on stand-by. It was their best hope yet to stop some cataclysmic terrorist or criminal disaster, and for the first time on this odd case, he felt optimistic. Whatever it was, the thing would start to impact very soon, and the Service had to take the initiative, rather than react to events. This was absolutely vital, particularly with the main target a high-profile British national. And especially with a new, cost-cutting Foreign Secretary to impress. At the very least, they needed something to look good in the Red Book.

Banto sat extremely still, even when locked up alone, like a small jungle animal trying to avoid attracting predators. The windowless room in which they kept him at the lab was some three metres square, with a low ceiling. Off it was a broom-cupboard-sized toilet and shower tray.

There was a bed and stool, which completed the jail cell quarters.

His arm ached from the daily drawing of his blood, and his head hurt as it never had before. For an athletic, physical man, the lack of exercise was debilitating. He needed to run as others needed to drink and sleep. His world had turned into a nightmare, but his survival instincts were helping him find ways, somehow, to compensate. There were no reference points any more. No rhythm. He understood nothing of what was happening to him, and everyone with whom he came into contact was brutal and frightening. Especially Bolitho, the chief warrior from the tribe who had captured him. As for the blood they kept taking, he reasoned that they were drinking it to show him he was defeated, like his own tribe when they beheaded and ate captured enemies. It was now his turn to find himself defeated, and he believed that any day now they would take enough of his blood to kill him, before devouring his flesh.

Death, even the prospect of a terrible death like this, held no fear for Banto. Barton had been right when he had said to Lydia that a tribesman's life mostly comprised hunting and killing and being hunted and killed. The death of mothers, brothers and sisters in childbirth was commonplace, and as a young warrior-hunter, his entire focus had been on death and survival. The slaughter of virtually his entire family in the raid had not hurt him emotionally, at least not in any way a Westerner could understand. The code of the tribe, and that of any warrior, decreed a short period of highly ritualised communion with the spirit world – through ceremonial dance, body decoration, a head-dress made from bird-of-paradise plumes, and the slaughter of pigs. But there were two over-riding emotions which kept Banto focused and looking for some way out. The first was his solemn promise to his village chief, the *kepala*, to return with warnings and information to help his people prepare for all the changes they soon had to face. The second was – Payback. He had been wronged. And without question, they would have to pay him back, on his terms.

Anger swept over him, and he now stood and started pacing the length of the cell, moaning the two-note chant, over and over again. The hypnotic mantra soon consumed him, putting him back in touch with the rhythm he needed to survive, and he began to feel invincible, a spirit army of ancestral tribal warriors at his side . . .

Suddenly the door flew open, and Bolitho came in followed by the two strong Caribs they used to hold him down. 'Stop that noise! It drives me crazy!' Bolitho barked, stooping, his face inches from Banto's. It was true. Banto had droned the chant for great lengths of their long journey together, and it had seriously got under his skin.

'No more take! No more!' Banto screamed, making to hit him. The Caribs quickly grabbed his arms, and Bolitho buried a vicious punch into his stomach. Banto folded, fighting for breath on the floor.

'Bring him!' Bolitho barked, and led the way.

Barton was waiting in the lab with Penny. A purple light created an eerie atmosphere in the small operating theatre. Banto had been strapped on to a hospital trolley by the Caribs, and was now being wheeled in. All eyes turned to Barton for some signal that they should continue. Banto noticed this. This man was obviously their big *kepala*. For a few seconds, the terrified eyes of the native met with Barton and locked on him. Barton looked away first, disconcerted by the experience. Then Banto tried to free himself, for a small man putting up a terrific fight, despite being well secured. Forcing him still again, Penny roughly shoved a needle in his arm.

'Does he always fight it?' Barton asked, worried about Banto damaging himself.

'No. He's normally passive – physically, that is. Mentally, though, he's fighting us every step of the way,' Penny replied. 'Tonight's the first time he's resisted like this. He seemed spooked by you for some reason. Look at him. Still staring at you. I don't like to sedate him, if we can avoid it. That way we get to keep as much twentieth-century junk out of his system as we possibly can.'

Barton watched impassively as they began drawing off the day's supply. 'How long can we go on doing this to him?'

'If we can get him to eat better, we can do it indefinitely. The body quickly makes up half a pint of fluid. That's no problem. It's the cells that take longer. But progress is fine. So long as we don't push it, and get greedy.' Penny drew Barton over to one side. 'But you *know* what I think of all this. It stinks. A lousy, phoney stock market scam. It's no more than a Jenner!'

'A what?' Barton did not like being patronised with other people's shorthand and jargon.

'Edward Jenner. The first man to use a vaccine. At the end of the eighteenth century,' Penny replied, sheepishly now, realising he had gone too far. 'He noticed that milkmaids who'd had cowpox rarely got the smallpox, figuring they'd developed some kind of immunity. So he made up a crude cocktail of bodily fluids containing the cowpox virus, then used a thorn to inoculate a boy. Weeks later he repeated the procedure, this time injecting him with smallpox. Jenner's experiment worked. The antibodies from the cowpox virus successfully attacked the smallpox. The boy was fine.'

'And . . .?' Barton snapped. 'What's your point?'

'Goddamn it . . . For all our advanced knowledge, you've got me copying exactly what Jenner did two hundred years ago. Using the native's bodily fluids as a fake vaccine, to *fake* the clinical trials.'

Barton looked sharply at him. 'And what's your problem with that? We've been over it a dozen times. You keep milking him. Farm enough of his natural antibodies for our so-called "vaccines" to impress in Phase One clinical trials. The world will believe that, miraculously, we've already cracked the genetic code. And that what we've been testing is a biotech, lab-produced copy of the antigens of disease-immune native cell lines. A miracle cure. All, of course, safely patented.

'So, yes, you're right. It *is* just a Jenner. But on even rumours of the trials going well, the markets will go crazy for the stock. And I'll be able to capitalise some of my holding to fund my other work, in Portugal. And for research funds to bankroll all the real clinical work you really want to do. In fact, I'm having a key broker flown out over the next few days. We've got to impress him. I need a strong "buy" recommendation from him – on the back of what he must see as our huge future earnings potential.'

Barton was right. Penny had already bought into the scam months earlier, in return for big funding for his own legitimate work on antigens. But he was someone who needed constant reassurance. 'I guess. But just so long as that money does come back here . . . Give me that, and OK, sure . . . I'll have them hailing you as the next Alexander Fleming.'

'I hope so,' Barton said with his shark's smile, and turned to leave the timid scientist to his worries.

Later, back at his vast ranch just outside San Ignacio, Barton took a long soak in his bath. Afterwards, having pulled on a cool silk dressing gown, he poured a large cognac and lit a cigar. Glancing at his watch, he called Tom Bates at the WMC offices.

'I'm in Belize, and need you out here,' he said to Tom, as though the row had never occurred. This was typical of Barton. He exploded ferociously, wounding and bullying indiscriminately one minute, and carried on the next as if nothing had happened.

Tom tried to empty his own mind of the bad blood between them, and to act for now with cool, detached professionalism. For once this did not come easily. He had been badly shaken by Mitchell's devastating accusations, and his own snowballing doubts about Barton. But tactics before temper, he counselled himself. 'What do you want?'

'Bring out the top biotech analyst. Someone the rest will follow. Bring Elkins. I want him here, to see what we're doing. And to meet Penny.'

'Why? What's the objective?'

'I need to get the share price jacked up again. To place some shares while we're out of the financial closed season.'

'How much are you trying to raise?'

'Not a lot. Just a couple of million.'

And this from a man who was bankrupt less than two years earlier.

'What do we need it for?' Tom asked, testing him.

'Things,' Barton replied tartly, obviously wanting to close the subject.

Mitchell's accusations rang true yet again. 'It'd have to be something pretty important to get someone like Elkins all the way down there. At such short notice.'

'It'd have to be something pretty important to move the price, given all the flak recently. It'd have to be. And it *is*. On both counts. Can you do it?'

'I can try,' Tom said, scrolling through his electronic diary. There was nothing he could not move.

'Good. This is what you do. Fly Concorde to Miami.

They've just introduced a new service. Have a night stop-over there. I'll fix everything. I know things about Elkins. I know how to give him a good time. How to make him grateful. So, Tom, you do more than just try. Get him out here. Whatever it takes. Call and tell me when.' Barton kept private detective agency reports on all the top analysts, fund managers and financial journalists, and was perfectly prepared to use them to further his aims.

'I can't guarantee anything . . .' Tom began, but Barton had already hung up.

Lydia was about to leave late to join her work colleagues for the party when the night line began to ring. As usual no one was in a rush to pick it up, and Lydia for once did not feel like being Little Miss Responsible. When at last someone did take the call, she was walking through the door as her own phone rang. A colleague was obviously transferring the outside call to her. She almost did not answer even then. But her conscience, as ever, got the better of her.

'About that OTS. You told me to call, and, well . . . here I am.'

'Tom!' She was surprised. Surprised and intrigued.

'I know it's short notice, but I'm at a loose end and thought . . . Well, how about that drink? Or dinner tonight?' Jim Barton's call earlier had prompted him to take her up on the invitation to ring.

'Sure. Why not? Only . . . Well, there's this office leaving party I was just off to. I have to show my face.'

'Sure. No problem. As I said, I know it's real short notice. I'm off to Belize soon. We can meet when I'm back. We'll fix some other time.'

He sounded genuinely disappointed. 'Look, why not join us?' she suggested. 'We just meet in a pub, so it's hardly private. These things usually end with everyone piling in for a Chinese or Indian somewhere. But we can skip off early if you like.'

An hour later, Tom Bates pushed his way through the crush at the Soho pub and caught her eye across the smoky room. Already two large gins the worse, she fought her way over and met him halfway. They looked at each other awkwardly, both hesitating over a phoney social peck on the cheek. Then Tom seized the moment. He kissed Lydia fleetingly on the lips, brushing her face with his hand, an arm around her waist pressing her into him. 'Hello, you,' he mouthed, before kissing her briefly again.

The sexual charge that surged between them signalled in that instant that they would at last sleep together that night. That their thus far ambiguous relationship had just irrevocably been resolved, for good or ill. She took him by the hand, leading him proudly over to her work friends. He was, she felt, the best-looking man in the place, and noticed with satisfaction the glances he got from some of the svelte, leggy agency beauties. Especially the two glacial receptionists, blatantly hired as interior design accessories to impress and flirt with clients.

By eleven o'clock she was happy drunk, and in no mood for a raucous balti house. As they left, there was no 'your place or mine' debate. The dog needed his last exercise. They could not keep their hands off each other in the cab over to Pimlico, and on arrival Oliver was subjected to the fastest walk of his life.

*   *   *

Maddie came into the Chester Street study, closed the door behind her and put her glass of Evian on her husband's desk. Some friends had asked her out to dinner at a new Mayfair restaurant they wanted to check out, and she had decided to wear her pearls. Along with the rest of her own and the Barton family jewellery, they were kept in the safe, for insurance reasons.

To her horror, as if in slow motion, she saw the glass tumbling over. Having carelessly put it down on the edge of his blotter, it spilled over a sheaf of papers on which he must have been working. Finding a box of tissues, she dabbed frantically to soak up as much as she could, but it had already made quite a mess. They would inevitably dry out with tell-tale crinkles and water stains. Yet another row when he got back and found them. Trying to make as good a job of it as possible, her eyes caught some of the headings, and she began idly leafing through them. The top sheets seemed to relate to cash-flow forecasts for the Stow plant – the xeno-transplant side of the business. This she now knew something about, having read the magazine article that had recently appeared on him. Curious now, she picked up the other documents. There was one from his lawyers about patent and intellectual property rights. Obviously, she reasoned, if you invented some new cure, you had to protect yourself from the pirates. All tedious stuff.

Satisfied that she could do no more to repair the damage, she walked over to the opposite side of the room, folded back the section of antique pine panelling, and exposed the Chubb wall safe. Having tapped out the code, she removed a file that had been stuffed in, put it on the chair, and took out the red velvet box holding the antique pearls. Her great-grandmother's. She held the four-string choker momentarily to her cheek loving its coolness, went to the mirror and put it on. As ever, the milky-white pearls drained her face of colour – an effect she sometimes liked. Set against her simple black couture Valentino dress, the consumptive, pre-Raphaelite look perfectly captured her vulnerable mood.

Having closed the safe and panelling, she collected her glass and was about to leave when she noticed the file left on the chair. Mildly annoyed, she picked it up, and glanced through the contents, suddenly curious at what was in these particular papers for them to have been locked away.

Perching on the chair, she began to read. The first document was a private detective agency report on a man called Elkins. Some kind of City analyst. It included a copy of his confidential medical insurance health file, with several AIDS tests ringed, copies of his personal bank statements and his latest annual appraisal from the broker employing him. She was appalled that anyone could get hold of such personal things. But was even more horrified when she turned over and saw grainy photographs of the man dressed strangely, performing homosexual acts. She threw the report to one side in disgust and started reading the next document.

This contained threatening letters from one of Jim's bankers. It warned of unacceptably high borrowing; Temple Bio-Laboratories had been put on what the bank called its 'critical list', and would be subject to detailed weekly inspections to ensure the firm met the cash-flow forecasts they had already imposed. The language was blunt and frightening.

It was clear Jim was in real danger of going bust again. That at least would explain his manic focus on making money, at any cost. And it would explain at least some of his moodiness and irritability.

The last papers were more difficult to follow. Some were in a foreign language. Portuguese, she thought. And others were technical, relating to the purchase of chemicals, the names of which she did not recognise. But then she saw a copy of a fax in English. Sent from Moscow. It was from someone called Rybinski, and referred to him accepting 'the Lisbon appointment', for half a million dollars. But it was the next phrase that sent her blood cold . . . *'To meet your brief, will need at least ten healthy males, 18–25. Destruction testing vital. You to supply and dispose.'*

Her eyes stared unbelieving at that single, telling stipulation. 'Eighteen to twenty-five' ruled out mice, rats, pigs or even apes.

Maddie's hand shook as she read it again and again until her head ached.

Lydia was woken by Oliver barking at her from the side of the bed. Looking at the clock, she saw it was almost nine o'clock. Horribly late. So late that Oliver was demanding his first walk and breakfast. Alcohol was still coursing through her, and her head pounded with the mother of a hangover. Then she remembered. Remembered everything! Throwing herself over, she realised she was alone. And no sign of his clothes. No sounds from the kitchen or bathroom. Jumping up, she dragged on her robe and rushed out, in a panic. The empty house sneered at her. Waves of guilt, embarrassment and self-disgust washed over her. This was why, this was *exactly* why she had stopped having short-term relationships. Why, why, why had she done it? And with Tom, of all people.

Could she trust him not to talk? Men always had to boast, or at least hint about these things. An easy lay. A *lousy*, easy lay. That was what he would now think of her. How could she possibly face him again? She would just have to avoid going to the Manor and Chester Street. She would have to lie low for a while, and then somehow just brazen it out later when they did meet again. And unprotected sex too! With a man who spent his life travelling. Who was always in the Far East. Africa even . . . How could she be so foolish? So girlishly *stupid*?

Then she saw the note, propped against the sugar bowl. White and sickly looking. Formal. How could words, any words explain? Let alone help? Stalking it, pacing, she dug deep for the courage to open the thing, to cope with the rejection it would inevitably contain. Pulling herself together, she finally tore the flap and read, steeling herself as if against a blow.

> *Darling,*
> *Had a seven-thirty appointment. So I've left for home, at the crack of, to change and pick up some papers. You were so deep in sleep I didn't want to wake you. I've tried to set your radio alarm for quarter to eight. Hope I did it right! But I can't even set my own video recorder properly!*
> *Last night was really special. Because you're a very special lady. Call you later. See you soon.*
> *Love, Tom.*

She read it once more, searching every word, every nuance to divine his real meaning. On the surface it seemed straightforward enough. There was none of the morning-after nausea or recrimination. None of the cold, self-centred hostility she had herself felt after a couple of meaningless one-night stands at university. She had always hated that empty Noël Coward, endearment 'darling', but how was he to know that? No. On balance, it seemed genuine.

A gossipy call to Philip about being an hour late, and a quick bath, left her feeling much better. And not a little excited about seeing Tom again.

Chapter Six

'**G**ary? Hi. Tom here. How goes it?' Tom pushed his computer key pad aside and reclined, putting his feet on his desk.

'Fine. And you? Still down-sizing corporate Europe for a living?'

'*Right*-sizing! Get it right, will you? That way it doesn't sound so bad.'

'Well excuse *me*. I'm sure the losers you people throw on the trash heap feel *so* much better, being *right*-sized and all.' The Texan accent had not softened even a fraction over the three years he had been stationed at the American Embassy. 'Anyhow, what is it you want? I'm kinda busy right now.'

Gary was ex-WMC, and like all the consultancy's old staff, was in everyone's Alma Mater networking database. 'You know people in the FBI and CIA over here.' They had talked about it on a number of occasions after Gary had confided in him that he had been asked to join the Bureau soon after his arrival in Grosvenor Square. 'Well, I need to know something.' He told him about his meeting with Mitchell, and that the Englishman had claimed to have cleared the approach with the embassy security people. 'Can you check it out for me? I need to know if it's official or not. And quickly.'

Gary promised to phone him back as soon as he found anything out, and was as good as his word. In less than an hour, following a visit to the FBI legat on the fourth floor, he was on the line. 'This Mitchell guy's genuine enough. They call him The Recruiter. Works for MI6, but he's now semi-retired and under cover of some commercial job. Big hitter in his day. His name gets a lot of respect from our people here. It seems he spent some time in the States as UK liaison officer with the CIA, after Oldfield. Until this semi-retirement, he continued as the main link between London and Langley, working out of Vauxhall.'

'And has he asked them about me?' Tom had known intuitively that Mitchell was genuine. But to learn that he was such a senior player only served to alarm – and intrigue – him all the more.

'Sure has. They gave him your file—'

'My— What goddamn file!'

Gary laughed at his old friend's naïvety. 'You don't think that people like you can globe-trot – Russia, China, the old Soviet bloc states – and whiz in and out of major defence and pharmaceutical corporates without being checked out, do you? Wake up!'

'Have you seen it? My file?' This whole secret world was beginning to draw him, a moth to the flame.

'I shouldn't have. But I did get to sneak a view.'

'And?!'

'Hey . . . I can't divulge a thing. No way,' he teased, before finally relenting. 'But . . . and this buys a favour back sometime when *I* need something. Well, you know your last trip to Moscow a couple of years ago, and that girl you somehow managed to charm into bed? The brunette dining next to your party at that restaurant by Gorky Park?'

Tom made a strangulated noise, a mixture of anger and fear. 'What the hell . . .?'

'Well, it seems she was FSB. That's the newly formed KGB. They were very interested in the assignment that took you over there. For Big Blue. You probably felt hung over in the morning? That right?'

'Why?' Tom was now defensive. He had most certainly felt desperately hung over and distinctly odd the next day.

'Because she drugged you, and after your . . . shall we say, tryst? . . . she made copies of just about everything you had in your document case. And lap-top.'

Tom felt sick. 'Are you sure?'

'Absolutely. But the Bureau checked things out with IBM's own security people, and it seems you could have given them nothing they didn't have already. So no big deal. Except you'll be forever categorised as an intelligence patsy. Someone who can't keep his dick in his pants. The people here are working on the assumption that she'll also have taken, er, interesting pictures of the two of you together. For possible future use. That's S.O.P.'

'S.O.P?'

'Standard Operating Procedures. Sap.'

'This isn't funny! And what else does the report say about me?'

'Just that you're someone who travels a lot, and has access to a wide range of important business people and bankers. And some political fixers in the east of Europe. There's a whole lot of guff about your relationship with Sir James Barton. They obviously have you down as someone open to routine honey-pot espionage techniques, but clean of drugs, and other illegals. Clean, but a piece of cake for the opposition. You have a "C" security grade as a result. An average risk, but not someone to be trusted with anything important without special training.'

'And what do you think? You know about these things. Should I agree to help?'

Gary snorted in disbelief. 'Hell no! It's all downside. That's why *I* didn't join the Bureau when they asked. Tell this Mitchell guy to go screw himself. You'd be crazy to put yourself at risk for these security types. They're all bastards. That's their job. And this Mitchell guy's one of the best there is. Stay out of it.'

'Hallo. It's me. Maddie.'

Lydia, surprised to hear her voice, looked away from her computer screen, glanced towards Philip to check he was too busy to eavesdrop, and focused her mind. The two women in Jim Barton's life rarely spoke one to one. 'Hi. This is a surprise. Where are you?'

'I'm in town. At the house. Look. I was wondering if you were free for lunch today. I mean, I guess you're real busy, but . . .'

Lydia's mind spun, trying to get a fix on what this could be about. Whatever it might be, it was certainly intriguing. 'Yes. Sure. But only a quick bite. I have got a lot on . . .'

Maddie mistakenly took this as an implied attack on her as a 'lady who lunches'. It had not been meant that way. Lydia really was very busy, and behind with things. 'Just a sandwich somewhere then,' she replied with an edge.

Lydia sensed that she had inadvertently hurt the woman. 'No, no. I'm fine for an hour or so. I know a very nice salad and pasta place near here. Veggie, I'm afraid. If that's OK?'

'Fine. I'll come to you then. Twelve-forty-five-ish OK? See you then.'

Lydia hugged herself nervously after Maddie had hung up. What could it be about? What would they talk about? Dad? The houses? The twins? Tom even . . .? Deep down she liked Maddie well enough as a woman, but all daughters had difficulties in relating to stepmothers. Especially young, attractive, title-hunting American stepmothers. But that all seemed to go with this particular emotional territory, and need not, surely, stand in the way of them getting closer.

Thinking this made her decide that it was time to stop sitting and waiting for Tom's promised call. She would call him now and judge how things really stood between them. Before she lost her nerve, she reached for the phone.

He was not in the office and she next tried his mobile.

'Bates.' His voice was clipped and businesslike.

'Hello, Bates,' she said. But as she spoke, the signal broke up, and she could not make out his reaction. 'Hello? Tom! Tom! Can you hear me?' Suddenly robbed of the immediacy of his response, she panicked. How was he reacting to her calling him like this, on the hop – and at work? After all, what exactly was there to their so-called relationship? A night of sweaty, drunken love-making, and a neutral letter on a sugar bowl. Was she really building some fantasy relationship on so little? Get real, she chided herself.

The line then went dead as the signal finally gave up the ghost.

Deciding firmly against ringing again, she reasoned that he probably would not even have recognised her voice over a bad connection. Cursing herself, she got on with some work and called up a TV contractor, giving him a hard time for letting her down. A minute or so later, Philip suddenly leaned over and stuck a mini Post-it sticker on the tip of her nose – something he often did, and which he knew annoyed the hell out of her. It would be Philip's turn to get a tongue-lashing when she was finished with her current hapless victim. Shooting him an angry look, she peeled it off and read the message he had neatly written out. 'Call Tom back. ASAP.'

Her heart leapt and she cut short her call and redialled the mobile number. 'Tom?'

'Lydia! Hi!' His voice sounded genuinely excited.

'How did you know it was me?' she asked, still unsure of herself.

'It was spooky. I was thinking of you a few minutes ago, hunting for your number, when there you were – on the line.'

'And what were going to say?'

'Just that last night was really special. That you are really special.'

'And I should believe this, should I? I mean, you do have something of a reputation, you know. Are you sure that it wasn't just some reminder call from your Psion to telephone last night's *femme du jour?*'

'Hey. You're not a client, you know. They pay me to be nice. On my free time I'm generally obnoxious. Ask anyone. Me being nice without a fee? This *must* be the real thing.'

She began to soften. 'I got your note this morning. Fact or fiction?'

'Fact.'

'Prove it.'

'How?'

'You're the smart consultant. You figure something out, something convincing,' she teased.

'OK. Dinner tonight. And later I'll be suitably – what? – Turandotian. You know? Ready to face any test.'

'There'll be only one test,' she laughed sexily. 'And for that – *nessun dorma* . . .'

Lydia had started to recognise he was the kind of person who had to talk about personal, emotional issues obliquely, usually using the prop of humour, irony or parables. 'But if there really was a dinner invitation wrapped up in all of that, you're on.'

'Nut cutlets at eight?' he teased, but the signal was beginning to fade again.

*   *   *

Banto had been quietly adjusting to the new world around him ever since his kidnap in PNG. That's what warriors did to stay alive. They watched, listened and adapted. At any cost, they survived.

As he could not run, he exercised his muscles instead by tensing and then relaxing them. And as he could not sleep deeply, he visited the quiet, very private hollow tree inside his head to refresh himself and become strong. The words aerobics and yoga were unknown to him, but he instinctively practised both to a high degree of sophistication.

Above all, though, he had been learning voraciously. His retentive memory had by now virtually remastered the basics of English, and the context in which words were used. At airports, on planes, there in the lab, between people not addressing him. In his head, and by whispering softly to himself – he was an extraordinary mimic, like the monkeys and birds of his forests – Banto practised the hundreds of words and sentences he had retained. Watching no less intently, he had also observed how they used small tools to eat, and a different kind to make marks on paper-leaves. He accepted without question that they could also talk to people not there by tapping and pressing banana-shape, shiny creations to their faces. And he observed the very clear tribal hierarchies. The big man who had just arrived – they called him Sir James – was obviously the chief: the big *kepala*, with his distinctive corn-coloured hair, blue eyes and pig nose. The other brutal man, Bolitho, who had killed the rascal and brought him all this way, was an important warrior. The man who now took from him – Dr Penny – was another tribal leader, a medicine man. And then there were the low people who, he observed, were treated with no respect. The women. And the blacks.

One of the Caribs now came in to his cell. It was the usual time to deliver the last feed of the day. The routine

had been set days earlier, and Banto was expecting him.
Ready for him. Tonight, he had decided, it was time to
show them what a warrior could do. The loss of blood
was making him weaker by the day, and he knew that
if he was to escape, it had to be soon while he still had
some strength.

Slamming the food and water down contemptuously,
the man made to leave, not even having bothered to look
at him. Banto had all along cultivated the impression of
a cowering, subdued prisoner, meekly doing as he was
told. Until that day he had never physically fought back
or resisted, even when he was beaten. As a result, the
guards took his compliance and cowardice for granted.
This was exactly as it should be, Banto knew. His enemies
under-estimated him.

As the man turned his back, leaving to lock the door,
Banto spoke for the first time. 'What is your name?' His
accent was American from the Christian missionaries who
first taught him, and from his exposure on the endless
flights to Bolitho.

The big man froze and turned his head slowly to stare at
Banto. To him the native was little different to any of the
other animals on which the lab technicians experimented.
'Wha . . .?'

'What is your name?' Banto repeated. He was still squatting
on the floor in his usual corner.

The Carib's hand now went to rest on the big, sheathed
knife on his belt. 'You! Quiet, man!' he spat, insulted at
being conversed with by something he considered no more
than a kind of ape.

Banto now stood up slowly. 'My name is Banto. What
is your name?'

Becoming angry, the Carib stepped towards Banto
and hit him hard across the face, his heavy gold ring

splitting his lip, which had barely healed from Bolitho's blows.

Banto had long since been trained to control physical pain. Only major broken bones could affect him as a warrior. Not even wiping away the gushing blood, he repeated, 'I am Banto.'

The Carib sneered and made to lift his arm to hit him again. But Banto sprang forward in anticipation, clamping his own immensely strong left hand over the man's right and simultaneously taking the knife with his other. There was an eighty-pound difference between the two men, but Banto broke his wrist as if it were a matchstick. The pain and shock immobilised the Carib, and before a scream of pain could leave his mouth, Banto had buried the serrated blade in his throat. He watched clinically, with deep professional interest, as the Carib slumped, mouthing and hissing noiseless screams that died in the severed windpipe. It had all been executed exactly as Bolitho despatched Chancey, and Banto was pleased with the outcome of his own experiment. Throat-slashing was an interesting technique. In the forest, it mattered little whether victims screamed or not. It was never quiet, with the constant calls and screeches of monkeys, wild pigs, birds and the rest. But in this indoor world there was, as now, much silence. More silence than noise. So warriors needed these special techniques, he reasoned. There were *some* small things to learn from the outsiders.

As the Carib writhed, bleeding to death on the floor, Banto calmly ate the rice and chicken, and drank the water. Then he went to the door and looked down the dimly lit corridor of the laboratory annexe. There was nobody else around, and the main door led straight out to the fields that surrounded the small, now deserted industrial estate on the edge of San Ignacio. Stooping to wipe the knife clean on the Carib's denims, Banto inspected the gaping wound. The man was close to death.

'Payback,' he said to him, not without a little respect. 'Payback.'

Then he got up and headed towards the door. The cool night air, and the familiar world of the dense rain forest called out to him from just a long walk away.

Maddie, as ever, made Lydia feel big and inelegant. Poise and deportment seemed to come to her naturally, and her dress sense was unerring. Today she wore a Burberry with matching scarf, and a rust-coloured soft tweed suit with brown leather boots and Hermès shoulder bag. It was an outfit you might see any I-wanna-be-Western Japanese woman wearing on her tourist bus. But on Maddie, it looked just right. That *style anglais* again, on a stylish American.

She had deliberately left her fur at home – something of a concession, for her. But not enough, predictably, for the ever-spiky Lydia.

'Cute boots, Maddie,' Lydia said, in greeting. 'I wonder if your handbag ever knew them.'

Maddie frowned. 'Do you absolutely *have* to?' she asked in despair.

'I suppose not,' she replied. 'I'm sorry. Bit on edge, I suppose.' Lydia noticed that the drop-dead gorgeous receptionists were fixing Maddie with cold eyes. This at least pleased her, knowing how the two harpies hated having anyone more beautiful than themselves around. First pulling Tom in front of them, and now lunching with Maddie: her star would be rising. Cynical as she was, she was not completely immune from feeling good about that. 'If Harrison Ford calls me *again*, tell him I've gone to lunch, girls,' she called, before turning back to Maddie. 'Come on. Let's eat. And I'll stop being a veggie PIA. Promise.'

No great meat-eater herself, Maddie happily ordered a pasta with pesto sauce, while Lydia went for a tureen of lentil soup with thick, crusty bread. 'Well. I know you don't want my views on animal testing. Or media inflation, I shouldn't think. And you definitely don't need the name of my hairdresser . . .' Lydia volunteered, to fill what she suspected would be the first of many long silences.

'Can't we meet just for no reason? Can't we just talk?' Maddie recognised that the distance between them still yawned too widely.

Lydia looked at her closely. For the first time in quite a while in fact. And on that close inspection, Maddie's face had become surprisingly lined beneath the immaculate make-up. And her eyes seemed smaller somehow, no longer those of a young woman. Even her hair was beginning to look manufactured rather than natural. Only another woman would notice, but for Lydia it made Maddie suddenly more human. 'How's the Manor coming on? Still a lot to do?' It was a peace offering, gratefully received.

'Oh, you know – it's like painting the Forth Bridge. I'll never really finish it the way I want. But we've got it back in good shape, haven't we?' The Manor had been her responsibility to get right: finding reliable builders, designers, landscapers, antique dealers and the rest. Even with an open cheque book, all this was still stressful. It had been the one thing she could call her own, and Lydia's opinion of what she had done to her family home mattered to her.

'The place looks great. Absolutely great. Just as it should. All the fabrics and furniture you've brought together look as though they really belong. Like they've always been there.'

Maddie leaned back, relieved. 'I do love the place, you know,' she said, smiling a thank you to Lydia. 'I mean love, too. I talk to it all the time I'm there. And tell it to look after itself when we leave for town.'

'Perhaps you're really talking to the spirits of all the others who lived there before us.'

'I've thought that myself,' Maddie replied, blushing slightly in embarrassment. 'And you. How are you? Still seeing that nice French boy?'

Lydia snorted. 'Maddie! That was *ages* ago! I haven't heard from him for nearly five years.'

Maddie looked deeply embarrassed. 'Sorry . . . But you don't bring people down any more. And we never really get to talk. So . . . is there anyone else special these days?'

Now it was Lydia's turn to blush. Ladling more soup into her bowl, she avoided Maddie's eyes. 'Maybe.' She was dithering over whether to tell her about Tom.

'Maybe?'

'Well, yes. I think so. But it's *really* early days.'

'I thought I detected a certain something about you. We girls can always tell. Anyone I know?'

This was it. Crunch time. Should she tell her – and risk it getting back to her father that she was sleeping with his closest business associate?

No way, she quickly decided. It was far too soon. This thing might not survive the week. Might not even survive dinner that evening . . . 'I will tell you. Promise. I just need to be a little surer. You know how it is.'

'I'll hold you to that, young lady. I hope it all works out for you. Really I do.' Leaning over, Maddie pressed Lydia's hand.

Unlike Maddie, Lydia was not a toucher, and freed herself as soon as she could without seeming rude. This was all getting far too personal and intimate for her liking, and she badly needed to change the subject. 'And how's Dad? Still racing around?'

Maddie's face clouded, remembering the unpleasant reason she was really there. 'He's in Belize again.'

'What does he do down there? It seems to be his latest toy.'

'It's one of his biotech labs. All secret squirrel stuff. Ask Tom next time you see him. He's the only one likely to know what's suddenly going on there. I certainly don't.'

Lydia's face also clouded. It was of course true. Not only her father, but he – Tom – was enmeshed in all the genetic work. No doubt entailing yet more animal testing. Strangely, stupidly, the obvious link had only just really hit her. 'I do so wish Dad would do something else,' she complained. 'I mean, his computer company days were dicey enough, but all this genetic engineering stuff . . . I know he's done terrifically well to discharge himself so quickly and pay everyone off, but why this? Vile medical research.'

Maddie gently shook her head. 'You're quite a cocktail of contradictions, you know. What started you out – on all your causes? I mean, we both come from privileged backgrounds. I conform. Become predictably preppy. *You* get passionate about animal rights and the rest. Yet still work in the world of advertising . . .'

It was something that had exercised Lydia's own mind often enough, and she had yet to find an answer that she could articulate. 'I like contradictions,' she replied. 'Life isn't simple, and neither are we. But when you think about it, I suppose it was strong-willed, ruthless people who built my family's fortunes. And yours. Father and me are at least true Bartons in that respect. Atavistic. But where he's hungry, I'm angry. Angry at suffering. Needless suffering. You want a glam fur coat, leather boots and a tasty lobster? OK. So minks get skinned alive, calves never get old, and a living creature gets thrown screaming into boiling water. I'm sorry, but you have to learn to play consequences in

life. You sure as hell wouldn't live like you do if you had
to do, or even witness your own killing.'

'And advertising. Doesn't that promote conspicuous consumption? Fuelling all your "needless suffering"?' Maddie
responded tartly.

'Like I said, I'm complicated. I guess I need some aggressive outlet, like any good Barton, and advertising is certainly
that,' Lydia replied, shrugging, readily acknowledging the
inadequacy of her response. 'Maybe I should take up squash
instead.'

Maddie smiled weakly. Despite entering briefly into the
repartee, Lydia's contradictions were not greatly exercising
her. Her mind was elsewhere, preparing what she had come
to say, and not knowing how to begin.

Lydia noticed, and realised that there was, after all, a
reason for Maddie's call that morning. 'What is it, Maddie?
There's something you want to tell me, isn't there? Is it Dad?
Is he ill?'

'Ill . . . How do you define ill?' Her eyes blazed briefly
with anger. Checking that nobody was close enough to
hear, she leaned forward, drawing Lydia towards her. 'Yes.
I think he is very ill. Not heart, cancer – nothing physical.
But ill in the head!'

'What are you talking about?' Lydia snapped. Despite
everything, he was her father. Only she had free rein to
criticise him.

'I glanced through some papers on his desk last night. I
wasn't snooping, but . . .' She held her hands up. 'Anyway.
And then at some in the safe.' Stooping to pick up her bag,
she took out a large, folded manila envelope, flattened it
out neatly and pushed it across the table. 'I found this.'

Lydia took it from her reluctantly. Whatever it was, she
knew she was not going to like it. 'What's in there?' she
asked, suddenly afraid.

'Proof. Proof of something I suppose deep down I've known for years. Perhaps known all along about him, but didn't want to confront. Read it and call me tonight.' Getting up, she pulled on her top coat. 'I'm leaving him, Lydia. I wanted you to be the first to know. Read the thing, and you'll understand. I don't know what's made him this way. Perhaps you'll make some sense of it, and forgive him. But I'm sorry. I can't. I won't.'

Chapter Seven

'So. You've got the picture? I'm a hard-nosed, arrogant stockbroker's analyst, specialising in ethical pharmaceuticals and biotech stocks. You've flown me out from London all the way to this dung hole to show me the really pioneering work you're doing here. OK? Off you go. Convince me.' Barton puffed on his cigar, ruined by the damp air despite his travel humidor. They were in the main ranch-house, the dinner plates from their indifferent meal of plantanos fritos and ceviche still in front of them.

Dr Noel Penny pushed the crockery away to make space, unable to work or think in an untidy environment. 'And how much can I assume he knows about biotechnology? A lot, or a little?'

'These people know more than you expect. But less than they think. A bluffer's knowledge. They're good at asking smart questions, but can't understand the answers – and probably don't even attempt to. Mostly all they go away with is an impression of how you handle yourself. They need to defend their recommendations if things screw up later. But deep down, never forget, they *want* to believe. They need to find winners to back.'

Little the wiser for all that, Penny decided to rehearse his analyst's presentation on the assumption the man would in fact really understand as little as Barton himself. All these business people could cope with were headlines in *Newsweek*. The attention spans of an amoeba.

'I'll stand,' he said nervously. 'I present better when I stand.'

'Fine,' Barton pushed his own chair back. 'And start by telling him about yourself. Your qualifications. What you've done before. I'll already have given him the basic company spiel on me, and why I started Temple Bio.'

'Right. Well. Welcome, Mr Mr . . .?'

'Elkins. His name is David Elkins.'

'Elkins. Yes. Then, welcome, Mr Elkins. Here to Temple Bio-Belize Laboratories. A plant we opened less than two years ago, with the support of a grant from the EU's European Development Fund.' He paused. Barton was smiling to himself at the delicious irony of all the EU money Tom had been able to get for him. 'Is it OK to say that? Is anything wrong?'

'No. Far from it. Carry on,' Barton said, pouring himself another cognac.

'So. My name is Noel Penny. I have a PhD in biotechnology from the University of Massachusetts for work on genetic engineering, and spent the years after working in a research capacity at various institutions in the USA and Britain. Sir James heard of my work in seeking cures for terminal diseases through biotechnology – I had by-passed the usual learned journals and published some early findings on the Internet, to try and find a sponsor to fund my research. He approached me two years ago to work with him . . .'

'Don't refer to the Internet stuff. I don't want him knowing you're anti-establishment, in case he picks up on all the controversy about you testing on yourself. Or your problems with the Federal Drugs Agency. They quite like nutty professor types, but not mavericks.'

Penny looked and felt hacked off with this. First he asks him to tell the man all about himself, then makes him leave out the parts of which he was the most proud. 'If you think so . . .'

'I do think so. And also, this stuff about spending years working at various research establishments . . . it doesn't sound impressive. Didn't you have some time at Cornell and Oxford?'

'Not really. Just a few weeks at each.'

'So what? Say you spent it all at Cornell. He might check you out at Oxford, but not Cornell. OK?'

'Cornell. I spent most of my research time then at Cornell. All right?' Penny ran his hands through his hair, fighting to keep the annoyance from his voice. 'So, Mr Elkins. As an expert on the sector, you know what an exciting world it is. Biotechnology. This is what is now at the very leading edge of scientific and medical discovery. We are to the new millennium what NASA and Moon travel were to the sixties.

'The theory, though not the application, is simple. Biological information can be passed from one cell to another as a chemical code, stored in large molecules – like proteins. Over a century ago, the great pioneer Miescher described the repetition of chemical units in proteins as a kind of language. "Just as the words and concepts of all languages can find expression in the letters of the alphabet", he wrote to an uncle. Half a century later Oswald Avery created a kind of Berlitz guide to understanding and speaking that language. He discovered that it was DNA – deoxyribonucleic acid – and not protein that stored and carried the information. He had discovered the very blueprint of life itself.'

'Good. Good!' Barton called out, encouragingly, beaming.

'Fine. Well, we now know that genes, which hand on physical characteristics, are part segments of DNA. And this has enabled us at Temple Bio-Labs to develop still further

the new technique of xenotransplantation, using transgenic
pigs, genetically engineered with human genes at our plant
in Gloucestershire. This is going to be big business. The
potential market for human organ transplants is put at £4
billion a year, with a serious shortage of suitable human
organs to go round. World demand is currently in excess
of 400,000 donor organs a year, with an ever growing black
market. From the limited publicity our work has received,
we already have a subscribers' list of almost a hundred
very wealthy individuals. All offering us open cheques to
be first in line to get their very own spare-part "self-pigs",
genetically tailored to meet any future need they may have
for replacement organs.'

'That's OK. But no need for too much detail. He knows
about Stow. I've already taken him around the plant,'
cut in Barton. 'Also, other labs are making big claims
for xenotransplantation. And anyway, he'll know that
the government's Ethics Group keeps slowing us all
down. So stress what we're doing there is not only
transplantation. What interested him more is how close
we are to a commercially viable cell-free blood substitute.
All right on that? But get on now with the real news. Our
work on new genetically engineered vaccines.'

'OK. OK. So, Mr Elkins. The *real* news in the sector is
breaking right here. In sleepy Belize. My own main field
of research is in what's called transcription. That is the key
linkage needed when attempting to copy a gene. It's kind
of like replicating DNA itself, copying information on, in
the form of the genetic code. It's technically possible now
to interfere with the transcription process to help create
remarkably effective cures. Actinomycin D, the anti-cancer
drug is one example. The antibiotic Rifampicin, for treating
tuberculosis, is another. Or – and this is what interests me
– you can try and re-create a gene that you think would

be helpful to fight a variety of illnesses. Cancers. AIDS. Hepatitis.

'This can either be done by copying certain original genes already found in nature. Or, as some pioneers are attempting, by using protein engineering. This is where they change DNA sequences to manufacture a completely new man-made protein. Here at Temple Bio-Labs, however, we own copyright on a series of *natural* proteins and cell lines, which give immunity to virtually all the remaining killer diseases of the age. Using techniques being developed here, we fully expect to be able to cure almost all the serious viral diseases known to man. And to offer the option of preventative vaccines. These would be not mere inhibitors, but actual cures. Making it quite simply the biggest applied medical breakthrough for centuries . . .' Penny now held his arms out to show that he had all but finished his carefully scripted presentation, something he had written and committed to memory earlier that day.

Barton permitted himself a broad grin, and clapped loudly. 'Bravo! Excellent. Spot on.'

'Not too technical?'

'No. Not a bit. Even *I* understood it,' he said, pouring Penny a drink. 'Let's now guess the questions Elkins might ask us. What do you think?'

Penny did not hesitate. 'Well, apart from time-to-market stuff, and questions about regulatory obstacles . . .'

'I can field all that.'

'Well, there *is* only one real question, of course. Where are we obtaining our supply of human host cells for development?' He thought guiltily of Banto, caged in like a laboratory baboon.

'So give me an answer. Something jargony, but credible-sounding.'

Penny sipped his cognac. He had already given the

subject a lot of thought. 'The truth is that healthy human cells are extremely difficult to culture, and are never used in commercial applications for genetic engineering. But if he's made any kind of study of the field he'll certainly know about HeLa cells.' He looked at Barton expectantly, probing whether he understood.

Barton glowered back, however. 'Remind me about HeLa cells,' he said, evenly.

'HeLa are the initials of a woman. The donor. She died of cervical cancer back in 1951. Culture cells were taken from the cancer, divided up and have been grown time and time again ever since for research use. We have a little of HeLa ourselves in the lab, right here. Along with cells from the lymph cancer of an African child. These have also been cultured and regrown many times to create interferon, a human protein that's used to treat some cancers, as well as viral illnesses – including herpes and hep. B. What I could do is snow Elkins with some junk about our being able to culture the original cell lines we took from the PNG tribes.'

Barton smiled fatly again. 'You certainly snowed me! That'll do fine.' Barton had got up, and Penny followed suit, assuming it was a signal for him to go.

'Well. I'll get back to the lab for an hour or two.' He made for the door. 'I'll practise that presentation, and get it much smoother. When are we expecting Elkin?'

'Elkins. He's flying out tomorrow. Tom Bates is travelling with him. On the new Concorde service to Miami – to save his precious time out of the office, helping him justify the trip with his bosses. It's a bribe of course, at our expense. All somewhat negated, you might think, by my ensuring they have a night's stop-over there before flying on here. I had a detective agency check Elkins out for me months ago. He's a closet homosexual.' Barton gave a wolfish grin.

'So I've got them staying at a gay hotel and arranged for a selection from the local scene to hang out for him in the bar. I want him showing up here with a nice, guilty secret. One we can use, if necessary. I can't leave anything to chance right now. Tom knows nothing about any of this, of course. Remember that. He's my Mr Clean. The acceptable face of Temple Bio. Don't tell him any more than you tell Elkins. Got that?'

Penny nodded, as ever feeling sullied by his involvement with the man. He strongly disapproved of so much of all this, and envied Tom's ring-fenced ignorance of the seamier side of Barton's business. He well knew that he himself was despised by many people for what he did, who accused him of the usual cliché of 'playing God' by manipulating genetics. Having worked through all the arguments, however, he was now happy to defend his case with anyone: that a great deal of suffering in the long term would be avoided by his real research there. The greatest good, Utilitarian argument. In his way, he still saw himself as extremely moral. 'I'll be getting off then.'

A maid came in to clear the table, having heard them moving about. She was a very beautiful Creole, in her early twenties. Barton noticed Penny looking at her. 'What do you do with yourself, down here for months on end?' he asked, pruriently. 'Do you have a regular woman? There are some gorgeous Lebanese and Sri Lankans around town.'

Penny stared at his feet, embarrassed. 'No,' he said, making for the door. 'You forget perhaps that I know rather more than I sometimes wished about medical nasties. Gonorrhoea is not exactly unknown here. Ask any of your British squaddies. And that's the least of it.'

The woman glared angrily at him, but he noticed with satisfaction a shadow of concern in Barton's eyes.

Suddenly there was a loud banging at the front door,

and the maid ran off to open it. It was Bolitho, who ran in, sweating heavily and looking worried.

'What the hell's happened?' demanded Barton.

'He's gone. Escaped!'

'Who? Pull yourself together, man. Who?'

'The native, Banto. He's killed his guard and escaped . . .'

Barton and Penny looked at each other in disbelief. The unthinkable had happened.

Barton sat down, his fist to his mouth. 'Where can he have gone?'

'The forest,' Bolitho said without hesitation. 'That's his world out there. The rain forest.'

Looking up, slowly, Barton held him with cold eyes. 'Get on his trail. Now! And don't come back without him. Alive. Because if we don't find him, or if anything happens to him . . . I'll have you shot.'

Lydia put down the slim file and sank her head in her hands. She had read it a dozen times since Maddie had given it to her the day before at their lunch. It could not be true. He was a rogue financially. That she knew. But this simply could not be true. She called Maddie, needing to talk to someone, to put some structure, some boundary on what she had just read.

'It's me. And I don't believe any of it,' she said, defiantly.

'That was my first reaction. But . . . I'm now really not so sure.'

'I mean, I know he's a bully. And cuts corners. But . . . not this!'

'Perhaps we should tackle Tom about it. He might be able to throw some light on things. Is he around? In the country?'

'No. He leaves today to join Dad in Belize. Taking out some important City analyst.'

'So. What *do* we do? Go to the police?'

'No!' Lydia snapped. She was still not ready to accept it. There had to be an explanation. It had to be some ghastly misunderstanding. It was after all written in telegraphese, referring to people and plans in Lisbon of which they had no real knowledge. 'We'll confront him, as soon as he's back.'

'And when's that?'

'He's due to fly back with Tom and the analyst in four days.'

'All right, if that's what you think. We tackle him together . . . But – wait, someone's just arriving. I'll see to it and call you back in a minute. Don't go away . . .'

Grabbing Oliver before he could escape her reach, Lydia hauled him to her lap for a cuddle. Never an affectionate dog at the best of times, he subjected himself to this for a few seconds before jumping down and shaking himself the way he did when wet, as if to rid himself of her unwanted sentimentality. Sitting by the door, he made his pathetic small animal noise, looking at her with big, brown expectant eyes. 'In a minute. I'll take you out in a minute. Down the Embankment and across to the p-a-r-k. In a minute.' She got up to make a quick coffee as she waited for Maddie to call her back.

The phone rang just as she was pouring the water out. 'Maddie,' she said, 'I think we should meet again before . . . Let's fix a time. Lunch or dinner or something. Here if you like . . .?'

'That's *real* noyce of yow,' came a sneering male voice, Sam Thrower's Brummie accent deliberately exaggerated. 'But yow'd have to shee-ow me which knife and fork to use.'

'It's you! What is it? What do you want?' She went cold, knowing full well what his call had to mean.

'Show-time,' he said.

'You mean . . .'

'Show-time is all,' he snapped before she could say anything more.

She shuddered. It was their codeword for tonight. 'OK.'

'You still up for it?'

She thought of her father, and what she had just been reading. 'More than ever,' she said, and hung up.

Perry Mitchell looked across the table at Tom Bates, his wide mouth turned down slightly in distaste. They were in the interview room MI6 still occasionally used in Admiralty Arch. The MOD had moved out in 1994, and soon even this last vestige of official use would end when the place became a tourist restaurant. 'This is a colleague of mine. His name isn't important.'

Tom took in Neil Gaylord. Tall, foppish hair, intelligent eyes and a sharp Savile Row pinstripe suit. 'Can we get on?' He tried to assert himself in his best consultant's manner.

'You have a plane to catch, of course,' Mitchell said, watching him closely.

How the hell did they know that? Tom wondered. It was another reminder of how serious they were about all this, however. 'I won't even bother to ask how you found that out, but yes. I do have a plane to catch.'

'Then you may be equally interested in knowing how we came to be in possession of this.' Mitchell pushed over a copy of a fax Tom had sent the previous afternoon to Barton. In it he resigned all his directorships and gave notice to terminate his long-standing consultancy contract with him. It also contained some technical paragraphs drafted by his lawyers designed to protect his stock options. Tom had looked into the mirror, and into his conscience, and decided he had been used and kept in the dark for long enough. He wanted out, and would use the Elkins trip to face Barton man to man.

Tom was shocked. 'I suppose nothing should surprise me with you people,' he replied quietly.

'We intercepted it electronically. And I have to tell you that Barton has not received it,' Mitchell replied. 'You see, we don't want you to resign. In fact, it's the last thing we want. But as you requested, I'll get to the point.' The anglepoise lamp was reflected in his spectacle lenses, preventing Tom from seeing his eyes. 'You've refused my request to help us. A refusal which seems to have been carefully and rationally thought through. And not one I'm likely to be able to change by way of any further appeals. Either to patriotism or to any Walter Mitty dreams of playing at spies. That's about where we are, I think?'

Tom's survival antennae were twitching. 'You got it. Like I said when I called you after our lunch, the answer's no. Not fair on my business associate. Not fair on WMC, my employer. And not fair on me. So. No deal. Tell Her Majesty, sorry, but I've resigned.'

'And that's really your final word?'

'Read my lips, Mitchell!' Tom snapped. They had not insisted on this meeting to just hear him refuse again, this he knew. Something was coming.

'And if I were to point out that the funds your team manages for Barton are almost entirely from the drugs industry?'

Tom looked defiantly back. He was confident on his ground here. 'Not true. I've checked it out. The money comes from perfectly respectable, mainly US travel and entertainment businesses. Hotels, restaurant chains, travel agencies, car rental ... Huge cash flow from the travel-voucher system. They use us as a clearance system for inter-company payments.'

'Very well. We tried. It's always better for everyone if these things are accepted voluntarily. And with goodwill on both sides. However . . . you're forcing me to, well, insist that you help. Help your country, and mine. Over to you . . .' Mitchell got up, nodded to Gaylord, and turned his back on them as if in disgust, looking out through the grubby net curtains at the thundering traffic decanting into the Mall.

'I have a DEA file here that proves beyond any doubt whatever that the companies channelling their money to your Curaçao account are indeed legitimate businesses. But fronts, all of them. Cash businesses laundering drug dollars through the travel voucher. You're welcome to look through it if you wish. But you *can* take our word for it.'

As he pushed the file over, Tom flicked through it half-heartedly. In truth, he did feel he could take their word for it. 'Assuming you're right, what makes you think that Barton or I knew anything about it?' he demanded.

Gaylord treated the question as rhetorical. 'The Aruba Alliance. What can you tell us about that?' he pressed.

Tom was genuinely fogged. 'Never heard of it.'

Mitchell shot a look at Gaylord, and nodded slightly. 'There's a lot you know nothing of, Mr Bates,' he said sarcastically.

'Like these photographs.' Gaylord was spreading out a selection of black and white half-plates on the table. 'Would you oblige us by looking at them?'

Tom put down the DEA folder and walked over. It took several seconds before he was able to assimilate what they were. Then he abruptly turned his head away, bile rising in his gorge. 'What . . .?'

'These are the largely decomposed remains of Africans found by our Lisbon Station over the past few days. They were in land belonging to Temple Bio-Labs, alongside your Oeiras plant. Each had died from exposure to varying amounts of a curious new strain of botulinum toxin. Mr Mitchell told you a little about it over your lunch, remember? These young men had been used as laboratory animals, we think to refine the toxicity levels to perfect biological weaponry.'

Mitchell walked over and passed Tom a glass of water. 'We'll leave you alone for a while. To read the file and think about things,' he said, before leading Gaylord out.

Tom had not moved when they returned three minutes later. He seemed in a state of shock. Shock at what he had seen and learned. And deep shock that he had after all been so comprehensively used by Barton. Putting his hands behind his swimming head he tried to get a grip. 'What do you want from me?'

'Rethink your refusal to help. Don't resign. Help us avenge yourself with Barton. Help us put him away for a very long time. Think about what I've said on your flight to Miami. I'll have one of my people contact you out there, to hear your decision. That's all I ask. OK? Deal?' Mitchell extended his hand.

After Tom had left, Gaylord looked at Mitchell curiously, shocked at the way he had left things. 'What the hell was that all about?' he asked. 'Are you going soft in your old age?'

Snapping the file shut, Mitchell smiled his sinister smile. 'I've almost got him. A few more hours will be a good investment. Believe me. A good volunteer is worth ten reluctant conscripts. And he's bright. If we get him on our side, he'll be excellent.'

'But if he still refuses?'

'Then all bets are off. He helps us, or he goes to prison. He helps us, or I break him.'

As Banto had padded down the deserted corridors to make his escape, he heard a pitiful screeching from one of the labs. Looking in, the dull light revealed three chimpanzees in individual cages. He started at the sight of them, at first thinking they were humans, even smaller than him. Chimpanzees are not found in PNG, just the spidery tree monkeys and tree kangaroos. But he quickly recognised them simply as frightened creatures, like himself. There were also rats and mice in cages on the long working surface. Pulling off the lids, he reached in and grabbed two of the fattest-looking rats, and pressed their throats, despatching them speedily and stuffing them in his pocket. He now had food for the journey. Then without a second thought he freed the chimpanzees, which shrieked excitedly, waving their arms up and down, baring their teeth at Banto in submission.

They followed him, bounding along on their knuckles, as he made for the door to leave the hated place behind. Pushing it open, the apes ran out without so much as a look back at him, but something made Banto pause for a moment before escaping. There was a captioned photograph of Barton, as chairman, displayed behind the reception desk. From the magazines and videos on his various flights, Banto had by now learned how to 'see' again, assimilating the shapes in photographs and identifying that they were likenesses of people or places. And he certainly recognised this likeness of the chief he had seen that day. The man to whom all others had deferred. This was the *kepala*. This was the one who would have to face Payback. Bolitho first. But Payback had to be given by the big *kepala*. That was obvious. Whatever it took, Banto could never return to his people without Payback from this man. Grabbing it from the wall, he had difficulty getting the picture out of the frame. Finally he threw it in the floor in frustration, where it smashed and he could pick out the photograph and shove it in his shirt pocket.

Banto's first act of freedom on quitting the compound had been to kick off the sandals he had been forced to wear. His wide feet splayed out and his strong, finger-like toes dug luxuriously into the wet soil, immediately drawing strength from it. Then, deciding against tearing off the loose denim jeans and shirt yet, he became very still, head up, catching the steady rain in his open mouth. Standing erect, a human aerial, he had focused his entire being on the forests around his village, so far away, and then on the deepest part of it that he had experienced there. As he became wrapped in its damp, foetal darkness he slowly divined the nearest place of safety to him now. There was no one instant when he knew. No flash of insight. No sudden shaking, like a water-diviner's willow. Gradually he simply knew. Safety was south. Two sleeps away. And south was *that* way . . .

The rain continued its steady fall all night as Banto half ran, his clenched hands held stiffly by his head, boxer-like. The lab was by the northern sports ground, alongside the Novelos bus depot, and he padded along the market place, past the petrol station and across the Hawkesworth Bridge over the Macal. Into Santa Elena his instinct took him south along the Cristo Rey road and on to San Antonio beyond. At first, leaving the urban sprawl of the town behind, he found himself in grasslands, keeping to the sandy roads. But by dawn he was back in the Macal River valley, now with more verdant pine forest and farmland, being drawn inexorably towards Mountain Pine Ridge and the Chiquibul rain forest beyond around Caracol.

Mid-morning and he had already reached Río On, having barely rested. Seeing the inviting river he at last decided to pause briefly. Taking off the denims, he swam in the clear, cold water before eating some hard and tasteless *pacaya* he found growing wild nearby. The carbohydrate filled him, and he snatched a light sleep. Half an hour later, and he felt completely rested and refreshed. Washing the guard's blood off the hunting knife, he used it to fashion himself a *lap-lap* loincloth from the shirt. Tidying the area to make following him difficult, he carefully stuffed the jeans and discarded strips of material under a rock and continued his journey.

Three hours later he had crossed the Macal yet again, this time at the Guacamallo Bridge from where he could soon see the Vaca plain beckoning him in the distance, with its dense blankets of rain forest. Beginning the ascent, he was glad to leave the acrid pines and their parasitic orchids and bromeliads behind. He was even more pleased to abandon the Reserve road and paths to begin to strike out on his own, as the Chiquibul primeval womb drew him nearer to home.

Chapter Eight

The industrial park was a mile outside Stow-on-the-Wold, just off the A429. The five-person team selected for the raid had arranged to make their own way individually to Gloucestershire, meeting up in the car park at the bottom of the hill, on the village outskirts.

It was dark and deserted when Lydia drove in, a far cry from the stream of buses and cars which choke the narrow streets on a typical summer's day. But there are few things more depressing than an out-of-season tourist centre, and the village's peeling paint and shuttered-up mood hung over all the unit members already there. Parking up, she walked over to Sam Thrower's mud-spattered Land-Rover Defender. It was a long wheelbase 110 County model, with no side windows. Lydia had been ten minutes early, but still the last to arrive.

'Now we're all here . . .' Thrower began, unfairly, 'we might as well make a start. Are you all OK? Know what you're going to be doing?' The group nodded back. They were all wearing dark, close-fitting clothes, as instructed. 'All right then. Tony, you stay here in the Land-Rover, and keep in radio contact for when we need you to come running.' The plan had been for him to remain parked up, and be ready to go through the motions of changing a tyre. Thrower had taken the trouble to have a flat wheel ready for him, in case a passing police patrol stopped to investigate. 'Chrissie and Joan, you follow behind Lydia and me after a couple of minutes. So. Now. First, switch on your radios, and check they're working OK.'

Each put the ear-piece in place, lifting the tiny black, foam-covered neck-mikes closer to their mouths. 'Beam me up, Scotty,' joked Tony from the Land-Rover, playing around with his volume control. This was followed by a piercing blast of feedback.

Thrower tore his ear-piece out until it stopped, then glared at him. 'What we'll see tonight will be science fact, not science fiction,' he cautioned. 'Let me hear the rest of you say something, to test these things.' Each muttered 'testing' in turn. 'Fine,' he said, satisfied. 'Keep in the ear-pieces, but don't broadcast unless you have to warn us about something. OK? Now. This is it. You all know what you have to do. Let's do it. Good luck.'

Now it really was the time to go, the mood changed. The tension was palpable, but Lydia was first to strike out. 'Come on then, Sam. Lead the way and let's get this thing over with.'

He looked at her with a hint of respect, and handed over a black canvas bag. 'All your toys are in there. If you want me to do it after all, I'd understand. You've had the bottle to show up. That'd be good enough for me now.'

'I said I'd do it, and I will,' she replied, acknowledging his peace gesture with a small smile. 'Let's see how good a teacher you are.'

They were walking away from the village and across icy fields to enter the industrial park from the open fields at the rear. Their reconnaissance had established that one of two security guards would be on duty that night. The younger of them spent much of his time snoozing in the neon-lit Portakabin office by the entrance barrier. When awake he used a Walkman or rang people, presumably his girlfriend or other insomniacs. He never toured the site, and just about managed to make the obligatory phone call every three hours to his control office in Cheltenham. This was the one Thrower hoped would be on this night's shift. The other man seemed to be in his late sixties, and was far more diligent. There was a small TV set in there, and he sometimes watched an old film. But at least three times a shift, and regardless of the weather, he would patrol the park, with its seven tenanted units, the ramrod back betraying a service career sometime earlier in his life.

It took them just over ten minutes to reach the four-foot-high chain fence which marked the outer perimeter of the park from the surrounding farm. It was in no way a security fence, but there to keep the sheep in. They climbed over without difficulty, heading for the Temple Bio-Laboratories plant one building in, along the private road. There were just half a dozen sodium streetlamps illuminating the park, but Thrower knew that the Temple building had a number of standard security sensors of its own which, if a beam was broken, would flood the place in light.

Exactly as rehearsed, when they reached the corner streetlamp the two got down on their stomachs and crawled commando-fashion the rest of the way to the side wall of the building. This was something Thrower had tested a week earlier to check out the sensor footprints. Lydia was numb with fear and deeply worried about remembering what to do. And would her shaking hands do what she told them, even if she could remember everything?

Thrower was in front of her and, on reaching the back delivery door, he took out what looked like credit cards, along with something resembling a small oblong-shaped torchlight. First he ran the torch object very slowly along the top edge of the door starting from the hinge side. When a red light flashed, just a few inches from the opposite edge, he firmly pushed one of the credit card wafers into the gap between the door and the frame at exactly that point. It seemed to stay in place when he took his hand away to continue running the torch instrument down the length of the front edge of the door. No red warning lights came on this time, and he next ran it along the bottom of the door again, from the hinge side. Once again, just a few inches from the opposite edge, and mirroring the top, the red light flashed. Pushing in the second credit card he stood back, looked at the door as if at a sporting opponent, and spoke softly into his neck-mike. 'You two. Don't forget to crawl at the streetlamp.'

'OK. Just coming up to it,' said Chrissie.

Lydia could hear the nerves in the other woman's voice even in these few words. She had to stop herself from saying something reassuring back. Instead she watched Thrower in action, impressed. He was now working on the lock with a set of skeleton keys. Lock-picking, something taught him by his burglar stepfather, had long been one of his party tricks, as well as a hobby. The skeleton keys had also been passed on to him by his stepfather: tools of the trade which, when married to the apprenticeship he had patiently given the boy, meant Sam need never be poor.

The lock was a basic pin tumbler. And, to his relief, a cheap Chinese make. This would allow him more clearance between the barrel and body, and with any luck it would also have larger than normal pin holes. Inside it were five equal-length pins, which in their locked mode held the barrel fixed in position. When the correct key was inserted, it would simply force the springed pins – each split at a different point – into line with the outer casing of the inner barrel. This could then turn freely to release the lock. What Thrower had to do was use his special tools to replicate this action, so opening the now hopefully dis-alarmed door.

Kneeling, he put his lips to the lock and blew hard to free

any grit from the mechanism. Then he selected a tension bar from his tool kit, delicately inserting it into the barrel and working it to and fro, judging the pressure needed to imitate the key action in turning the barrel. Next he eased a rake into the keyway, over the tension bar, as far as the rear of the back pin. The tension bar was now supposed to replicate the normal key's bottom shaft, as the rake, when quickly pulled out, aligned the five pins, so allowing the tension bar to turn the inner barrel and open the lock.

With a look to the heavens, Thrower applied light tension and whipped out the rake. The lock however stayed stubbornly in place. He knew immediately that he had applied too little pressure, allowing the pins simply to fall back in place. A good mistake though. Too much pressure could have complicated things by binding the top pins. After one more failed attempt, worried, he put his ear to the lock and raked again, leaving the bar in place, listening for the tell-tale sound of a pin sticking. Happily, he heard nothing and so tried once more. A painstaking clockwise turn of the bar brought a smile of relief and pride to his face. But only for a fleeting second. Still kneeling, he knew it was not over yet. The door would now open but – had he properly disarmed the alarm?

Edging the door fractionally ajar, millimetre by heart-stopping millimetre . . . it was long, long seconds until he was sure. Then . . . Yes. Yes! It was safe. Thrower stood up, dizzily gulping air, realising suddenly that in his concentration he had been holding his breath.

'Are you all right?' Lydia asked, worried.

He nodded, flushed. 'The lock's open. Before we open the door though, pray the sleeves hold that I put over the alarm contact sensors. These things can be bloody unreliable.'

'What? Those credit card things?'

'Yeah. The theory is they mirror back the contact on the

door edges, so that when we open the door the circuit stays intact. And the theory also is that the electromagnetic field holds them in place.'

'The theory . . . And how well tested *is* this theory?'

'I've had a success rate of about seventy per cent.'

Now you tell me, she thought bitterly. 'So we have a three in ten chance of the alarm going off, here and at the police station?'

'Worse than that. That seventy per cent was just my bench-test results on them reflecting back the contact. There's also a one in four chance of the magnetic field being too weak to hold the top one in place,' he replied matter of factly. 'Ready?'

She glowered at him in disbelief, then watched with a kind of fatalistic, detached fascination as his hand, still on the handle, began to inch the door open. Her headache was now in danger of turning into a blinding migraine. Then suddenly, there was a loud electronic howling filling her head and she screamed, dropping the bag.

The blow nearly broke her nose, but the searing pain cleared her head like smelling salts. Opening her eyes to focus, she saw Thrower mouthing silent obscenities in her face. His hand came back to slap her again, but she caught it in time. The electronic howl, she now realised, was simply radio feedback from her ear-piece. Still snarling at her, he pushed the door wide open and in the same flowing movement gaffa-taped the cards in place.

The security alarm was silent.

'What happened . . .?' she whispered.

Pulling her roughly inside, he closed the door behind them and put his back against it. 'You screamed, you stupid cow! And you dropped your toys.' His face was thunderous with anger. 'Detonators in or not, you *don't* drop fire-bombs on the bloody floor!' Then, turning his head away in disgust, he spoke into his neck-mike. 'How loud was that scream? Did you hear it, Chrissie?'

'I'll say! What happened?'

'Never mind that. Get out of view, quickly, before the guard comes to check it out. Do it. Now! And if you see him, whisper to me where he is and what he's doing. We're now inside.'

Lydia slumped to the floor in the darkness, furious with herself for justifying all his 'stupid cow' stereotyping of her. Her confidence shot to pieces, she felt she could do nothing right any more.

'Sam!' she heard Chrissie bark in her ear-piece. 'The guard. He's on his way over!'

'Which one is it? An old guy or the other?' Thrower demanded.

'He's old-looking.'

'Shit!' he spat. He knew the type. Old school, knew his job, took his responsibilities seriously and had the irrational courage to execute them to the letter.

Lydia hugged herself miserably as she felt Thrower's eyes boring into her through the blackness. It had all gone wrong because of her. Because of her! And it was not over yet . . .

The helicopter pilot looked over at Bolitho. 'Ready?'

'Hit it.'

They were in the ancient Bell Ranger regularly chartered by Temple Bio-Laboratories for ferrying people and freight to and from Belize airport. Its owner, or rather the man trying to pay off the monthly lease payments, was a late-middle-aged Lancashire man, an ex-RAF pilot. As a Flight Lieutenant he had completed four standard seven-week tours in the late seventies flying helicopters in the then colony, loving every minute. Mostly it had been in the large transport helicopters, the Pumas, delivering supplies to Gurkhas and Queen's Infantry units – the main run being to and from the airport camp at Belize International and Rideau Camp. Sometimes he had been up in the smaller Gazelles and night-flown wiry, tight-lipped SAS men to their map references for routine exercises, although on other occasions, and especially when he dropped them near the Guatemalan border, he had known this was not just training, but active-duty covert operations.

The pilot activated the starter switch and immediately the starter motor whined to life, kick-starting the turbine. Having checked his gauges – exhaust gas temperature, oil pressures for engine and transmission, torque – the blades now spinning invisibly above them, he pulled at the collective pitch control lever and lifted off. Once airborne, he pushed the left pedal then moved the cyclic stick to the left, carrying them south towards the Vaca plateau.

Bolitho had guessed that the native would head for safety in the nearest rain forest, and his hunch had been pretty much confirmed. His men had been sent out first thing to ask around, and they had soon found people who had seen Banto mid-evening, running down Burns Avenue, and minutes later past the Shell station alongside the market by the Hawkesworth suspension bridge. He had crossed the river, heading east to Santa Elena. Then a final sighting had him jogging south towards Cristo Rey, the 800 square kilometres of Mountain Pine Ridge Forest Reserve and possibly as far as the Chiquibul rain forest.

'How well do you know the area?' Bolitho asked the pilot over the headset.

'Pretty well.'

'You RAF?'

'Was. Now I fly for money. Tourists, archaeologists, wildlife ecologists . . .'

'I'm a 'Nam vet. And miss it like hell. You?'

The pilot smiled to himself. Did he miss RAF life out there? He thought back to the five-mile runs, wearing boots. The gins in the mess, followed by the horror B-film shows. Friday night 'Bad Taste Parties' at Airport Camp, with the water-pistol shoot-outs and punch served in a lavatory pot. The free condoms for Saturday night specials, when the camp bus was sent to the city to bring back local, poxy girls. And the Sundays spent scuba diving at the Cays. But there was the serious side that haunted all the schoolboy fun. The fear of the Guats actually doing it. Actually invading. And the Royal Artillery Chestnut Troop's big guns at Holdfast, Rideau and Salamanca being fired in anger. There was always the violent weather, changeable in minutes from clear blue skies to ferocious tropical storms which could toss a Gazelle around like a child's toy: torrential rain lashing the craft, lightning suddenly illuminating the cockpit before the rib-shaking thunder signalled a plunge back into disorientating, smothering blackness. The nightmare landing sites, some just thirty feet square with 1,500 feet sheer drops on three sides. And the fatalities . . . the terrible night-time loss of the Puma in 1975, after which routine night flying was stopped. 'Sure. I miss some of it,' he said at last.

Bolitho sensed the other man's mixed emotions about the military, and respected them. They flew in silence for a while as the farming landscape around the town gave way to pine forests, the River Macal now a silver thread pointing them south. The journey to the ruins of Caracol was one the pilot made regularly, especially in the wet season when 4WDs could not get through. His main income was from archaeologists working on the vast eighty-eight-square-kilometre Mayan site. By road, even when passable, it meant an overnight trip. Even the

Daimler Benz Unimog could take ten hours. 'How far do you think he may have got by now?' Bolitho asked after a few minutes.

'He's had how long? As much as sixteen hours? These natives have incredible stamina. He'll be able to grind out six or seven miles an hour all day, on very little rest. He's over a hundred miles from San Ignacio by now. And he may even have got a lift from someone. We just don't know. If he really was heading for rain forest, as *you* think, then he's over halfway there. Why are you after him, anyway?'

Bolitho was ready for this one. A native man-hunt would, he knew, seem Uncle Tom-ish. 'We've been helping cure him of a rare cancer. Using a new treatment. We have to get him back. For his own sake.'

The pilot seemed satisfied with this gibberish. 'Rather you than me, going in there,' he said, nodding to the thick blanket of rain-forest cover in the distance. The plan was that Bolitho would be dropped to track and capture Banto, before radioing the pilot to fly back out for them. 'Have you used a TI before?'

The thermal imager laptop control was in front of Bolitho. Under the aircraft's nose was a two-foot-diameter dual sensor pod, comprising both a daylight video camera and a TI. It was one of the early Forward Looking Infra-Reds, known as FLIRS, and served as the other earner for the pilot. It helped wildlife professionals and eco-tourists search out the endangered big cats down there. The ecologists to trace, tranquillise and radio-collar the jaguars and pumas, and the tourists to snatch photographs and video footage of them.

'Sure. No problem.' Bolitho had used far more sophisticated kit than this with the Kopassus special forces in Indonesia, including remote infra-red sensing technology employed in small pilotless drones. All crude stuff alongside the spy satellites he had been able to use hunting Free Papua Movement rebel tribesmen around Irian Jaya. 'And you. Have you used it before to track a man?'

'More times than you'd think. Barely a year goes past without some young tourists getting themselves lost in there. But of course, we can't penetrate deep forest with this. In the lighter cover and clearings though we should be able to pick him out.'

'So we should be able to locate him OK? It's not a needle in a haystack?'

'If he's already made the rain forest, then the canopy will protect him. If not, as I expect, it depends how smart he is. Most people I look for *want* to be found. But if your man's clever . . . If he hears the chopper and hides in a cave, or in a river . . .'

Bolitho snorted. 'Smart? He's a dumb native! Can't even figure out how to take a shower.' The thought of the diminutive primitive getting the better of him was laughable. 'Better yet. He'll probably climb a tree and start *worshipping* you. I mean it! The PNG tribes made up a religion after seeing war planes drop cargo. You heard of that? The Cargo Cult. Figured if they mocked up little air-strips, then the God of Cargo would drop down steel axes and stuff. Like from heaven, and no need to work for a damn thing!'

The pilot had worked with South American natives off and on for the past fifteen years. They might think differently, but stupid and lazy they were not. He could see that the American was making a big mistake by patronising and under-estimating the warrior. Just as he doubtless had in Vietnam all those years ago. 'We're in the kind of range now for us to start sweeping. I'll take her down to 800 feet and forty knots and go into slow orbit. Get ready.'

Bolitho looked over and gave a thumbs up sign. He was still laughing to himself at the very idea of Stone-Age man

out-smarting the most sophisticated technology available.
Of out-thinking *him* . . . If the image intensifier worked
efficiently, he had no doubt whatever that he would have
the native back in his cell again by the next nightfall. No
doubt whatever.

'James. Sir Barton. What's happening?'

Barton immediately recognised the voice of the Mexican,
Dino. The most mercurial and least committed of the Aruba
Alliance. He was on his guard, and hit the switch which
would record the call. 'Everything's fine, Dino. And you?
Business still good?'

'Getting a lot of heat from the Tijuana cartel and the
Juarez because I got some of their people to come over.
They're madder than hell!'

'Competitive world. At least my Stabiliser deal must
be helping,' Barton remarked, referring to a mutual aid
scheme he had got the Alliance to support. Through it,
Alliance members, the most powerful in their respective
markets, agreed only to deal with other Alliance members
– effectively creating a closed shop, and at a stroke reducing
the threat of local coups and the internecine fighting that
traditionally plagued their lives.

'Yeah. That's working real good. But the money I earn,
I sweat for. You know?'

'I *do* know, Dino. And your money's not just safe now,
it's also sweating for *you*. Earning you even more money.'
He knew then why the man was calling. He trusted nobody,
and had been bullied into the Alliance by his Colombian
cocaine suppliers. 'Do you want to know how much is
in your account?' He stretched out his arm to reach the
keyboard of his PC, calling up Dino's reference.

'Sure. Why not?'

The powerful machine, linked up real time to London,

quickly threw up the astronomical figures. 'You've been depositing on average $100 million a week. Net of outflows, $70 million. For thirty weeks that gives you $2.1 billion. Plus interest of $140 million. All in a secure offshore account no one can touch. And all hedged against bad currency movements, and avoiding South American inflation. Pretty good, don't you agree?'

Dino did not reply immediately. 'I guess,' he finally said, uncertainly.

'Anything else you need from me?'

'I just want you – to *know*.'

This was a man who had trusted nobody all his life. Who was only alive because of his acute suspicion of everyone and their motives. For him now to be entrusting most of his fortune to this alien Englishman, and pooling it with cartels even bigger than his own, was extraordinary. He had agreed to it only to stop them going to one of the other two big competitor Mexican cartels and cutting him out. But now, like an animal, he needed to keep physically touching base.

'Don't worry. I do know. Believe me I know.' That he was dead if there was ever even a suspicion of double-dealing.

'Good.' There was no manic laughter this time. The line went dead.

Sweating heavily, shaken as ever by the unpredictable Mexican, Barton reached for his notebook and dialled Tom Bates's home number. But the answerphone reminded him that he was already *en route*, flying out via Miami to Belize with the analyst. The call had worried him. In fact, things generally were suddenly not going his way. Banto, his meal ticket, was free. He slammed the phone into the cradle so hard that the handset cracked. Somebody would suffer for all this.

But the spectacular assault he was preparing would see to that. It would be talked about for decades, maybe centuries to come. He was going to leave his mark on history; his attack would be on a par with any other single outrage of the twentieth century, on the scale of the Romanov murders, the Kennedy assassinations, Khomeini's overthrow of the Shah, and Saddam's contemptuous and brilliant cat-and-mouse gamesmanship with the most sophisticated military powers on the planet.

The lab seemed much larger than it had on the plans. Lydia was exploring the building alone, Thrower remaining by the door, now relocked, and deciding how best to handle the officious, diligent old guard. Chrissie and Joan were in the shadows outside, keeping Thrower briefed on what the man was doing.

'He's coming over to your door,' Joan hissed.

'Well make sure you're hidden behind something. He'll trigger the security lights out there any time now!' he warned. Seconds after he said this, the windows flooded with light. Lydia looked up in horror as the standard photographic Chairman's portrait of her father over the reception desk was suddenly lit up. Then, half a minute later, the door handle was being tried, the old man's laboured breathing clearly audible to Thrower on the other side.

'There *is* nowhere! Just grass banking along the side of here,' Joan cried, just stopping herself from dropping out of a whisper and into normal speech. 'And the whole area's now lit like a film set.'

'There! Behind the bins,' Chrissie cut across. 'That's all we have. Come on!'

A bang like a pistol shot echoed inside and out the building, freezing them all. The guard had slammed the flat of his hand hard on the door before moving to the window to the right of the door and shining his powerful lamp inside. Thrower was pressed hard against the outer wall, shaking. If he had to go out and hit the man, he would. It was something he had faced before. A guard's cracked skull was a small price to pay for the cause. He would do it if he had to . . . even though face-to-face violence, unlike impersonal bombings, did not come easily to him.

From the erratic flashes of the lamp, Thrower realised that the guard was now walking round to the western side of the building, presumably to check the other door. This would take him straight past the women, cowering by some kind of refuse area. There was no way he could miss them. And when he raised the alarm, the police would be on their way in a matter of minutes. They needed help. He simply had to go out there after all . . .

Taking out the small cosh he carried for exactly this purpose, Thrower silently slipped the lock on the latch and went out, blinking into the lights. It took him a frightening few seconds to adjust his eyes, and was relieved to find no sight of the guard when at last he focused properly. Keeping to the wall, he edged to the corner and looked round. The uniformed figure was gingerly walking along the grassy surrounds towards the small tarmacked refuse area where the women were hiding. He was already shining his lamp at the nearest wheely-bins and overspill black-bagged rubbish, and making towards them to check the area out before continuing on to the other door.

He was only about twenty-five yards away, and Thrower figured he could comfortably cover that distance and set upon him before the old man could get any coherent message out to his control room. The guard was just feet away now from the nearest row of bins; it was time to launch into the dash and beat him unconscious. Taking a deep breath, Thrower began to sprint . . .

A piercing scream tore into the night and froze them both. It sounded exactly like the scream of a baby, but louder. Much louder. Then it rang out again, and Thrower darted back behind the wall. The guard shone his lamp ahead to a second grouping of bins twenty yards further on. As he did a fox and vixen shot across the grass, both looking accusingly at him, before running off. They often came there to raid the bags and bins, in which they sometimes found the remains of lab animals. And sometimes, having fought over scraps, they would mate. Noisily and painfully.

The guard followed the animals with his torchlight as long as he could before losing them in the misty night. He had seen them there before, and often heard the terrible screams of the vixen as the fox withdrew, tearing her raw. Stabbing a finger at his radio, Thrower heard the man's message back to the control centre. 'Panic over,' he said, relief in his voice. 'Just foxes rutting.' There followed some ribald and predictable response from the duty officer, to which the guard laughed and replied, 'Not at my age!'

Thrower padded back into the building, locking the door behind him. It had been a wonderful stroke of luck; he hoped a good omen, too. Three minutes later and Chrissie reported that the guard had disappeared back towards his office, and they were coming in. They had no need for the moment to worry about setting off the lights, for they were still blazing.

Lydia had come back to the reception by the time they were inside. She hugged the two women emotionally, having lived their ordeal with them over her headset. 'That was too close for comfort,' she gushed. 'You must have been petrified.'

'All in a day's work, *girls*,' Thrower sneered. 'We're not here to knit squares, you know. We've got serious work to do.'

Breaking away, Chrissie's temper flared, her nerves still jangling from their ordeal outside. Despite her slender frame she pushed him hard against the wall, her snarling face an inch from his. 'Listen to me, you misogynous, homophobic little creep, we've all had it with your insults. I've warned you before. Because me? *I'm* mysophobic. I can't stand dirt, or filth like you . . . So, I'm telling you – keep right out of my way when this thing's over. You got that?'

Thrower let her free him before standing away from the wall. Still holding the cosh, he fought the urge to sink it into her skull. Barely able to speak with rage, he shoved past her and glowered back at the three of them. 'Let's get this thing done. After tonight I work alone. And you three cute little Charlie's Angels can do what the hell you like,' he spat, deliberately provoking Chrissie further.

Lydia put herself bodily between the two of them and tried to impose some leadership on the group. 'We're going the right way to get caught here,' she warned. 'All this can wait for another time. And Sam's right at least in saying that we're here to do a job. I've recced the place and there's a lot to do. Joan, you stay and keep watch in case the guard returns. Sam, Chrissie – follow me.'

They meekly did what they were told, relieved that someone had re-established order. Then she led them along the central corridor to a set of double doors. 'Sam, you need to get the monkeys out. There are only two. Young macaques. Chrissie, you box up the rats and mice. They're in the lab on the left side. I'll set the incendiary first, and then see to the pigs. OK? When we've got our animals ready to move, Sam, I'll let you know. Then get Tony over here with the Land-Rover. OK? Let's do it.'

The three electronic incendiary devices were as sophis-ticated as any used by the IRA. In the early days, the AFW were very much at the Heath Robinson end of the terrorist

market, cobbling crude fire-bombs together at safe houses
in Leeds and Birmingham, avoiding London and the far
greater resources of Scotland Yard and Special Branch
there. At first they went on bomb-and-run missions, but
by the eighties they were having patchy success using
tomato-shaped kitchen timers, following instructions put
out on the Internet by American anarchists. The new units,
however, were bought via a middle man from the prolific
bomb-makers in Bulgaria.

Having selected three combustible areas, Lydia set about
the simple job of arming the bombs and setting the delays.
At her first site, she took out the flat device – $12.7 \times 8
\times 2.5$ centimetres – and then the first three ampoules of
high-octane fuel. These always reminded her of the green
Sparklet capsules used in soda syphons. They had to be laid
diagonally across the back of the unit. Then she pressed
in place the double studs of the battery connector on the
top right side before wrapping the tape around to hold
everything firmly in place. Turning it over, she set the
delay period they had pre-agreed – an hour and twenty
minutes – and slid the start button to 'on'. Moving rapidly,
and with increased confidence, she armed the remaining
two units and then ran over to the room where she had
found the pigs.

Steeling herself – her first sight earlier of the two animals
had reduced her to tears – she went into the sterile sty, with its
noisy air-filtration system. Once more they looked up, their
intelligent eyes twinkling, happy to see her. If they were
not actually smiling, she had no other way of explaining
the entirely human expressions she was encountering.
They were less than a year old and, if her father was not
stopped, she knew they would soon be killed for a whole
variety of their organs for spare-part xenotransplantation
research. They had started life when her father's team

had injected DNA into a host pig embryo, thrusting him into the front line of medical ethics. 'Bio-ethics' had now joined abortion and euthanasia as a popular topic for the chattering classes. Sickeningly though, most of that debate had nothing remotely to do with animal welfare, centring instead on the risk of transmitting animal viruses into the human chain, as some feared had happened through BSE in cattle and Creutzfeldt-Jakob disease.

But to Lydia, bio-ethics was a side issue for now as she looked at the excited animals, their big ears up and twitching, noses waving to and fro in friendly excitement at human contact. Taking out two harnesses and leads, she went across to the first pen. Over it was a code number. At least Dolly, the genetic sheep, had been given a name. 'Come on, my beauty,' she said encouragingly. 'Let's have you out of here. And *quietly*, if you please.'

For all their great intelligence, 'quiet' is not a concept readily understood by an excited pig; first one and then the other began squealing happily, the noise deafening in the small room. Thrower came running in. 'Keep them quiet! They'll be heard outside.'

'I can't. Help me get the harnesses on. All we can do is get them out and away as quickly as possible.'

It took them less time than she feared, however, and the pigs did quieten down once out of their sties. Thrower had already instructed Tony to drive over the fields, lights extinguished, to the perimeter fence, and when he got the message that Tony was in place, he checked they were all ready: Chrissie with the holdall of her little, squeaking charges; the two macaques lying still in hessian sacks. He had not wanted to use the tranquilliser gun, but the brutalised little platyrrhines had been fiercely aggressive, and even noisier that the pigs.

Joan recced outside, and confirmed that the guard was

still safely in the gate office. The exterior security lights
had now extinguished, and as they made several journeys
to the Land-Rover each had to make sure they stuck close
to the wall before crouching very low by the streetlamp to
avoid triggering the sensors again. Mercifully for Lydia, the
pigs just snorted, pulling madly at their leashes – just like
Oliver dragging her to Green Park on a Sunday morning.
Then, at long last, it was all done, and Tony was bouncing
them violently across the fields, back to the car park and
their own vehicles.

Sam Thrower and Tony now had a long night drive
up to Carlisle, where a fellow AFW member would tend
the various creatures, the 'saves' as they called them, on
his isolated smallholding, until permanent places could be
found for them amongst their network of supporters. The
mood as they made to go their separate ways was subdued,
Chrissie and Thrower still prickly with each other.

'I'll make the call then, from a pay phone. As agreed,'
Lydia confirmed. She at least felt good and excited about
freeing the animals and putting the horrible place out of
action. A few minutes before the incendiaries went up,
she was to call the guard at the gatehouse and find some
reason to keep him talking until detonation. They did not
want a death on their hands. And with any luck, the place
would be burned to a shell before fire officers even arrived.
Compassionate commandos was how she saw them. And
it had, despite the falling out, been a successful raid. If,
that was, she had correctly armed the incendiaries. That
nagging doubt would be with her until she had confirmed
the place really had gone up.

With one last look back at the two pigs, now huddling
together for warmth in the back of the Defender, she briefly
hugged each member of the team in turn and got into her
car. Thrower's softly whispered 'well done' gave her more

job satisfaction and pride than she had ever felt at the agency. She drove away elated, ready to tackle anything. Even Maddie and her damned file.

Chapter Nine

David Elkins was hard work. Tedious hours with him at airports and on board the flight to Miami had stretched Tom's professional charm to its limits. It was not that he was obnoxious. Or unintelligent. Or even that boring. It was just that they had little in common outside their mutual professional interest in Barton and his Temple Bio-Laboratories business. And Tom had decided to avoid saying too much about even that until they got to Belize. Things seemed to be moving so quickly out there that he was worried about putting his foot in it, giving out wrong or old information.

They were in the stretched limo Barton had arranged to collect them from Miami International, sedately cruising down the North-South Expressway towards their Miami Beach hotel. 'You know Miami well, David?' Tom asked, sipping a glass of Diet Coke from the bar.

Elkins was in his early forties, but his thinning sandy hair and worry-lined face made him seem much older. He replied, 'I know Key West better. I have friends down there.'

As they finally pulled over outside the hotel Barton had also arranged for them, Tom's sexual antennae immediately began to twitch. The art deco confection was on Ocean Drive, and the limo door was opened by a bottle-blond black guy wearing skin-tight leather pants and a mauve blouson top.

'Welcome y'all to the beautiful Miami Bonaparte Vista Hotel,' he lisped in an inept attempt at a Southern drawl – *Gone With The Wind* meets Harlem – and proffering his hand. Elkins took it and got out of the air-conditioned car, the humidity immediately steaming up his spectacles. Tom declined the offer and got out unaided with unconscious manliness, creating exactly the opposite effect to that he had intended. The doorman winked at him. 'You ladies have a real good time with us, you hear? My name's Peter. It says so right here.' He pointed a long, manicured finger theatrically to his badge. 'And you can call on me for whatever you need. Your bags will follow you right in. Have a nice stay.'

The interior of the place was mercifully more understated, but the orientation of its clientele was clear from the Greek statues and gigantic Murillo-influenced mural on the far wall. All the staff wore the same leathers and blouson uniforms as the doorman, and by the time Tom had checked in and got to his room – the Dorian Gray Suite – he was fuming at Barton for putting him through this. A short nap followed by a shower and large gin, however, helped relax him and he was ready for dinner when they met, as arranged, in the bar at seven.

Elkins had changed into a white tropical suit and seemed like a different man – happy and confident. Breaking off talking to a couple of men, he got up to greet Tom, the look of a naughty schoolboy on his face. After a cocktail, the limo took them to the hottest restaurant in town: the Twisted Pier. Aston Martin Volantes, Porsches, Jaguars, Ferraris and Bentleys littered the entrance. It was the only place for Miami's beautiful people to be seen on Wednesdays. Tom involuntarily ogled the stunning women parading around the restaurant, struggling to keep his mind on his job. They had an excellent meal and even better wine – a 1982 Margaux, washed down with a half-bottle of Château d'Yquem – before leaving for the Queen Mojo. This was a disco off Washington Avenue which Elkins especially said he wanted to check out. Tom stayed less than the ten minutes it took to down a gin and reassure himself that Elkins was OK in the packed, pulsating gay night-club. As he left, he looked back and saw two men immediately join Elkins. The same two who had been talking to him in the bar at the hotel. With a shrug, he hailed a cab. Their flight to Belize was not until late morning. He'd had no idea . . . but good luck to the man. It was his life.

There was a message for him when he got back to the hotel. Tearing it open, it simply asked him to ring a local number as soon as he got in. Whatever the time. No name was left. Back in his room, Tom made the call. 'Bates. Who is this?' he said.

'Goodness, it's humid, isn't it? Not really my cup of tea . . . But, there we are. I know it's latish, but I did say one of us would be in touch with you out here. Well, I decided to come myself. Just got in. Sub-sonic – to save taxpayers' money. But this thing really is that important. Mind if I pop over for an hour? Now?'

Tom sighed wearily. 'Very well, Mr Mitchell. Come on over. And I'll see if this place can brew you up something that *is* your cup of tea.' The man was wearing down his resistance. It was something they both recognised. Slowly he knew – despite all his instincts – he was moving inexorably towards becoming a part-time, unpaid spy for Her Majesty's Secret Service. Mitchell as ever, would get his man.

They had found something that was almost certainly Banto. Using the river as the base around which to conduct the search pattern, it had proved far easier than they had expected, helped by the native's unerring ability somehow to take the most direct route towards the nearest deep forest. On the twelve-inch TI screen in the control panel in front of Bolitho, the black and white image clearly showed a human figure. On these units, white areas identified surfaces giving off heat. So a police patrol in a city would see cars as black shapes overall, but with white tyres and bonnets. Below them now, however, in the light forest, along riverbanks and in clearings, Banto's head was white as his dark body moved ahead much more quickly than any archaeologist or tourist trekker would.

'That has to be him!' the pilot concluded triumphantly. 'I see very few solo images down there. It's highly unusual. That's your man. No question.'

'Get me down!' Bolitho shouted – unnecessary over the headphones. 'Close.'

The pilot frowned. 'I saw one possible clearing that would give me enough space, but that would leave you five miles behind him.'

'Then drop me in front. Let him come to me.'

'Hopeless. He's almost into the deep canopied rain forest. It's a carpet over there. Nowhere to put down.'

'OK. Let's get it done. Drop me as close as you can. And quickly. The longer we're up here, the further away he gets.'

They descended minutes later in a forest clearing barely twenty yards square, the pilot having readied himself for the slight bounce sometimes caused by a thermal above the trees. Unbuckling his harness, Bolitho reassured himself that he could trust the pilot to come and find him when he had captured Banto. 'So. I have altitude flares. Three hundred footers. I have a Day-glo landing marker. And a firefly strobe, on top of my geo-sat tracker. OK? And *you* keep open radio contact with me. OK?'

Following a thumbs up from the pilot, he got out. The

man passed his rucksack and shotgun down to him. Then, after another thumbs up, Bolitho, crouching to avoid the deadly rotor blades, cleared the landing area and turned his head away to protect his eyes from the fifty m.p.h. downwash winds. Then the cacophony was over, and the helicopter became a fading drone as Bolitho was left alone in the clearing. One part of him was looking forward to the challenge that lay ahead, but he desperately wished that he still had the fit young body from his Vietnam days of jungle training. He had been on very recent jungle missions, as a field trainer for the crack Kopassus special forces, but training was training. Now he was pitted against a young warrior, who despite being weakened by all the blood extraction, still seemed capable of forty miles a day through this stuff. He was going to need all his experience to pull this off. The bullying threat from Barton had meant nothing to him. He was dying anyway. But the challenge certainly did. No young native could be seen to get the better of him: the best jungle fighter of his day, with the highest man-hour kill ratio of his unit.

The forest here was nothing like as dense as he knew it would become a few miles ahead. It was important to make good time, to close that distance down between them, while the going was relatively light, and while he felt at his fittest. Consulting his compass, he struck off immediately south-south-west, clearing his mind to focus single-mindedly on the job in hand, hacking out a route through with his long, curved kukri, the tool-cum-weapon he favoured over the machete.

Tracking in jungle and rain forest was difficult, and Bolitho had always preferred to use native visual trackers or dogs. But in the short time he had, having asked around San Ignacio that morning, the helicopter had been the only SAR show in town. Besides, he still prided himself on his

own skills as a tracker, which he had learned in the field,
and later codified to train others in Asia and South America.
Since 'Nam, this had always remained his local patch. He
had never even set foot in Africa, and had no desire to
go there, where, with its different wildlife and plants, he
would be less special.

A visual tracker basically has to find and then interpret
the 'signs' humans leave behind as they pass through an area.
These are categorised first into 'temporary sign', which in a
few hours or days might disappear – disturbed ground cover,
human defecation, mud suspended in water that has been
traversed – and 'permanent sign' – macheted branches, camp
fires, scored rocks and man-made, durable items dropped or
discarded, such as plastic packaging or bullet casings. Then
secondly into 'top sign' those made by the upper body of
the prey – disturbed or broken vegetation, scuffed moss
on trees from rucksacks and rifles – and 'ground sign' –
such as sand kicked up on ground cover, broken sticks
and dry leaves, scuffed soil and worm casts, and of course
footprints – known in tradecraft jargon as spoor.

How he wished now he had with him a tracker dog's
sensitive ears and nose. Its sense of hearing is a hundred
per cent more acute than man's, and its power of smell almost
a thousand times greater. This can create a dream team for an
experienced hunting party, combining the human tracker's
reading of visual signs and the audile and olfactory skills
of the dog. But that was a team game. He was alone.

The subtle skills of tracking were some hours ahead,
however. The first priority was still to close down the
distance between the two of them. Looking at his battered
old Rolex Explorer, he calculated just four more hours of
daylight in the already gloomy forest. The darkness need
not necessarily stop his progress, but it would inevitably
slow him down, and expose him to far more deadly and

efficient night hunters than he could ever be: snakes like boa constrictors and the killer *fer de lance*, poisonous spiders and big mammals – the jaguars and pumas that would also be out searching for fresh prey. In the jungle all hunters were also themselves the hunted: simply a fresh supply of meat, there to be taken.

'This is unbelievable! I've warned you before. Don't *ever* call me on an open line again!' Barton was furious and worried that the stupidity of Ladislas Blacher, the chief of his Portuguese plant, in calling him direct in Belize, might already have compromised him. Belize was a backwater, but there was still a substantial military presence there: the Belize Defence Force, 1,200 registered troops, an infantry battalion and a half, plus the British Forces there under agreement, including a detachment of Harriers. Because, despite the agreement, still nobody really trusted the Guats. International calls might very well be routinely monitored.

Barton hung up on the man before he could say any more, and then called him back using his portable scrambler, one compatible with that permanently installed on Blacher's direct line in his Oeiras office at the plant. All the fool had needed to do was throw the switch at the side of his desk.

'Sorry. It won't happen again,' the older man said. He did not sound remotely sorry, however. In many respects he realised that Barton was afraid of him – he knew so much, especially about their work on perfecting the biological weapons. 'But I did think that this is important.'

Barton felt nervous now. Until its closure, the old doctor had worked at the Ministry of Defence's top-secret chemical and biological warfare centre at Portreath, and then at Porton Down. The man was not a panicker by nature, and would not have made the call without good reason. Quite enough was going wrong in Barton's life right now without even more bad news. 'What is it? Couldn't it wait?' He planned to be in Portugal days later.

'I thought you would like to know immediately. That maybe you would be as excited as I am.'

'What is it?'

'To put it simply . . . we've done it. The system's worked. I've successfully grown the base toxic agent. Those special double-jacketed fermenters I designed worked perfectly. And very soon now, we'll have your 15,000 litres of botulinum toxin. It's all gone exactly to plan. We're there.' The doctor could not keep the excitement and pride out of his voice. 'I thought you'd want to share the good news with me as soon as possible.'

Barton's heart leapt. Having steeled himself for a nasty shock, this was indeed absolutely stunning news. 'Well done! Absolutely marvellous,' he gushed. 'Bloody tremendous.'

'It was not really so difficult,' Blacher responded modestly. 'After all, I had prepared this particular weapon before. It was simply a case of following my private notes, and then improvising with the laboratory plant.'

'Nonsense. That was all a long time ago. And in those days you had a team of, what, twenty crack technicians helping you? In purpose-made official labs. Is Rybinski there? Congratulate him too. You've both done brilliantly. Especially you, Ladislas. Replicating all that with just a handful of young Portuguese lab technicians. People who you had to keep in the dark about what you were really doing. How on earth did you pull it off?'

Blacher snorted, mostly at sharing any credit with the arrogant Russian with whom Barton had insisted he work. Someone who, Barton claimed, had helped the Gulf War Allies, having earlier installed specialist plant for the Iraqis; billing him as 'the man who stopped the biological Scuds'.

'They think we've been producing a new top secret biotech intelligent fertiliser. One that adapts itself to whatever soil conditions it finds,' he replied. 'That explained away the fifty-gallon drums of biological growth medium we've been getting through. It's not so crazy actually. Some of the ingredients and processes are very similar. That's how we convinced the Portuguese inspectors, remember.'

Then Blacher's mood changed. 'We celebrate, but we should not forget the terrible accident. Those poor young men. I will never forgive myself. We were working too quickly. Cutting corners. But it was, you still assure me, vital for us to finish as quickly as possible. Absolutely vital for Israel's security.'

'*Sine qua non.* That I assure you. And those people, they were just illegal immigrants. North African Arabs. Angolans.'

'Don't ever talk to me that way! Don't include me in your racism!' Blacher shouted. 'I don't hate Arabs or Angolans or anyone! How dare you make me feel like some camp doctor!'

Barton realised he had misread him. 'I'm sorry . . .'

'Just because that imbecile Russian assistant you forced on me, Rybinski, misread the trial dosages!'

'I've said I'm sorry. Me, *I* hate the bloody A-rabs. That's partly my reason for doing this. But I *know* it's not yours. You want to help keep Israel secure. I know that. I'm sorry.'

He had enticed Blacher out of retirement by representing himself as an intelligence go-between for the Israelis, convincing Blacher, a lapsed Jew, that Jerusalem had requested his help. They needed a biological deterrent for a deadly intelligence poker game with Iran. It was public knowledge that Tehran had a £525 million deal for

Russia to complete the Bushehr nuclear power station. An Israeli intelligence report, openly circulated to journalists to put pressure on the USA and EU – a copy of which Barton showed to Blacher as evidence of his credentials – alleged that some hard-line Mullahs also expected the Russians to leave behind know-how on using the plant's enriched uranium, raising the spectre of the long-feared Muslim Bomb, to set against Israel's two hundred stockpiled nuclear warheads.

The whole game, Barton had assured him, was no more than a text-book 'Emily' intelligence tactic: CIA-speak for the deliberate leaking of accurate intelligence to the enemy. And to add further credibility, Barton – an ex-Foreign Office Minister, after all – showed Blacher now published KGB reports from the early 1970s, when the Soviets were redoubling their work on biological warfare. Just as the West was destroying its stockpiles, a CIA double agent informed the Soviets that both the USA and Britain could rebuild them within weeks. And that Western scientists remained far ahead in their research, with secret new strains that could devastate livestock, plants or people. It had been, Blacher himself well remembered from his days at Portreath, enough to force the Soviets to make important policy changes. A highly successful 'Emily'.

'But the deaths ... They make me ashamed,' Blacher continued. He was still utterly convinced that he was clandestinely working for Israel, just as so many of his nuclear scientist friends had done for so long.

'Accidents. All of them,' lied Barton. 'Ladislas, please ... this is a day to celebrate, even as you remember the tragedy. By creating the base toxin in commercial quantities, you're helping prevent a dangerous weapons race with Iran. They will soon know that if they proceed with nuclear weapons production at Bushehr, then Israel will up the stakes with biological deployment. Rejoice in that. You've performed a great humanitarian service!'

'If you say so,' Blacher replied, uncertainly.

'I do. Relax today. Take a holiday. You are a great man. And I will see to it that your work is fully recognised in the secret corridors of Jerusalem.'

This pleased Blacher, a child of an orthodox *frum* family. A man guilt-ridden for abandoning his faith for the racy mistress of science. And a man now in his early seventies, thinking more and more about his own death – something for which that faithless mistress still had no answer.

Mitchell had made no concession to the climate or the late hour, and arrived dressed in a dark navy suit and waistcoat, his tie impeccably knotted in a half-Windsor.

Waving him into his suite, Tom remarked, 'Aren't you hot in all that?' He was himself wearing the trousers from his cream linen suit, and a dark mushroom Sea Island cotton polo shirt.

'There's so much air conditioning out here that I could happily wear my old army greatcoat,' Mitchell complained. 'I've always had a hankering to write a Hemingway-style adventure story down here, and call it *Frostbite in the Tropics* . . .'

Smiling, Tom showed him over to the two easy chairs positioned around a low coffee table by the window. Offering him a drink, he noticed that even in this, Mitchell's choice was singular, almost from another generation: 'A dark rum and water. Cold will do, if you have no hot. But please, no bloody ice.'

Staying now with mineral water, Tom sat opposite him in the corner chair Mitchell had deliberately left for him. 'You're a queer bird, Mr Mitchell. An English expression, I think. I hope it doesn't offend.'

'It's not something I'd thank you for saying too loudly downstairs in reception,' he replied. 'But you're not the first person to find me – what? Opaque?'

'And is that how you see yourself?'

Mitchell immediately recognised Tom's attempts at amateur psychology. Reflective responsing: answering a question with a question. Probably picked up on an expensive management course. He decided to play along for a while, for fun. 'Perhaps. Think of me as the black coating on the mirror. Enabling others to see themselves.' He was pleased with this bit of nonsense. Your move, he thought, sipping the rum.

Tom looked slightly puzzled, but ploughed gamely on. 'Me, I'm a dilettante at heart.' He leaned forward conspiratorially. 'The truth is that we consultants are on the whole a pretty bogus lot. Fifty per cent of what we do is a con. We breeze in, then breeze out, leaving the management we've just rubbished to do all the real work.'

Page two, thought Mitchell. Tell a stranger a secret to make him like you . . .

Then it suddenly occurred to him: Tom might be so brainwashed with techniques that he no longer recognised them as devices. Perhaps the man no longer simply met people, but 'encountered standard psychographic types'. Perhaps he did not have friends, just certain people to share his 'quality time'. 'It's only recently that dilettante has been used pejoratively,' Mitchell batted back, starting to enjoy himself. 'The original Age of Reason dilettantes, the Grand Tourists, understood all the arts and sciences. Fully rounded men. You can see it in their faces. The portraits of the Dilettante Society members are now in Brook's.'

Tom too was enjoying this, warming to the man and totally failing to spot that Mitchell, with cold calculation, had already turned over to page three. Deliberately reflecting back Tom's own values and interests to make *him* comfortable. 'You're right,' he said. 'Education should have remained holistic. Separating arts and science was a cultural disaster. In fact, this was what attracted me to consultancy. We're encouraged to think in the round. Like the Dilettantes. To be a kind of intellectual Swiss Army knife, you know?'

Mitchell had by now had more than enough of all this garbage, but did his best to hide his feelings. 'People see *us* less as a Swiss Army knife, and more a blunt instrument of state,' he went on, now pulling the conversation round to the point. 'But that's really not true. Staying with the simile, I'd describe us as a surgeon's knife. Used by highly trained specialists, and only after the most thorough diagnosis of what needs cutting out. For the health of the body as a whole.'

'And that's how you see Jim Barton, as some kind of malignant cancer?'

'That's exactly how we see him. Our job is to act, before it spreads.'

Tom had already given a lot of thought to what Mitchell and his man had shared with him at their last meeting. He had since also done a trawl on the 'net and various databases on biological warfare in general, and botulinum toxin in particular. It had made for sickening, terrifying reading and helped finally make up his mind to agree. But first, before he showed his hand, he needed some reassurances and safeguards. Immunity from prosecution by Barton – or WMC for breaches of his service contract; and a categoric assurance that they would not knowingly put him in any physical danger. 'Let's talk turkey, Mr Mitchell. I'm tired and it's late. As I see it, you want me to use my access to Barton and his business affairs to supply you with intelligence. Intelligence you'll use for what, exactly?'

Mitchell moved his chair inches closer to Tom's, literally

forcing him into a corner, making him feel trapped, and willing to agree to anything to escape. This was Mitchell's page four, and a tactic known to all good salesmen as they go in to close. 'We need to prevent Barton from letting those biological weapons loose. That's it. We don't yet know why he's developed them, who's commissioned the stuff, or whether there's a link with this Aruba syndicate.'

Tom took a deep breath. This was it. The commitment. 'I'll help, but I want some promises in return from you people,' he said. 'We all remember Matrix Churchill . . .'

Mitchell was heartily sick of having that thrown in his teeth every time he tried to recruit someone. But time was fast running out for him. Bates was the only show in town. He would now somehow have to lick the American into shape, and make him into an effective field operative, in a matter of days. Thrusting out his hand and baring the tombstone teeth, he forced a tired smile. 'Deal,' he said. 'Welcome aboard. We'll look after you. And really, I'm only tasking you with one thing. One over-riding priority. Really get Barton to trust you – with *everything*, and find out why he's developed the biological bomb. Tell us why, and for whom – and you can leave the rest to us.'

Banto had no plan, other than to escape to the deep forest. It was important to feel safe, back in his own world, and to recoup his full strength after all the blood they had taken. But if he had no real plan, he did have a clear and simple aim. Payback. From the big *kepala*, Barton. And then he could return home to his village. To warn and prepare his people as he had vowed.

But now he had to sit. It was almost night-time, and he knew he had to stop and wait for a while. There is a startlingly common belief shared by primitive nomads the world over – aborigine, Inuit, African plainsmen, Bedouin

– that if they travel too quickly, for example in a car or plane, then they have to wait for their soul to catch up with them before moving on. If not, and they leave their soul behind, it will wander lost, for ever.

For Banto, the deep forest was in any case full of spirit life. Ancestors in *dimanples* – the die man place – separated from their bodies. In limbo. In the forest around his village he knew all the dark places to avoid at night – special clearings where the spirits would hold *sing-sings*, chanting mantras and beating deep *kundu* drums; giant trees which had the power to steal your senses if you walked by them at certain angles. And he knew that ancestors, *ol tumbuna*, could became birds of paradise to fly above you, watching, watching . . .

This forest was strange however. And it felt, after all his efforts to get there, unwelcoming and dangerous: its sounds and smells alien. The jungle itself was made up of a different balance of trees and vegetation: the colossal guanacastes, breadnut *ramon* trees, strangler figs, the piggy-backing epiphytes, the black orchids. There were sounds of creatures he did not recognise: the caterwauling of a distant jaguar; the clicking from tropical rattlesnakes; tapirs crashing noisily through the underbush. Macaws, parrots and the beautiful ocellated turkeys. The howler and spider monkeys. The bats' soft, incessant peeping. The maddening frogs.

But for some miles now, he had felt himself being drawn towards a strong spirit. A kapok tree had been benignly but inexorably reeling him in. It was a 700-year-old ceiba, the world tree, the Wacah Chan, Gateway to the unseen world of Xibalba, sacred to the Maya, its buttress roots at the base of the huge trunk twice his own height. Approaching it he could sense the presence of powerful spirits, spirits of ancient warriors, wise and protective towards him. He knew he would be safe here.

Here he could rest, and let his own spirit catch him up with him.

And then, as soon as he had arrived and marvelled at his unwitting destination, all became blackness. There is no dusk in the deep forest, and it had gone from day to night in ten minutes. It was as if the tree had deliberately held back the veil of the night until he safely arrived.

Before he slept, he planned what he must do the next day. Above all else he needed hunting weapons. A bow and arrows would have to be fashioned. Then, using the friendly world tree as a kind of extra-sensory, atavistic transmitter, he would seek guidance from his own village tribal spirits on what he should do next. He would have to hold a *sing-sing* the next day. But for now, he needed sleep. Having made a leafy mattress in the deep buttresses, he ate the last of the cooked food he had brought with him and threw away the dead rats. He had not needed them, and would catch fresher, better meat tomorrow. And he would in any case need to hunt out a pig to sacrifice at his *sing-sing*. He had caught sight earlier that day of a group of peccaries, a kind of wild pig. One of those strange-looking beasts would be fine. Then, cutting off a type of vine he recognised, Banto drank the cool water inside and fell into his best sleep since leaving his village just seven days earlier.

His short, but stocky, broad body was curled tight, his back nestling, protected in the tree. And his face, with its deep-set eyes and broad nose, its tattoos and manhood initiation scars, relaxed at long last. The native, at twenty-five, was already over halfway through his life expectancy. Forty-five years was the average for his race. But this was now no ordinary young warrior. He had travelled eleven millennia from the Stone Age in a week. And he was becoming stronger and wiser by the minute.

* * *

'Is it really so terrible? I mean, whether we rear pigs for human transplants or bacon sandwiches, it won't matter very much to your porker friends, will it?' Maddie said all of this while flamboyantly forking a salade niçoise. Sipping now on her Evian, she pressed on. 'And besides. I bet the millionaire's pigs, those with their own DNA – what did you call them? – xenotransplant pigs . . . I bet they get treated really well. Looked after like VIPs. Very Important Pigs!'

Lydia groaned inwardly. She had arranged lunch with her to discuss further what to do about the file, but before that Maddie had launched into the usual simplistic logic about animal testing. The newspapers were full of the story of the fire-bombing of her father's lab, halting his xenotransplant experiments. And the one thing she did not need right now was having to rehearse the same old debating topics yet again. Not with someone, she thought unkindly, whose greatest daily intellectual challenge was whether to order Sauterne or Barsac with her pudding.

'Five per cent of people are already veggie, and fifteen per cent rarely eat meat. Wait and see the next generation coming through from the schools. These figures will treble. But in the end, it all comes down to philosophy,' she said wearily. 'You can argue that animals lack the power of reason and choice. You can cherry pick bits of Bentham and Descartes. You can point to Plato and Aristotle's contention that our intellectual life is at a higher level than other animals. And if you really know where to look, you can find enough in Aquinas, Hegel and even Kant to make the case for man as a higher species.

'Fine. Except if you knew what else was caught and tortured in your tasty tuna's drift net, you'd think again. If you actually saw the lives of calves in veal crates, you'd think again. And if you realised what was really going on in genetic experiments . . . a mouse with a human ear grafted on its back, or the big selling oncomouse. They've bred it to be born with a cancer gene, making it more susceptible to tumours. In fact there are now over 250 strains of mice deliberately bred with genetic defects . . . It's horrific. And Dad should have nothing to do with it.'

'So you condone these people?' Maddie waved her *Daily Mail*. 'Going around fire-bombing perfectly legal companies. Risking lives?'

Lydia recognised she had to be careful not to make Maddie suspicious. 'I don't believe in risking human life. Of course not,' she replied, cautiously. 'But I do believe in animal *rights*, not just plain animal welfare. I do think that the rights of animals have a direct parallel with Thomas Paine's *Rights of Man*. And I do detest speciesism, no less than I do in racism or sexism.'

Maddie looked unconvinced. 'Well it's because of people like you that I'm afraid to be seen out in my furs these days. Put it to the vote. Make wearing fur illegal, and I'll burn the things. But why should small groups think they can over-ride the democratic process? What if we all chose to act like that? Anarchy,' she said, indignantly. 'Besides, I'd have more respect if these people threw paint at big, hairy-assed Hell's Angels in their leathers, instead of at frail old ladies in fox stoles.'

Lydia smiled. It was a fair point. '*Touché*,' she said. 'But please, let's change the subject. You mentioning fox stoles is absolutely guaranteed to get me on to you again about you and your hunting set.'

'The uneatable . . .?' Maddie teased, nodding at the unappetising vegan-friendly mess of pulses on Lydia's plate.

'The hunting quote *I* prefer is Jorrocks's: "The image of war with only five and twenty per cent of the danger",' Lydia responded quickly. 'We hunt saboteurs are just trying to raise the odds. Make it even *more* fun and exciting for you . . .'

They had by now each comprehensively put the other off their food and had the plates taken away for coffee. Lydia was still high on the success of the attack on the plant. She had telephoned the guard as agreed and ensured he was safely away from the lab when it went up. The incendiaries had worked perfectly, virtually razing the building and its hateful equipment and records before the fire service arrived. Thrower had called her to confirm that they safely got the animals up to Carlisle, and repeated his praise for her. 'I'll work with *you* in the future, but not those two clowns,' he had said, and promised to be in touch again soon. But with the raid behind her, she knew the priority now was to tackle her father head on – about something even worse than his animal experiments. That document – ambiguous though it was – had definitely pointed to human testing. '*Males, 18–25* . . .'

'So. What do we do about the file?' Maddie asked. She had not fully understood the technical references, but the meaning had seemed obvious enough. Her husband was involved in producing biological weapons. Her husband, the man she thought she once loved, the father of her twins, was a monster. He was someone she can never have really known. And who had married her, for reasons the whole world could see, but she had not believed – for her family money, and to try out a new womb for the son he so desperately wanted. There had always been a mystery surrounding his divorce, but she had put his unwillingness to talk about it down to some deep hurt, something intensely private between the two of them. Perhaps, though, it was as simple as that. His first wife had not been able to give him a son, so – Henry VIII style – a new model had been required. That she too would leave James was now certain, but for the present the logistics of what it all meant were overwhelming and frightening. They needed someone they liked and trusted to lean on, to help them decide what to do. Someone like . . . 'We could ask Tom what he thinks,' she suggested.

The sound of his name made Lydia start. 'Tom? Whatever for?' she asked, furious with the involuntary blushing that had plagued her from early childhood.

Maddie noticed and was puzzled by it. 'It's just that he knows so much about Jim's businesses. I thought he might help us.'

Lydia was quiet for a while before deciding to tell Maddie the impulsive plan she had formulated over-night. 'Worth a try. It might well be a good idea. Actually, what I was thinking of doing was flying out to Belize and confronting Dad. To his face. He's out there for another week. And Tom arrives any time now too. I could talk to him first, before facing up to Jim.'

'How long would you be away?'

'There's a new direct charter flight to Belize. Just one out and back a week. Saves half a day. And it's tomorrow. I either take it or I wait until he's back. Although his secretary says he's then flying straight on to Lisbon.'

'It sounds as though you've thought it all out,' Maddie said. 'At least you can try. See what he says . . .'

'I'll go then,' Lydia said, relieved to have finally made up her mind. 'I'll call you when I get there. All right?'

Chapter Ten

'Jim. It's me. Everything seems to be going pretty much to plan out here.'

'So, you haven't heard, then?' Barton snapped. 'I thought you consultant people were supposed to follow the news.'

Tom felt exposed. The hotel reception had called first thing to say a fax had come in for him from London. Rather than have them deliver it while he was taking a shower, he had said he would collect it on his way to the breakfast room. 'What's happened?'

'The Stow plant. It's gone. Burned to the ground last night.'

'What? I don't . . . Do they know what caused it?' Tom was shocked, his quick mind already playing over the various crisis management options.

'It was fire-bombed. The inspectors are crawling all over the place, but unofficially they're telling me what I already know. Animal rights terrorists.' Barton had received a stream of personal and corporate threats over the past year from several of the fragmented militant groups. And even more since that damned article on Temple Bio-Laboratories had run in the weekend supplement. He had already fired his City PR company for talking him into doing the interview against all his instincts. The piece did nothing for the share price, but made him a magnet for all the bleeding heart cranks, and worse. He had not told anyone about the warnings, however. Certainly not the police. The last thing he wanted was to invite attention and surveillance. And certainly not Tom or his own management people. If it got out, it could only hit the share price and push up his already crippling insurance premiums.

'What's the media making of it? This is share sensitive.'

'No group has claimed responsibility yet, and the fire inspectors will take some time to get to an official conclusion, but the press is already speculating about a suspected fire-bombing attack. From the Animal Liberation Front, the Animal Rights Militia, some ALF offshoot called The Justice Department . . . or a newish group, the Animal Freedom Warriors. Whoever it is made a hell of a job of it. Two years' work up in smoke.'

'You kept back-up records though.' They had talked about just such a scenario for a disaster recovery programme.

'We've got the data backed up, sure. But it's the actual work . . .' Barton moaned, genuinely upset. Despite his nakedly commercial reasons for entering the field, he was none the less deeply proud of what the teams he had assembled were achieving, leading the world. 'The transcription, where we were replicating the pigs' DNA. Base pairing. The chimera rats we'd developed. And especially the work we'd done with the transgenic haemoglobin. We were *months* away from a commercially viable cell-free blood substitute. Imagine the worldwide market for that! One animal had blood that was sixty per cent human, forty per cent pig haemoglobin. With protein engineering we had all but cracked the problem of low oxygen affinity, and side-effect kidney problems. All this is the *real* cost. It's the actual specimens. Not the notes. Everyone knows the theory behind all this. What we had was the practical, physiological proof.'

'There might be some hope, you know. If this *was* an

animal rights attack, then the good news is that they will have "liberated" them. They won't have burned *them*, will they?' Tom reasoned. 'And if I'm right, your pigs are probably roaming around free range on some hippy smallholding in Glastonbury, or some damn place. There's still a decent chance that the police will find them, you know. They take these militant animal rights people very seriously.' He just stopped himself adding that MI5 would also almost certainly have been brought in by now. Mitchell would hardly thank him for putting Barton on notice of Secret Service interest in him.

'I've thought of that,' Barton said. 'I'll put the private detective agency on the case as well.' He retained the company to sweep his offices and home regularly for listening devices, as well as compiling the reports on anyone who could help or hinder his ambitions. 'As for the impact of all this on Temple Bio, the new PR people are putting out a statement saying we had everything backed-up, including specimens – to settle the market. We've had enough of a hammering without all this. And you, I want you to tell Elkins the same story. OK?'

'Sure. I'll handle that.'

'How did last night go. You know . . . after the dinner.'

'I assume your PI found out that Elkins was gay? Hence the hotel,' Tom replied with an edge. He now needed no signposting on how Barton was using him. 'I left him in a gay bar surrounded by some beautiful boys. I've checked that he's actually back. Got in about five. But I haven't seen him myself yet this morning. I'm about to call and chase him. We need to be out of here in an hour.'

Barton laughed. 'Don't worry. He should be in a really good mood.' One of those 'beautiful boys' had just called the private detective with his report. The threesome had got through mountains of coke and poppers.

Tom felt unclean at ever being a part of Barton's dirty way of doing business. 'That side of this trip is all your department. More seriously, are you happy that he's going to be impressed with what you're doing out there? Without any need for blackmail?'

'Not a phrase I want to hear you use again, Tom,' Barton cautioned. 'Big business using job insecurity to cow young-sters and fifty-year-olds – is that blackmail? Governments tying Third World aid to defence contracts, or to attacking drugs barons – is that blackmail? Don't suddenly turn into Mother Teresa on me! But yes, to answer your question, we're ready for him. I've rehearsed Penny on what to say, and how much to show him. Just get him over here happy. I'll have the helicopter fly you down. See you later.'

But Tom knew that all was far from well at Temple Bio. In his job he had often witnessed what he called the 'bandwagon of success' working for clients. Things began to go right for some reason, and then almost magically everything else also starts to go their way. Winning contracts by a whisker instead of losing them. New income and new opportunities seeming to come at them from all sides. Currency movements working for rather than against them. The best people are suddenly desperate to work for them, whilst their own high-fliers stop taking calls from headhunters. It was a genuine phenomenon, he thought, one with empirical legs – something he would like to study seriously some day on a sabbatical. Success really *could* breed success. But there was the other side too. The bandwagon of failure, and Murphy's Law, when everything that could go wrong, did. This was what was happening now to the company. Unaccountably, everything now seemed to be going belly-up again for the once untouchable Barton.

And now on top of all this, through the formidable Pere-grine Mitchell, Tom himself was spearheading a powerful

MI6 campaign against the man and the outposts of his sprawling empire. Mitchell had briefed him to 'go native' with Barton. To get him to bring him fully into his confidence at last on Lisbon and this Aruba Alliance. It would not be easy. Barton obviously had him pigeon-holed as a convenient front man for the legitimate side of the companies. What was it he had called him? 'Mother Teresa'. On another occasion it had sarcastically been 'Tom the Baptist'. Mitchell's plan was for Tom now to show his streetwise side, and make a play for a lot more money. Show Barton some naked greed, and use a little blackmail of his own, to plant them firmly on the same moral plane. It was a role an angry Tom was more than ready to play. He would take the greatest pleasure in bringing the monster crashing down. Permanently this time. And if Barton thought he, Tom, could not play dirty pool, then he was in for one very big shock.

Bolitho looked around urgently for a safe place to spend the night. The light had just started to go, and he knew how little time he had left. The temperature had also dropped substantially. Jungles, however, held few surprises or terrors for him. He was pleased with the distance he had already managed to put in, the going so far not being as difficult as he had expected. Trekking on into the night had been an option, but given his good start it was not worth risking a fall and a broken leg.

Having spotted a fallen banak tree, lying at an angle against a group of others, he decided this would be his first resting place. Swinging off his rucksack, he quickly strung up his nylon hammock before collecting wood. Satisfied with the security of his bed, he now set to work on a fire before the light finally died. The wood was damp, so he took a couple of tampons out of the rucksack pocket and placed them together on the ground. It was an old

Air Force survival trick he had picked up years earlier: the cotton wool made excellent tinder. He lit it with a varnished survival match and carefully added the wood. Then, using his powerful torch, he turned his attention to one of the jobs he least enjoyed in jungle operations. Removing the leeches.

These slug-like creatures survive by attaching themselves to passing animals, sucking out as much as half a pint of blood at a session. Even more horrific, however, are aquatic leeches, which can lodge behind the eye, in the vulva and vagina, the male urethra or, if they have entered through the mouth or nostrils, on to the trachea and bronchi. Bolitho was extremely respectful of the hated things, and now he checked himself, finding three on his legs. Two had not got a hold, and he simply shaved them off with the knife. The third, however, had burrowed in deeply. Dragging them out is dangerous, as the jaws can be left behind, risking ulceration and gangrene. For this one, along with another he felt but could not see on the back of his neck, he applied some anti-insect cream. In half a minute the creatures had left the wounds, leaving behind their bloody trail, and he gratefully flicked them away. Next he reapplied his insect repellent to try and avoid problems with mosquitoes and other bugs.

Afterwards he made a coffee, drinking it directly from the scalding, charred billy can, swallowed a fistful of his pills and then chewed on some high-energy dry biscuits. He was confident he would not be out there long enough to have to worry about living off the land. Changing his T-shirt, he staked the sweat-soaked one he had removed by the fire in an attempt to dry it. The temperature was plummeting and he knew that wet clothing loses heat twenty-five times more quickly than dry. Before making for his mosquito net and hammock, he decided to radio the pilot, to keep him on his toes.

Sure enough, the man answered the Tacbe unit almost immediately. 'Everything OK?'

'Yeah. I put in maybe eight miles. Pretty good. But it's fairly easy going in this valley. I was able to walk along a small trib quite a way. Now I'm just turning in.'

'Fine. Anything you need?' The pilot desperately hoped not. The less he had to do with Bolitho the better he liked it.

'What you do is this. Get over here tomorrow, real early. Five, latest. Locate the native again. And me. And radio down precise compass directions. I don't want to spend any more time hacking through this stuff than I need. Also, I want to know how far ahead he is now. Have I closed on him, or stayed about the same this afternoon? Got that? I'll hear you up there. Call me when you have the information.'

'That's fine,' the Englishman replied, relieved. 'Oh, but just one thing for tomorrow. Mid-day.'

'What?'

'I have to pick up two people from the airport. They're due in at twelve-forty-four. Then I bring them over to San Ignacio. VIP treatment. Sir James's orders.'

'No problem. Carl Lewis couldn't get to the Mother that fast. I won't need you until a lot later.'

Although at odds with his feelings, the pilot felt an unexpected pang of compassion for the man. He had been on night manoeuvres himself often enough in his service days, but always with others. Mates. Bolitho was alone out there, and not young any more. Also, for all his toughness, he had the pallor of a seriously sick man. 'I'll be here for you when you need me. Good luck, pal.'

'Yeah. Sure,' Bolitho said and flicked off the handset.

Despite the gnawing pain, and the noise of the forest –

water flowing, monkey screams, frogs, birds and a Luftwaffe of flying insects – Bolitho fell easily into a light sleep. It was something he had trained himself to do years ago, using his own bastardised form of yoga. The mosquito net was as tight as he could make it, the hammock as comfortable as any hotel bed, and after an inky coffee, a slug of bourbon and a cheroot as a nightcap, life could have been worse.

And then suddenly it was. Much worse. His highly developed sense of danger woke him, and he opened his eyes, not moving a muscle of his body. He held his breath so as to hear better. Inside the sleeping sack, his thumb eased off the safety on the Army issue Beretta. His straining senses told him nothing. But there was danger. Though he could not hear or see it, he could taste it, as strongly as the coffee.

What he had in fact tuned in to was danger being picked up by the far more acute senses of the small creatures around him. They were busy warning their own species and young. And this subtly different jungle noise was what had woken him. Calmly he began to work through the options, as a process of elimination. Poisonous snakes, like the rattler or *fer de lance* – known as the tommy-goff in Belize and the pit viper in the States – would not attract this kind of forest attention. Deadly, but not big enough to cause nocturnal panic. The same went for poisonous spiders and scorpions. A boa constrictor could grow to eighteen feet, but it moved lethargically and was not likely to spook a whole area like this. There were crocodiles in the region, but not high as this, he reasoned.

Far more likely was another human. Banto himself may have turned and come looking for him. He would have heard the chopper, and must have figured out that he was being tracked. Bolitho cursed himself for lighting the fire. That and the aroma of the coffee would pin-point him to any halfway decent tracker within a few miles. Had not his own field instructor in Vietnam taught him to respect the skills of Vietcong trackers? Anyone in the bush who so much as used soap, deodorant, hair cream, toothpaste, boot polish, smoked or chewed gum, he had stressed, might as well stand up, yell and wave a flashlight to these people. And if not Banto, there could be local drug runners, heading for the back door to Guatemala. They would have taken the chopper's long hover over them to be the security forces . . .

He screamed inwardly at himself. Despite all his experience, he had acted like a rookie. All because he was still treating natives like dumb gooks.

Then he heard it. The sound of something big and confident moving through the jungle towards him. This was no human, he now knew. It was one of the big cats.

A jaguar. Or a puma.

Bolitho felt a claustrophobic panic rising in him. He was trussed up in his sleeping bag and strung up in his damned hammock. Very slowly he eased out both his hands and peeled back the net. Next he began to shimmy free, out of the constricting strait-jacket bag and to the ground. Then he froze, making far too much noise as his feet sank into the fern forest bed. Both hands now on the Beretta, he opened his eyes wide, willing his pupils to open even more to help his night vision. There was a sudden crashing sound as the animal leapt forward in attack on the small clearing. A big shape flew at his T-shirt, still staked out by the fire's dying embers. It shook it violently for a while, knocked over the billy can, then disappeared again into the blackness.

Bolitho grimly recognised it as a puma, one of the world's natural killers. Known also as the mountain lion, cougar or panther, it is the Americas' answer to Africa's leopard. Just like the leopard it kills many more animals than it devours, to slake a desire for warm blood and its instinct to destroy. Not for nothing had major South American ranch owners each employed one or two lion-hunters, *leoneros*, until laws came in to protect the endangered beasts.

His mind racing, Bolitho forced a calm on himself as he planned the best form of defence against the animal. It was still near by. The strange purr-like growl seemed to be resonating all around him, from no one direction he could identify. The beast had seemed fairly average size, from what he knew of them: about 150 pounds, three foot high, and a body of some four feet, not counting the thick, long tail. One thing was clear though. It knew all about him. And exactly where he was.

There was something that he had read or been told that he needed to remember. He knew it was important. Something about a situation just like this ... But all he could remember was that he had something to remember, Goddamn it! And then suddenly it came back from his distant memory. It had been in a book about one of his military heroes, an expert jungle fighter in the Second World War. John Hedley had been in the British special services in the East. One night, behind Japanese lines, he had been sleeping when his native guides saw a tiger stalking him, just three yards away. They had guns, but knew they stood a high chance of just wounding the animal, making it even more dangerous for being the more unpredictable. Also, of course, they did not want to advertise their whereabouts to the enemy. Instead one of them shone a torch directly at the animal's face. And, in Hedley's own words, 'he beat it'; adding that it was 'a trick worth remembering'.

If he could have got to his shotgun, it would have been different, but Bolitho decided to put his life in Hedley's hands. His Beretta, not a great stopper, was accurate, at best, to around thirty yards. And a fast moving cat – at night?

The deep-throated, terrifying purr-roar seemed to be getting louder, the puma becoming angrier, when, unexpectedly, it stopped – and there was an uncanny silence. The whole noisy forest was holding its breath, waiting, watching . . .

The attack came from his right; Bolitho's only warning the three or four crashing bounds as the puma raced at him. Rolling over, he grabbed the powerful, high-intensity lamp and shone it at the beast, now just feet away. He saw with pin-sharp clarity its four dagger canines bared, its ears perked, its head perfectly still as it flew forward, accelerating beyond twenty miles an hour from its standing start with its huge paws flaring. Bolitho screamed and screamed at it, the lamp in his left hand, the shaking Beretta in his right. He prepared to fire now, panicking that the torch was not going to work, when suddenly the puma straightened its front legs. It dug them in, throwing up debris, and shook its head as its back half skidded round like a car in a drift. Then, regaining its poise, it darted off into the forest and was gone.

Bolitho remained immobile for minutes as he strained his senses again to be sure he was safe. And slowly, progressively, the jungle noises started up again as this little world within the great forest closed over the threat like quicksand.

Elkins woke to the phone ringing. For a while he was completely disoriented, unsure of where he was. It was a feeling he knew well, and waited the few seconds it always took to get his brain in gear.

Then the bitter-sweet memories came flooding back, and he closed his eyes again. The lids felt like sandpaper, and made them smart. Squinting at the clock-alarm he grabbed the phone to kill the noise, his head pounding.

'Welcome to sunny Miami!' Tom said with a disc jockey's forced cheerfulness. 'It's seventy degrees on the beach today. That's Fahrenheit, for any Limeys out there.'

'Morning, Tom,' Elkins croaked, sitting up very carefully. His back and genitalia were stinging sore. The guys had been into a heavy pain and humiliation trip. Not his normal scene. But, as one of them had said last night, 'When in Rome, do as Caligula does.' In fact he had enjoyed great sex, which had challenged all his old prejudices and, frankly, his fears. Nothing could change the fact, however, that it was simply not an option for him to go home after every session with a body covered in marks. Neither was all the body-piercing. Rubber and plastic, along with cross dressing, were his favourite scenes in London, and he had found a couple of clubs in Soho and Charing Cross that suited him well. But the rough-trade treatment meted out to him until early that morning had been his best session ever. They had a fully equipped 'cell' at some apartment they had taken him to, and at the time – his senses heightened by the coke and amyl nitrate poppers – he would happily have died at their hands.

'We don't have too much time, I'm afraid. Can you make it down here, packed to leave in an hour?'

'No problem.'

'Shall I have some coffee and juice sent up?'

'Throw in some paracetamol, and I might just survive the day,' he said. Hearing Tom chuckle, he hung up and cautiously eased himself out of bed. Catching sight of himself in a mirror, he went over to open the curtains. In the strong light, the weals and clamp marks looked horrific. Then, seeing his suit and clothes on the floor, he realised that the last part of the night was a mental blank. He had no memory of leaving the cell, and none of how he had got back to the hotel. Suddenly sick with shock and terror, he went over and picked up his jacket, convinced that he had been professionally rolled. Had to be. Stupid! Hadn't they seemed like professionals from the moment they picked him up in the hotel bar? His money and charge cards were sure to be missing. How could he have been so gullible, so bloody naïve, at his age . . .?

But no . . . there they were. His expensive Breitling watch was also safely in his side pocket. Relief washed over him, soothing away the worst of his fears, and turning it inwards to his familiar feelings of self-loathing and contrition. Flicking through his wallet, he checked the cash and his collection of charge cards. All there. Then he noticed something odd about the photograph he carried of his wife and two teenage children. There were felt-tip pen marks on Michael's picture. Looking at it more closely, he saw that someone had crudely drawn a moustache and cap, the cliché gay symbols, on his son's face. Tearing it out he stared down, smudging the hateful ink with his thumb.

But removing the family picture had exposed something even worse. A new photograph. One he had never seen before.

There he was. Stupid, reddened head and hands thrust through the stocks. Sweating, eyes rolling, naked, his lacerated back bloodied . . . He no longer needed his memory to remind him of what they had done to him. He stared at the Polaroid briefly before dropping it and running to the bathroom to throw up.

It had been a long way and eaten into a lot of Mitchell's time. At least the Service's front tour company, still operating out of the last vestige of their old offices in Vauxhall Bridge Road, had kept the cost down. They had got him a trade AD75 air ticket, and rack rates at the downtown Omni International.

Had it been worth it? He could have sent someone else out, or got one of their stringers down there, or even had the CIA meet up with Bates. But no. It had all been too damned important to get right. And he knew that he personally had broken through to the man at their last meeting. By flying out personally, he had begun to create that all-important bonding with him that was going to be necessary if things got hot. His flight back from Miami was still four hours away, and he opened his briefcase in the small office they had made available to him.

Taking out his Service-issue laptop, he plugged it into the telephone line and switched on. The 64-bit gas plasma-screened unit had been produced to the Service's own specification based on a CIA Wang desktop machine, with special encryption software developed by MIT and the Weizmann Institute. The brief to them had been deceptively simple. Create a closed user group with passwords and cryptography that neither GCHQ's Communications and Electronic Security Group nor the Sigint experts at the US Defense Intelligence Agency could unscramble. As a result, even a technological illiterate like Mitchell could now log in securely to headquarters through the ATHS at a station or embassy anywhere in the world, pick up e-mail, send messages, file a report and access a limited menu of databases.

He had decamped the Omni for the Service's sometime outpost in the region, the British Consulate's suite of offices on South Bayshore Drive, precisely to use the Service's Automatic Telegram Handling System for filing his CX – his field agency report. But Mitchell was also there as an old hand to cement FCO relations. He had spent a lifetime forwarding reports from embassies and consulates, and he knew that some of the personal relationships developed during these times often proved invaluable later. The middle-aged Consul had certainly been pleased to welcome him for the morning. Mitchell's considerable reputation in King Charles Street went before him, and a spot of SIS business made a welcome change from helping out sunburned Brits.

'The ATHS works a lot better than our old Folio system,' he remarked cheerfully.

'Technology certainly marches on. And thanks for finding me a corner,' Mitchell said.

'Always happy to help a Box 850 "Friend",' he replied, using some old FCO jargon for MI6 to show he was in the know.

'You're kept pretty busy here, I imagine, with Mouse pilgrimages.'

'It's a popular place. And not just for Disney and the other parks. We're getting a million British tourists a year to Florida.' The Consul smiled. 'And we see a fair percentage of them, one way or the other. People who have lost their passports, or been robbed. Tourists *still* insist on believing that we'll lend them money. It's one of those great urban myths. There are also Brits to visit who've got themselves arrested – mostly for drink or drugs offences. More seriously, we also get involved with some victims of rape, serious assault, and murder.' He explained how he had over recent weeks become a highly reluctant TV face, following the murder of two British tourists. Despite the excellent signage, they had taken a wrong turn soon after leaving the airport. It was late evening, and tired, jet-lagged and a little drunk on free in-flight booze, they had just picked up their hire car. While trying to find their way back to the expressway, they were hit from behind. Against all the advice, the man stopped to check out the damage and got them both shot dead resisting the muggers. 'Terrible for the families, of course, but also for the State.

Miami gets an unfair press for these things. They've really
cleaned up their act for tourists. Hard to see what more
they can do, really.'

They gossiped for a while longer, Mitchell envying him
rather. An interesting, important job, but with some good
lifestyle compensations for all the pressure.

When alone again, he scrolled through his e-mail messages, ignoring most of them for now, just dipping into a
handful that seemed either urgent or interesting. Then he
went into the latest report submitted to the Cabinet Office
Assessments Staff by the CIG on Russia. The news was all
bad. Their worst fears had been confirmed by an asset being
run by Moscow Station in the Sluzhba Vneshnoi Razvedki,
Russia's overseas intelligence service, which was to the FSB
what MI6 was to MI5. She had reported that it was Andrei
Rybinski, the Deputy Director of Volchov, the country's
leading biotech research facility, who had been recruited
some months earlier by Barton to work alongside Blacher
at the Oeiras Temple Bio-Laboratories plant.

To refresh his memory, Mitchell did a word search on
Volchov. Seconds later his screen was filled with referenced
source options, much of it from hard intelligence obtained
from inside the Research Institute for Especially Pure Biological Preparations in Leningrad. The Institute had been
one of four satellites in the powerful Volchov empire in the
old Soviet days. From all he read, it was clear that frenzied
work had continued, despite the USSR's signature on the
1972 Biological Weapons Convention. The most sensitive
research revolved around growing bacteria and viruses at
the highly secret labs at Obolensk.

Tapping into another data source headlined 'Sverdlovsk',
Mitchell read the top line report from 1979 on the accidental
release of anthrax in the Urals town. There had been scores
of deaths, which TASS had described as being due to an

outbreak of E. Coli toxin in a supply of meat. Then he saw another headline that took him back twenty years. It drew him into reading once more of the *poligon* on Vozrozhdeniya, an island in the centre west of the 27,000-square-mile Aral Sea. The Soviets had used part of the island – comfortably far away from Moscow – as a test range for experimental viruses and delivery weapons. Hundreds of animals, tethered to posts, had been killed to test killing power and dispersal capabilities.

He could still vividly recall the first time he had learned about this place. And the satellite photographs the Americans had got of one of the test firings. The imagery of the scene on the ground – the frightened, uncomprehending suffering of the farm animals and apes – was still too strong for him, even after all this time. 'Avoid Aral Sea caviare', he had written flippantly on the file at the time, before throwing it gratefully in his out-tray for the next recipient. It had been an act of phoney bravura to hide what, at the time, he considered a worrying and uncharacteristic sign of sentimental weakness in himself. Certainly, he had by then seen and witnessed much worse than this in the field. It was just that some things get through to a man. There was no rhyme or reason why one horror should affect an agent more than another. But that was how it was, and the sight of those bewildered animals had never left him.

So now, reasoned Mitchell, Barton had teamed a top Western expert, Blacher – someone with practical applications' experience – alongside Rybinski, and all his Volchov experimental research knowledge. And further married all this to the leading-edge genetic work going on at his own laboratories. Conceivably, all underpinned by the Aruban billions. The man was acting exactly like a foreign power. Yet why? What would he do with his biological weapons? Load them in Russian-built Scud missiles? But aimed at whom?

There were far too many questions. It was vital that Tom Bates came up with some answers – fast. Because if he failed, the Special Boat Service would within seven days be tasked to destroy the Lisbon plant and make it safe. So reducing immediate tension, but simply pushing the unknown problem back a matter of months, before like a hydra it reared another head. Time was running out. And corners would have to be cut. Bates would have to take more risks than he would be allowed to realise.

Chapter Eleven

Banto had sensed that a battle was coming. And before it did he needed weapons, and the protection of the spirits.

He was pleased with the powerful sturdy longbow. His father would also have been satisfied that his eldest son had learned well from him. It was six feet long, had a powerful sixty-pound pull, and was fashioned with the dead guard's knife. Steel had made the job fast and easy. It was much, much better than his village knives, made from hard wood or a sharpened cassowary thigh bone. The right kind of strong, flexible species of willow had been easy to find, although the strong vines needed for the bow string were not quite the same as in his forest. The six *pitpit* bamboo arrows had razor sharp point-heads, fixed with rubber sap. Vital, but time-consuming now, was the careful preparation of the poison for the tips. For this he hacked off the stringy red bark from a *tiki uba* tree. It looked like the entrails of an animal, but its sap was an anticoagulant curare that would cause his victims rapidly to bleed to death. It needed hardening by fire, but this presented him with a dilemma. Leave an easy sign for the hunter he knew would follow him, or have his warrior tools? The answer was in the end simple. Above all else, efficient weapons were essential. The risk was necessary.

The steel also made the slow job of making sparks from

flint rock easy – much easier than using slim shafts of wood as fire drills – and after less than an hour the lethal arrow point-heads were ready. The next priority was to catch a pig to kill for the spirits. During his search at first light for the weapons' materials, he had looked for signs of pig. Spoor, fresh droppings, mounds of loose earth where they had been rooting for food . . . but nothing. In his own forest he could hunt for eleven hours some days and still not be successful. A sacrifice was vital, however, because without the spirits' protection he knew the *dimanples* would let the hunter kill him.

A three-hour hunt had so far revealed only birds, maddening red-eyed tree frogs and assorted ugly-looking creatures – iguanas, anteaters and fat armadillos. Spider monkeys looked down lazily, howlers let rip their deep-throated roar, and Technicolor toucans and parrots flitted in the forest canopy. But Banto needed a sizeable mammal if he was to please the spirits. There was a fleeting chance of a small brocket deer, but not one good enough to risk a precious arrow.

Then he heard it. Standing perfectly still, weight forward, balanced on the balls of his wide feet he tuned his ears to this one noise, excluding all else. Whatever it was, the timid animal was not very big. But not small either. No pig, but maybe . . . Its snout pushed through the vegetation first, sensing something wrong but not finding any obvious warning signals. Nothing moving. No noise. No scent. Banto had as usual when hunting stained himself with mashed vine leaves, blocking out his scent. At last the gibnut appeared, foraging in the small clearing. A nocturnal herbivore, feeding early, it was nosing a particularly pungent root. The creature was brown-spotted, a kind of badger-sized guinea pig. Known locally as a *paca*, it is a regional delicacy. When served to the Queen on her last visit to Belize, the UK tabloid press had great fun describing – erroneously – how she was forced to eat a rat.

To satisfy the spirits of ancestors, only one arrow is allowed for the kill.

Only one was needed, as the animal was skewered by the long arrow, writhing, unable to run back to the dark safety of the deep jungle. Banto walked over, dispassionately pushed the arrow in and out and finished it off. Satisfied, he slung the gibnut over his shoulder, its blood dripping down his back, mingling with the green slime of the vine mash.

He had weapons. He had hunted down atonement for the spirits.

He was now invincible.

She was in no mood to watch the in-flight movie, a soppy romantic comedy. An uninspired, tourist-class vegetarian meal lay untouched in front of her as she forced down another paracetamol to fight off the threat of migraine. The fat man next to her window seat was asleep, snoring wetly, and she needed to get to the toilet. Her pounding head and general nausea were not helping her sudden misgivings about what she was doing. Flying alone into the unknown now seemed a very stupid, spur-of-the-minute idea.

For a start her boss, the Media Director, had been none too sympathetic to her request for a short-notice holiday. It was still the tail end of her team's busiest time of the year. TV Buying Group Heads simply don't take holidays in November, December or early January. And the Metropolis deal was still in the air. Knowing he effectively had no choice, he had agreed without much grace to her few days off, while making it clear that she had just cashed in a lot of her hard-earned Brownie points with him. This thing with her father was in danger of taking over her life, and serious though the bigger issues appeared, this did worry her. A woman alone, the job was her only anchor.

The stewardess caught her eye and intuitively understood. From her pallor and the analgesic bottle she knew that Lydia needed to get out. Waking the grumpy man for her, she asked if Lydia needed anything after she had climbed free.

'Thanks,' she said, gratefully, giving her a woman-to-woman smile. 'There is one thing. Does this flight have those air-phone things? Or are they only for the people up front?'

'This is charter. There *is* no up front! Come and find me in the galley when you're ready. I'll show you.'

Tom was signing the hotel bill when her call came. He was taken aback to hear her voice. 'Lydie! Great to . . . But how the hell did you know I was here?' he asked. Elkins had just gone out to the limo, and he knew they had to hurry to make the Belize flight.

'I got your itinerary from your office. Before I left London.' She felt better hearing his voice. It seemed at last that there was someone on her side. Someone she could talk to about things; someone with whom she could be weak and uncertain.

'Before you left. Where are you? On business somewhere? Sunning yourself in Cannes with the rest of your crazy industry?'

'I wish . . . I'm on a flight – to Belize.'

Tom's immediate reaction was that she was flying out to see him. Great as their early relationship was, he would be disappointed and alarmed if she now turned out to be too clingy. Too serious too soon. 'Why? What brings you out?' he asked cautiously.

She noticed. 'I can't stay away from you, lover boy. I want to have your babies, grow old and die with you,' she replied with an edge.

Not sure what to say, he stammered, 'That's what all the girls say. But . . .'

'But. But – *seriously* . . .' she cut in, finishing for him. While understanding his initial panic, she had not liked it much. 'Hard as it is to believe, I'm not actually flying halfway around the world to see you. There's a big, older guy with touched-up fair hair out there. Answers to the name of Father.'

'When do you get in?' Lydia could be unnecessarily aggressive at times.

'Sevenish.'

'Does he know you're coming?'

'No. And don't tell him. I want to surprise – or rather confront him. But I'd like to see you first, Tom. Can you get away tonight?'

'Late, probably. Yes. Yes, of course.' The spikiness of their conversation now began to melt away for both of them. 'Where are you staying?'

'I've booked a room at the Hotel San Ignacio. The travel agent said it was the best in town.'

Tom, like Elkins, was staying in one of the luxury cabanas on Barton's ranch, a couple of kilometres outside San Ignacio. 'I know it. On Buena Vista Street, up from the police station. It's fine. Nice and high. And cool. How are you getting out there from the airport?'

'They booked me a driver. Don't worry. I'll be fine. Come over to the hotel any time you can get away. Any time, no matter how late. I won't be going anywhere.'

'Great. Look forward to seeing you. We'll make a night of it,' he said enthusiastically, hanging up.

The ache in her head became more intense again. No chance, she said in frustration to the dead line. *No* bloody chance of that.

* * *

Peregrine Mitchell was also caught by an unexpected phone call just before leaving for his plane.

'I've just got your postcard.' It was Neil Gaylord. Mitchell's short CX report had just a few minutes earlier pinged, announcing its presence on his screen.

'That was damned quick! I've only just sent it.'

'If you look at your watch, you'll notice it's also damned early over here.'

'Well, I don't get to fill out anyone's appraisals these days, so don't expect any house points,' Mitchell replied. 'Anyway, what is it? You didn't call to praise my literary style.'

'It's just that now I know you've had a positive result, we have to talk. Real quick when you're back,' Gaylord said tersely.

'Something up?'

'Cousin David's cutting up rough. Won't wait long for us.'

'Understood. I'm on a red-eye. I'll call in to see you as soon as I get back in.' Mitchell hung up, said goodbye to the Consul and got in the car they had laid on.

So. Now Israel was also pressing for early action. Briefed almost certainly by the Americans who kept little going on in the region from them. No doubt they would be threatening to go it alone to eliminate any threat from Barton if Britain did not move soon. After the long-held fear of biological Scud attacks from Iraq, Syrian chemical weapons, and the worry now about Iran's theoretical nuclear capability, he certainly did not blame them. But it all added massively to the urgency for a fast result.

The humidity was unbearable but Bolitho resisted the temptation to wipe the sweat from his face. It's the body's cooling system working efficiently, he told himself, as he pressed on through the now increasingly dense forest. The pilot had, as instructed, flown over first thing with the excellent news that the native had not moved at all since yesterday and was still moving around a small clearing. He must have found a base that suited him, at least for a night or two. Armed with a precise compass bearing, Bolitho was now within a three-hour march of his prey.

Struggling over long-fallen trees, he fully recognised the strain he was putting on his failing constitution. Not only his gut ached, his varicose veins felt about to burst with the heat and his heart was thumping dangerously. Every mile felt like ten. Despite all this, however, his earlier years of training had taught him a fluid technique which still enabled him to set a pace fit but inexperienced younger men found hard to better. There were, he prided himself, still a few more fights left in that hulking old frame.

Looking up to the high canopy, he was watching patches of bright blue turning to grey, thick cloud. With regular checks on the compass, he forced his way through the mangled roots and rotting vegetation, his hands one minute grabbing tangled vines – some barbed and painful – and the next disgusting, fleshy fungi, its sweet odour nauseous, or a large twig that became a stick insect. Land leeches seemed to fall like blood-sucking hail, especially from the large ferns near streams where animals drink. Epiphytes flourished everywhere, piggy-backing other species like mistletoe on an English apple tree. From time to time he rested, eating figs and drinking vine water.

When at long last he estimated he was within a few kilometres of Banto's last sighting, he began to look more carefully for sign from his track. It was half an hour until he thought he had some success, before deciding the trampled vegetation was made by an animal. The disturbed forest-floor vegetation was that of a quadruped. But it was footprints twenty minutes later, in the soft soil of a stream bank, that first gave him cast-iron evidence that Banto had passed that way. The bootless spoor showed the characteristic wide, splayed prints of a native. Having at last picked up the spoor, the task now was to keep the trail when the few footprints soon disappeared into the forest. At first his practised eye was easily able to keep it hot, spotting fresh scuff marks on the moss enveloping rotting logs. And in the densest patches, Banto had left clear holes, not yet closed by the forest. But when cover became a little lighter, it was again very difficult to pick up the direction. That was when he had to rely on spotting cobwebs broken above animal-head height, cobwebs already being frantically spun back, but with still enough damage for his sharp eyes to read like a rambler's footpath sign. He did lose the track completely once, however. But confident of his direction, he did a cast, backtracking and sweeping in a five-metre circle from the last evidence of sign. An unusual scattering of dry broken leaves, and a clean break in a twig – all things he had unaccountably missed earlier – suddenly screamed at him, and he was hot on the trail once more.

Now confident, feeling he really knew how Banto's mind worked, seeing *his* hacked-off vine water stems, his discarded figs, the tear marks of fistfuls of berries, he knew he was close. Very close. Maybe within half a kilometre. Slipping off his rucksack, he climbed a tall, straight ebony tree to gain a vantage point, and to try and figure out exactly where the man was, before his own unavoidable noise of approach warned him. He could not hope to climb even near the fifty metres into the top canopy, but getting into the forest's secondary ceiling would, he hoped, be enough to help pin-point the native.

Having barely got a third the way up, he smiled and relaxed. He had easily scented the alien smell of Banto's long-extinguished camp fire and the mouth-watering aroma from hours earlier. The roasted gibnut acted exactly like a McDonald's neon. But his deeper question of why here? why stop at this specific bit of the wilderness? had also been answered. The magnet that had drawn the alien native unerringly towards it was now towering magnificently above Bolitho, a few hundred metres away. The huge, brooding ceiba tree. A living fossil that had first taken root on that spot when, back in Britain, Edward I was still fighting Robert Bruce. Its unearthly presence must have long been a powerful spiritual beacon to anyone in its range, drawing man to it with the same awe their brothers, in different countries and in different times, were drawn to Everest, the Grand Canyon, Niagara and later the elemental man-made monuments like St Peter's and the awesome Apollo space rockets.

Bolitho did not have a religious bone in his body, but he had seen much in his action-crammed life. He had witnessed in wars too many inexplicable and extraordinary things not to recognise another now, dwarfing all around it. It had created a cathedral in the forest, a holy place which infused even him with reverence – and a little dread for what he was about to do in its presence.

It had been gone one o'clock when Tom finally pleaded exhaustion to escape Jim Barton and Elkins. And exhausted he was. On arrival at the ranch in the helicopter, they had been shown to their cabanas and, with barely time for a shower, rushed on to dinner with Barton at the main ranch-house. Penny had not been invited, Barton not wanting Elkins catching him off guard with any questions before he made his rehearsed presentation the next day. The good doctor was, Barton had long since decided, highly intelligent – but stupid in business terms. A phenomenon he had observed amongst not a few of the 'geniuses' he had employed, and made money from, over the years.

At last Tom got to Lydia's hotel after a worrying half-hour walk in the black night. Taking one of the ranch 4WDs had not been an option if he was to avoid awkward questions. Luckily there was still someone on the desk who rang Lydia's room for him. Having been told to go straight up, he ran excited at seeing her again, and – his exhaustion now forgotten – at the prospect of some unexpected steamy sex.

All thought of that evaporated, however, when he saw her. White-faced, yet a little flushed, she was clearly unwell. 'What on earth's wrong? You look dreadful,' he said straight out, not thinking.

'Thanks a million. That's just what a girl wants to hear.'

'Sorry. I didn't mean it to come out that way. I'm just worried about you. What is it – travelling sickness? Can I get you anything?'

She looked at him more warmly. It was true. He did look worried. Worried rather than horrified to see her like this. 'I'm fighting off a migraine. I'll be a lot better in the morning. You'll see.'

He came over to her and kissed her gently on the forehead. Kindly. 'It *is* the morning.'

Hugging him for a while, she broke away and examined his face. 'You look pretty bushed yourself.'

'Just what a boy wants to hear . . .' he teased, smiling.

They sat on the bed, arms around each other, and talked about nothing much for ten minutes, before she finally steered the subject round to her trip. 'Tom, I'm here because I'm really worried about Dad. He's doing terrible things. I have to find out more, and get him help.'

'What do you mean? The animal testing? You've known about that for a long time.' He looked at her, then something suddenly crossed his mind for the first time. 'You've heard about the fire, I suppose. At the lab in Stow?'

'Yeah, yeah. It's been in all the papers.' Her eyes avoided him and without realising she was doing it, she let go of his arm.

His trained eye read the body language. 'I don't suppose you had anything to do with it?'

Standing up suddenly and holding her arms across her stomach, she walked out to the balcony. 'Oh sure. I bought an incendiary from "Bombs 'R Us". Planted it, and went home to paint my nails,' she called back derisively.

Oh no, he thought. She *was* involved. Her every movement and tone screamed it. 'So. If it's not animal testing, what's Jim's doing that's frightening you?'

She came back in, feeling cold, and closed the balcony door behind her. 'This is going to sound crazy if I just blurt it out. But Maddie and I had lunch the other day, and she told me that she came across some papers Dad was keeping in the safe. She decided to go through them. And found this one document that seems to make out . . .' Her voice trailed as she took a copy of the hateful thing from her bag, and handed it to him.

He skim-read it and looked back at her. But his eyes showed no shock. No surprise. No disgust. He had been confronted with evidence of human experiments, and was showing no sign of anything . . . 'Tom!' she shrieked. 'You *know*. You *know* about it! My God no! You're a part of all this . . .' Completely wrong-footed, she ran to a wall, facing away from him, afraid. The man she had asked to help her was as guilty as her father!

Tom rushed over to hold her, but she shook him off. Tom's head was racing. Mitchell could not have made any clearer the absolute importance of watertight security. Any leak would put in danger the life of the agent getting information out of Oeiras. The whole complex and vitally important operation could be ruined.

'Listen to me,' he said firmly, turning her round. 'It's not what you think. Trust me. Trust me until I've had a chance to make a call. Get some rest and I'll come back over here and see you after lunch. Can we do that? Is that OK with you?' Mitchell had given him a London number of someone who could trace him in minutes, wherever he was.

Avoiding looking at him, she said softly but firmly, 'Go. Just leave me. Please.'

'I'll make that call. We'll talk tomorrow. It's not what you think. OK?'

But she just stared at him with sad, wet eyes.

The next morning David Elkins sat through Penny's presentation, and had begun asking searching, informed questions as they now toured the lab facility.

'You're not testing on apes?' He had been surprised to see none in the lab. The DNA of chimpanzees, he knew, differed from humans' by only one per cent.

Ever quick to turn a disaster, like Banto's freeing of the chimps, into an advantage, Barton shook his head gravely. 'No, no. We really don't like to test on primates where we can avoid it. They *are* an endangered species after all. Have you ever visited the Primate Research Centre in Holland? Heartbreaking,' he said, with an utterly convincing look of concern on his face. 'And, of course, we work to the letter and spirit of the British Government's 1986 Animals Act, wherever we operate in the world. And that gives special added protection to primates.'

'Very laudable,' Elkins replied, with a hint of sarcasm. He was not that easily fooled. 'So. To summarise – excuse me, Dr Penny – in language even a Fund Manager might understand . . . What you're doing here is copying the genes from the cell lines you've patented of the PNG tribes. You've cracked the DNA codes and are transcripting some for use in vaccines, and others for gene therapy – treating and preventing diseases from cancers and viral killers – like hepatitis B and HIV/AIDS. Is that about it? Is that what you're claiming?'

Tom could see that Elkins was sceptical. But that, after all, was his job. 'Just because others have promised and disappointed before, doesn't mean that we will,' he said, catching an angry look in Barton's eye. He knew how much the man hated the power people like Elkins wielded.

'And exactly how have *you* succeeded in protein engineering identical cell lines, when so many others have failed, Dr Penny?'

'Temple Bio-Labs. Not me. This is a real team effort. We use X-ray crystallography, like everyone else. But with a modification. One which we must for now keep to ourselves. But call our crystallography four-dimensional, not the usual three-dimensional. That's as near to a clue as Sir James would want me to let slip,' Penny replied, shooting a worried look at Barton.

Elkins knew flannel when he heard it, and shook his head. 'So, to be absolutely clear about this. You're not using human cells for commercial development.' He had read, of course, about the PNG government's allegations against Barton.

'Of course not. Using human cells for anything other than research is illegal,' Barton answered. A little too quickly, Tom thought.

'And you've not gone the trendy new *de novo* route – designing new proteins on your drawing board?'

'No. All that's still fledgling science. And some way from commercial application,' Penny replied. 'To repeat. We're simply applying our own modification to well-proven protein-engineering procedures. And through this, making the changes we need to create *different* proteins from the original DNA sequences we got from the tribes. Cell lines with remarkable immunity to many killer diseases, and the ability to avoid developing the full-blown symptoms of others, like AIDS, even where they *do* carry the virus.'

'And finally, what about time to market?'

Barton took over now, relieved to have left the technical side behind. 'As you'll know, there are very different routes for gene therapy than for drugs. We first have to identify and clone our target genes from the DNA. Then select our vector, the virus, to carry it into the cells of our host organism prior to creating a transgenic animal to test its effectiveness as a treatment. This is the stage we're at with some cancers and hep B. Herpes is a few months behind this. But for HIV, we're in the early stages of human testing – for Phase One. This is crunch time. And the preliminary results are extremely encouraging. I'm confident we have a real success. Dr Penny shared with you the first trial results. We now have to check the treatment is not only effective, but safe – and what, if any, side effects it might throw up. You'll be familiar with the three phases of clinical trials, each with larger numbers.'

'I know it's a long process. If all goes to plan you're looking at, what, six years at best to any commercial launch? And before shareholders get sight of a dividend. What chance of success do you think you have?'

'The average chance of a commercial launch after Phase Three is about sixty per cent. For us, I'd put it higher. Eighty-five per cent,' Barton replied. 'With patent protection to 2020, and a very strong royalty stream potential. Like most biotech stocks, we'll be a bumpy ride for your investors. Long years of losses and cash calls, more than compensated by a rocketing share price every time we announce some news. And, most importantly of course, backed by really phenomenal potential future earnings. No portfolio is complete without an exciting biotech stock. And we're the most exciting of them all. I've done all this before, in the equally helter-skelter software market of the eighties. I made investors and myself a lot of money – before my one well-publicised crash. The Americans don't care about previous failures. It's just we Brits who never forget. But nobody need doubt my ability to ride out *this* sector. Temple Bio-Laboratories is a winner, David. I'm a winner. Tell them to buy and you'll be a hero. Promise.'

Tom was watching Elkins carefully throughout this last, ill-judged piece of old-fashioned hard sell. It had obviously back-fired, revealing only Barton's desperation to raise the £2 million he said he needed. The analyst was still far from convinced. But – he knew – if Barton's attempt to play it by the book had failed, then the man would blackmail and bully until he got the result he needed. How the hell had he ever got mixed up with the monster? he asked himself yet again. And why had he not seen this criminal side to him much earlier?

It was high time he made that call to Mitchell to warn him that Lydia was about to confront her father over Oeiras and the human experiments. But should he also warn Mitchell that she might have bombed one of her father's labs? For her own sake? Perhaps the Security Service people could make some kind of deal for her, some US-style plea bargain in return for helping Mitchell out. It might be worth a shot.

He was just making his way back to use the phone in his cabana when he saw the battered old Ford taxi arrive at the ranch house. Lydia got out, looking much better now, and strode purposefully up to the main door. She had decided that she had not flown all this way to delay any longer what she came out to do. Tom Bates or no Tom Bates.

Chapter Twelve

Banto knew that the hunter was approaching him an hour before he had any visual sign. Perched high in the ceiba tree, he first heard distant birds in the forest canopy as they followed something big moving below. They were not warning each other, simply swooping down joyfully to feed on the disturbed butterflies, moths, bugs and, for the buzzards and hawks, the frogs, darting lizards and disoriented bats. Then, soon after, the extreme upper register of his auditory nerves – long since vestigial in modern man – began to pick out the faint high-frequency sounds given off by breaking wood and steel severing through vegetation. So that by the time medium-register sounds were in range – Bolitho easing carefully through the spongy mass of roots, decayed wood, mosses and fungi of the forest floor – he already knew exactly his pursuer's direction, speed and distance.

Bolitho's painstaking approach work would have been good enough to surprise army buddies in field training. Good enough to steal up undetected by the Vietcong, or any of the other guerrillas he had faced in battle. But nothing like enough to evade the extraordinary instincts and senses of primitive man. He could have had no knowledge of a Stone-Age warrior's hearing range. No modern man could. Any more than Banto could understand the devastating killing power of Bolitho's Remington Model 870 pump-action shotgun.

The battle lines were becoming clear. The advantage of ambush against brute firepower. There was a progressive thinning of the forest where the ceiba's hulk had created the small clearing. Banto had a hide in a sapodilla facing the hunter's approach, and with his vine-mash smeared body he utterly disappeared, camouflaged from sight and scent. Occasionally his hand would reach out for the sweet brown fruit he had got a taste for. It had the flavour of chicle, the tree's sap used in chewing gum. His bow and poison arrows were laid in firing position, and the guard's knife was at his side. He knew precisely how long he must wait for the hunter, his sounds now audible to the ceiba tree's catchment of wildlife, startling and exciting them on the ground and high in the canopy. It was all as deafening to Banto as it would have been unnoticed to an eco-tourist. But in turn he now needed to maintain complete silence himself. After a few minutes, he even abandoned the minuscule arm movements needed to reach out to graze. Besides, he chided himself, the aroma of the ripe fruit was attracting midges and flies to his mouth and sticky hands. A good warrior might hear, smell and see all of this. Worse still, a group of the inquisitive, fruit-eating black howler monkeys might swing down to investigate. His father would have been angry with him for such carelessness, and he resumed his motionless state again, invisible to all but the inevitable insects. Waiting patiently to kill the hunter.

It was Lydia's first visit to Belize, and with the darkness blocking out any real sight of the country on her drive from the airport, she had woken that morning to the view from her hotel balcony overlooking the misty Macal valley. The forest-carpeted Maya mountains stretched to the blurred horizon to the south, and rolled on to the border with Guatemala. And, later in the taxi, she had soaked in more of the area, with its fast-flowing river and streams, its verdancy, its tumbling wild orchids, until at last they drove down the long approach road to her father's imposing white ranch-house. She noticed from the sign at the entrance that he had called it Temple Ranch, as if it were some kind of colonial outpost to his manor and estate in the Cotswolds.

A houseman-cum-guard swaggered over to find out, a little aggressively, who had arrived unannounced. Showing up in the battered taxi, wearing denims and a white T-shirt, hair stuffed in a baseball cap, she realised that she did not cut an authoritative figure. For a young woman to command immediate respect anywhere in this chauvinistic region, she had to dress like a powerful man's tart. As soon as she explained who she was, however, she saw fear in the young man's eyes and the belligerence turned at once to sickening deference.

He showed her in to a vast, wood-panelled room. A pool table was in one corner, a gleaming black concert grand piano casually filling another, with a vulgar-looking full bar in a third, to the left of an open fireplace big enough to roast an ox. Having gone out to tell her father she was here, the flustered man returned with the news that he was on a phone call and would be down directly.

It was then that Tom had rushed in, face flushed. 'Lydie. Out. Now! Don't ask why, just leave with me now!'

She was too shocked to be annoyed at being ordered around. His pleading face told her that whatever this was about, it was no prank. Without a word, she got up and left, following him to his cabana. Then once inside she glowered at him. 'This had better be good.'

Tom had decided to tell her everything. 'We've got just minutes before Jim tracks you down here. So listen and don't ask questions now. I'll answer them all later when we have more time. OK?'

She nodded, suddenly afraid. 'Go on.'

'Point one. I do know something about what he's doing in Portugal – but only because I've very recently been briefed on it. By your Secret Service. MI6. Point two. You must *not* tell him that you, Maddie or anybody knows about what he's doing in Oeiras. If you do, it will put a very brave woman's life at risk. That's it. That's really all you need to know for now. So think up some other reason for flying out here. Say you needed a break. Anything. Tell me you agree. That you'll help.'

Sitting down, head swimming she felt weak. '*Of course*, I agree,' she said with some indignance. There came the sound from the open window of someone running towards them. 'Just what kind of trouble is Dad in?'

He shook his head sadly. 'Just about as bad as trouble can get.'

Then the door burst open and the guard came in, followed seconds later by a sweating, flustered-looking James Barton. He took in the scene, the two of them talking, obviously for once in his life thrown by events.

'Dad!' Lydia got up and gave him her normal greeting kiss. 'I bet this has surprised you!'

Collecting himself now, he gave her a bear hug before holding her in outstretched arms as he examined her minutely. Then, with a curious look over at Tom, he said, 'It's the kind of surprise I like. But, what – I mean, tell me, what are you doing out here? Why didn't you *tell* me you were coming? I would have met you. Got things prepared.'

'Spur of the moment thing. I needed a short break. There's no decent snow in the Alps. And then I saw Belize in a winter sun brochure and decided a spot of snorkelling in the Cays would fit the bill nicely. I knew that you two were out here, of course, and decided to give you a Lydia-style shock. And it's a bull's eye – if both your reactions are anything to go by! Look at the pair of you. Fly-catching!'

It was true. Each was open-mouthed. Barton in shock, Tom in awe at her ability to sound so plausible at literally a minute's notice. 'Correction,' Tom said, trying to match her performance. 'Mosquito-catching.'

She laughed. 'So can either of you drag yourselves away from butchering baboons for a couple of days to join me on the coast?'

'When do you go back?' Barton asked.

'Wednesday. There's a non-stop charter flight. I'm on that.'

Barton shook his head. 'We can't. There's an important City analyst we've flown out here specially. We're trying to convince him I'm to be the new millennium's Bill Gates. Why not stay here with us instead? There's lots to do around here. Treks into the forests. Mayan ruins. And we can at least spend some time together in the evenings, over dinner. Say yes. Eh, Tom?'

Tom looked at her, trying not too obviously to discourage her from agreeing to this. It would only increase the risks of something being said, of something going dangerously wrong. 'We'd love to have you, of course. But if you've set your heart on a few days in the beautiful Cays islands, then we'd understand. After all, you can look at old ruins like us two anytime at home! And frankly, Jim,' he said, turning to him, 'if she got to meet our City VIP over dinner, and treated him to one of her polemic little lectures on animal testing . . . Think about it. It might confuse our message, don't you think?'

She recognised the signal Tom was sending, but was not about to turn tail and head meekly for home without a lot

more answers. 'Oh, I can be quite a house-trained guest
when I try,' she smiled, sweetly. 'I'd love to stay here a few
days, Dad. Thanks. I'll cancel the rest of my package and
move in here. I imagine there's the odd spare bedroom in
this modest little place of yours?'

Barton grinned widely. 'Oh, I think we might squeeze
you in somewhere. But I need to hold you to your promise.
You can be your normal obnoxious self to the rest of us, but
be*have* in front of our Mr Elkins. Deal, young Barton?'

'Deal, old Barton,' she replied, their familiar, affectionate
banter making what she now knew about him even harder
to accept. Risking a look at Tom, she saw he had resigned
himself to her staying around. In fact, if her intuition
was not mistaken, he seemed pleased despite his better
judgement.

Banto watched impassively as the hunter edged his way
out of the deep primary forest and on to the perimeter
of the small clearing. It was only when the light struck
the man that his heart leapt with joy, recognising him as
his tormentor Bolitho. Payback. Payback! It was going to
be sweet . . .

The American had the shotgun in his hands, ready for
use. Guns were nothing new to the native, having seen
and heard from the missionary all those years ago the way
a rifle worked. It had then been a Lee Enfield .303, however.
Not the kind of pump-action modern weaponry that had the
firepower of a small army. Staying in the half-light, Bolitho
froze motionless while his senses searched for any sign
to confirm that Banto had indeed been there or whether
he was still near by, also listening and watching. After a
few minutes, satisfied, he paced forward painstakingly,
placing one rubber boot-sole after the other carefully on
the undergrowth, not putting his weight down fully until

confident there was no avoidably noisy material under there. As he did, he was unknowingly inching closer to Banto's chosen killing ground – the triangular area into which he could fire his poisoned arrows at the man without repositioning himself and risking noise. All he now needed to do was silently draw his right arm and bow-string back to his face, before launching his own deadly biological missile at its target.

Bolitho had by now got the strong scent of the fire he had detected back in the forest, and risked walking more quickly over to the charred remains. He was now just feet from the killing zone. Prodding the ashes he found that they were cold, but the forest and insects had yet to take them over, suggesting its use less than a day earlier. There was animal fat in globules around one edge, and five partly charred hardwood sticks that had clearly been used as some kind of spit. There were no bones, entrails, fur or feathers nearby, nor human defecation, suggesting that the native had intended using the ceiba tree camp for more than one meal, more than one night. Creating a latrine and rubbish tip away from the fire, and hence sleeping area, told him that much, and made him stiffen up again and look around carefully. If he was right, the warrior was somewhere very close. Watching. Realising now that he would already have been detected, he decided that there was nothing to gain by his stealth any longer, and potentially much to lose. Picking his way slowly about like a chameleon was simply presenting an easy target.

Pulling back the pump load noisily, he stepped out and began to move quickly and low across the clearing to begin a concentric search pattern. The first arrow slammed into his left arm, throwing him around. The shotgun boomed, sending birds and monkeys screaming up towards the canopy, which exploded into life above them. Then the second thudded into his heart. Curiously, Bolitho barely noticed it until he lifted the gun to aim at Banto, who had now begun moving away from the hide to avoid return fire. The long bamboo shaft deep in his chest stopped him taking a proper firing position, and he loosed off three rounds rapidly in Banto's general direction. The shot peppered Banto in the head and chest and his green body began bleeding extensively. He threw himself behind a fallen log, before crawling rapidly on, snake-like, into the dense forest undergrowth. He felt no pain, but a pellet had missed his left eye by millimetres, and blood from the deep wound was pouring down, partially blinding him.

Both men remained still, as they took stock of their injuries and position. Bolitho was still exposed, and having heard the native's general direction, lurched suddenly behind the great ceiba tree. He recognised from the numbness spreading from the wounds that the arrows had to be poisoned. Either toxic poison, or one of the native anti-coagulants. The arrow in his heart was also already making him weak and breathless. The pain was masked by the numbing poison, but Bolitho was an experienced-enough bush warrior himself to know that he was dying. And he was damned if he was going to die alone.

Taking out the radio from his side pocket, he called up the helicopter pilot.

'That's quick. Ready for me to come and get you?' The Englishman's voice sounded so normal, so matter of fact, giving him a momentary hope that maybe he, Bolitho, could be normal again. Images of his parents and Ohio home came to him. Of summer camp, the Army. And then scenes of death and burning. Of pleading round faces; of beautiful Vietnamese sunsets after the horror of a raid . . . 'Do you receive me?' the pilot persisted.

'Let me tell you something. People should know this.

You want to know my platoon's motto? It's this. "Marines never die. We just go to hell – and regroup." You hear that?' Bolitho laughed, becoming delirious. 'Have a nice life, Airman.' There was nothing more he wanted to say, and nobody to say it to anyway. But he had needed to touch someone, one last time. Fortified by it, he gripped the arrow in his chest, closed his eyes, and in a sudden movement yanked it out. The harrowing scream he roared had the forest canopy teeming again with panicked wildlife, but when he finally looked down he saw just a bloody shaft. The head had broken off, and was still lodged deep in his heart.

Banto drew the serrated hunter's knife. He had now silently circled around Bolitho, whose scream and death-rattle breathing broadcast both his location – and his desperate state. Banto's own injuries appeared worse than they were, but with his blood-streaked green body, and his betelnut red-stained teeth he looked like some kind of forest monster. Now behind Bolitho, he began creeping forward, exposed in the clearing, but ready to spring forward for the kill. And Payback.

But seconds before the attack, Bolitho stood to his full height, and with some sixth sense turned from the tree to stare wild-eyed at Banto, unfazed by his appearance. Both men froze momentarily, before Bolitho suddenly moved with lighting speed. 'Screw you!' he snarled.

Aiming the shotgun at the native's chest, his fingers closed on the triggers, his left palm cupping the pump action, ready for rapid fire. Knowing he too was about to die, the native also now stood erect. Proud and unafraid. Head up. Ready to perish a warrior, in battle. Seeing this triggered images in Bolitho's mind's eye. Images of other men he had literally ripped in half this way – the impact of both barrels at this range was truly terrible. The faces of inexperienced, frightened teenage kids came back to haunt him. Kids that he had vaporised into a red mist, to rain back down on him as gore. But then, over-riding the horrors, driving them away, a calm yearning for release washed over him. He knew he was now just seconds from death, its coldness and oblivion already cloaking him. And still Banto stood proudly and waited. Like a tin soldier. Waiting for death.

All became clear. It was time . . .

In a flowing movement he put the barrels in his mouth and pulled the triggers.

The blast decapitated him, spraying the ceiba red with his blood. Banto looked on wide-eyed as the headless body staggered a couple of paces before crumpling to the floor in the tree's great buttress roots.

Death, especially violent death, was natural to the warrior. But what Bolitho had done truly frightened him. Suicide was unheard of in his world, and he knew that the hunter's soul would now never rest, in *dimanples*. In limbo here, with all the others.

He was also very angry. The self-killing had taken away Payback. He had not slain him. There had been no Payback. And that was bad. Full Payback, however, remained an absolute necessity. The image from the now badly mildewed photograph of Sir James Barton filled his head. The face of the man who was the big *kepala* to Bolitho.

This was now the real target for Payback. Barton would have to pay. And that meant retracing his steps. Back to where they had imprisoned him, and where they took his blood. The idea made him afraid, but there was no choice. He knew exactly what he now had to do.

'Why did you stay? You should have gone off, as if you were on that holiday break to the Cays.' Tom was mildly annoyed at her stubbornness, but pleased for himself that she had stayed. 'This can only complicate things here.'

They were in her hotel room to pick up her things before returning to the ranch. 'Look, I did exactly as you asked. And did it pretty damned well, all things considered. So you shouldn't be surprised if I stay on to find out more. I mean . . . that *is* why I'm here, remember?' Lydia retorted, throwing her few things untidily back in her suitcase.

Tom knew what he was about to say was courting danger but went on anyway, taking a calculated risk. 'So you're here strictly for enlightenment, not to burn the place down?'

She turned, hands aggressively on her hips. 'Meaning?'

'Meaning that I think you were involved in the fire. In fact I more than just think it.' He frowned and went over to her. 'Lydie, it's cards on the table time here. I'll go first, then you. Right?' He looked very stern, and she wondered what was coming. 'Here goes then. This thing we've barely just started is, well, really important to me. Maybe all it adds up to is sex, and the usual getting-to-know-you stuff. And if so – that's fine also. But for me, I think it's more. We've known each other since your student days. I think I've got to understand you pretty well by now. You're someone who's grown up, but still kept faith with her student ideals. And that's not easy for most of us.

'What I'm trying to say is that I'm proud of you for what you did. I only wish to hell *I* cared enough about *anything* to do something like that. And I'm also trying to tell you that I care for you. You can buy what I'm saying or not. This isn't a presentation I've ever made before. But I just want you to know you can trust me. With anything. I'll *be* there for you.'

She was silent for a while as she digested what he had said. He claimed he knew she had bombed the lab. And more than that, he said he actually admired her for it. 'So what are you asking me here? Whether I'm a terrorist? Whether I trust you? Whether I *love* you?' She went over to him and held his handsome face in her hands. Examining him with a curious gaze, she replied, 'Well . . . Yes. Yes. And—'

He hugged her hard. 'That's terrific,' he said. 'But if I ever talk like that again, like some New Age Romantic geek, you have my permission to shoot me.'

'Or fire-bomb you?' she volunteered, smiling.

'Whatever.' Now, at last, he kissed her, but gently, drawing her to the bed.

David Elkins ran a spell check over the draft he had just finished typing into his laptop. It threw up biotechnic as a word it did not recognise and he tapped in 'skip always'. The machine had better get used to it, just as the world needed to get used to the breathtaking impact the new science was destined to have.

It was his preliminary report summarising his conclusions on the potential of Temple Bio-Laboratories as a high-growth stock. The sector as a whole was retaining its speculative go-go image and rating. No self-respecting institutional investor could be without a portfolio of shares in what remained the fastest-growing section of the market. In the UK many, like Temple Bio-Laboratories, had begun with listings on the AIM market for smaller or fledgling businesses in need of outside capital. One of the legends of the sector, however, was British Biotech, founded in 1986. When the company floated its share price was 425p, valuing it at £150 million. At one point, a few years later, the shares were over £38, putting its market value at almost £2 billion, after reporting positive Phase Two trials on its cancer treatment, Marimasat. All this in a sector which typically posts little or no profits for years.

Credited as the first analyst into the industry, he had made his clients a lot of money over the years. But as in any fast-moving industry, he knew he had to keep being right and to stay ahead of the market. There was no question of basking in the glow of past glories. Markets, like playing cards, have no memories. And Elkins had now come to believe there was too much froth in the sector and that it was overdue a rerating. Down. More and more knotty issues were being raised about it. Unfortunately for Temple Bio, many of these problems were precisely those lining up against the company. Animal rights activists were one. He had of course been told of the fire-bombing by his office when he had called in, and found Tom's game attempts at damage limitation unconvincing. It could have happened to any drugs or biotech company, he had claimed. Elkins knew, however, that some types of work attract more attention than others, and that genetic animal experiments and xenotransplantation – one of Temple's main business streams – was way up the list.

Then there were other ethical questions facing the sector, like 'bio-piracy'. That challenge to Barton's cell-line patents by the PNG government was very publicly rumbling on, with no sign of an early settlement. Unluckily for Temple Bio, a new unrelated but parallel furore was keeping the general issue firmly in the public eye. The Indian government was going to court challenging an American patent on the use of turmeric as a substance with healing properties for cuts. This was claimed as one of the country's ancient herbal remedies, and officials were supporting their case by citing thirty-seven other patents held by Western companies for neem tree by-products, such as pesticides.

No, he had decided, Temple Bio-Laboratories looked decidedly accident-prone. And the flamboyance of its chairman was in today's more austere market no longer

an asset. For a company losing millions year in year out, and
still borrowing like a drunken sailor while waiting for some
Phase Three boat to come in, the public image of Barton
in his stately home, and piloting helicopters to his 300-foot
yacht, was doing nothing to impress his dividend-starved
shareholders. Especially after a stream of rapid-fire rights
issues, milking even more cash from the virtually captive
investors. What he had heard there in Belize about the
wondercure had certainly been interesting, and Dr Penny,
at least, was impressive. It did seem that using the cell lines
of the Stone-Age tribe to replicate their natural immunities
was technically possible. And the early results they were
asserting from Phase One trials already supported Barton's
claim to have somehow got round the usual obstacles. But
it was a very long road before anything got to market, and
Elkins saw Barton as a man in a hurry. The whole set-up at
Temple Bio-Laboratories smacked to him of opportunism,
and this short-notice trip as crude share-price ramping.
In summary, his report had concluded that the company
was a highly speculative stock, and one – with so many
other quality stocks in the sector – which he did not
recommend.

The draft report ran to 1,200 words of reasoned argument
and technical back-up on PE ratios and projections – against
the sector and the Footsie as a whole. It needed more
work, which he could easily do on the plane back.
Then his report and strong 'Sell' recommendation on
Temple Bio-Laboratories would be released electronically
the morning after they got back, holing the stock below
the waterline, and quite possibly sinking it in days.

Saving what he had just written and logging out, he
switched off the laptop and began to get ready for dinner.
It was the final night before they flew back to London, and
knowing what he was about to do to Barton, he wished

he did not have to sit through it. Especially as he had now been told that Barton's daughter was unexpectedly joining them. Hard as he had to be on occasions, he did not enjoy this side of the job, and was cursing himself for coming and putting himself in this invidious position.

As things turned out, however, the dinner began as great fun after all. No shop was talked, and Barton was on good form, recounting some hilarious self-deprecating stories from his public school and Army days. Elkins could well see why Barton had had little problem raising capital over the years. The man was witty, charismatic and genuinely funny when he chose to be. His daughter was in some ways so very like him. Not just the facial characteristics, but in their personalities. An ability to schmooze married to firm views and a clear personal agenda. They all joined in the slightly drunken fun and banter, and despite the agreement to keep off the subject, there was even some gentle teasing of her about animal welfare. But nothing too serious.

They were finishing the evening with coffee, liqueurs and cigars as they played a little not very good pool, when Barton was called away. It was fifteen minutes before he returned, and in a markedly changed mood. His local computer expert had got into Elkins's laptop, quickly cracking the log-in code – predictably DAVID E – and password, still set to the default PASSWORD. Having copied the report on to a floppy, he had printed off the devastating draft for Barton to see. He had shaken with rage as he read every damning, albeit perceptive, word. If this hit the screens, it would spell disaster. Far from engineering a share-price boom, it would cause a further slump and lead to a stampede out of the stock.

He had tried nice, and nice had not worked. Time now to call on the insurance he had taken out for just this eventuality. He rejoined them, with the time well gone one o'clock. When Lydia left to go to bed the rest of them soon began to break up for the night. As Elkins was saying his goodnights, Barton took him to one side and handed him a videotape. 'Something to help you remember your trip,' he said, with no discernible menace.

Elkins made a face. 'Not yet another corporate video, I hope. Full of gleaming new equipment and directors reading an autocue.'

Barton's chilling reply blew away all the phoney urbanity of earlier. 'There was plenty of gleaming equipment, but no autocues in your rent boy's dungeon. Remember? But you'll see that for yourself. There's a player in your suite.'

'What are you saying?' Elkins had gone white.

'To avoid any possible misunderstanding, I'll spell it out for you, Mr Elkins.' Barton now manifested an aura of pure malevolence. 'I've read the draft report in your laptop. And it's not saying what I want. Again, for the avoidance of doubt, a floppy disc of what I do want you to file is in your room. You look at that and then tweak it *only* to match your own normal style. Your first unfortunate draft has already been deleted from your machine. Replace it with the new one, use all your influence to ramp my share price . . . and your wife, children and employers don't get to see your interesting hobby.'

Elkins was traumatised. He knew, *knew* he should have come out years earlier. His marriage might just have survived it then, and the children been too young to be hurt by it. What was happening now was something he had feared for a very long time. He had nowhere to go. Barton was good. Very good. Not being the suicidal type, Elkins's only options were to do as Barton instructed, or ring his wife straight away. The firm, ironically, would probably be OK, for refusing blackmail to protect the integrity of his reports for them.

This was the crunch. Ring his trusting wife, or file a stock recommendation with which he did not agree?

The decision did not take long. 'You get away with this just once, Barton. I'll file your garbage. But never, ever expect anything again.'

Barton did not smile, and had no air of triumphalism. 'I promise. I'm a man of my word.' He offered his hand to Elkins, who took it with a look of incredulity. Though it beggared belief, it was clear that despite what he was doing the man did indeed consider himself honourable. A man of his word. That insight scared Elkins almost more than the crude blackmail. Without question, the man was capable of the most sophisticated self-justification: the self-delusion freeing him to do anything he wanted. He had become that most dangerous of animals. A powerful man completely devoid of conscience.

Lydia nestled in Tom's arms. 'I don't think you should agree to it,' she said.

'You and me both. But someone's got to stop him.' He had been completely open with her, feeling a little show of selfless heroics would not go amiss. She had just told him everything about the AFW and her part in the fire-bombing, making her seem braver, more alive somehow than him, and he had wanted to respond.

'And what happens next? What exactly does this Mitchell man expect you to do?'

Tom rolled over on his side, resting on an elbow, and looked at her. It was as if they were already old lovers. Always a sign of something good happening in a relationship. 'I can already tick the box on the first mission he set me. I get to go to Portugal with Jim. We fly out tomorrow. Once out there, I'll be contacted by one of Mitchell's people and briefed about what exactly they want me to do. It seems that's when I really do become a spy. But in broad terms I already know. I'm to find out who the biological weapons are for, why, and when they're due for shipment. Hopefully by getting Jim to take me into his confidence on this. Or if he won't, by getting access to the files and paperwork.'

'I still don't like it. If Dad really is guilty of all these terrible things, why don't these people just arrest him? And destroy all the dangerous viruses and the rest?'

'I asked exactly the same thing. And the answer is that unless they find out who commissioned the stuff, then whatever outrage is planned will still go ahead. With weapons acquired elsewhere. They can take Jim out any time.'

'Take him out?' She sat up, pulling the sheet over her breasts.

'Sorry. I didn't mean it to sound like that. That was my clumsy phrase, not Mitchell's.'

'Maybe. But it's true, isn't it? These type of people wouldn't think twice about killing Dad, if that was easier or more convenient.'

He did not reply, afraid any reassuring denials would sound insincere. Mitchell had used the phrase 'special forces' to him when raising the option of a raid. And if by that he had meant the SAS, then he also feared for Jim's life if he got between them and their mission. 'And you? What will you do? Go back to London, back to the agency?'

The agency. How remote and foolish it all seemed from this distance, and knowing now what she did. 'What's he up to here in Belize?'

Pleased that the tack had been changed, he replied, 'This is his great hope for rocketing Temple Bio into the big league. And he's using it to ramp the share price. He told me he needed some big money, fast. Two million. For what, I don't yet know. But the irony is, having talked to Penny, it's clear he may really be on to something important out here in his own, proper research. If your father does nothing else right in his life, funding Penny at least could prevent a lot of suffering.'

'He's saving lives with things like this, and killing people in Portugal,' she sighed, perplexed. 'How can any of it make sense?'

'Oh, there's no mystery in that. It makes perfect sense on one level. The level of money. Saving lives and weapons of destruction are two of the biggest money-spinners in the world. Just look at pharmaceutical and defence stocks. Even primitives had medicine men as well as pretty damn lethal weapons. These things are right up there with procreation and finding food in just about any civilisation's priorities. Your father isn't really involved in making people well, or in making war. Just in making money. Big, big money. I think it's become a fixation at the very heart of his illness. Think about it. He's come from a long line of hugely successful people, only to find himself a disgraced bankrupt. And the last male heir in the baronetcy. Imagine it. The weakest and maybe final twig of your towering, deep-rooted family tree. Incapable of producing an heir. The laughing stock of the county. An embarrassment to his old school tie and political friends. And a complete non-person to his dowager mother. Damn it, I'm not sure I wouldn't have turned into something pretty strange carrying all *that* baggage.'

She lay back again, thinking about all of this. It did make sense, she had to admit. Her father's Lazarus-style comeback from ruin could only have been made with iron determination and fanatical, brass-necked application. And with a kind of fatalism. Perhaps the only options open to him at that time had been suicide, or some kind of screw-the-world success at any price. 'What will happen to him?' she asked hesitantly, for despite everything, she still carried deep, if ambiguous, feelings for her father.

Tom rolled over and put his arm around her as if to protect her from what he was about to say. 'I think that unless he confesses, and co-operates, then he's finished for good this time. With no way back. He's involved with some of the most violent and dangerous people around. And that goes for the good guys as well as the bad. Unless I help Mitchell stop him, he could get himself killed.'

'We,' she said, quietly.

'Excuse me?'

'I said, unless *we* help him . . .'

'Oh no!' Tom leaned over her. 'This is something I have to do. Not you.'

She kissed him and smiled enigmatically. 'We'll see.'

Chapter Thirteen

Banto had after all decided to carry out the traditional victory ceremony over his defeat of Bolitho, despite the man's suicide. The Mayan ancestors and spirits of the ceiba would communicate with him. Had Bolitho taking his own life really cheated Banto? The spirits would tell him whether or not the dead man amounted to Payback. Because if there was still no Payback from this death, there was much work to do.

Taking his time, and painstakingly following the ritual order, he first dug a pit and built a large fire inside. Then, when it was blazing, he put on hardwood logs. After an hour they were glowing like coals, just how he needed them. Next he prepared himself, covering his body with the thick oil of a swamp togaso tree, a fern in his hair, and with an elaborate face decoration using white clay he found on the bank of a stream.

Now he was ready to cook the body. For his *mumu* feast.

Dragging Bolitho away from the roots of the ceiba and into the clearing, he used the serrated combat knife to hack off what little there was left of the head, the messy loose neck flesh and sinewy entrails. Then he cut off the clothing leaving the man spreadeagled on the ground. This was the first time he had actually cooked a human body himself, although he had watched others do it many times. There was nothing unusual about the butchery involved. Preparing meat was

preparing meat, be it a pig, deer or chicken. Getting down
to work, he set about jointing the body, starting with the
arms and then legs. The hands were severed and discarded,
but not the feet. These were a delicacy, just like pig's feet.
The rest he also discarded, before ramming the selected
limbs into large bamboo cooking tubes to steam over the
glowing coals for an hour.

An important symbolic part of the body was missing and
might, Banto feared, ruin the ceremony and displease the
spirits. Not having the head saved him from the additional
chore of wrapping it in thick palms to cook in its juices.
Eating brain tissue during funeral rites and at cannibalistic
victory ceremonies such as this meant, until recently, that
as many as one in a hundred of groups like the Fore and
Okapa people in PNG were affected by the terrible killer
illness, *kuru*. Known to the natives as the laughing disease,
it attacks the central nervous system making victims scream,
bray and crawl like mad animals before the final blessed
release of death.

When the meat was nearly ready, Banto improvised the
victory ceremony which should have featured at least six
other warriors. Crying out a repetitive 'wa, wa, wa, wa'
mantra, he lost himself in a short-stepped dance, his mind
soon floating above himself in what Western adults would
have recognised as a self-induced out-of-body experience,
and what their young children would have known as
commonplace *Through the Looking Glass* play. Life to
Banto was a kind of ritual dance. Rhythm and repetition,
repetition and ritual gave him the order and balance that
he needed. Without it, Banto would drown in a bewildering
sea of choices. Freedom of the will was an alien concept, one
for future civilisations. Stone-Age Banto neither knew nor
desired it. He was a forest creature of rhythm, who expected
and wanted no more in his short years on Earth.

The meat from Bolitho's thigh tasted like pork, only a little sweeter. The Melanesian pidgin name for human flesh is indeed 'long pig'. Banto sat and ate several mouthfuls before throwing the upper leg away. Spitting the flesh out, he knew that it was all wrong. Despite all his careful, ritual preparation, the spirits were not pleased and there was no sense of the rhythm. The *mumu* was a failure. This was, he knew now for sure, because the man had taken his own life. Something *he* should have done. There had been no Payback. The man was in *dimanples* instead, with the others around the ancient tree, and Banto knew now for sure that to restore the rhythm he must retrace his journey and take Payback from the *kepala*. His first instincts had been right all along. There was nothing else for it.

Barton marshalled his thoughts before making the call to Colombia. Caldente's English was only ever as good as he wanted it to be, and sometimes Barton found it difficult to make himself understood. Especially explaining some of the complicated financial structures and capital transfers they now had in place. But Caldente was the *de facto* chairman of the group, having been the one who called together the first Aruban meeting. And Barton knew he would ask how the fund was performing. He always did, sometimes ringing twice a week for reassurance and an update on the value of his own share.

'It's James Barton.' He attempted no small talk or charm with these people. All the inter-personal skills which had served him so well throughout his life simply had no effect on them. 'I need to agree with you how we want to play the summit next week.' He spoke openly, their sophisticated telephone encryption never having been penetrated. So far at least.

'You still got the Africans?' Caldente asked. The Nigerians

were important to him in obtaining large quantities of good quality heroin.

'And the Russians and Sicilians.'

'Sure. OK. What do we need to discuss?'

'Well, we should review how my Stabiliser agreement is working out. And, of course, I'll give a report on the financials. But most important is what we agreed in Acapulco when you told me to find a way to fight off the US anti-drugs taskforce. This is the main subject. And I have some pretty big news for you.' The excitement showed now in his voice. 'I'm sinking over £2 million of my own money setting this thing up, and I'll want big bucks from the Alliance to see it through.'

'And you think you can stop a US President with this thing?' There was incredulity in Caldente's tone.

'I'm sure of it.'

Caldente barked a short laugh. 'Coming from anyone else, I'd say that was crazy talk. But so far, you've delivered good for us.'

'And I will again. But at a price.'

'You do this for us, and you can name any price.' He meant it. Already a new Justice Minister had been appointed in Bogotá, one nobody – not even he – had been able to buy or threaten. Against all the odds, the new US trade and diplomatic threats were biting hard. There had been major DEA-inspired border seizures of cocaine and cash, and the twenty-six-nation Financial Action Taskforce, armed with the new Syfact fraud-protection software, was closing down scores of long-established money-laundering channels, including such favourites as car dealerships, travel agencies, chemist shop chains and pharmaceutical companies. Worse still, the US Treasury had now reduced from $10,000 to $750 the amount that remittance shops had to report on when, for instance, immigrants in the US wire money back home. This had choked off a billion dollars a year that Caldente's Cartel had laundered back that way for years. It was all starting to hurt. Bad.

Barton smiled to himself, mightily relieved that Caldente remained as keen as ever on somehow fighting back. 'I think when I tell you about it, you will be impressed,' he said.

'Yeah. Sure. We're all learning to trust you. And through your Stabiliser agreement, each other. You're doing a good job.'

Barton felt as proud as he had ever had at this rare praise. These were not easy men to impress. 'Thank you.'

'OK. See you soon. Make sure security is real tight.'

'We'll have you all protected by a small army of mercenaries.'

'Good. Like I said, you're doing good, Sir Barton.'

'Sir James,' he responded automatically.

'Whatever,' Caldente snapped. Nobody corrected the head of the Santander Cartel.

A driver met them at Lisbon Airport and took them straight to Oeiras, half an hour away.

Tom knew the area fairly well, having visited Lisbon many times on WMC and Temple Bio business, and as a student having stayed just down the bay in Estoril one whole summer – teaching tennis at a big hotel through the day, then blowing his wages each night at the casino. As they drove through, following the coast road, bars and familiar corners of the area as ever evoked happy, carefree memories for him. That period in his life all did now seem a true age of innocence, compared with the dangerous, duplicitous work he was now involved in. Oeiras itself, however, had changed little since then. An outbreak of long offices, along with the modern-looking lab, had sprung up opposite the beachfront, but everything else was still as

pretty and picturesque in this somehow very English corner
of north Portugal.

Barton was more cheerful than Tom had seen him for
years. His call to Caldente had tee-ed up his big pitch to
the Alliance perfectly. Also, Elkins had been as good as
his blackmailed word, and electronically filed the glowing
report on Temple Bio-Laboratories's 'wonder vaccines'. The
short-memoried markets had immediately discounted all the
previous bad news, and poured into the stock on both sides
of the Atlantic, enabling Barton easily to place £2 million
of his shares without so much as a raised eyebrow from
anyone. Although the native was still missing, Barton now
cared much less. The blood they had already taken and
successfully used in Phase One trial 'Jenner' vaccines, along
with Elkins's report, had bought him all the time he had
needed. He did not care if Bolitho and the native never
came back. In fact, he would now prefer it.

'You never explained what you needed the money
from the placement for,' Tom prompted, as they cruised
round the Rio Tejo, the Atlantic winter grey, flecked with
white horses, ghostly tankers seemingly suspended in the
horizonless torpor.

Barton threw a quick look at him. 'Expenses. CGT. Things
like that.'

Mitchell, in his briefing, had made it clear that Tom would
have to be intrusive and more than usually persistent if
he was going to be of help to them. 'Anything I should
know about? Call me old fashioned, but I *am* a director
of Temple Bio-Laboratories, remember? With all the duties
and responsibilities that entails under the Companies Act.
I don't want to get dumped on, Jim.'

'I don't think there's a risk-taking bone in your body,'
Barton replied, without malice.

Considering the very dangerous course on which Tom

was about to embark, the comment was ironic. But he simply replied, 'Hey! I'm *normal* here, and proud of it. It's you who's risk-crazy. The kamikaze kid. Remember? That was how we first met. You giving the entrepreneur guest lecture at INSEAD.'

Barton smiled, and took a swig from his hip flask. 'I need the money for some special supplies. And to pay some people off out here. For extra-curricular work they've done – way outside their job description. Call it a performance bonus, for Andrei Rybinski.'

'A bonus for him, and none for Blacher? His boss? That won't go down well, surely.'

Laughing, Barton replied, 'Blacher's usefulness is at an end. All I needed him for was to bring Andrei up to speed on some production processes. Ploddy stuff, but it saved us reinventing the wheel. But it's Andrei who's the genius. Who's delivered the impossible.'

'So he's done it?' Tom probed, nervous now. This was crunch time. 'He's produced a genetically intelligent fertiliser?'

A slight smile still flickered over Barton's lips. 'Yes. Sure. A terrific new fertiliser.'

Tom sat quietly for a few miles before gathering his courage to press on, knowing once he did, there would be no turning back. Taking a deep breath, he screwed his eyes up and took the leap. 'Balls!' he said at last.

'Excuse me?' Barton still looked amused.

This was it. He now had to play it for all it was worth. Barton had to believe the worm really had turned, and that Tom wanted in. 'I said balls! I'm sick of it. Let's start with Rybinski, shall we? You know, and I know, that Russia's leading biological weapons expert has not just spent five months making a better horse shit. The only horse shit around here is what you've been expecting me to believe!

I've had it, Jim. I'm either in or out on all of this. As a director, I'm taking the same risks for none of the real action. OK, my share options might now be worth a few hundred thousand dollars. But that's not enough. Not *nearly* enough.'

The smile had now gone as Barton leaned forward to close the glass divider to the limo driver. 'And what else do you think you know?'

'What am I? Blind? Let's look next at that $15 billion fund I'm having managed for you. You know what some of my new traders call the bank? The laundry. The goddamn laundry. Look at the non-dollar currencies they're dealing in. The Colombian peso. The Mexican peso. The Burmese kyat. The Nigerian naira. Russian roubles . . . Give me a break! At first, OK, I figured you were being kind – not telling me things to keep me clean. To protect me even. But we're way past that now. I'm in over my head with your cocaine and biological weapons. You once boasted to me – right after your bankruptcy hearing – that you'd bounce right back and show the bastards. That you'd make yourself the richest man in Europe. Well, I now know that was no idle boast. I think you're about to pull it off. And I'll be damned, after all I've done, if all I get are those poxy options.'

Now it was Barton who was quiet, as he furiously thought through how to play this. And he had just accused Tom of not being a risk-taker! Could Tom possibly realise what he had done? In a very real sense, he had just thrown his life down like a chip at the Estoril casino. Barton was left with only two stark options. Have Tom killed. Or involve him in everything, as a full partner.

'Is this why you met up with Peregrine Mitchell?' he asked, at last.

The sound of Mitchell's name nearly sent Tom into catatonic shock. It was his death warrant. Barton knew about Mitchell, and so he was dead. There could *be* no other outcome. 'Mitchell?' he parried, the panic cracking his voice.

Barton watched the reaction to what he had said and puzzled over it. 'You met a headhunter from Management International. At some Pall Mall club. So you *are* serious about leaving. What's he offered you? Some nice safe corporate job? Pension? Job security? Isn't that really what you want?'

Slowly it was becoming clear that Barton did not know headhunting was just Mitchell's cover. Perhaps he was safe after all. In fact, he could make it work for him. 'So. Even I get followed by your damned private detectives!' His feigned outrage sounded convincing. 'Well good! Now you can see that I'm in demand. I *have* other options. But no, I'm not interested in being some corporate desk jockey. If I'd wanted that, security, the white picket fence syndrome, I wouldn't have stuck by you all these years, would I?'

'My private detective reported something else.' Barton's cold, washed-out blue eyes held Tom, playing with him, like a cat with a bird. 'It seems you spent the night with my daughter.'

The blow across his mouth threw Tom's head against the side window, and blood gushed from his lip, split by Barton's Masonic ring. The big man's face was now hard against his, the stale cigar breath acrid, making Tom feel sick. 'You sleep with Lydia, the one person I care about in this whole stinking world! What was it? A one-off . . . a quickie? Or was screwing her your way of hitting back at me?' The second blow was less hard, but sent spasms of searing pain through his nose.

'No!' Tom called out, grabbing Barton's collar and shaking him viciously. 'You don't understand. I like Lydia. A lot. But I figured you wouldn't want me seeing her.'

Barton contemptuously brushed off Tom's grip, and moved back a little, calmer now. His mood swings were lightning quick. 'She likes you. Always has. It's written all over her. Every time she sees you.' He was panting slightly. 'Why do you think she fagged all the way out to Belize – to see me? To snorkel at the Cays? No way.'

Tom shook his head, stemming the blood with his handkerchief. 'I don't know what to say to you.'

But this was something Barton had been thinking about a lot, since reading the detective's report on their night together. He had not intended to confront Tom with it just yet, but a vague plan, ambition even had been formulating in his scheming, hyper-active mind. 'But you really do like her?'

'She's special. Yes.'

Suddenly Barton was grinning. 'Then everything's solved,' he said, handing Tom his own handkerchief. 'Everything's tidy.'

'I don't understand.'

'It's obvious. There's no way I could involve a regular partner in what I'm doing. I simply couldn't trust anyone that much. Not even you. But a son-in-law . . . Now that would be someone I really *could* make a full partner. As one of the family. And I certainly need some help. The kind you give me on my legit businesses. You said you were in or out. Well . . . agree to marry Lydia, and you're in. Right over your head. Deal?'

Tom stared at the offered hand. It was typical of the man's megalomania to offer such a thing without even a thought to whether Lydia actually wanted to marry him. But the unstated alternative to the bargain hung heavily in the air.

'Deal. If she'll have me,' Tom heard himself saying. Barton's burst of violence had really brought home to him just how unstable the man had become. More so even than all the cold frightening facts from Mitchell.

'Good!' Barton smiled. 'And I'll tell you everything – everything, tonight.'

Lydia had stayed on at the ranch, to kill the remaining four days before her flight back to London. All around her workmen were raising electric fences to encircle the inner complex of the ranch-house and the cabanas. Two more helipads were being marked out by the landing strip, and four tall, stilted guard posts were going up. A group of fifty military-looking men had also arrived, wearing fawn and green fatigues. They erected their own tented village in a morning, and by afternoon were jogging and drilling like the small private army they were.

'What's happening here?' she asked Penny as he drove her off in his buggy. He was taking her to his lab again. As, thanks to Banto, there were now no animals left there for testing, her father had hit on the idea of getting her to see what actually went on in a genetics lab. In this way he hoped to reduce her prejudices against the science. And himself.

'They're getting the place ready for an important meeting. Some international VIPs.'

'Scientists? They must be expecting one hell of an attack from the animal rights people.'

'No. This all has nothing to do with my side of things. It's one of your father's other businesses. Some investment syndicate. That's all I or anyone else around here knows about it.'

She pressed him, knowing any additional information would be useful to Tom and his people, but it was clear that he knew no more. Despite herself, she had enjoyed all the time so far spent with Penny at the lab, and they had held long and mutually enlightening debates over the hot topic of bio-ethics, not least because the USA, unlike most of Europe, had yet fully to ban human clone experimentation. Penny dismissed the hysteria over the possibility of human cloning, pointing out that mice were much closer genetically to humans than sheep – and no one had come close to cloning one of them. Despite this, he did confess that rumours persisted in the profession of the Chinese already conducting human clone experimentation.

On her first visit to the lab, she had donned a white coat and been given a thorough induction. This began with her performing Penny's party trick. Following his written-out recipe, she put an onion she had finely chopped in a cooking dish, and stirred in a half-pint solution of water, two and a half tablespoons of washing-up liquid, and a teaspoon of salt. This she cooked in a cool oven for five minutes, regularly stirring, before liquidising it at a high temperature for five seconds.

Having strained the remaining liquid, she added a few drops of fresh pineapple juice, while vigorously mixing it. This she then, as instructed, put into a tall, chilled glass before finally smoothly adding a little freezer-cold vodka to float on top. After a few minutes, a cloudy layer appeared where the base liquid met with the vodka. This had brought her to the end of the recipe instructions, and she looked at the mess disappointed, convinced it had all gone wrong. She called Penny over, curious to know what she had just done. And why.

He looked at the mixture and beamed. 'Well done! Right first time,' he said, before handing her a spatula. 'Now, try very carefully to fish out that milky stuff.'

As she did as instructed, it turned into a fibrous web which she lifted out. 'Well?'

'Congratulations! That stuff's known as deoxyribonucleic

acid. You've just created DNA.' Applauding, he gave her a T-shirt featuring the DNA double helix spiral. 'You're now an official member of the DNA club.'

Later she had learned how to assist as one of the technicians used X-ray crystallography in their attempts in earnest to replicate genetically antigens of the disease-immune PNG cell lines. Penny's genuine research work, funded by her father, was progressing well. It was Penny's price for masterminding the 'Jenner' scam. By the end, it all served to confuse her, challenging her prejudices. From what she had learned, there was obviously much potential benefit from genetic research – for animals as well as humans. And she had also come to realise that the process was not as alien as she had thought – cell division, meiosis and binary fission all occurring naturally in bewilderingly diverse ways in plants, insects, mammals and man.

Perhaps her most startling discovery of all, though, was that someone like Penny was not a one-dimensional monster, but a thoughtful, well-read man: motivated only by his vision of a better, disease-free future. Even a future with food-chain animals bred with low/no pain thresholds, and temperamentally programmed to cope with the trauma of factory farming. The two of them were of course worlds apart in their visions, their paradigms, but overlapped far more than either had expected in terms of ethical humanism. It was a discovery that for a fleeting time even made her reappraise her father. Until of course the appalling truth came flooding back to her . . .

The next day, she decided not to return to the lab, opting instead to take a horse from the ranch. She might as well grab a tiny holiday exploring a little of the area, having turned down her father's offer to pay for her to fly back with them.

As she cantered down the drive to pick up a nearby trail,

she did not feel the eyes watching from the bush. Eyes that had tired from long hours of watching for Sir James Barton, but which had none the less seen the deference with which everyone treated this mere woman. Including the man who had taken from him. And he had seen the *kepala*'s face in hers. The corn hair. Blue eyes. Pig nose. Dimple chin. She was *wantok*; she was family with the *kepala*.

She was the chief's daughter.

After a three-hour meeting with Blacher and Rybinski at the lab, the driver had taken them back to the city. Barton always stayed in a suite at the Ritz in Lisbon, one of his favourite hotels in the world, and as they checked in, he arranged to meet Tom at eight in the piano bar.

Tom's room was a mini-suite and he quickly unpacked, showered and collapsed on the bed to think. His split lip had swollen badly, but mercifully his teeth had escaped damage. Head swimming with all that was happening to him, he began to drift off, still jet-lagged, into a light sleep. Until something woke him. It was not the phone. Not someone knocking at the door. But something, someone had woken him . . .

He opened his eyes, and shot up with a start. Staring down at him was a woman he had never seen before. Clamping her strong hand on his mouth, she shook her head and hushed him, waving a finger at her lips. Wincing as pain again shot through his tender lip, he sat up, nodding that he understood.

'I am Hortense,' she said, now moving her hand from his mouth. 'I work with the British. At the Oeiras lab. Mr Mitchell will have told you about me.'

He looked carefully at her. Mid-thirties, olive-skinned, black page-boy hair, short, strong body. Mitchell had certainly told him about a female agent MI6 had got into the lab. But what to do? How was he to know this was she? Should he trust her, and risk revealing his own involvement? He felt completely unprepared.

'I don't know what you're talking about,' he replied, cautiously. 'And how the hell did you get in here anyway?'

She ignored the question. Standing in corridors and knocking at hotel doors was not something they taught you in training school. 'I have no time. Rybinski suspects me. You have to help.' Her eyes were pleading.

'I've told you, I don't know what you're talking about.' Should he ring the number Mitchell had given him? Even that would be tantamount to conceding his involvement if she *was* one of Barton's private security people, testing him.

'OK then. Don't say anything. Just listen. OK?'

'Go ahead,' he replied, sharpening his mind.

'I have to disappear tonight. I pushed my luck yesterday trying to get samples out of Rybinski's private lab. I can't go back again. They're already watching my flat. This I know.' She now sat down on a stool, obviously exhausted and afraid. 'You'll be at the lab again tomorrow? As planned?'

He nodded.

'Good. Then you have to do something. Something I failed to do. Rybinski has been conducting his own experiments. Experiments he keeps from Blacher. The Englishman thinks he's simply producing botulinum toxin. As a deterrent for Israel. But Rybinski has been modifying it somehow. Genetically engineering the virus. We don't precisely know how, and we don't know why. After all, what can be the point? Botulinum toxin is itself one of the most devastating viral killers in the world. But I'm certain that Rybinski has created some new strain. I was tasked to get a sample out for analysis. So we could understand it, and create an antidote.'

Tom decided now he had no alternative but to trust her now. 'What is it you want me to do?'

With a look of relief, she smiled weakly. 'Thank you. It is this. Rybinski has a private lab, which nobody is allowed to enter. Supposedly because it's dangerous and sterile. It's the one next to the ground-floor store room with a radiation warning sign on the door. You'll find it. Even Blacher does not go in. He knows the Russian needs his own space. And besides, they hate each other. I have been in this lab twice. The first time, last week, I got out some samples. But they were nothing we did not expect. This afternoon – when you were at the plant – I was intending checking out his paperwork too. But I dropped a phial and got disturbed by the guards. Rybinski will by now have been told. I can't go back. I'm blown.

'So *you* must try and help. It's almost too late. I heard him telling Barton that he's finished his experiments, and succeeded in whatever it is he's been trying to do. And he and Blacher yesterday had a terrible row. I think Blacher now also suspects that Rybinski has been doctoring his work somehow. So you see, there is very little time left.

'This is a key to the lab and one to a filing cabinet in there. Take them. *Don't* try and take out any phials. You won't know what you're doing, and it could be very dangerous. And not just to you. But his research notes should be in the cabinet. They might give our people all they need.'

Tom shook his head. 'I'll only be there half a day tomorrow. During regular working hours. How can I possibly get in there?'

The woman got up and went to the door. Opening it and looking cautiously up and down the corridor, she shot a parting glance back at him. 'Figure something out, Mr Bates. Many lives depend on it.'

*   *   *

There has been a close, if at first informal link since the War between MI6 and DI6 – historically *M*ilitary *I*ntelligence, *D*efence *I*ntelligence – cemented later in clandestine campaigns such as Borneo, the Yemen and the Gulf. In Northern Ireland, the exchange of senior officers has continued, alternating between SIS, military intelligence and the SAS headquarters in Hereford. Despite all this, Mitchell still did not like the special forces. Never had. And was not comfortable at having been appointed commander of the assault operation.

The regiment's technical skills, their training and commitment were as impeccable as they were legendary. But in the final analysis MI6 and the SAS generally moved in very different worlds, with different priorities, as MI5 had also found with Operation Flavius, ten years earlier in Gibraltar. The officers and men, to whom the 'troop' is everything, were of necessity utterly tunnel-visioned on a mission. Their priorities were *their* priorities, their part of the operation, and Mitchell had always felt uncomfortable working with them on potentially messy jobs like this. Jobs where goal posts might have to change mid-game.

The group's first meeting was in a windowless Ministry of Defence secure briefing room, off Whitehall. Sitting around the table were Neil Gaylord, representing both his own Service and the Cabinet Office Proliferation CIG; the Service's Director of Counter Intelligence and Security; the head of its Global Tasks Department; a lieutenant colonel and a major from 'G' Squadron SAS, the Special Projects Team on stand-by as a counter-terrorist force; a commander of the Special Boat Squadron; an officer from the Special Forces HQ; a professor from the Defence Intelligence Staffs Scientific and Technical Directorate; and a lone Foreign Office man carrying the brief for both the Portuguese and Central America Desks.

Having let the nine of them – all men – study their numbered files, Mitchell summed up before opening the meeting up for questions. 'So. All in all, it doesn't make very pretty reading for HMG, does it? Sir James Barton, Bt., a former British Treasury and Foreign Office Minister, about to host the next Aruba Alliance meeting in Belize. Our Station Officer in Belmopan tells us the additional security work at the ranch is almost complete – he's sending full details of what's been installed for you, Colonel, along with maps, building blueprints, and aerial photography.' The SAS man nodded, but knew they would not use it. Having got wind of what today was about, he already had his own reconnaissance underway, using a team coincidentally down there on routine jungle training. 'At the meeting Barton will present his normal management report on last quarter's performance by his treasury management team. Plus a "bank statement" for each Alliance member, detailing their inter-group trading and capital balances. Neil, we've got them pretty well monitored, haven't we?'

Gaylord was not expecting this and looked a little flustered in front of the powerful group. 'We've had access for some months now to his dealers' computers. A copy of all the financial information is also in your packs.'

Mitchell nodded, looking around. 'On the back of this, at the same meeting he'll go on to sell them another of his ideas. One designed to make him one of the richest men in the world. They'll pay him anything he asks when he explains what he's done. It's his answer for the Alliance to the American drugs taskforce. An initiative driven personally by the US President, remember. It's the thing for which he wants his second and final term of office to be remembered. The man who cleaned up America.

'To stymie all this Barton, at huge personal cost – funded

by a recent £2 million share placement – seems to have perfected for the Alliance a formidable deterrent. Biological weapons. Certainly botulinum toxin. But possibly – *probably* we think – something even worse. We were hoping our agent in the lab would have got out some hard intelligence on exactly what we may be facing. But we've had to pull her. Cover blown. I'm hoping one of my recruits will be able to do something today. *Hoping.* Because with Rybinski involved, I can promise you whatever's out there will be something very tricky, and very nasty. This, gentlemen, is what we have to stop. And with only a week to the Aruba summit, not much time to play with. It will have to be a co-ordinated simultaneous attack – on Oeiras, led by SBS, and Belize, led by SAS. For the former, current thinking is not to pre-brief Lisbon, hit hard, have the boffins make it safe, and worry about EU diplomacy later. And the latter, to arrest the drugs barons for extradition to the States. We think we'll be able to get the Belize PM to have his Chief of Police formally sign over control to us.

'So. Before we task ourselves, any questions on this whole bloody mess?'

There was the usual early silence as members of the inter-departmental group sniffed out their own territorial boundaries, making their assessments, and figuring out positions in the pecking order.

It was the SAS leader who spoke first. 'Who's IC overall?'

Mitchell smiled inwardly. 'I've been asked to head up the operations centre here in London. But responsibility for the two missions – planning and on the ground – rests of course with yourself, and the SBS.'

The dour man looked less than impressed at this. 'And what are our . . . terms of engagement?'

'Hard arrest,' Mitchell replied sharply. 'And I want that clear from the outset. Both these missions are taking place on friendly soil, and I don't want "undue force" used. There will be no such thing as clean kills out there. We'll have surprise on our side. I won't accept any post-rationalised wets. Not on my watch. Is that understood?'

The two commanders nodded back. Each knew of Mitchell's formidable reputation in the field over his long career, but they now had him firmly pigeon-holed as an old war-horse, out to grass.

'With your Lisbon agent out of it, how good's this DP4 of yours?' It was the old Foreign Office hand.

Mitchell looked amused. DP4 had been one of his earliest postings in the Service, and was what had got him into the fast track Sovbloc stream. Based in a red-brick mansion block, opposite New Scotland Yard on Victoria Street, his job had been to identify suitable businessmen travelling to the USSR, and then recruit them to work for him. More than thirty years later and *rien ne change*. 'He's a management consultant. American. Bright but cautious. OKish, but don't expect too much from him. Who knows, though, he just might surprise me. I'll be making him available to you tomorrow for briefing when he flies in. He's unique in being familiar with the layout of both Oeiras and the ranch in Belize. And of course he knows Barton.'

'Can't wait to get our hands on him,' the SBS Commander said, catching his SAS counterpart's eye and then looking despairingly to the heavens.

The plan had been for Tom and Barton to meet for lunch the next day with Rybinski before going on again to the lab. Barton wanted a full update without Ladislas Blacher there.

Rybinski was already in the Saisa restaurant, just off the coast road and overlooking the bay. There was nobody else in the place yet, and they ordered their meal, grazing the bread, nuts and olives and sipping white port. 'So. How's it *really* going?' Barton demanded.

The Russian shot a look at Tom. 'How much can I say?' He had the same irritating American accent of many international streetwise Muscovites.

Barton nodded his acknowledgement and turned to Tom. 'Give us a few minutes alone. I need to explain to Andrei why I've now involved you – as a partner. OK?'

Tom nodded and reluctantly left them, heading for a breath of sea air outside.

'How much does he know?' Rybinski was not happy.

'He knows *almost* everything. Tom's now family.' Barton had briefed him over dinner the night before on the Aruba Alliance, the US-sponsored threat to the drugs money and the work here in Oeiras on the biological weapons. 'I've told him everything – except the real nature of what you've been doing.'

'But he knows about Blacher's work?'

'He now knows we're offering the Alliance a credible biological warhead. But believes it's purely botulinum toxin. He also knows we plan to launch a small warhead, demonstrating the power of the deterrent, to frighten off the President's taskforce. And to rake in serious money from the Aruba members.' Barton knew the naturally suspicious Russian was annoyed at this change, but he was in no mood to be challenged. 'That's it. So. Your turn. Shoot. I need to know just one thing. Will it work?'

'Yeah, well . . . the biological agent is ready. My special one. It worked fine on the small test group. The right people died.' Rybinski picked out another olive, sucked noisily on it and placed the stone neatly on the edge of his side plate alongside the others. 'Overall, for a small sample, it worked out pretty good. My new weedkiller wiped out the daisies.'

'And you're sure Blacher knows nothing of what you've been doing?' Barton asked, anxiously. 'The old fool still believes he's helping Israel!'

'He's suspicious. Gave me a hard time yesterday. But it's OK. He just thinks I've just been experimenting with different levels of toxicity. Which in a way I have.'

Tom had come back deliberately quickly, and was hovering just outside earshot. Barton waved him over.

'So no problems, then?' Tom said as he sat down again. He felt for his own safety that he had better seem to enter into the spirit of things, and be excited by it.

Rybinski looked at him, still suspicious, and then back to Barton. 'I wouldn't say that. We've produced the agent and germ cultures for the warheads. It's a credible enough threat. But the lab here is hardly what I was used to, you know. Our weaponisation – delivery and dispersal – is completely untested. At Leningrad we had an entire complex with big teams working on these things. With our own scatter chamber, and sophisticated *poligon* test-firing facilities. All we have now is a very crude option. Untested delivery on Scud B missiles, from a Maz-543 launcher. Range 350 kilometres.'

Tom's eyes widened. 'So you've actually got the missiles?'

Both Barton and Rybinski laughed. 'We've got dollars – and they buy just about anything we want from our Russian friends. And I mean anything,' Barton grinned.

Tom knew this to be no idle boast, recalling recent press reports of a $6 million deal in Florida. US agents had frustrated an alleged attempt to buy two ex-Soviet nuclear-powered submarines and six military attack helicopters. 'And where's our target?' he pressed, knowing this was the key information Mitchell would want from him.

But now even Barton seemed suspicious, and as the waiter

brought their food he pointedly changed the subject. It was a warning bell not lost on Tom, the nursery-slope spy.

As they were finishing their meal, Rybinsksi's pager buzzed, and he read the short message. His face drained of colour and, throwing down his napkin, he stood up. 'Some big problem at the lab. Come on. We need to get over there!'

Minutes later, they were hurrying through the entrance, Barton's portrait photograph as usual beaming down on them. A young woman met them, her face telling them something major had gone wrong. Tom wondered whether it had something to do with Hortense, Mitchell's agent. He also wondered if the damn place was safe. 'This way!' she called, running in.

The lab had two wings, broadly split between Blacher's work and Rybinski's. But she led them to the rear of the building and towards the loading bay. Then she stopped, panting.

'What is it?' demanded Barton, his face blotchy, breathing hard.

'Through there.'

Barton slid open the big double doors, and immediately cried out loud in shock. Inches from his face was that of Ladislas Blacher, the noose and rope creaking as he swung. Blacher was suspended from a gantry high above the bay; his bulging eyes stared accusingly at Barton, following him as he swayed, and his mouth hung in open-mouthed horror.

It was the face of an old man who had just seen hell.

'Somebody cut him down!' Barton screamed.

Chapter Fourteen

The call from Maddie had surprised her. There was a big problem at the agency over her attempt to snow Metropolis. The DIY client had found himself sitting next to the TV sales contractor at some Marketing Society dinner. Unsurprisingly the £5 million spend with Metropolis had quickly been raised, to the obvious confusion and embarrassment of the client. Unable to track down Lydia at the package holiday hotel, Philip had in desperation called Madeleine with whom, he saw from Lydia's Schedule Plus electronic diary, she had recently lunched. The Media Director was demanding to speak to Lydia, furious. And the high-profile client was close to firing the agency, something that *Campaign*, the industry trade magazine, had already picked up on. A big, damaging story was being threatened.

'I simply can't get excited about some bloody DIY shed right now!' she exploded. 'Whether they spend £5 million or five pence flogging their poxy mixer taps and paint brushes . . .'

'Don't yell at *me*!' Maddie responded. 'I'm just the poor messenger. And anyway, I had kind of been expecting a call from you, you know? All things considered.'

Lydia came down off the ceiling. Maddie was right, of course, and she suddenly felt guilty and selfish. 'I know. And I'm sorry. Really I am. But if you knew . . . When I get to tell you everything, then you'll understand.'

Maddie got the coded message that she did not want to talk on the phone. 'Sure. When you're back we'll fix a lunch. But what do you want me to do about this Philip man? I said either I'd ring him back if I didn't track you down, or I'd get you to.'

'I'll call him. Don't worry about it.'

'Fine. Jim's back in Europe now, I gather. With Tom.'

'Yes. They flew on to Portugal.'

'When's Tom due back in London?'

'Tomorrow, I think. Why?'

'Oh, nothing. And you call me as soon as you're back, you hear?'

With that Maddie was gone, and while the mood took her, Lydia checked her watch, and realised she would have to talk to Philip at home.

'Philip. It's me. Sorry to call you so late,' she said.

'Lydia! Where are you? Still in Belize?'

'Sure am. And my wicked stepmother's been on saying everyone wants to congratulate me on the Metropolis deal.'

'This is serious.' Lydia's half-hearted flippancy fell flat. 'The chairman's hopping mad. And the account's about to walk.'

'It was walking anyway. To a media independent. I was just trying something to keep them in.'

Philip did not know what to say. Her job was on the line, and he knew she had fought to keep the DIY account largely to protect him. 'What do you want me to do?'

Lydia was getting mad now. 'I'll tell you what to do. You call Mike for me, and tell him we want £2 million at the same discount. If he asks why the hell he should agree, just tell him because of "Sleepless in Sienna". Got that?'

'"Sleepless in Sienna". Sure. But what does it mean?'

It means I'm really not much better than my father, she

thought. Perfectly capable of using blackmail to get her way. A year earlier, there had been a European media congress in Tuscany, and rather than stay at the usual boring conference hotels, a bunch of mates had decided instead to rent a villa and make a week of it. They had found a Renaissance castle on the outskirts of Sienna. On their last drunken night, Mike had staggered into her room naked, and – not wanting to scream the monastic place down – it had taken all her strength to fight off being raped. In the morning each, for their own reasons, had wanted to pretend it never happened. And neither had referred to it since, despite almost weekly telephone contact. 'Never mind what it means,' she said wearily. 'Just tell him.'

Later, not now feeling energetic enough to spend her day exploring on horseback again, Lydia decided to take one of the ranch's open Jeeps for a leisurely drive into the hills to find some cool air. Dressed in comfortable, loose-fitting khaki chinos and a matching cotton shirt, wearing her Ray-Bans pushed into her hair, she asked the houseman for some general directions before setting off. Countless pairs of eyes from the security contractors and mercenaries followed her braless figure as she climbed in the Wrangler. She realised this and tartily played to the gallery a little. Praying she would not ruin her image by pathetically stalling the left-hand-drive car, she was relieved when she accelerated hard away, the wind feeling good in her flowing hair.

As she came to the end of the long driveway, she slowed to join the road towards town. Fiddling with the radio, she found the Friends music station and turned up the volume to the old Rolling Stones hit, '*Honky-Tonk Woman*', joining in at the top of her voice. It was then that she saw him, sitting under the Temple Ranch sign. Blacker than most locals, he was wearing only a tanget made from fraying denim. Embarrassed at being caught singing, she smiled at him. Standing now, the small man bared his upper teeth, in a kind of submissive smile. Then he waved a piece of coloured paper and came towards her. She knew she should drive off, but a lifetime's polite English conditioning and a liberal's fear of appearing racist or patrician fatally delayed her. Banto was sitting beside her before she knew what had happened, thrusting at her the now hopelessly torn and rotted picture. 'You' father? You' father? *Wantok*?' he asked excitedly, still with his ingratiating grin.

Taken aback, her common sense still deserting her, she nodded, recognising the standard company portrait. 'Yes. Yes it is. Do you work here?' she gushed.

But at her words, the grin evaporated and the knife was at her throat. 'Go town. Over river. Go town. Go!'

Ashen, and cursing her stupid gullibility, she did as instructed, turned right and headed the few miles to San Ignacio. All her attempts to communicate further with him were met with fractionally increased pressure from the knife on her neck, so that with every pot-hole she feared it would puncture the skin. As they approached the town, he moved the knife to his right hand and pressed it now against her side, hiding it with his folded left arm. 'Over river. Over river,' he repeated.

He could only mean one thing. Cross the Hawkesworth Bridge towards Santa Elena. She was much too afraid to call out to the people pressing around them as they drove down Burns Avenue towards the junction. But in her head she screamed to them. Could they not *see* she was being kidnapped? But the stupid men were just ogling her bouncing tits, not the terror in her face. As they approached the bridge she did think about simply throwing herself out of the moving car, figuring that once they left the town, she had no hope of rescue or escape. As if he had read her mind, his left hand moved over, grabbed her leather belt firmly, and she felt the knife pressed a fraction harder in her ribs.

It had to be kidnap and blackmail, she kept telling herself. He obviously knew her father was rich. And kidnapping, she knew, was endemic in South America. Was he part of a gang, or working alone? Would he treat her well while negotiating? Or would he rape her . . . Rape! Her skirmish in Sienna with Mike now seemed very tame in comparison. Glancing over at him, she began to think through her chances of fighting him off. Probably about her own age, he was shorter than her. That was something. But he was obviously extremely strong. There was not an ounce of fat on his naked upper body, his sculpted pectorals glistening with sweat, arm muscles bulging, the thick neck bull-like. His wide face was showing no tension, the large, liquid unblinking eyes looking confidently ahead, his naturally curled, black hair buffeting in the breeze. It seemed hopeless. He looked the kind of man she could hit with a baseball bat and still not be able to hurt.

His directions were curt but effective, and two hours later, with Cristo Rey and San Antonio behind them, she could see the carpet of rain forest towards which they seemed to be heading.

The key Hortense had given him felt heavy in his hand. Heavy like his conscience at his duplicity. However much Tom had right on his side, entrapping his long-standing business friend still felt dirty.

But he knew this was his chance. The place was deep in confusion over Blacher's suicide. An ambulance and the police had already been called before Barton had got over from the restaurant, and as the emergency services arrived, within minutes of each other, Tom realised he had to grasp the opportunity to get into Rybinski's private laboratory. The two men were giving statements to the police, and he figured that the Russian in any case would keep out of his lab while they were there, for fear of giving them a reason to enter the place.

The yellow and black radioactive warning symbol on the door and the red light glowing above added to his nerves as he fumbled the Ingersol key into the sophisticated security lock. Looking constantly to each side, checking the corridor, he let himself in the room. Low-energy blue lighting gave a science fiction feel to the standard-looking lab. On the long central bench were rows of labelled test tubes, presumably containing cultures, and a large electronic microscope. The lighting was too dull, however, to make out very much else, even as his eyes grew accustomed to it. Cursing himself for not bringing a flashlight, he knew he had to risk turning on the light. Taking off his jacket, he laid it carefully along the bottom of the door, blacking out the gap, and switched on.

The ancient-looking filing cabinet was by the far wall, and he took out the second key he had been given. Sweating heavily now, he fumbled it into the brass lock, freed it and, trying to steady his hands, opened the top drawer. It was packed with papers and buff files. And so were the other two drawers. More than he could possibly carry or get out. Nervously, he janked a couple of files out, dropping one, which hit the floor like a rifle shot, spilling its bulging contents. Scanning at random he found papers in a variety of languages: Portuguese, English, Russian, French . . . Some were mostly in words – written reports, others in figures – accounts. It was a hopeless mission, with far too many things to look through. His mind swam with uncharacteristic indecision. What to do . . .?

The loud bang on the door made him start.

'Meester Rybinski! Meester! You there?'

Tom froze. The female Portuguese voice sounded servile. It was obviously some lab assistant looking for the Russian, someone who knew better than to try and enter. Holding his breath, he heard her call just once more before muttering some expletive and rushing away down the corridor.

Swallowing deep breaths of air, he focused his consultant's mind once more on the precise task in hand. He decided he wanted to be in there no longer than another ten minutes. Maximum. There were perhaps thirty files in there.

A twenty-second scan each. Go!

Working diligently, he soon realised the majority of the paperwork was irrelevant – the last few years' accounts, old lab trial results, tax and legal documents required to be kept by the pedantic Portuguese authorities. Discarding these left just three files that interested him. One in English, detailing orders and shipments of materials and equipment from mainly British and French suppliers. He removed the last dozen pages. The next was in Portuguese and from the little he could make out, seemed to be detailed medical reports on a series of men. They included photographs of organs, presumably taken at a post-mortem. The last file was hand-written in Russian, and listed rows of figures, each followed by annotated comment. The entries were dated right up to the previous day. He once more took out the last dozen or so pages from these two files, before stacking them with the rest back in the drawers. Shoving the papers inside the back of his trousers, like a schoolboy facing the cane, he stuffed back his shirt tail, turned off the light and put on his jacket.

Easing the door open, he froze as he saw Rybinski standing at the end of the long corridor, talking to two people. From his body language, he was obviously trying to get away from them to head for his lab. Tom closed the door, feeling the panic rise in him again. There was no other way out of the room. And nowhere to hide. When Rybinski came in, he was finished. If the police were still there, perhaps he could shout and get their help . . . Or should he hit the Russian? Knock him unconscious, and escape? His mind played over the options. All frightening, and fraught with danger.

Then his eye fell on the phone, and an idea came to him. Dialling O for the switchboard, he told them to send an urgent pager message to Rybinski: 'Meet Sir James now in his office'. Inching open the door again, he risked another quick look down the corridor. The group had already broken up and the Russian was striding rapidly towards him . . .

But then, there it was. Surely! Or was it just wishful thinking? Tom was convinced he had heard a faint, persistent electronic bleep. Closing the door, he grabbed a small, heavy pestle from Rybinski's bench, and waited, quaking. Far from sure he could bring himself to sink the thing into the man's skull, he prayed for his diversion to succeed.

Time became elastic as he stood there, palms sweaty, the smooth stone feeling like wet soap. Rybinski's footfall became louder outside on the terracotta tiles, but then so did the blessed bleeper call signal. He had not imagined it! The footsteps stopped . . . and then began again, becoming fainter. Tom opened the door and, seeing the corridor now empty, shot out. Light-headed with relief, he was almost back in reception before realising the pestle was still in his hand – gripped tightly like some comfort blanket. He almost dropped the thing in fright, then shoved it into his jacket pocket.

Gary, his cynical Texan friend at the embassy, had been absolutely right. He *had* been crazy to put himself at risk like this for the likes of Mitchell. Amateur spying was for fools.

And after this, Tom now wanted out at the first possible opportunity.

The tone of Noel Penny's voice told Barton there was even more bad news to come that day. He had just got back to his suite from a very late dinner, having spent most of the evening giving yet more statements to the Portuguese police about Blacher. 'How are things out there?' the American went on, dreading having to tell Barton, and delaying the moment for a few seconds longer.

'Pretty good, on the technical side.' Penny knew nothing about the biological weapons' development, believing the group's Oeiras lab was simply working in a different, highly confidential specialism of biotechnology to himself. In the way he knew Stow did on xenotransplantation.

'Good. I'd really like to visit sometime, and get to learn more of what we're doing out there.'

'Sure. We'll fix it. Sometime . . . But what is it?' Barton pressed. 'It's almost three in the bloody morning here.'

'Sorry. But I thought I should ring. I'm getting worried.'

'Is it Bolitho? Is he back yet with that damned native?'

'No. But that's another concern. It's been almost a week now, and his last contact with the pilot was pretty worrying. Nothing since. It doesn't look good.'

'But that's not why you've called me.'

'No. It's Lydia.' He closed his eyes. 'She's missing.'

'What!'

'She went out in one of the Jeeps, before lunch. For a quick cruise up to the mountains. But she hasn't yet returned. It's night-time now, and she's nowhere in town. She may be perfectly safe, but I felt I should tell you.'

'Was anyone with her? You didn't let her go out alone?' Barton thundered. 'In an open Jeep!'

'It seems that's what she wanted. I was working in the lab, as usual,' Penny replied defensively.

'Are the police looking?'

'Yes. I called them. I hope that's OK. We've also got our own men out, and the chopper on stand-by for first light.'

'Is there any other news?'

Penny had been dreading this. 'Some people questioned in town saw her around twelve-thirty. Driving towards the bridge and out of town. And a few said there was a black guy sitting beside her.'

Barton's heart lifted a little. 'Then it could be a kidnapping? If so, we pay. No negotiating. We just give them what they want. Fast. Money doesn't matter. No arguments with the police. And no cock-ups. You hear?'

'Sure. But I don't think that's it. You won't want to hear my real worry. But here it comes. The description I've heard of the black guy sounded familiar.'

'What are you saying?'

'The description was of someone young. Not a local. Very short. Semi-naked . . .'

'Who?'

'Jim – I think it could have been Banto.'

Barton went silent as he thought through the shattering implications of this. The way they had treated the man. Kidnapped, beaten, drugged and systematically drained him of his blood. His state of mind could only be imagined. And his hatred for the Bartons would be all-consuming. He remembered now the way the native had stared at him. It had been pure malevolence. If Lydia was in his hands, she was as good as dead.

'I'm flying straight back. Stop at nothing to get her back. Whatever it takes. Hunt him down and kill him.' Then he hung up, sitting on the edge of the bed, his head in his hands. Suddenly, becoming the richest man in Europe was empty and hollow. But as a wounded animal, he was now even more dangerous. Even more unpredictable. Even angrier at the stinking world.

Perry Mitchell put down the files and looked at Neil Gaylord. 'Is this your first operational involvement?'

'On something of this scale.'

'Well, the thing to remember is this. Once all the political decisions are out of the way, these things simply boil down to logistics. We gather as much intelligence as we need – more usually. *We* seize the initiative and then, the permutations and probabilities on what might follow are all predictable. Just like in those war games you'll have played at Ashford centre on your training.'

'No room in your book for battlefield flair? Bravery? Charismatic leaders?'

'No room for recklessness, or big egos, if that's what you mean. Take the SBS plan for Oeiras. Amphibious night landing and withdrawal in the bay, vehicular support to an emergency alternative pick-up two kilometres towards Carcavelos. Road blocks at each end of town, to close the coast road for the twelve minutes they need. The two night guards restrained and moved to a safe distance. DIS scientists inspect the plant, remove bench cultures for study, and direct the troops where to locate the high-temperature incendiaries to vaporise the vats. A button job, electronically detonated from the sea. No civilian buildings in the immediate area of the plant. In and out, twelve minutes. It all seems straightforward, doesn't it? But what are the permutations? Let's hear your ideas. Run through what could go wrong. "Think evil", as the SAS boys say.'

Gaylord thought hard. 'There's a force twelve blowing. The communications system goes down. Or they've been tipped off to expect us. More guards than normal. Armed, and they exchange fire. Or activate an alarm, also waking up the town. A passing police or military patrol challenges the road blocks. The scientists need a *lot* more time. The incendiaries fail to detonate. How's that for starters?'

'Pretty good. And do any of those scenarios call for unpredictable heroics? No. Just pre-planning, training and repeated rehearsal drills. That's why the best special forces people are as ordinary as hell. Not to say boring.'

Gaylord had to agree, having been stuck with some of them in assorted pubs and messes over the years. 'What about Belize?'

Mitchell looked grim. 'They've been told this is a hard-arrest job. I want these drugs barons and their goons arrested. For deportation and trial. That's their brief. Left to me, I'd go for air intercepts for those on short hops over from the States, Mexico and Colombia, with the long-haul people picked up on arrival at the airport or *en route* from Belize City to San Ignacio. What I wouldn't do is what their ops planning group's come up with. Let them all get to Barton's ranch and then mount a raid. Security there will be head-of-state standard. And we know he's hired a team of mercenaries, with serious firepower.'

'The SAS argue that taking them in one location minimises risk. You don't buy that?'

'No. That's not what I'm saying. My way *would* be more fragmented, and risk frightening one or more of the others away. But then arresting Barton and just one or two of the others is more than good enough. We're going to freeze their funds under UK management anyway. I don't need a clean sweep. But that's what they're shooting for, the bloody moon, and I don't like it. These drugs barons will have their own serious protection with them, in addition to that laid on by Barton. There's no way this can be a clean, hard-arrest operation given that background. It's got all the hallmarks of exactly the carnage I want to avoid. The Gadarene swine.'

The SAS ops planners had come up with an early evening assault plan, for the first night of the Alliance meeting. They figured that the minders and mercenaries would still be getting in each other's way, sniffing each other out, and all of them still disorientated. No line of command. Barton himself would be completely preoccupied with his VIPs. They would use a Trojan horse tactic to get the ten-man assault team through to the inner security circle at the ranch. Tom Bates had briefed them on a huge firework display planned for that first evening to impress the guests. The SAS 'team job' would replace the Californian pyrotechnic crew, due to arrive earlier that day. Sporting the right paperwork and equipment, courtesy of the CIA, and showing up in a large truck, specially equipped with false floors and walls, five of the SAS team would spend the afternoon setting up, leaving the rest, with their own no less pyrotechnic equipment, hidden in the truck.

'Can't you have them rework it? After all, you are heading the joint ops centre.'

'Surprisingly enough, it had been informally seen and "liked" by the head of JIC, before it ever got to me. Who Dares . . . eh? I've spent my life fighting Britain's enemies abroad, but pit me against the Whitehall Warriors, and I'm still a rookie.' Mitchell's menacing mask of a face looked anything but. 'So. We'll just have to help make it work, won't we?'

Banto made her leave the Jeep several miles before they had to, but he was feeling bad and needed the ground under his feet.

It was still night, and pushing Lydia in front of him, he made her run. Run and run. Not the fittest of people, it was just five minutes and half a mile on before she abruptly stopped, her lungs heaving. He thought she was ill, not comprehending that someone could possibly be tired after such a short time. To be marooned between the village and his forest was dangerous though, and he made her stand, lifted her over his back, and ran on at exactly the same pace. Lydia's body was draped over his neck like a stole, her face bouncing into his chest, his huge hands gripping her hand and foot vice-like. His animal scent, pungent and manly, was almost overpowering, yet the strength of his body, and the realisation of what a machine it could be, was somehow both exhilarating and comfortingly protective. It was like being carried by a pit pony.

Finally, even he needed to rest, and he gently put her down as they reached a stream. Kneeling, he drank. Then he turned, offering her water in his hands, cupped as if in prayer. He urged her with his hands and eyes, knowing now she was weak and would need to drink often.

'No. Thank you.'

'Drink. Water. It's good.'

She noticed he spoke his obviously limited English in the gentle, naïve way she had heard before in native, missionary-taught Africans. 'Who are you? Why are you doing this to me?' she pleaded.

He sat open-legged on the grass opposite her, his face lost in the darkness. 'I am Banto.'

'Banto. OK. Well, Banto, where are you from? Belize? Guatemala? Venezuela maybe?'

The concept of nationality was alien to him. 'I am Banto. My people, my village is Chenga.'

Lydia was puzzled, never having heard of the place. Trying another tack, she asked, 'Why did you take me? Why me?'

'*Kepala*. Big Man. Payback.'

The meaning, crystal clear, was extraordinarily contemporary. 'You're taking revenge on my father. Why? What has he done to you?'

Banto shuddered and made a whimpering noise, like a small wounded animal, hugging himself defensively. 'He *take* from me.'

'"Take"? I don't understand, Banto.' She was losing her fear of him.

'Take. Take!' He jumped up and grabbed her arm roughly. '*Take.*' He pinched her hard at the point they had rammed in the endless needles. Then he scampered the few yards to the stream. Returning with a little water, he carefully poured it slowly on her arm, so it flowed down and dripped to the ground.

Lydia felt sick as she thought she understood what he was trying to tell her. 'He's been "taking" your blood. Is that it?' Suddenly his wide face and aboriginal features began to make some kind of horrific sense. 'Banto, where is your village – what was it, Chenga?'

'Long time. Long time.'

'It's a long time away? OK. I think I understand you.' The realisation hit her. 'Banto, do you know the nation called Papua New Guinea?'

'Gav-man. Gav-man, missis!' he confirmed, excited. It was a name the American missionaries had used a lot. To describe some big village which 'governed' everyone. Governed all the tribes. It was a name he had also heard Chancey use, when he had been encouraging him to leave his village.

Since she had learned of it, her father obtaining cell lines from primitive PNG tribes had haunted her. But now it was she being forced to live the nightmare he had created. She had one more question for now. 'And Payback, Banto. What exactly is Payback?'

Uncomfortable talking to a woman, and naturally shy of any form of directness, he shifted his weight nervously and stood up. 'Time we go,' he said, unwittingly answering her question by avoiding it.

Lydia hauled herself up, now knowing the worst. This glimmering of a fresh dawn may be her last.

Four exhausting hours' trek later – he with his fluid, unhurried movements, she jerky, quick, and wasting energy – he at last allowed her the first decent rest period. She was completely exhausted, and as she lay back, her head against a rotting log, deep blessed sleep came immediately.

She was woken by the physical nearness of Banto. He was kneeling by her right side, with a strange look on his face: a sharp threatening look that froze her. Then his enormous hand was on her right breast, sliding slowly across her open shirt top, the other hand gathering her hair holding her head back, so that she had to look upwards. She fought to stifle the involuntary scream rising in her throat. The fear of Banto now raping her had anaesthetised all her feelings and she became limp, incapable of effective resistance, physical or mental.

But then she realised that something else was happening. The physiological stock-in-trade of pick-pockets and magicians had been at work on her. Banto's hand on her breast had diverted her attention away from something else. There was some other pressure on her left breast. Something was moving under her shirt. Something big and warm was settling there. Nesting!

The tarantula is also known as the wolf spider, from its hairy body and wolverine face. It feeds mostly at night on insects, small frogs and mice. Not with the help of webs. Tarantulas, like wolves, pursue their prey, and kill it not with venom, but a bite from its powerful jaws. A bite highly painful to man, and which risks fatal secondary infection or parasitic attack in the jungle. In the day-time, however, they are timid creatures, burrowing to safety and away from the light – as this one, which, having explored her sleeping body for orifices in which to hide, had finally been attracted to the beat of her heart, burrowing instead under her shirt. Its body length of three inches, and leg span of five, was now resting contentedly over her breast.

Banto had spotted the movement under her shirt as the spider had settled. Crouching at her side, and seeing now that she had realised what he was doing, he released her hair, freeing her to look down. Then, with a slight nod of warning, he tore off the shirt with his left hand and swept the tarantula off with his right. The roughness of his hand chafed her like sandpaper. Shaking, she sat up, arms behind her, her exposed breasts glistening with sweat. A part of her suddenly actually wanted him to scoop her up and hold her protectively against his beautiful body, the boyhood initiation scars deeply sculpted on his arms and back. He had saved her, and if he now claimed his prize . . . The moment was elemental, as a heady cocktail of delirium, exhaustion and fear suddenly aroused her, her nerve ends craving those over-sized, rough hands . . .

Banto looked away, the centuries yawning between them. Breasts were not sexual to him. He remembered his mother regularly holding orphan piglets to her, letting them suckle. As for sex and relationships, their experiences and conditioning could not be more different. For Banto, displays of affection were to be avoided at all costs. And sex for him was strictly for procreation, not recreation. Men and women in his village did not live together. Indeed, some PNG tribes, like the Huli, had bachelor villages and the men would not even let women grow or cook food for them. When the Christian missionaries had come to Banto's village, they had tried to encourage men and women to cohabit, but it had never caught on. There remained the practical business of limiting the number of mouths to what the village could feed. Women were only allowed additional children after their last child had become self-sufficient. If for whatever reason there were too many children, sexual relations stopped completely, with 'mistakes' left exposed to the jungle, to die.

Added to all this was the simple fact that Banto – at last looking at the semi-naked Lydia, sensing the fleeting wantonness in her – found her pink skin, blonde hair, and especially her sickly sweet smell, repulsive.

She quickly covered herself, coming to her senses and getting a grip back on herself. Blushing, she avoided his eyes and simply said, 'Thank you. Thank you for saving my life.'

He stood up slowly and began shifting his weight in obvious discomfort at all this. 'We go,' he said, gruffly, pounding his fist on his thigh in agitation.

Chapter Fifteen

Tom Bates was met plane-side at Heathrow by a security man and taken in a buggy to an area used only by authorised airport personnel. He did not clear immigration or customs, and was soon speeding down the M4 to London in the back of the anonymous-looking Ford Scorpio. Neither man spoke much on the journey, and with the reassurance that they would get his suitcase to him later, he was taken down to Mitchell's MOD ops room within an hour of touching down.

Peregrine Mitchell looked grim-faced, tired, and somehow older. Offering Tom a coffee, he forced a half-smile. 'Well done,' he said. 'Very well done. Those papers you got out of the lab were exactly what we needed.'

Tom had called the number Mitchell had given him on returning to the Ritz, and young Manuel Ferez from the Lisbon Embassy had called soon after to collect them. 'How's the woman? The agent who came to see me? Is she safe?'

'We got her out of Lisbon. But it was a close-run thing. Barton's security men had been watching her apartment.'

Tom was relieved. Seeing the fear in her eyes had first brought home to him the seriousness of what he had got himself into. Grimacing at the stewed, strong coffee, he asked, 'So. Those papers were really worth all the trouble, then?'

'Invaluable.'

'Good. Because that's it from me,' he said firmly. 'I've

done my bit. You can count me out from now on.' It was
a decision that he had made the night before. A decision
which in truth had needed very little debate with himself.
He was not cut out for heroics. Oeiras had taught him that
much. That momentary panic attack had been the first in
his life. He had survived it, and in the end – as Mitchell
himself had just acknowledged – acquitted himself well.
But Tom knew the truth. Knew how close he had been to
bottling out.

Mitchell shook his head wearily. This was not what he
wanted to hear. 'But we badly need you over in Belize.
Alongside Barton. And you have to brief our special forces
with your inside knowledge of both Oeiras and the San
Ignacio ranch. It could save many lives.'

'I'll brief your people as much as you like. No problem.
But I'm not going back over there. I quit. And nothing,
nothing you can say will change my mind.' Tom scowled
at him, determined not to be talked round.

Mitchell shook his head, and went to the phone and
dialled the internal number. 'It's Perry. Would you come
down please, doctor. Right away.'

They maintained the awkward silence for the few minutes
it took for the man to arrive. 'Mr Bates, this is Dr Merrick.
The doctor – a bacteriologist – is one of our leading experts
on biological weapons. One of the world's leading experts,
based at Porton Down.'

The small, neat man looked more like a country vet. In
his forties, the wispy, sandy hair, somewhat loud tweed suit
and thick rubber-soled brown boots seemed altogether too
rural for the heart of Whitehall. His handshake was firm and
dry, and his penetrating brown eyes looked troubled.

'You must be curious to know what was in those papers
you got out for us yesterday,' Mitchell said.

'No,' Tom lied. The truth was he was desperate to know,

but shrewd enough to realise that if they shared it with him, he would once more somehow become ensnared. 'I've told you, I want nothing more to do with any of this.'

Mitchell sat down heavily opposite him. 'You'll credit me, I think, as being someone with experience of the uglier side of this world of ours. I've seen many things in my life – in the old USSR, in Africa and Indo-China. Things that I wish I could forget. Wipe clean, like a video-tape.'

Tom nodded respectfully. 'I'm sure you have.'

'Then when I tell you those papers show the most repulsive, the most frightening threat I have ever come across . . . That it was the reason Blacher took his own life. That what Barton and Rybinski have developed really *is* terrifying enough to stop the US President and all the Allies in our tracks . . . then what? Would you at least reconsider?'

'There's such a thing as crying wolf, Mitchell!' Tom snapped, feeling this damn man's tentacles enveloping him once more.

'Mr Mitchell is in no way exaggerating,' Merrick cut in sharply. 'What Rybinski has attempted to develop is truly horrifying. Believe me.'

Clenching his fists under the table, Tom closed his eyes tight. What more could they throw at him? 'OK,' he heard himself say. 'But this had better be good!'

Relieved, Mitchell nodded instructions at the doctor to carry on.

'Mr Mitchell tells me you're already to some degree familiar with the devastating power of biological weapons. He's told you something about botulinum toxin?'

Tom nodded. 'It all seemed barely credible. That so little could be so dangerous.'

'Oh, it's true enough. And like everything else, there are always people working to refine and make even more efficient weapons of mass destruction and death.

Biological warfare has been no different,' Merrick went on. 'Some of the most innovative work was taking place in the old Soviet Union, at an organisation called Volchov. Under the direction of Andrei Rybinski. Since the fall of the USSR, people like him have been cast aside, and he made his services available on the open market to the highest bidders. Bidders, of course, like Sir James Barton.

'By teaming him up with my misguided, gullible old colleague Ladislas Blacher, Barton has been able to create not just a huge scientific quantum leap in biological warfare, but also the practical weapons application for successful delivery. Something the Soviets struggled with.'

'What? Some more powerful kind of biological bomb?' Tom was feeling frightened now. The genie was about to be released.

'Not more powerful. No,' Merrick answered, grimly. 'But more selective. It's based on specially cultured "intelligent" viruses. Viruses that seek out certain DNA codings before attacking. Mr Bates, Sir James Barton has commissioned the most terrible weapon since the atomic bomb. By bringing together the worlds of biological weapons research and genetic engineering, he has created the world's first bio-ethnic bomb. In the way the neutron bomb was designed to kill people while leaving buildings intact, so this viral biological weapon will kill distinct racial groups without harming others. The age of bio-ethnic cleansing is about to dawn.'

Tom's mind raced to digest what he was being told. The memories of crude ethnic cleansing in the former Yugoslavia, Africa and Asia were all too vivid, as well as the Holocaust and Stalin's massacres. Barbaric TV images from Bosnia and of the Hutu massacres flooded his mind. Such a weapon would find a ready market amongst many of the world's dictatorships, separatist and terrorist groups.

And such a weapon was indeed a formidable deterrent, even against the world's most powerful nation. 'How can you be sure?' he asked, still barely able to believe it.

'Those papers you got out included details of Rybinski's clinical trials. With post-mortems on his victims.' The doctor took out his copy of them. 'He had a control group of young male Africans. Mostly Angolans. And a same size group of racially pure Jews. North European Ashkenazim and North African Sephardim. I know of some recent genetic research that has established measurable differences in the frequency of certain male Y-chromosome halotypes between traditional Cohanim priests and lay, non-orthodox Jews. So modern-day descendants – the Cohens – do seem to have some slight genetic difference, thanks to this particular male chromosome being passed down from the original priesthood for three thousand years. And that's a difference *within* a racial group. Establishing genetic differences *between* racial groups is even more straightforward. No, Mr Bates, those clinical trials are unquestionably a precursor to some form of bio-ethnic bomb.'

'It's even cleverer than you might think,' Mitchell cut in. 'Barton got himself the open cheque commission from the drugs barons to threaten the President of the United States. To force him to call off the dogs. Well, any nation state attempting to do this has just one chance. Given America's complete dominance in conventional and nuclear weapons, given the sophistication of her Star Wars interception capabilities, the only hope is to threaten in an area where they've slipped behind. Chemical or biological warfare. Especially when threatened – as I now expect – via random terrorism. It's the one Achilles heel, their one soft area of under-belly. And your man Barton has gone straight for it.

'Now, Mr Bates. Will you help?'

'And you think the attack will be on Israel?' Tom replied, deflecting the question.

'Not necessarily. If indeed the first bio-ethnic weapon does target Jews, it could be centred on any major US city.'

Tom stood up, and helped himself to another mug of the foul coffee. 'Tell me what to do,' he said, his back to them.

Mitchell signalled for Merrick to leave them. When he had gone, he got on to the next piece of difficult news for Tom. News that he knew would hit him hard.

'You left for the airport at what time this morning? Early – sixish?' he asked. 'And you did not see Barton before you left?'

'No. Why?' Tom immediately sensed that something more was coming.

'We're monitoring all calls at the ranch and Oeiras. At 02.57 this morning, Barton was called by Dr Penny. I'm afraid it looks like Lydia's been abducted. Barton's already *en route* to Miami. A private jet's being arranged to fly him straight on to Belize.'

Tom's heart sank. He felt he could not take much more. Why had he not insisted she came back to Europe with them? Why? 'Is it certain? Has there been a ransom demand?'

'Not yet. And they don't seem to think there will be. You see, Penny told Barton that the man seen with Lydia in her car was known to them. He described him as "the native". And used the name Banto. Does that mean anything to you?'

Tom looked puzzled. 'Banto? No. Absolutely nothing. Look – I want to turn around right now and get back there too!'

Mitchell had been prepared for this. 'You're already booked on Concorde to Miami tomorrow morning. That's much the quickest way out there. And gives us all night with you to work on the operations planning. Your up-to-the-minute intelligence is absolutely vital to both teams. I meant what I said earlier. It really could save lives. All right?'

Tom only upset Mitchell's plans for him by insisting on calling at his flat before starting with the ops people. He wanted to pack another case of fresh clothes and check his mail. As if to hurry him, Mitchell stayed in the car, engine running, while he went up to the apartment in Chelsea. The place seemed smaller somehow, and instead of helping him touch base with normality, had an unreal, dolls' house feel. Having hurriedly packed, he flicked through the pile of mail that had almost prevented him pushing the door open, panicking him over the alarm. Five minutes later, and he was about to leave when he remembered to check his phone messages. There were seven, all now out of date or ignorable – except one. Maddie's voice had startled him, as she simply asked him to touch base with her as soon as he could.

Having first tried Chester Street, he learned she had left that morning for the Manor. 'Hi,' he said. 'I just got back, briefly. How are you?' Should, could he tell her about Lydie? What would Mitchell want?

'I'm fine. And you, and everyone else? I spoke to Lydia a couple of days ago out there. When's she back?'

The hell with what Mitchell would want. Anyway, Jim could drop the bombshell any time to her about his crass match-making – trying to bully them down the aisle. 'Maddie, I'm afraid there's some worrying news about Lydia. It seems she's gone missing. It's only a few hours so far. But she didn't return last night from a drive around San Ignacio. And everyone's concerned.'

'No!' she gasped. 'Is there anything else you know? Any sightings?'

'She was seen with a man beside her in the Jeep. But so far there's very little to go on. A full search is underway.

Helicopters, search parties, the police . . . It may all be nothing. She may simply have broken down, and bunked up in some hotel nearby.'

'Or bunked up with this man. You know how headstrong she can be.'

It was not meant unkindly, and until recently he would probably have thought the same himself. Now, however, he felt he had to defend her. 'Oh, I think that may have been true of the old Lydia, but she's changed a lot.'

Maddie sighed in worry. 'You're right. There's someone in her life right now. She told me. Someone really special.' Tom reddened. He should have told her about the two of them, but now was hardly the right time. 'She said she'd tell me when we lunched again when she got back. I just hope the guy is worth her. She deserves the best.' Maddie was now sobbing with worry. 'We've got real close over the last few weeks, you know. Dear God, please let her be all right . . .' The sobs now collapsed into bitter tears.

'I'm flying Concorde to Miami in the morning to join Jim. He's already on his way down. I'll call you the whole time, and tell you everything. Promise. Try not to worry too much. You hear?'

The car horn from way below made him cut the call short to rejoin Mitchell. The driver took his suitcase from him as he raced down. 'All OK?' Mitchell asked, looking closely at him.

Deciding against telling him about calling Maddie, he just shrugged. 'Just bills and junk mail.'

But as they motored back to Whitehall, he felt Mitchell's suspicious eyes watching him.

The giant ceiba worked its centuries' old magic on Lydia.

Banto had force-marched her mile after painstaking mile through the dense rain forest and, drained by the humidity, she was now close to complete physical exhaustion. But the sight of the living cathedral, the small cloister, the clearing its brooding presence had long since created, gave her a much-needed second wind. He did not need to tell her they had arrived at their destination. It was simply something she knew.

She was about to collapse to the ground when suddenly she sensed Banto staring at her again. He came over and gripped her arm. What now? Had she been right the last time about his real intentions? Had he even *put* the damned tarantula in her top as she slept? Fighting him off with her kitten strength, she pushed hysterically as he grabbed her left leg with those sandpaper hands, pulling her roughly to the ground. He was pushing up her chinos . . . From somewhere she found the strength to scream, pummelling ineffective blows at his head, tearing at his hair. He snarled, and viciously slapped her face, nearly breaking her nose and dazing her. Despite this she knew what was happening, what was about to happen. He really was going to rape her after all. To avenge her cursed father's crimes. *This* was to be his Payback. Rape and ritual murder!

Now he had clumsily freed her belt and was pulling down her trousers. And then, satisfied, paused to look carefully at her legs. His opaque, liquid eyes were impossible to read as he unsheathed his fiercesome knife. Clenching her eyes tight, she tried once more to be somewhere else, to distance herself from what was about to happen to her body. He could rape and tear her flesh, but not *her*. This is not me, this is not me, this is not me! she kept repeating. Over and over, to make it true. His rough hands were now all over her legs, touching them, stroking them.

But after an eternity, she began to realise that there was no pain. No rape. Just a feather-light brushing sensation . . . Opening her eyes, she steeled herself to look down.

Banto was kneeling over her legs, frowning in concentration, and delicately shaving off leeches. As he finished one leg he moved to the other, repeating the exercise. Then, avoiding her eyes as ever, he moved up to her exposed arms and neck, his face inches from hers, until satisfied she was free of the things. Finally, he roughly pushed back up her trousers, and lifted her effortlessly in his arms before gently setting her down to recover in the protection of the ceiba's buttress roots.

Then, as if nothing had happened, he immediately set about remaking camp, fashioning a hammock for her by stripping *nari nati* tree inner bark. It was mid-morning, and he knew he needed to make many more arrow-points and poison for what lay ahead. He had also decided that a sacrifice to the spirits of another pig creature would be necessary, to thank them for his success so far in capturing the *kepala*'s daughter, and to ask for their help in turning this prize into true Payback.

It was three hours later when Lydia awoke with a start. A large beetle had run over her face, having failed to burrow into her ear. Shaking her head, she fought to clear her mind and get her bearings. The grim reality of where she was hit her like a blow, and she almost fell out of her hammock in trying to stand. The clearing was quiet, save the usual cacophony from the forest canopy. No sign of Banto, who was still out hunting and gathering. Easing herself down, she began gingerly to explore, nervous of the impenetrable, dark forest walls beyond the clearing, imagining bestial eyes watching, and fearing snakes and scorpions under her every step through the matted debris covering the ground.

The clearing covered a radius of some fifty feet around the ceiba, and teemed with insects. There was no sign of anything that could be useful to her, however. No sign to her untrained eyes of previous habitation. Even the remains of the fire had already been absorbed by the living carpet of vegetation. There was one thing that seemed slightly different, however. Perhaps. Was that a louder than usual drone of insect noise, a few yards into the forest proper? Picking out a stout stick, she pushed her way towards it, filling the air with a dense cloud of insects. Afraid that she had disturbed a wasps' nest, she froze until they began to settle, seeing now they were only mothy flies. Continuing, her foot stubbed painfully against something solid. Something, somehow, unforest-like. Curious, she prodded at it with the stick. Sure enough, it felt hollow. Not a rock. Steeling herself, she thrust her hand into the vegetative slime and pulled the object out.

The radio had until a few days earlier been held in a leather carry-case. That had already rotted away. Wiping the thing on her trousers, she examined it carefully, marvelling how it could possibly have got there. It had to be Banto's, and this clearing obviously his lair. But there, at the side of the Tacbe unit, she had now revealed the on-off button. Her hand shook. It was impossible. The radio surely would not work. But . . . she had to try.

When it suddenly crackled into life, she almost dropped it as if it had given her an electric shock. 'Hello?' she called, collecting herself. But nothing. And the volume of the initial static was already fading. Fast. The rotting batteries, having been briefly shocked back to life, were about to die. 'Please! Hello. Anybody!'

Then, there it was! The faintest of metallic replies. She was *sure* she had not imagined it. She had heard it. She *had* . . . 'Hello! Hello!' she cried, but already knew it was too late. The forest had finally done for the batteries, absorbed the life from them to feed itself. The sophisticated radio was now no more useful than a hunk of rock.

Pushing on, emboldened by her find, she whipped up

another mist of flies as her stick struck something dull, and then on a second blow metallic. Definitely metallic. Excitedly she thrust her hands once more into the mucoid slime, pulling hard at the object she had found.

Bolitho's hand hit her in the face as the decomposing arm suddenly belched free. Banto had only cooked part of the body. The Rolex rattled down the now mostly skeletal limb, and as the remaining pus-ridden flesh came away in her fingers, she dropped it and let out a full-blooded scream. Barely able to believe what she had fleetingly seen, she ran back to the comfort of the tree, cowering in its buttresses.

But the nightmare was not over. Her own scream was as nothing to that she now heard, just yards behind her in the forest. An animal scream of terror and fury . . . The canopy of startled birdlife and howling monkeys exploded above her in their own noisy panic. Crouching in a foetal position, cowed and shaking, Lydia was by now close to a complete breakdown. Wide-open eyes, open-mouthed, waiting . . .

Barton arrived at the ranch in a foul mood, barking orders at everyone.

The defence work was behind schedule, with just two days to go before the Alliance started to arrive. And their *mañana*, he knew from bitter experience, did not mean 'tomorrow', simply 'not today'. Also, he was still waiting for a whole stack of figures and account statements from Tom's treasury management team. But most of all, Lydia was still missing.

Penny was waiting in the study to bring him up to date. 'We found the Jeep quickly. Abandoned at the approach to the Chiquibul forests, on the Caracol track. That's also where Bolitho went in. Looking for the native.'

Barton sighed heavily. 'So it looks as though your theory was right. He has taken her. What else is happening?'

'We've had air searches sweeping the area using thermal imaging. But nothing. If they are in there, they've either reached the deep forest, or maybe holed up earlier in one of the many caves. Parts of Mountain Pine are limestone and it's riddled with them. Large and small.' Barton nodded. He had himself visited some at Río Frío. 'The police have taken the Jeep and got the man's prints. But they don't match any on record. They've got two search parties out with locals – trackers who really know those forests. Plus, I've sent out three of the security men you hired. I spoke to the guy in charge, and he said he had people with jungle experience. I hope I did the right thing.' Penny looked unsure of himself. He knew how important the Alliance meeting was to Barton, and that the last thing he might have wanted was police involvement and some of his security mercenaries redeployed.

He need not have worried. 'You did *exactly* the right thing. I'd have sent even more of the mercenaries out. And there's nothing else? No contact? Ransom demand? Nothing from Bolitho?'

Penny was in two minds whether to mention it, for fear of falsely raising Barton's hopes. But deep down, he realised he simply had to tell the man all he knew. 'In my opinion, Bolitho's not coming back,' he said. 'He was chronically ill, you know. Should never have gone out there.' Barton looked uncomfortable at this. 'Either he's died of his illnesses – that fits with his last message to the pilot. Or the native killed him. But then something real strange happened earlier today. The pilot we use, the English helicopter guy? He picked up a snatch of something – he thinks from Bolitho's radio. No more than a squawk. Then nothing.'

'And? What does it mean? That Bolitho's not dead?'

'I don't think so. He had flares. The guy was well equipped and experienced. If he was alive and wanted to be found, we'd have heard from him. I don't *know* what it means. But I got the pilot to drop our search team off at exactly the place he put down Bolitho. That last contact was something over a day out. So we can assume he either died, was killed or himself captured within no more than two days' march of there. These security men are supposed to be the best. Ex US Marines. If Banto and Lydia are in there, they'll find them.'

Barton looked pensive. 'We've got radio contact with them, I assume. I want to talk to the team leader. Now.'

Penny led him to the room commandeered as an operations centre for both this and the rest of the Aruba security planning. When they had got radio acknowledgement from the jungle team, Barton told Penny to clear the room of everyone – himself included. Once alone, Barton asked the team leader his name.

'Pitcher, sir. Mike Pitcher.'

'Well, Pitcher. You know who I am and why I need you to succeed out there. Anything to report yet?'

'It's going well, sir. We've made real good time, heading for the last TI sighting by the pilot.'

'Have you picked up any kind of trail yet?'

Pitcher laughed. 'No need. He's sending us smoke signals!'

'What do you mean?' Barton snapped.

'We've picked up smoke, sir. Probably a day's march away.'

'Great! And listen to this, Pitcher. You get my daughter back safely, and there's a half-million dollars for you and your men. You hear that?'

'I *copy!*' Pitcher replied, delighted.

'But one thing. The native doesn't make it. Whatever happens, the native does not come back alive. Do you also copy that?'

There was no hesitation. 'I read.'

'Good luck, soldier. Keep me posted. Out.'

Tom Bates sipped the ice-cold champagne. It was too early in the morning really, but after the long night of relentless questioning, he needed something to refresh him.

The two operations teams had been all that Mitchell had warned. And more. Persistent, pedantic, slipping in control questions the whole time to see how he answered the same point expressed a different way . . . But he had explained, described and drawn the layout of both targets patiently time and time again, until at gone three in the morning they had finally let him grab some sleep on a camp bed. Then at five, the SAS ops man and Mitchell had woken him, to explain what they needed from him two days later in Belize. He was becoming an integral part of what they had called CTR – their close target operation.

His job was to communicate with the SAS leader throughout the day, using a messenger-sized radio they gave him, to confirm numbers of guards, their deployment and weaponry. Then, as the night-time firework display was scheduled to begin, he was to find some way to get Barton back into the ranch, and keep him there. His own return outside would be the signal for the attack to commence. The rationale for this was obvious enough. When the highly organised confusion began, the SAS did not want anyone from the other side taking control and co-ordinating an effective response. Only Barton, they calculated, would be able to attempt that. The rest – seven mistrustful factions, each looking out for only themselves and unsure even who was attacking them – would fragment shambolically.

As for Barton's mercenaries, with American help they had now identified their leader – a disgraced ex-Green Beret commando. He would be 'disfunctionalised' in the opening seconds of the attack. Not quite the 'hard arrest', no 'wets' policy Mitchell had laid down, but the commander on the ground had decided it was vital to protect his men.

Touching the radio in his side pocket for the hundredth time, Tom tried to relax and enjoy the experience again of Concorde, the aircraft as ever feeling incredibly narrow and small compared with the cavernous 747s. Having chatted with the British Airways stewardess about the new Miami service, he downed a second flute of the superb pre take-off vintage Bollinger, refusing the heinous offer to mix it with orange juice. But the early morning alcohol and his physical and mental exhaustion soon had his head slumping involuntarily as boarding continued.

'Champagne again, Tom?'

The voice and sound of his own name abruptly dragged him back to gritty-eyed consciousness. Looking up he could not believe what he saw. Wide awake again and automatically trying to stand, he bruised his hip on the fastened seat-belt. 'Maddie! What the . . .?'

She looked gorgeous, and knew it. Straight off the pages of *Vogue* in her flowing, generously cut Christian Dior cream woollen topcoat and matching Cossack-influenced hat. Even Concorde had effortlessly been reduced to no more than just a back-drop for her, a supersonic cat-walk. 'Nice to see *you* too.'

'I didn't mean that. It's just, well . . . What the hell *are* you doing here?' For all kinds of reasons he did not like it.

The stewardess took her coat and Maddie sat down, those endless legs turned towards him, her cold lips on his cheek. 'I thought I'd come and keep you company,' she said mischievously, but her eyes then took in his tiredness.

She saw he was in no mood for their usual banter and mild flirting.

'But seriously . . .?' he asked wearily.

'Seriously . . .? Partly because, like you, I'm worried sick about poor Lydia. I just want to be out there. And partly because . . . I've finally decided, Tom. To divorce him. And I need to confront this thing while I still have the courage. To tell him to his face. He desperately wants to be the richest man in Europe. You've heard him say that often enough.' She smiled distantly. There was a hard, petulant aura about her he had never sensed before. 'Well, I've briefed my lawyers. And I'm going to take the bastard for every cent he's got. I'm going to break him again.'

The paca's squeals would haunt Lydia for the rest of her life.

It had come blundering through the jungle, skilfully driven by Banto, and into the clearing. There it backed into the ceiba in front of her, panting, and faced the native defiantly, pawing the ground. As before, only one arrow was permitted: only one arrow in the heart to despatch it. Banto stealthily closed in on his prey until he was within twelve feet. Lydia wanted to scream, to interfere, to save the frightened animal, but she knew it was hopeless.

The killing had not been quick. Although the arrow slammed into its mark, the little paca ran off, frantically trying to escape, running its only method of defence. But fatally it stayed in the clearing and, when it was dazed and exhausted, Banto walked over and pushed the arrow in harder to finish it off. Even then it refused to die, fighting many minutes more, frothing at the mouth and snorting noisily, until at last, mercifully, it was all over.

Having made a fire, and burned the body hair off, Banto had next dug a shallow hole in the ground and lined it with wet vegetation, covered the charred, bloated carcass with clay, put the glowing hardwood coals on top, before covering the whole lot over with earth. After an hour he estimated the feast would be ready, and he eagerly broke open the earth oven with a pair of sticks he then used to pick the meat out. The aroma of the juices was in all truth mouthwatering, but Lydia had still been in a state of shock from the trauma of expecting at any time to be raped and killed, from the horror-movie experience of finding the dismembered arm – and now being witness to the killing. When he hacked off a leg and offered it to her, she made a soft scream and ran off to the other side of the clearing, falling to her knees, trying to control her heaving stomach.

This had made Banto angry with her for the first time. He had been treating her well. Honouring her, even, with the first, choicest offering from the ceremonial feast. And it had been their first substantial food. Her refusal was bad. Insulting to the very spirits he was seeking to win favour from for his mission. Standing over her he aggressively thrust the greasy leg into her face. 'Eat!' he roared, tugging her hair and forcing her head back. 'Eat!'

She had looked into his thundery face, but recognised in it hurt and incomprehension, not real menace; recognised in it the non-verbal messages his limited English could not communicate. This was something very important to him. Pulling herself together, she began to appreciate the millennia yawning between them. A small, proud native, someone who had carried her miles on his back, who had looked out for her in the jungle, allowing plenty of rest periods which he certainly did not need, and who now had caught some special food and cooked it, offering her the first morsel. His incomprehension at her behaviour, at her vegetarianism, was as understandable as his anger.

Especially considering who she was – the daughter of his tormentor. Partly in fear, but mostly in recognition of all this, she took the leg and, steeling herself, bit into the leathery skin through to a layer of fat, making a real attempt to chew.

He had watched intently, nodding vigorously. There was now nowhere to hide. No way to fake it by spitting out the smoky mess. With a Herculean effort she swallowed and prayed for the self-control to keep it down. Still watching, he looked on sternly for a minute longer before breaking into a beautiful, childish smile. 'Good. Good,' he giggled, falsetto, before returning to the carcass at last to feed himself.

Lydia had immediately run into the jungle and involuntarily threw up, pleased none the less rather than ashamed at her temporary tumble from veganism. For once she had seen a more powerful moral reason to eat flesh than to abstain: to acknowledge the native's cultural heritage; even to show respect for the brave little paca, so that its death would not have been pointless after all. There had to be a meaning to it all, some way to reconcile the moral dilemma, but that would require a lot of thought, a lot later.

Several hours on, just before the light went, she had tried to talk to him. Establishing he had somehow got a smattering of missionary education, their first common ground was Jesus, and snatches of the Sermon on the Mount. 'Jesus here?' he asked.

'He's everywhere,' she had replied lamely. It was exactly like talking to an intelligent, inquisitive Sunday School child. As a long-lapsed communicant, however, she wanted to change the subject, afraid of losing her credibility as some kind of sage. 'And you. You have a wife? And children maybe in your village?'

He burst into his falsetto giggle again. 'No, no!'

She had smiled back, wondering now how she could

ever have been afraid of him. 'But why? You *handsome* boy. Strong.'

Looking away, painfully shy, he giggled on. The native used about a quarter of the eye contact of modern man, and her direct gaze disconcerted him greatly. Attempts to encourage him to explain what had happened to him largely failed – perhaps for the same reason. He clearly did not like any kind of directness. The only slight progress she made was when she found oblique ways to question him. But that was painfully slow. At last, for the question she really needed answering, she reverted to her usual in-your-face-approach to see where that led. 'So, Banto.' She touched his arm to force him to look at her. 'What do we do now? Do we stay here, with your giant tree? Or do we go back?'

Not happy at being touched, he drew away sharply, but answered this once as a way to escape her directness. 'Go back. *Pay*back,' he said simply.

Then suddenly he had shot up, standing rigid to his full height, his senses straining, spooked like a timid forest animal by sounds she could not even hear. 'What is it?' she whispered.

But he ignored her and climbed with astonishing speed high up in the tree, higher and higher towards the gloomy forest canopy roof. She lost him from sight for a while in the rapidly gathering darkness. When he came down, his mood had radically changed. No giggles now. This was the hard warrior Banto. Moving quickly but somehow, as ever, succeeding in not rushing, he went to a cache where he kept his new arrows and brought them out with his poison. Very carefully he redipped the points in the curare.

'What is it?' she had repeated, worried and afraid again.

Not looking at her, his face now a mask, he said, 'Hunters. They smell fire. You stay with tree.' Then without even a look back he was gone as the forest nightfall completed its rapid descent.

Barton's three-strong crack pursuit team had pitched camp alongside an angular outcrop of limestone. They had not lit a fire, chewed gum or eaten any of the processed food they carried. The scent of everyday consumer products – from toothpaste, coffee, hair cream, an open can of beans or a cigarette – is alien in the jungle, detectable from surprising distances by animals and primitive man. It was the same with sounds. Animals crash through jungles, breaking vegetation, and a man's voice is not so different to that of other creatures. But a bottle smashing or metal striking is foreign and jarring.

And so it had been with the high frequency electronic squawk of the team leader's radio; broadcasting sounds beyond the acoustic range of modern man's hearing, it had acted like a beacon, directing Banto. By the time he had actually got within a quarter-mile of them, they were no longer using the thing, already sleeping. He had pin-pointed their location for this final leg as a result of another mistake they had made. The men had used the same area as a latrine in their unconscious need to create some kind of Western normality.

Banto's splayed feet delicately picked his way over the forest floor, shifting his weight, delicately probing and testing before each pace forward. He made no sound that did not lose itself in the ambient background hubbub of the night. When he saw the first man's hammock – the first warrior hunting him – he paused briefly, scanning the area with his acute bush baby eyes. When finally satisfied, he drew the knife and silently despatched him in his sleeping bag. The huge hand covered the mercenary's face as the throat was cut, again as Bolitho had taught him – the windpipe severed to extinguish any vocal noise. Despite this something woke the next man as Banto lifted the mosquito net from over his face. The giant hand and dripping knife were silently about him, however, before his brain even registered any comprehension of danger. This time, though, his body desperately thrashed in its death throes, and fell out of the hammock, crashing to the floor. The noise immediately woke leader Mike Pitcher and had him freeing himself, his hand already holding the automatic with which he always slept.

Seeing Banto's figure stooping over his comrade, he fired four rapid shots through the bag at him. Banto disappeared unhurt into the shadows as the explosion of sound once more panicked the forest above and around them. Desperately recognising his vulnerability, Pitcher kicked off the bag, ran crouching to the nearby rock-face and turned, his back to it, desperately wishing he had the night-sight from his Bergen. His pump-action shotgun was also resting on the rucksack, but he knew a dash to retrieve it was far too risky. The thirteen-round Browning, now reduced to nine, would have to do.

The first arrow slammed into his chest with such force that it hurled him back against the rock. The second, a heartbeat later, flew into his stomach. Pitcher staggered uncomprehending, turning, as a third hit him in the back, throwing him on to his knees. The Browning fell from his limp hand, and his last memory was of his hair being pulled back, a flash of steel and black, emotionless eyes.

They were the non-triumphal eyes of Stone-Age man who had, in seconds, taken out three of the most experienced, highly trained and best equipped jungle fighters in the world. Once again, Banto had been under-estimated.

He returned to the ceiba an hour later, blood-stained and carrying one of the rucksacks to show Lydia, as a kind of trophy. Her heart sank, knowing immediately what it must mean. Rescue was not coming. She was still completely at his mercurial mercy.

But later, as Banto spilled the contents of the Bergen on the ground, her optimism raced. Amongst the clothes and rations she saw a flare gun. And a pack of batteries. Batteries that might just fit ... Banto had picked up a powerful flashlight, and as she showed him how to work it, he giggled, and swept the forest canopy with its beam, sending birds and monkeys into clattering confusion high above them. As he ran and played, she grabbed her own treasures and hid them under a bush. The flare was a lethal weapon in its own right, as well as a means to attract any other search parties. And the batteries might just fire up the two-way radio she had found near that nightmare severed arm. She had left the unit out there, but was confident she could find it again, perhaps with the help of the torch later. This semblance of a plan cheered her up to an irrational degree. A little hope for the desperate, she now knew, went a very long way.

Chapter Sixteen

Andrei Rybinski had sounded uncharacteristically stressed over the scrambled line. 'Pressure getting to you?' Barton sneered.

'I am dealing with very dangerous people,' the Russian protested.

'None more dangerous than me!' Barton spat, menacingly. 'So I hope you have spent my £2 million wisely with your friends.'

'It's done. Exactly as I promised. We have six Scud ballistic missiles. And a Maz-543 mobile launcher. An experienced launch crew. And of course the chartered ship.'

'The warheads. You're confident?'

'I've told you many times, no. No! I'm not confident. The old Soviet weaponisation was always the weak point. Getting the right concentrates of filler powder, the right dispersal and scatter . . . We never tested enough. That was the problem. But with Blacher's lessons . . . Maybe we will succeed.'

Barton smiled to himself. 'When will they be in position?'

'The ship will be off Cyprus tonight, the missiles available for gyroscopic launch almost immediately. To follow your instructions.'

'And those instructions are clear? Crystal clear?'

'Absolutely.'

'Good. You've done well, Andrei. There's another £100,000 for you when this first phase is completed satisfactorily.'

Rybinski was pleased with the praise, but not the additional bonus. After a lifetime being stifled by the Soviet Union, all that now motivated him was big money, to ensure the last fifth of his life at least was worth living. He had a lot to crowd in to so little time. As for that extra £100,000, alongside Barton's billions it was nothing like enough. A couple of million pounds would be more like it. Enough to make this his last risky adventure. He certainly wanted nothing more to do with the Moscow gangsters through whom he had negotiated to buy the military weapons. Two million. That was what he wanted. Barton had no option but to agree. The Englishman no longer scared him. Not one bit.

'No,' he said, his voice firm.

'What do you mean, no?'

'I mean it's not enough. Two million – pounds. I want two million. Or everything's off . . .'

There was a long silence on the line, as his heart pounded. For a while, he feared the connection had been lost, and that perhaps Barton had never even heard his threat. His confidence now evaporating, he prayed this had happened, not daring to speak and ask if he was still there.

Finally, however, Barton broke the silence. 'You are a gambler, Andrei. This is something I did not know about you,' he said, evenly. 'Me too. I also gamble. And I accept your wager. If this goes exactly to plan, I will give you your two million. But if it fails, I will not *have* the money to pay you anything. Making you very dangerous to me . . . while you live. You have just bet your life, my friend. Let us both hope it is a long and prosperous one.'

The line went dead, leaving Rybinski white-faced and afraid.

* * *

'What's the news on Lydia?' Tom asked.

Neil Penny had met him as arranged at Belize Airport, and was thrown at seeing Madeleine with him. Barton, he knew for sure, was not expecting her. 'Nothing. Our helicopter pilot thought the man we sent in looking for her may still be alive though. Apparently his radio briefly came to life a day or so ago. But then nothing again.'

'No ransom demands?'

'No word at all. The police have teams out searching. And we've also put a crack squad in there. The best people available. They're sure to find her. Lady Barton,' he said, turning to Madeleine, still worried about her showing up unannounced. 'I hadn't realised you were flying out.'

'Neither does my husband. I thought I'd surprise him.'

Penny and Tom caught each other's eyes, recognising the understatement.

'How are arrangements going for the Alliance meeting?' Tom asked, as they walked to the helicopter, a porter following with a luggage trolley. He saw that Penny was surprised at the question. 'It's OK. Jim's finally briefed me up on everything out here.'

Penny still looked unsure, but replied, 'They arrive the day after tomorrow. Just for one night, thank goodness. The arrangements are going just fine, as far as I can tell. Not my patch really. But I have heard some yelling over the firework technicians arriving late. That apart, all seems to be going to plan.'

Fifteen minutes later, the pilot helped them in for the short flight to San Ignacio. Tom sat next to the Englishman, chatting to him as well as he could above the noise. The sea around the Cays sparkled its incredible blue as they took off, but soon they had left the coast behind heading inland south-west.

The flight was uneventful, hot and soporific, the sun beating mercilessly down on the goldfish-bowl cockpit,

when the pilot suddenly became excited. 'Listen!' he
called out.

Over the tinny speaker came a voice they all recognised. An English, frightened voice. 'Come in! Come
in! Anyone. Please! This is Lydia Barton. Lydia Barton.
Anyone. Please!'

'I read you,' the pilot said, his cool professional voice
contrasting with her obvious panic. 'Confirm please. You
are Lydia Barton?'

'Yes. Yes! Who is this?'

Tom burst into a huge smile. 'Can I?'

The pilot handed him the spare headset. 'Go ahead.'

'Lydie, it's me. Tom! This is tremendous. How are you?
Where are you?'

'Tom . . . thank God.' She was crying now in relief. 'I'm
in the rain forest somewhere. Being kept here by a native.
Someone Daddy's been using for experiments. It's all too
horrible.'

'Are you safe? Has he hurt you?'

'No. The opposite, in fact. He saved my life. But I'm afraid
of what he's planning. Some ritual revenge. And I have
to be quick. He's away hunting, but could be anywhere,
near by.'

The pilot cut in now. 'What about an American called
Bolitho? He was sent looking for the native and never
returned.'

'This must be his radio. I think he's dead. There's a body.
The native butchered him. I think in some kind of cannibal
ceremony.'

This silenced them as they all attempted to come to terms
with what she had said – and its possible implications for
herself. At last the pilot continued, keeping his professional
tone in tact. 'When you left the Jeep, how long did
you walk?'

'A little over a day.'

'That helps a lot. And can you light a fire, or somehow use the radio again when it's safe to signal to me? I'm the helicopter pilot who dropped the man we sent in to find the native.'

'Better than that. I have a flare gun. But we're still in deep forest. And even if the thing penetrated the canopy up there, you'd never find anywhere to land. But listen, I'm pretty sure that later today he's going to head back with me towards San Ignacio. For this revenge of his. Payback, he calls it. It sounds crazy, I know, but he seems to think he can just walk back into the ranch, and get to Dad.'

'He got to you easily enough,' Tom warned. 'It sounds like it would be a mistake to under-estimate this man.'

'You're right.' She of all people realised that. If he set his mind on doing something, he had to be taken seriously. 'Look. I have to get off this thing. My best guess is that we'll head out later for the pine forests. And then travel the road at night. I'll either radio you or use the flare and hope to hell he doesn't know what's happening. But then – come running. Fast! Got that?'

'We'll be there for you,' Tom promised. 'Meantime, take care. Fire that flare in his face if you get scared. Anything. But just keep safe. For me. You hear?'

'I've missed you. Missed *us*.'

'Me too.' Then there was just static. Hissing. She had gone.

Maddie put her hand on Tom's shoulder. That last brief intimacy between them had spoken volumes, and explained so much that had not added up. It would certainly take a little getting used to, but she was pleased for them. When she left Jim, she was going to need both to help her get through the divorce and the fight over the estate – Lydia's estate and heritage every bit as much as her own . . .

* * *

It had been like taking candy from a baby.

By feigning a tummy upset, Lydia had kept the pilot regularly updated on their long trek back towards the road. Then as soon as she and Banto broke into light forest, he told her to stop risking the radio calls. He had picked them up on the thermal imager, and in turn radioed to another three of Barton's best men their exact location and ETA at the road.

When it happened, she had been glad Banto was taken completely by surprise in the ambush, knowing her father would have given them instructions to kill him if necessary. As it was they were unnecessarily brutal, handcuffing and leg-ironing him. Tom and Dr Penny had raced to her from the people carrier. She and Tom had embraced, hugging each other, not needing to talk, taking comfort from their touch and closeness. Penny left them alone, watching what was obviously much more than a display of close friendship. The men had been about to throw away Banto's weapons when Penny stopped them, deciding to take back the arrow-tips and the container of poison. It would, he thought, be interesting to analyse the stuff sometime back in his lab. Nature's own biological weapons might have much to teach him.

The plan had been for Penny to check Lydia over for any immediate medical attention that may be necessary. Then the three were to fly back to the ranch in the helicopter which had now put down near by. She had, however, flatly refused to leave without Banto, fearing the mercenaries might still kill or further mistreat him. So instead, they all travelled back together in the Unimog, Penny asking her endless questions and Tom just holding her hand, massively relieved to have her safely back.

Lydia, although pleased to be with Tom again, was feeling oddly equivocal about her rescue. And especially her part in Banto's capture. It was something she badly needed to resolve. On one hand she had been genuinely afraid in the jungle: of its obvious inherent dangers, and for most of the time of the native himself. He had been like a Martian to her. At no time had she ever felt she knew what he was thinking. Her inter-personal skills and social antennae, things that made her who she was – all of these had suddenly ceased to function. It had been a totally disorienting experience. On the other hand, despite her early fears, he had in fact protected, and never once abused her.

She turned round and caught Banto for once staring at her. Her mind played over half-remembered 'primitive man' references – from Rousseau to Maslow, and she smiled back benevolently – still unconsciously patronising him. But he simply went on staring a second longer, before averting his black eyes to the window.

The phrase operations room still conjures up Second World War film images of low-ceilinged underground bunkers with naked lightbulbs hanging over a huge table map littered with miniature battleships and planes. Of baggy-eyed servicemen wearing Bakelite earphones, and trim-waisted, uniformed girls with BBC accents parading before some lantern-jawed supremo barking Churchillian orders.

Things have changed.

Peregrine Mitchell's ops centre was little more than a suitably equipped meeting room on the fourth floor of the Stalinesque Ministry of Defence building off Whitehall. The only concessions to cinematographic convention were the four twenty-four-hour wall clocks, labelled GMT, Belize, Washington and Jerusalem. Twelve communications officers were designated to work eight-hour shifts in teams of three, but all had to take their sleep and rest time for the duration of the mission on call in the building. There were sleeping quarters in the honeycomb of subterranean rooms and tunnels that runs the length of Westminster and Whitehall. Their desk-top comms equipment linked them to the SAS and SBS headquarters, GCHQ, and via its secure network of geo-stationary Inmarsats to the Chiefs of Police in Belize and Lisbon, the RAF camp at Belize Airport, to 'watchers' from MI5's A4 Section – chosen above MI6 people for their local knowledge from colonial days – the two SAS and SBS operational commanders, and Washington. At the press of a button, Mitchell could patch himself in to whoever he needed to talk to, with the additional facility of conference calls. The line of command was clear to everyone. Mitchell was effectively a commander-in-chief, and once the respective Police Chiefs signed over control to him for the short period of the attacks, the strategic decisions were his alone, with tactical responses those of the field commanders.

Patching in Hereford, the SAS major and the watchers in Belize, Mitchell asked for a sit-rep from the field. It was now the eve of the Alliance meeting. The day before the two raids.

It was the SAS man who led. 'A4 reported the Nigerian, Italian, Burmese, New York and Russian parties arriving at BZE over the last two hours. Three of the groups have now arrived here at the ranch by helicopter, the other two in transit. All are people we expected. A private jet has flown in the Colombian group direct to the strip here, with the Mexicans *en route*. ETA fifty minutes.'

'Weaponry.'

'Except for the Burmese, they're all clean,' replied the MI5 watcher. 'We upped the first-leg airport security, and unless they have plastic weaponry, they were all flying clean. The Burmese though have some heavy metal: machine-pistols, AK-47s, DHSK machine-guns and RPGs. They must have blackmailed or bribed a very large number of people to get as far as they did. But we X-rayed and then opened their baggage freight from the hold.'

'And you seized it at Belize?'

'No. In discussion with SAS, we decided to sabotage the equipment and let it through. The guns won't fire efficiently, and the rocket-propelled grenade launchers should explode on use.'

'And your end? What about the locals?'

'Barton's mercenaries have been depleted on some search-party work. His daughter was missing. But she's been brought back . . . We still count them three men down though. And there's still no sign of Bolitho.' The SAS had an impressively long and respectful dossier on the old vet, and the American's disappearance was still worrying them, for they suspected that he had gone under cover somewhere. 'They're well equipped. Mostly pistols and machine-guns. The Colombian brought an entourage of six men, all known as part of his private army. They unloaded boxes almost certainly containing heavy weaponry. The guards are all staying in a tented village, and one of our men, fluent in Spanish, is mixing with them to try to get them to brag about what they're packing. We've also got one of Barton's maids on board with us. One that Barton apparently attempted to rape one night. She detests him. We'll also use her to get them to brag. That apart, we expect the Mexican, Dino, to show up with some flashy weapons. That's his style. And he's the craziest, least predictable of them all.'

'And your men, your plan . . . it's still on track?' Mitchell asked.

'Yes. The firework display cover is proving ideal. Got everything in as planned in the truck. We'll be ready. And the cavalry's on stand-by if anything unpredictable goes wrong.'

'Good. Thank you, Belize, for now.' He patched next into the SBS headquarters and the ops commander, off Lisbon. 'Sit-rep please, gentlemen.'

The SIS Lisbon Station answered first. 'Positive response back from the Interior Minister following my briefing with the Ambassador. They're *more* than happy to have our special forces and scientists covertly lead, and will pass control to you tomorrow when SBS is ready to go in. They're warning the local police to stay away from what they're being told is a short NATO exercise. And also helpfully suspending the coastal train service from late evening just in case it ran late and got in the way of things.'

'Commander?'

'Weather reports are fine. Windy, but plenty of cloud cover expected. No moon. And my men familiarised themselves yesterday with the general area, as tourists. Also, I took advantage of our new-found official Portuguese support late yesterday afternoon. With your Station's help, we got the Lisbon police to make another unscheduled visit to the labs. Saying more investigations were needed around Blacher's suicide. I tagged along with one of the boffins, and we got to crawl all over the place from the inside too. We've never had it so good.'

'I don't want the night guards hurt.'

'Understood, sir.'

'Finally, the boffin. Having now got in there, was he happy about what needs to happen?'

'Affirmative. He wants our men to take samples of the cultures, so that Porton Down can work on antidotes in case any has already been shipped. And then they'll direct where we put the high-temperature incendiaries. One thing has occurred to me though.'

'What?'

'There's going to be a stiff breeze tomorrow, and these

types of incendiary are extremely intense. The nearest other buildings are less than thirty yards away. As we've got the government on our side now, it might be worth them having some military firefighters on stand-by in case it spreads. It might avoid unnecessary questions later.'

'Good idea. Will you arrange that?' His Station man quickly agreed. 'Anything else?'

'No change on the timing?'

'No. As soon as SAS go in – we expect at around 03.00 hours GMT, late evening in Belize – I'll confirm your order to go.'

'Understood.'

Mitchell took off his headphone, and nodded his satisfaction to his comms team. He did not like coffee, but he had never yet been in an ops room that had managed regular streams of drinkable tea. At least the stuff was weak and watery, and he swallowed half a plastic cup, a sour look on his face. Everything was going *exactly* to plan. And it worried him.

'What is it, sir? Something's bothering you,' Gaylord asked, also helping himself to a coffee.

'Perfection. I'm worried about perfection. It only comes to fools and geniuses,' Mitchell replied. 'And I'm neither.'

Lydia was enjoying the longest, most indulgent bath of her life. She had washed her hair twice already, and the tub was brimming over with Badedas bubbles. Apart from a few bites and grazes, however, she was fine. In fact she had lost a very welcome half-stone and had not felt fitter in years.

Her father, waiting for her with Maddie, had engulfed her when they got back, hugging her emotionally to him. His guilt over his own actions risking her life had been haunting him, pushing all his many other concerns aside for the moment. Promising to tell him all after a good soak and rest, she made him vow that Banto would be properly looked after. The native had killed men, and would have to be kept somewhere secure while they decided what to do. This she appreciated. But she did not want him hurt – or to be told later that he had mysteriously died in captivity.

She had also whispered an assignation to Tom and, now drowsy with the hot water and lack of sleep, she half heard him opening, shutting and locking the door to her cabana. Then she felt his soft kiss on her neck, and his hand as it slipped into the water and drew her to him.

Their love-making, spiced by abstinence, was even better for her than their first time together. New layers of depth had been added: she growing in confidence, he in tenderness.

'Who'd have thought this?' he asked later, as she lay protected in his arms on the vast bed.

'What?' She looked up at him dreamily.

'This. That you and me could stop fighting long enough . . . for this finally to happen.'

'We've never really fought . . .'

'Not fight-fight. But we certainly sparred. All the time. I mean, we were, *are*, strong individuals. It goes with the territory in our jobs. And over the years, let's be honest, we've fenced with each other. It was fun, but . . . hard work. No way to spend your life.'

She sat up. Those words 'spend your life' sounded as if they were about to ring either warning bells or wedding bells. She could not decide which. 'You're right. Perhaps we're just a little older. And wiser,' she ventured, looking curiously at him.

Each knew that the signals they were sending the other were leading to something serious. It was no casual word-play this time. Perhaps it was the raw intensity of what they were going through – the kidnap, her father's terrible crimes, Mitchell, and the SAS raid the next evening. It all seemed to have put their fledgling love affair on a kind of war footing. Life and death dramas were throwing up black and white choices that had always before been grey. Or perhaps it was more simple than that. Perhaps this really was what it felt like to find someone with whom you wanted to spend your life.

Tom wanted to kiss her and propose right then. The moment was right, he knew – for each of them. It should happen exactly like this . . . But thanks to James Barton, there was some messy baggage he had to clear up first.

He did kiss her, but then broke the spell when he said, 'If we're getting serious about this thing, there's something you need to know.'

She stiffened in his arms, and then sat up, drawing the sheet around her. He looked uncomfortable, and it was obvious she was not going to like whatever it was. 'If you're about to tell me you're married, HIV positive, or are my estranged brother, I need a drink first,' she said, steeling herself. 'You want?'

He nodded, asking for a bourbon. Slipping on a dressing gown made her feel slightly less vulnerable, and having fixed the drinks, she passed him the glass, sat on a bedside chair and stitched on her trader's face. 'OK, buster. Shoot.'

Taking a gulp for confidence, he launched in. 'Jim's more or less attempted to bully me – into marrying you.'

'What! He knows about us?' She was shocked.

'Just let me get all this out. There's a lot to tell. Then ask me all you need. Deal?'

She nodded sulkily.

'All right then. So here it is . . . I've told you I've been helping out your Security Service people. MI6. Spying on him.' Her poker expression did not change. 'I'm not proud of that. But when I realised why he needed that £2 million of Temple money – for the biological weapons work – and when I realised the funds he had me managing was all stinking drugs money . . . I had to help. Maddie and you came to the same conclusion by a different route. That's true, isn't it?'

Pushing her hands through her hair, she frowned. 'Go on. You said you wanted to get it all out.'

'Sure. Well, what happened was this. They needed me to get even closer to him on the illegal businesses he always kept away from me. So I threatened to quit, telling him I wanted a share of the *real* action. I called his bluff. These people needed fast results. And it was then that he made me the offer . . . a kind of bribe. He said he really could *use* my help on the drugs syndicate, the Aruba Alliance. That I could definitely earn big bucks that way – as his right-hand guy. But only if he could really trust me. Only if I became family. He'd trust a son-in-law in a way he couldn't trust some outside consultant . . . even me.'

'He offered you *money* – to marry me?'

'Yes – but it was just his warped mind at work again. Acting like some medieval despot. Thinking that money, fear, can make everything he wants happen.'

'And what did you say?' She was suddenly angry and afraid. Had she really misjudged Tom?

'I wanted to tell him to go to hell! But remember what this thing's all about. We're all trying to stop him. And there's so much at stake. More than even you or either of us yet know. So in the end all I said was I didn't need his money to want to marry you. But, yes – before you ask – I *did* leave him with the impression that I'd agreed.'

She got up and paced by the window. 'And what now?' she asked irritably. 'Do we tell everyone? An announcement in *Tatler*? Throw an engagement party? I mean, if a job's worth doing . . . Or have the two of you already set the date of the wedding?'

'That's not fair,' he said, hurt, getting up to go to her. 'I don't deserve that.'

'None of it's *fair*!' she snapped.

'I was about to ask you about the future right then. To ask how you want this thing to go. But I needed to get this baggage with your Goddamn father out.' He tried to hold her, but she shook him off and, turning, hands on hips, she confronted him.

'Where you want exactly *what* thing to go? We screw a few times and, what – we're suddenly Barbie and Ken? Get a life. And get the hell out of mine!' She knew she was being unreasonable, but her nerves were raw.

Breathing deeply to calm himself, he kissed her on the cheek, wet now with silent tears. 'That sounded like the old in-your-face Lydia. But better in my face than in my past. Try and get some rest. We'll talk tomorrow.'

She heard the door close quietly before throwing herself on the bed.

Life without Jim held almost as many terrors for her as life with him.

Despite her lawyer's easy confidence, Maddie knew that nothing could be taken for granted in a divorce. Not custody of the twins. Not the money. And not even her reputation. And even when it was over, what then? Should she return home a failure to her elderly, strait-laced parents in Philadelphia? Might she be awarded the Manor? She would keep her title, and finishing off all the work she had begun there would be her first-choice option. Perhaps Lydia – in whose name it remained in trust – would spend more time there. If she and Tom really were an item, it would be wonderful to have

them both there with her. They could have Jim's wing
to themselves . . .

But first she had to face him. Tell him their marriage
was over. Non-confrontational by nature, she felt sick at
the thought of what she was about to do. It was not
something she could have sprung on him while Lydia
was still missing. She had seen how distressed he had
been, and despite everything, she could not have added
to his worries then. With Lydia now safe, however, there
were no more excuses for delaying what she had flown so
far to do. Before he was distracted next by the arrival of
his precious guests, she had to use this tiny window of
opportunity.

It was almost seven, and she had changed into a dark
brown linen suit for dinner – not too dressy, but still serious
for the showdown. Checking herself nervously yet again in
the mirror, she left her room for his suite.

Pumped up now, she cursorily knocked once and
sashayed right in. 'Jim,' she called brightly.

The sitting room was empty but stank of a cigar, half
finished in the ashtray.

'In here!' His booming, arrogant voice punctured her
fragile confidence, and she ran yet again over the words
she had so carefully been rehearsing.

Fighting her rising panic, desperately wanting to keep
control of her voice, she strode into the bedroom.

The sight that greeted her changed everything. He was
sitting on the edge of the bed in his dressing gown,
a young Creole in an untied robe standing over him,
towelling his hair. Maddie recognised her immediately
as the prettiest of the maids. The girl's own dripping hair, and the damp circles in the silk over her
curves, removed any question of ambiguity. Their shower
may have been before or after their love-making. It

really did not matter. They might as well have been in bed.

He looked up, his dishevelled hair robbing him of any remaining dignity. The maid also half turned, covering herself, before running shamefaced back into the bathroom, her bare feet slapping on the marble floor. Making no attempt to flatten his hair, not even caring that much, Jim simply stared back at Maddie, a look of mild amusement on his face. 'Don't pretend you're surprised,' he said.

She somehow found the strength to keep her voice steady. 'Thanks,' she replied. 'Thanks for making this easy.'

With that, she walked over to him, placed the letter from her solicitor on his bed, and left, closing the door quietly behind her.

Chapter Seventeen

L ydia looked at Banto sadly, guiltily, and wondered what was to become of him. They had put him in a windowless room at the back of the ranch-house where they kept household stores, a hefty-looking bolt newly fitted on the door. She had demanded that her father let her see him that morning, and – hugely preoccupied with the arrangements for the Alliance meeting later that day – he had agreed, although much against his instincts, and only on condition there was a guard present.

True to their word, they had not harmed Banto, and he seemed to be well enough. Whether he was glad to see her again she really could not tell. He did not move and barely looked at her when they came in.

'Hi! How are you today?' she asked cheerfully.

He made some grudging noise in response, still avoiding her eyes, still uncomfortable with the directness of the outsiders.

'We have to decide what we arrange for you. This is important, Banto. Look at me! I'm trying to help. I may be your only friend.' It was true. The Stockholm Syndrome is well known to police psychologists the world over, describing how captives can bond with their kidnappers. 'What do *you* want?'

'No more take?' he asked, eyes wide.

'No more. I promise.'

'Payback. Then I go home. To tell the *kepala* about the outside. To help us fight.'

'No Payback, Banto. Forget that. It's hopeless. It's just not going to happen. No Payback. You understand me?'

'No more Payback,' he repeated, without enthusiasm. The killing of Bolitho was a token Payback. But he still wanted more. He wanted Barton. *Their* big *kepala*.

Satisfied, she pressed on. 'I can *try* and get you out of the country, and back to PNG. I've no idea how right now. But I could try.' She knew she would have to make it happen quickly though, before the truth of his forest killings became known. 'Or you could stay in the new world, Banto. You learn really quickly, and your English would soon improve. Do you want to think about that?'

Lydia had. A lot, over-night. She had toyed with the idea of taking him back to England and semi-adopting him, acting as his teacher and guardian. Between this and puzzling over what to do about Tom, she had got virtually no sleep. On both counts, she was terribly undecided, her confidence at a low ebb and her normally assertive self in rapid retreat. As for Banto, she needed to conclude what was best for him and had just discussed her vaguely formed idea to take him home over breakfast with Neil Penny. He in turn had thought for a while before recounting the story of an American anthropologist. After spending twelve years in the deep Amazonian rain forest, the man had married a beautiful Stone-Age tribeswoman before, in 1987, taking her home to New Jersey. The girl, just some four feet tall, took English lessons, removed the white sticks which pierced her nose and cheeks, changed her loincloth for regular clothes, had a fashionable hairstyle, allowed her feet to grow soft in modern shoes and worked hard to come to terms with the trappings of the West. There were three children from the marriage. But in 1993 she chose to return to her jungle alone, back to her tribe. The last Penny had read, the loving husband was still hoping to find her and reunite the family.

This moving story was very much in her mind now as she looked protectively at Banto. But he had by now started rocking himself, chanting the two-note mantra that she had heard so often when, she suspected, he too was unsure and afraid of things. She nodded to the guard that she wanted to leave, and followed him out.

Nothing had been resolved there. Next stop Tom.

'Dino! Great to see you. Good flight, I hope.' Barton smiled broadly, his own confidence not affected one bit by Maddie's news the evening before. He made no attempt to introduce Tom, who was hovering self-consciously by his side.

'Hey! Sir Barton! How's the Queen? She doing good?' The short man, energy bursting out from him, was as usual dressed all in white. Right down to his shiny, big-heeled boots. He giggled his irritating laugh.

'Her Majesty's very well. She especially asked to be remembered to you.' There was, he knew, every chance that the mad Mexican would think he was serious. 'The rest are all here. My people will show your men to their quarters, while you come and join the rest of the Alliance.'

Dino stopped him, looking directly into his eyes. 'You got good security here? I mean real good?'

'The best money can buy. Top mercenaries on top pay. The place is tight as a drum. Don't worry. Please.'

'Mercenaries suck,' Dino spat, deadly serious now. 'Pay them a dime more each and they'll shoot you in the back. You need men from families you grew up with. Chihuahuan brothers, whose mommas cry with your momma when someone gets hit. This money *can't* buy. The one thing. That's why I brought some of my own people. No offence. But that's the way it is.'

'I know this. No problem, Dino. The more the better. I just want you and the rest to feel safe here and at home.'

'Who else brought their own people?'

'Just the Santander boys. And our Warlord. He seems somehow to have shipped enough hardware all the way from Burma to start a small war.'

'Figures. Those Golden Triangle guys are crazy.'

Crazy as Dino also was, he knew what the man meant. The Warlords were in a medieval time-warp, reminding him of the terrifying Mongol leaders like Genghis Khan. The Western mobsters, ruthless and coldly efficient murderers as they were, at least worked to some agenda he could understand. The Asians – like the Burmese and the Triads – came from another world entirely. 'The Alliance is a broad church,' Barton replied.

The mad laugh rang out again. 'Yeah, church! Yeah! I like that.'

Barton then sent Tom to check for some urgent encrypted e-mail message he was expecting from the States, before taking Dino straight over to the ranch. The rest of the Alliance members were grazing from a vast buffet. 'Dino's arrived, everyone!' he called, clapping his hands. 'We're all here now, gentlemen. So, relax, enjoy your meal. But not too much! I've got a very special dinner and show for you tonight. The best fireworks you've ever seen, to welcome you all in true Aruba Alliance style. After lunch, we'll begin the first part of our meeting, concluding tomorrow. I've got some exciting things to tell you. Not least about a communication the President of the United States will be reading' – he looked at his watch for dramatic effect – 'around about – now! A communication that should help guarantee all of you long and happy retirements in which to enjoy your money and your grandchildren. This I have done for you. I'll tell you all about it this afternoon. Have a nice meal.'

Tom's relationship had changed from that of Barton's senior strategic counsellor and fellow director to what now felt like the family poodle. And he did not like it much. On the other hand, there really was no one else the man could trust or get support from. No one else who had the big picture of what he was trying to do. And it was exactly the role Mitchell would have wanted him to play. On the inside. Indispensable.

The main agenda for the Alliance top men was undemanding, but belied the amount of work that had been put in. And now, having been exposed to the sheer scale of money Barton stood to make from his adventure, Tom could at least understand, if not condone what he was attempting to pull off. Quite simply, he had brilliantly identified a new market sector for consulting and treasury management services. That huge, and growing, high-margin global business: the illicit drugs industry. One run by streetwise, but financially inexperienced people whose main preoccupations were local turf wars, and fighting off whichever politicians and security forces they could not buy off. It was a new market sector closed to the great strat and financial houses of the world, but with earnings potential each would die for. Better still, by the skilful manipulation of his biotech company – another get-rich-quick sector he had shrewdly spotted very early – Barton had been able to put some serious capital of his own on the table to leverage the astronomic returns he now expected from the Alliance for holding the Americans in check.

Patching through the nearby special forces signals man, Tom had kept Mitchell briefed on what was happening, using the radio they had given him. He also kept the SAS team – the 'firework crew' – updated on numbers, and who was where. Unfortunately Barton had refused to share with him the nature of his 'détente' threat if the US President did not now stymie the work of his drugs taskforce. That was something he was due to hear later that afternoon, at the same time as the Alliance members. Tom may, in Barton's books, now be almost family, but even that did not count for much with his billions of dollars at risk.

Taking the second shower of the day in his cabana, skipping lunch with the boring Alliance members, Tom was drying himself when she let herself in. Lydia was wearing a white cotton suit with a simple black T-shirt. Her hair was scraped back and up, giving her a brusque, businesslike air. His own nakedness made Tom feel vulnerable. 'Are we still talking?' he asked defensively.

Sitting down primly on the edge of the bed, she looked up at him, her face softening. 'I must still be pretty stressed out,' she said, 'to react like I did. I just didn't like the feeling of being bartered somehow. But I can see you didn't have any way out.'

'I was wrong-footed,' Tom admitted. 'And all this spying business is stressing me out too. I'm kind of making it up as I go.'

'And what you said to me last night about wanting to ask me about our future . . . were you making that up?'

Tom felt immense relief, took her in his arms and kissed her hard. They hugged, holding on tightly for several minutes, not speaking. Each needed the other. In their different ways they had been through gutting emotional turmoil. During her kidnap, each had feared they would never see the other again. 'Now *this* is the kind of making up I do like,' he smiled.

Lydia smiled back, but the strain was still obvious on her drawn face. 'I can't take much more of all this,' she said. 'If Dad thinks we're engaged, let's leave it like that.'

'And does it feel good – being engaged to me?'

'Compared with what?' she teased, not ready to be drawn.

Tom smiled and gave her a peck on the forehead. 'I have to get ready,' he said, standing. 'Jim needs me to present the latest quarter's treasury management performance to them. That's the first thing on the agenda after lunch. How their combined portfolio is performing. And how their own shares stack up.'

She watched as he dressed. 'And how is it performing?'

'Just as they want. Safe and unspectacular. We're staying ahead of inflation and outperforming interest rates. Basically tracking blue chip equity performance and gilts. They don't need to speculate. All they want is a safe return – one that's tax efficient for dividends and laundering.'

'So Dad's doing well for them. CEO of the world drug industry . . . Not really any worse than our ancestors in the Bristol slave trade, I suppose.' She looked pensive. 'And what else has he got planned for them?'

Tom looked anxiously at his watch. 'Look. I have to hurry. And there's something I need to warn you about.' His face told her their joking and teasing was now over. 'What I'm telling you must not get back to your father, Penny or any of the rest. You understand what I'm saying?'

She nodded, shaken. 'Go on.'

'A big budget, state-of-the-art firework display's planned for tonight. To impress the Alliance members. Jim will decide the timing, but probably around nine – before the gala dinner. Just before it starts, I have to get Jim back inside, and keep him there somehow. When I go back out, and show myself – all hell will let loose. And the SAS go in.'

'The SAS!'

'There's a special services unit out there right now. They've replaced the firework crew, and have more than a few fireworks of their own, I imagine. They plan to arrest your father and the drugs barons, some of them for trial in the States. Your father, for deportation back to Britain – unless the Belizeans demand a show trial here. You'll have seen the mercenaries Jim's shipped in as extra security. And the bodyguards some of the Alliance people travel with. The SAS men want to avoid a serious fire-fight. They figure my taking Jim out of the loop will frustrate any semblance of a chain of command, leaving the various guards confused and ineffective. I'm not an expert in these things, but that's their theory.

'But there are no guarantees. Some of Jim's mercenaries get a lot of respect from the British, and it could get very messy. That's why I need you and Maddie somewhere safe and away from all this. So – as soon as you see me returning, the two of you immediately move back into the ranch. Go to the plant room. It's below ground and should be the safest place there is. I've already checked it out. You can lock the steel fire door from the inside. Do you know where it is? Well – go down and find it. Promise me. Familiarise yourself with it. And *don't* come up until you're sure it's safe. I'll come and get you. Have you got that?'

'But what about—'

He took her by the shoulders and looked her in the eye. 'No buts. And don't ask me any more. For once, don't question. Just do. OK?' He held her again, realising they would not now get to talk again until after the attack. He also realised that given the firepower of the SAS and the private armies, there was a real chance of things going badly wrong. It made these last few minutes together precious. 'Let's get this thing done.'

She looked up at him, seeing the worry in his face. 'And this "thing" tonight isn't just a formality. It's dangerous, isn't it?' she asked.

He avoided her eyes. 'I'm late,' he said, breaking off. 'Please. Just do as I say, and we'll all be fine.'

The Prime Minister's official study is on the first floor in Downing Street, behind the famous black front door. But the architectural puzzle that is Number 10 seems to defy logic. That 'front' door – now made of bomb-resistant plate steel, not wood – is in reality the back door to the rabbit warren. And this Prime Minister, like others before him, had made the ground-floor Cabinet Office – the old library – his workplace.

The Foreign Secretary and Allan Calder met in the black and white marbled entrance hall and walked down the narrow corridor. This widens into a lobby, a holding area, with Churchill's portrait over the fireplace and busts of William Pitt and Disraeli looking across. Calder made for the Gents, just off the lobby, and the Foreign Secretary followed him to snatch a few words before they were called in. Neither could cast any light on why they had been summoned, however. They returned to the lobby, minds racing at what could be so important for the PM suddenly to haul them out of other meetings.

Calder smiled at one of the veteran 'Garden Room Girls' as she came out of the Cabinet Room carrying some papers. 'What's the flap, Muriel?' he asked. But she simply shook her head, and told them to go straight in.

They were both immediately alienated on entering the Cabinet Office to find the US Ambassador there, accompanied by the new CIA London Station Chief, a man Calder had not yet got to know as well as he would have liked. Or as well as he should. But it was the diplomacy that was upsetting the Foreign Secretary. The proper channel to the PM for any ambassador was through his department. Period. Whatever this flap was about could not alter that, and he and his department had been seriously slighted. Something that would not be raised today, but which would never be forgiven or forgotten by King Charles Street.

'Prime Minister,' he said, with deliberately exaggerated formality. Calder and he nodded greetings to the two Americans.

If he noticed the frost, the PM did not show it. Something much bigger than departmental sensitivities had arisen. 'Gentlemen. Thank you for interrupting your schedules. As you will see, it's not for nothing. This is a copy of an e-mail message to the US President, received at the White House a few hours ago. Take your time to read and digest it.'

They took their copies, selected one of the sea of red leather, buttoned chairs, and sat with the other three men grouped around the end of the long, highly polished table.

The message read:

Mr President,

In a matter of hours, a missile armed with a biological warhead will be launched at a sensitive, heavily populated target. There is nothing you can now do to stop that happening. Subsequent analysis of the fall-out will reveal a formidable new form of biological agent: genetically engineered bacteria which target only the genes of races we choose to attack. The world now has a new Domesday threat to replace the nuclear bomb. Bio-ethnic cleansing. Whereas you cannot stop our first attack, you can easily prevent further launches. Do not prosecute your new powers against the global drugs syndicates. And, at their twelve-month review, do not seek to renew the anti-drugs treaties you forced on the governments of Mexico, Colombia and Burma. You can confirm your

agreement to us by using the word 'coronach' in your
official media response to our first and, we hope, final
attack. Our terms are not negotiable, and there will
no further communication.

'If I may, Prime Minister?' the CIA man said when he saw
the others had finished digesting the communication. 'Let
me answer the obvious questions. Yes – we are taking it
seriously. It marries with our own intelligence on Sir James
Barton and the Aruba Alliance. Second, the e-mail was sent
from a PC at a large commercial computer-training centre
in Chicago. These machines are virtually public access. We
have no leads, nor do we expect any, on who physically
sent the thing.'

'And the threat of bio-ethnic cleansing. Is that technically
feasible?' the Foreign Secretary asked, visibly shaken.

'Sure. We've looked at most things ourselves over the
years, and this is fairly easy technology – for anyone with
some capital and the determination to drive it through.'

The Ambassador, a pugnacious ex-fighter pilot, cut across
him. 'The blunt fact is this. The US is as near as damn it
militarily untouchable these days – in terms of weapons
technology. Europe, the Middle East, Russia, China are –
by our standards – all low-tech armies. Our C4 command
control and communications IT is way out on its own.
We have GPS cruise missiles, our "stealth" radar evasion
programme, F-117s and laser-guided bombs ... Then
there's the JSTARS ground-surveillance system showing
– regardless of weather conditions – anything deployed
over an area 200 kilometres square. Our multi-dimensional
warfare options include electro-magnetic pulses to screw up
enemy computers and telecoms, microwave beams, as well
as computer viruses and a bunch of anti-satellite weapons
the Pentagon don't even tell me about any more.' He looked

around at the discomfort he knew his words would have on his British hosts. 'I say all this purely because it goes to the heart of a danger which, I think, this very supremacy has thrown up. Something I've discussed with the President more than once. It's this. If our enemies can't touch us with modern weapons hardware, then sure as hell they're going to do it some other way. The *only* way they can. By tearing up the rule book on chemical and biological weapons. Dirty weapons. And *hell* . . . I think your James Barton is about to prove me right.'

'Anything more to link Barton with this?' asked the PM. He was far from happy at a Brit, and an ex-member of his government to boot, being prime suspect in what was obviously now a major international incident.

'The language and cadence of the message is English. Definitely not American,' the CIA Station Chief said. 'Take the choice of the key word they want the President to use. Coronach. No American would use it.'

Seeing the Foreign Secretary looking puzzled, Calder – a *Times* crossword enthusiast – came to his rescue. 'A Scotsman like me might,' he said. 'It's a Highlander's funeral lament. Originally. But is now used to describe any kind of spontaneous public outcry of grief.'

'And the target for this threatened attack?' The PM again.

'We think it'll be the US mainland. Any one of our big cities. America's one big gene bank for ethnic groups. Africans, Poles, Jews, Irish, Greeks, Hispanics, Asians . . .' the Ambassador replied, wiping his face with his hand.

'And what do you think?' The PM was looking at Allan Calder.

'I'd like to hear the Foreign Secretary's opinion, of course,' Calder countered, diplomatically. 'But on the information we've got I'd doubt very much that it's the

USA. Delivering what they call a warhead suggests use of a ballistic missile. And that almost certainly points to a Scud. With the shambles in Russia's armaments inventories, they've become the black market Kalashnikovs of the skies. We've frustrated the freelance sale of several systems over the last two years. But given the sophisticated defences the Ambassador described, the US is far too ambitious a target for some crude Scud attack.'

'Where then?'

'I think it will be targeted at America's conscience, not its soil. At a small country with the most hostile and difficult borders in the world.'

'That was our second assumption,' the CIA man agreed. 'We've already shared all we have with the Israelis.'

'As have we,' Calder replied. 'All the information from the labs in Oeiras. They'd anyway, over his last days, belatedly recruited Ladislas Blacher as a sayanim. And it's clear that if we don't go in hard and soon over there, then they will.'

'What about the risk of civilian casualties?' The PM had one eye firmly on his public image. TV pictures of innocents in body bags had to be avoided at all costs.

'Low. A couple of night guards at Oeiras. As for Belize, there's the house staff at the ranch, Barton's daughter Lydia, his wife, and the US citizen helping us. Tom Bates.' Calder opened his hands in a gesture that spoke volumes.

'How's this Bates guy doing?' the CIA man asked.

'He's nobody's fool, and has been pretty half-hearted from the start. But he did well for us in Oeiras, getting out some vital information. And now the balloon's really going up, we think he'll do all we ask.'

The group of powerful men sat uncharacteristically quietly for a while, before the PM at last spoke. 'The two raids tonight. They've suddenly taken on very much greater importance. I was consulted some days ago on

Lisbon's sensitivities. But I have to say that until seeing this communication with the President, I had certainly not realised what was at stake. How confident are we?' The way he directed the question now at his Foreign Secretary defined their uncomfortable working relationship. There was the implied criticism for not keeping him properly briefed. It was clear to everyone that if things went well, the credit would be the PM's alone. But if there was a screw-up by the special forces, the fault would lie squarely with the SIS's sponsoring minister.

The Foreign Secretary stood up to leave, fully under-standing the political terms of engagement in all this. 'The Chief and I have a busy few hours ahead of us. We have one of the Service's most experienced men running the ops centre for both missions . . .'

'Perry Mitchell. Yeah. I heard that. A real old pro,' the CIA man chipped in, feeling for the Foreign Secretary and trying to give him a little support.

'Yes. I understand he is. And as to the chances of success, you'd better ask me in about six hours. Have a pleasant evening. If we succeed, we'll get a message to you. If we don't, you'll doubtless enjoy watching it all on CNN.' With that he turned to leave.

Calder stood up to follow him. The angry politician he figured was either going to be the next PM, or rapidly exiled to the back benches. Hedging his bets, as he must for the Service's sake, he gave the PM an old-fashioned look, shot a watery smile to the Americans, and left. It was time to touch base with Mitchell. A lot was riding on the 'real old pro'. He just hoped he was still up to it.

The Aruba Alliance members clapped loudly, a few waving their papers in the air.

Sir James Barton gestured modestly to Tom, and sat down,

holding his hands up in mock diffidence. The two of them had just opened the meeting with a well-rehearsed presentation summarising the last quarter's treasury management successes. Using computer graphics to bring the dull figures to life, they had shown a better-than-predicted growth in earnings, on the back of strong world equity markets, and then painted a very rosy picture for the rolling year-end predictions. On the table in front of each of them had been a sealed envelope containing that individual member's statement, written in their native language, and with the dollar conversions to their own currencies.

Standing again, Barton quietened them, indicating that he wanted to continue. 'Gentlemen. Thank you for that. Thank you for your confidence. As you see, I have not let you down,' he said. 'What these figures demonstrate is exactly what I said to you when we began our relationship. That yours is one of the biggest, fastest growing and most profitable businesses in the world. Five hundred billion dollars a year. And that by structuring yourself as any other multi-national, and working to a jointly agreed business plan, you can and will go from strength to strength as a true Alliance of congruent interests.

'But this is only the beginning. The treasury management of your cash and working capital is just a building block, a foundation on which to base our wider ambitions. With that now in place, it's time already to look ahead. In the business plan I originally put to you, the key need we identified was to protect the core business from attack. You individually fight off your local market competition from other cartels, from other warlords. And my mutual aid Stabiliser agreement has, I know, been very helpful already to some of you in your own territories . . .' The men nodded. Only weeks earlier, in a turf war, one of Dino's many Mexican competitors tried to push him out, and the other Alliance members *en bloc* had refused to deal with the new man, effectively giving Dino a monopoly in his territory of quality Colombian supply, and to the money-laundering channels. With Stabiliser, Barton at a stroke had made each of the Alliance leaders feel far more secure. Something that no one else, not even their private armies, had ever given them. It was on the back of this insight into their vulnerability that he had now developed what he knew would have them cheering him even more loudly. At a price . . .

'Stabiliser helped me big. Thank you, guys,' Dino said, with a humility they had never expected to hear from him. 'And thank you, Sir Barton.'

Still he got his title wrong. 'Part of the service, Dino,' he went on, building himself up to the big news. 'But Stabiliser is not enough. You now have the biggest threat to your own security, and that of your families, that you have ever faced. In the shape of a US President determined to leave his mark on world history. As the man who made a difference to drugs. You – all of you – are his public enemy number one. Not the KGB any longer. Not the Ayatollah, Saddam or Gaddafi. Not the Vietcong. Not the North Koreans . . . You, gentlemen, have supplanted all of America's bogeymen. And all the awesome technology, power and wealth of that great nation is on the point of being channelled into bringing you down. The new taskforce has a degree of cross-border pursuit capabilities; treaties have given the US extradition rights and the power of asset and financial sequestration; and in return for trade and aid benefits, the courts and enforcement agencies of Colombia, Mexico and the rest are going to have to hit you and your businesses hard. In a word, this is *serious*.'

Caldente, the pock-marked Colombian Santander chief, raised his hand like a schoolboy. 'You're good at picking holes in our socks. But we know these things,' he said with some sarcasm. 'Are you also going to tell us what we should do?'

Barton knew that this was the member he most needed to convince. In many ways the Colombians were more worldly wise than the rest. 'I don't just know what to do, my friend,' Barton replied, raising his voice. 'I'm about to do it.'

There was a murmur of comment as the men took in what he had said. 'What you do?' Predictably it was Dino who shouted out.

Barton pressed the remote computer mouse and the text of his message to the President appeared on the screen. 'This will have caused great consternation in Washington. And in a few other capitals by now.'

He let them read it carefully. 'What does it mean?' the cautious Russian asked.

'It means that on your behalf I have – with my own money – devised and constructed a deterrent that will force the President to call off the dogs. Just as the nuclear deterrent for over forty years prevented any serious territorial ambitions from any of the superpowers, so my – *our* – deterrent will oblige the USA quietly to abandon its new fight against drugs. When the first warning attack takes place in a few hours, you will hear the President use my code. To tell all of us secretly that we've won. And the new taskforce will be a paper tiger. Thanks to this, thanks to me – you will be able to rest easier in your beds tonight. And every night.'

There was a burst of excited interchange between the members. 'What exactly are you planning to do?' the Russian pressed.

'Nothing, unless this group agrees. Agrees to pay me fairly for your own security.' He now had their undivided attention. 'I want an immediate $5 billion payment, agreed now. And 0.1 per cent of your annual combined turnover thereafter. This is approximately a further $3 billion a year.

For as long as my deterrent remains effective. In return, I fire my ballistic missile at its target tonight, fully armed with my very own brand of bio-ethnic cleansing. You will want to discuss this proposal, I know. So Mr Bates and I will withdraw. Call us back when you have reached a decision. But please, do so within an hour. Time is tight. Thank you.'

With that, Barton and Tom left the Alliance in stunned silence to return to the comfort of his study – and listen to the 'private' debate over his hi-fi speakers.

Mitchell always secretly suffered from well-suppressed nerves before a major operation. But this time they seemed worse than ever.

Perhaps he *was* too old to be fronting this kind of work any more. After all, they had put him out to grass as a recruiter. Then Calder had press-ganged him back into service, just as he himself had press-ganged so many other reluctant spies over the years. Like Tom Bates. *Unlike* Bates, though, his own life this time was not on the line. He had turned into exactly the kind of armchair general he had always hated: playing with other people's lives from a safe distance.

Bates's last snatched report had still not given them any information on where the Scud – if Scud it were – would be launched from. Or at. US spy satellites had found nothing new so far on the Syrian, Iraqi, Lebanese or Egyptian borders. Nothing in Jordan, the Palestinian areas, or in southern Cyprus ... Tom had pressed Barton hard to tell him, as proof that he really was now his complete confidant. But he had been refused. It was, Barton had insisted, water-tight, strictly need-to-know information. Given this, Mitchell now had a decision to make. In addition to Tom's report, made minutes ago from the men's room, the SAS team had also wired-for-sound the games room where the Alliance was meeting, recording the ghostly fibre-optic images of the group as they argued over what to do. The heart of Mitchell's decision was whether to order the SAS team in right now, before the Alliance agreed to the offer Barton had put to them, in the hope of preventing Barton giving the order to launch. Or risk the launch and stay with the well-rehearsed operational plan, one studiously designed to capture the Alliance group with minimum loss of life. Going in now, he knew, would have to be a crude tactical attack, with a high probability of a heavy fire-fight, and major loss of life on Belizean soil.

Neil Gaylord came over with a tea he had found for him. 'Tough call,' he said. 'What do we do?'

'No choice to make,' he said brusquely. 'Everyone out there is expendable. We go in hard. Now.' He put his headphones back on and had the SAS leader patched in. 'Major. I want you to abort the plan and go in now. Priority one, take out Barton before he can give the order to launch. Understood? Please confirm.'

'I hear you – but wait, London . . . Wait. I'm being passed new intelligence. Wait please.' The major's voice had the familiar echo and fractional delay as it bounced 44,000 miles in space to and from the geo-stationary Inmarsat. After a very long thirty seconds, he continued in his clear, slow, unemotional voice. 'Barton has already been called back to the Alliance. They had nothing really to discuss. Unanimously agreeing to his plan and his terms. He can do no wrong with them right now. But hear this, London. He's just told them that the launch is going ahead. That it was to anyway. Because he had no way of stopping it – even if he wanted to. Advise please.'

Mitchell knew it was getting away from him. If in doubt in battles of any kind, act decisively and firmly. That had always been his creed, from his own Army days. 'We go in now while they're all together—' he began, but was talked over by the major.

'They're breaking up – sorry, but . . . He's just told them to meet on the terrace later for the firework display. To celebrate early. Advise please, London.'

'No. Hold that,' Mitchell called out, the new information changing his mind. 'Original plan. Repeat. Revert to original plan. Confirm.'

'Confirm.'

'Good luck, Major.'

The man, an ex-Para in the 5th Airborne Brigade's crack Pathfinder Platoon, replied, 'Thank you, sir. The Regiment tries not to acknowledge luck in its planning. But it all helps.'

'Have you still got your special guest appearance, Major?'

'Sure have, if she shows up on time.'

'Then you're right, Major. You shouldn't need luck with *her* on your team. She'd certainly frighten the pants off me! Out.'

The mental imagery of what they had planned made him smile, despite his butterflies.

Lydia had told Maddie a loose version of what was about to happen, warning her to stay close as soon as they were called down for the firework display. That she seemed unsurprised spoke volumes for what she already knew about the state of Jim's mind.

'You and Tom certainly know how to keep a secret,' Maddie said, changing the subject. Part of her was genuinely pleased for Lydia. Another part was less generous, feeling annoyed at the way they had excluded her. 'So Tom *was* that new man you were going to tell me about. I figured that you'd suddenly got interested in him.' They were in

Lydia's room in the ranch, and Maddie sat down on the edge of the bed while she fully digested the news.

'It's not really all that sudden. We dated a few years ago, but it never went anywhere,' Lydia replied, sitting next to her, fidgeting with her bracelet. 'We were both afraid of what Dad would say, I suppose. And then a couple of weeks back, Tom called me – kind of out of the blue . . . and it just seemed to work. We were comfortable with each other. Talking shorthand. Or not talking at all. This time we weren't competing the whole time.' She did not even hint at the great sex, sensing that Maddie had been hurt somehow by the news.

Standing, Maddie turned away. 'Well. While we're sharing things, I told your father last night. About the divorce. The man I married disappeared along with all his assets. The bankruptcy changed him. Really changed him. He became driven and bitter. Those bailiffs also took away our marriage. And the twins.'

'How did he take it?'

Maddie paused before answering. How *had* he taken the news that their life together was over, that their young family was splitting? 'With complete indifference,' she said at last. 'I gave him a solicitor's letter – and today he's not even mentioned it. Lydia, he's sick. We both know it's got worse over the past year. It's as if he's just a shell. The person who used to live inside there has gone away someplace. I really do believe he has no feelings for anyone or anything. No conscience. He's your father, and I know you've always been close. But I don't recognise him any more. That – that monster is not the man I married. He's dangerous.'

Lydia frowned and looked away. Of course she knew what Maddie was saying was right, but it was something she still hated to confront. The bankruptcy and public humiliation *had* been too much, and he had fought back in the only way he knew how. In the way Banto was also responding to the unspeakable things that had happened to him. Payback. Pure, cathartic, time-honoured revenge. Maddie *was* right, of course. And the best thing that could happen now was for Tom's SAS people to arrest her father, smash the evil things he was planning – and then get him some medical help.

After a further emotional half-hour, Maddie left at last to change and Lydia, her head now spinning, went through a mental check-list of what she had to do. An inveterate list-maker, she now tick-boxed briefing Maddie. Earlier on a recce she had, as instructed by Tom, found the underground plant room. However, the claustrophobic place was noisy and smelled of nauseous hot machine oil. No way could she spend any time down there. Hunting around for an alternative, she finally discovered the entrance to the labyrinth of wine cellars her connoisseur father had built down there. That would be much better. It too could be locked inside and out, with a strong, fire-proof door.

The thought of all the potential dangers, of what could go wrong, suddenly reminded her of her responsibilities to the other man in her life. Taking out her Psion, she found the number and dialled out. It was night-time, and the old security man would be on.

'Is that George?' she asked.

'Who's this?' The Welsh accent was obvious even over just two syllables.

'It's Lydia Barton. I'm abroad. Down Mexico way. Sorry to call at this time, but how is he?'

'Oh, Oliver's just fine. Don't you worry none, miss. He howled when you left him. As usual. To make you feel bad, see? But within minutes he was right as rain. Leaving his calling card everywhere, barking to let everyone know who's top dog.'

She smiled, relieved. Tom or no Tom, Oliver remained no less important to her. 'George, I don't know how to say this, and please don't ask me anything – but I'm involved in something a bit dangerous down here. I mean, I'm just being melodramatic, I'm sure. But if anything happened to me, you'd see that Oliver was well looked after for me, wouldn't you? There'd be plenty of money to help, but I still haven't got round to putting anything in my will.'

The old man knew something was very wrong. Lydia had been taking Oliver to the kennels for over six years, several times each year for her many overseas business trips and holidays. She, and he, were popular and valued customers. 'Miss, if it pleased you, I'd look after Oliver myself if, Lord forbid, anything happened. It'd give my Jack Russell something to think about – having Ollie living with us!'

Hugely relieved, her eyes were moist at the thought of Oliver there, sleeping in his run, nuzzling the old comfort blanket from his puppy days that she always left with him. She tearfully thanked George profusely, and then began finally to think about her other charge. Yet another man now in her life.

When the shooting started, she was not happy about leaving Banto exposed in that ground-floor tool room. His place was below ground in the wine cellar, with Maddie and her. She would move him out right now, and lock him down there, while the guards were distracted on other security duties.

As she hurried on, tension mounted inside her at the thought of all she had to do. And at what was facing Tom – so much in the front line of things. Tom, the reluctant hero, on whom so much now depended.

Chapter Eighteen

Mitchell had completed the legal niceties. The Chief of Police in Lisbon, sitting with the head of SIS Lisbon Station, signed over control of the raid on the Oeiras Temple Bio-Laboratories to the SBS Commander at 17.02 GMT. Listening in over the radio links at the Belize Defence Force Ladyville barracks was Belize's Deputy Prime Minister, a role also encompassing that of Minister of National Security, Attorney General and Foreign Affairs. With him was his National Security Adviser, the BDF Chief of Staff along with the Chief of Police. Also there was the British High Commissioner, up from Belmopan. At 17.14 hours, the Chief of Police, following a last-minute heated discussion in the room, also signed over control of the San Ignacio raid to the SAS major.

SBS and SAS, through the Mitchell's ops centre, now had full authorisation to prosecute the assaults. Nothing could stop them.

Mitchell wanted Belize successfully under way before instructing the SBS to go into Oeiras. He put them on stand-by as he at last gave the operation theatre to the SAS major.

This was the drama silently unfolding when, at gone nine o'clock, Barton gathered his Alliance guests on the terrace. Vintage champagne was flowing as the guards completed another tour of the ranch perimeter, confirming that all was quiet. The men in the watch-towers were equipped with state-of-the-art night-surveillance equipment as well as radar and searchlights. And in turn the rest of the private security personnel of the Alliance members were on full alert as their charges mingled together outside, on the cloudy, starless night.

Barton seized the microphone and called for their attention. 'Alliance brothers, you have today done me a great honour, making me in effect a full partner. I will not fail you. And I pledge that my protection will be the best 0.1 per cent you ever invested. For you and your families. And so, as part now of the Alliance family, let me introduce you to my *own* family. First may I present my beautiful wife. Lady Barton. Madeleine to you all. Maddie, come over here, please!' To loud applause she walked across, looking at him curiously, shell-shocked by the man's irrepressible showmanship. Lydia had told her to dress sensibly, knowing what they may have to face later if things went wrong. She had chosen a simple black shift dress and flat velvet pumps, and his look showed his disappointment at her unaccustomed lack of glamour. 'Next, I have my darling daughter here, Lydia. Our twins are with Nanny back at the Manor. Lydie, come and say hi!'

Lydia did as she was instructed, unlike Maddie entering into the spirit of things, not wanting to create any distractions. Taking the mike she called out, 'Hi, everyone!' and waved, like some air-head game-show hostess.

'And finally, someone who's about to join my family. You know Tom Bates as my assistant. Our financial genius. Well, pretty soon he's going to become even more important to me. When he marries Lydia. Folk, please raise your glasses in a toast. To Lydia and Tom. And all the grandchildren I know they'll soon be giving me! Lydia and Tom!'

Tom took his cue from Lydia's play-acting, and with an embarrassed smile, he went over and theatrically kissed

Lydia, lifting her off her feet and swinging her round. There were cheers and some ribald shouted remark from Dino, as Barton got the four of them to link arms for a happy family photograph. As Tom's hand was releasing Lydia's he squeezed it gently, and gave her a smile several degrees braver than he actually felt.

'Now, friends, before our very special gala dinner, I have what I'm promised will be the most spectacular display of pyrotechnics ever staged. That's fire-crackers to you, Dino!' he explained, to good-natured laughter. 'Recharge your glasses, take a seat over there, and in just a few minutes – enjoy the show!'

Tom was by now plain scared. He had been given the simple-sounding mission to get Barton back in the ranch and keep him there. How exactly he achieved that was his decision, and it had been worrying him incessantly. Tricking him into the study and locking him there would not be enough. He could easily escape from the large windows, or call for help. As for knocking him senseless, Tom did not much like that as a route, figuring he would either not hit him hard enough, or far too hard, killing the man. And if it came to a brawl, with Tom attempting to tie and gag Barton, he was far from sure he would win. This was still a fit and powerful man.

Instead, he had decided the best plan of action would be to lure him down to the cellars.

Palming the transmitter behind his handkerchief, Tom spoke into it, pretending to wipe his mouth. Then he drew Barton over to one side. 'Jim,' he whispered urgently. 'Before you give the signal to start, you need to see something. Urgently.'

Barton was on a high, adrenaline coursing through him. 'You take care of it,' he grinned. 'Like a good son.'

'Not this time,' Tom replied, a worried look on his face.

'You're not going to like this. You'd better come see. Decide what you can salvage.'

'What is it? What's happened?' he demanded.

'Don't get too mad now, but there's been an accident in the wine cellars. Your sommelier just told me. Too scared to tell you himself. The place is flooding for some reason. Under about three foot of water already, and rising. You need to get a team down there and tell them which expensive vintages to get out first.'

Barton howled, 'They're *all* expensive vintages!' and started to run into the ranch. 'Come on!'

Seconds later, he flung open the cellar door, and raced down, throwing the switch to the intentionally very dull lighting. His eyes tried to adjust to the gloom. But his feet crunched on the gravel. Dry gravel, he realised, as he picked up a fistful. 'What . . .? There's nothing wrong down here!' he roared, partly in relief, and partly in anger at having his time wasted like this.

The crash of the heavy door slamming, and the rifle-shot sound of the lock being closed stopped him dead. 'Tom!' he roared. 'Tom! Get down here. NOW!'

Racing up the stairs he pummelled the door with his fists, the sound echoing through the rabbit-warren of dark cellars. But he knew it was hopeless. Tom had already noisily closed the cellar-access door to ground level. No one would be able to hear a thing. All kinds of permutations raced through his mind as he attempted to make some sense of what had just happened. Was Tom blackmailing him for a share of the Alliance billions? That *had* to be it. Money on that scale did crazy things to people. He, of all people, knew that well enough. That had to be it. That – or Tom was some kind of informer. Was he working for the police? The taskforce? Or was it one of the Alliance competitors? The Cali mob, maybe, in Colombia . . . Whatever it was, he would somehow be able to fix it. With money. With charm. It had always worked in the past. It would again now. Nothing to fear . . . He was a survivor.

Then he heard it. From one of the distant cellars behind him. The sound of feet crunching on the gravel. Wide, bare feet . . . approaching slowly.

Tom's heart was racing so much that he had to fight to seem normal when he returned to the terrace, standing by a light to show himself to the watching SAS men. This was their signal. He had already been mightily relieved to see Lydia rushing back inside, as instructed, with a white-faced Maddie. To make absolutely sure the men had seen him, he again risked a quick word into the transmitter through his handkerchief. Slipping momentarily back into the darkness he mouthed, 'Barton inside and secure. Do you read me?'

'I read,' the Major replied. 'Take cover, Bates. One hundred and twenty seconds, and counting . . .'

Just two minutes before all hell let loose. There was nothing more he could do out there. He may as well take cover himself, down in the plant room, with Lydia and Maddie. Walking rapidly back, fighting the urge to run, he already sensed confusion and suspicion growing amongst the Alliance members and their security people. At Barton's sudden disappearance, and now that of his family. 'Hey! When's the show start, Bates?' yelled Dino.

'Any second. We're just sending the crew the message to begin!' Tom shouted back. 'Take a seat. Enjoy!'

Once inside, he ran down to the plant room, and was surprised to find the door open. He had expected to have to yell at them to let him in. And he was even more surprised to find the place yawning empty inside. Letting fly a stream of expletives, he looked at his watch. A minute maybe to go! Where the hell were they? Running back upstairs he jogged quickly through ground-floor rooms, and then back to the terrace, desperately searching them out.

Barton felt as though his head was being ripped off his shoulders.

The native's baseball-mitt hands had shot out from the darkness and seized him from behind. Thrown to the ground by the unearthly power of the tiny man, Barton looked up terrified into Banto's searching stare. The native was carrying out one final check, to make absolutely sure this really was the big *kepala*. The image in the picture he had carried for so long. The face he had given to his daughter. Then, after just a few seconds more, a small smile came over his face. It was.

It was the *kepala*.

Time for Payback.

But as Barton recovered from the shock, he also prepared to attack. Banto was the height of a mere child. And seemed unarmed. At six foot two and sixteen stone himself, he was damned if he was going to be over-powered by the little warrior. It was inconceivable that this diminutive man could defeat him.

Grabbing a wine bottle with his outstretched hand, Barton whipped it viciously across, catching Banto on the side of the skull. The bottle did not break, and sent him floundering on the gravel. But now Barton deliberately smashed it against the wall and stabbed at his head with the jagged bottle neck. Banto's hand deflected Barton's arm just enough to avoid it gouging his eyes, but instead it tore deep into his right cheek, carrying a wide strip of flesh with it. Roaring in pain, the native sprang to his feet, and disappeared again into the gloom.

'Come on!' screamed Barton, pumped up for the kill, his fat arms beckoning like a street fighter.

But there was only silence from the long rows of dusty wine bins.

The two men then froze, as they heard the sound of people outside. Lydia had opened the ground floor cellar door and was leading the way for Maddie. 'Close that after you,' she called. 'And then be careful. It's pretty dark once you're in the cellars. Even with the lights on.' She then ran noisily down the stairs and snapped open the lock in the door, the sound echoing inside like a rifle shot.

Barton and Banto, both now in the shadows, watched as the outside light briefly shone in.

Barton immediately recognised them. 'Lydia, Maddie! Get out. Fast!' he yelled, rushing over to escape with them.

'Dad?' Lydia called out, shocked and disorientated.

'Jim. Is that you?' Maddie followed up.

Just feet from them now, Barton cried, 'The door. Keep the door open!' His feet slipped and stumbled in the gravel.

Banto had silently climbed on top of the tall bin nearest the door, also recognising Lydia. More confirmation that this was the *kepala*. Nestling in his hand was the only effective weapon that he had been able to find during his time alone in the cellar. But what a weapon. The jeroboam corkscrew had a spiralled, blackened draw, designed to penetrate the long necks of the huge bottles. With no hesitation, he threw himself down at his enemy. Hitting his back with his dead weight, he floored and winded Barton, and in one smooth movement pulled the dazed head back exposing the throat. The metal flashed down, sinking deep into his neck before he immediately ripped it out again. Lydia and Maddie looked on, numbed in horror, as they were sprayed with blood.

'Payback!' Banto roared, blood from his own torn cheek still pouring down his chest. Flipping over the body like a rag doll, he next sank the screw, double-handed, time and time again, ferociously, in and out of Barton's lower stomach, disembowelling him as, still alive, he mouthed silent goldfish screams.

Maddie was the first to fight off the shock rooting them both, and flew at Banto, kicking and clawing his semi-naked body, gouging at his eyes. Anything to stop him. This also got Lydia moving, and she ran forward, grabbing a bottle. The screw flashed defensively into Maddie as Banto fought her off to go in for the kill on Barton. Maddie screamed and fell back, clutching her stomach, blood spurting through her hands.

Lydia put all her weight behind the blow, and Banto dropped, his face drowning in Barton's gaping stomach.

'Nightbird. What is your ETA?'

'21.07.'

'Thank you, Nightbird. Stand-by Unit. Activate now, Now, Now!' the major called.

Immediately the searing, hugely powerful lights snapped on.

The Alliance members, mostly now sitting to watch the display, were temporarily blinded by three one-million candlepower Dragon searchlights. This was then followed up with a barrage of concussion grenades and hovering very magnesium flares, dangling on their small parachutes. Simultaneously the four watch-towers collapsed as the electronically detonated plastic explosives blew away their bases. Unnoticed, small groups of men in anti-blast gas-masks and body armour had raced forward, and as some of the more alert mercenaries and bodyguards began firing blindly at the lights, the muted sound of the Regiment's lowered velocity Heckler & Koch MP5 AZ self-loading carbines could just be heard, silencing them.

One SAS man had got himself mid-way between some of Barton's mercenary guards and a group of the Alliance bodyguards fifty yards away. Lying low, he fired a burst first at one, and then turning 180 degrees, at the second group. Each thought the other men were firing at them, and he crawled away, bullets whistling over his head, having started an intense fire-fight between two friendly groups, using up their ammunition and effectively removing them from the theatre for the first vital minutes.

Dino was the first to realise that this was no firework display, and signalled to his men to gather round and get him out of there. The Warlord's men had also already grouped, and a loud explosion told the major that one of their booby-trapped RPGs had just blown up on use. Dino's plan was simple. Reach his private jet and get the hell away. But even had he been able to get past the SAS line, it would still have proved fruitless. All the aircraft had long been immobilised.

The major's calm but firm voice boomed out from the PA they had installed. 'Hear this. You are to abandon your arms and walk forward towards the light. Hands behind your heads. Slowly. We are British special forces supporting an official Belizean police operation. You are to do as I say. I repeat. Abandon your arms and walk forwards towards the light. Now. Your hands behind your head. Do it. Now!' He then repeated the message twice in his excellent Spanish.

'Screw you!' Dino yelled using Barton's feeble PA on the terrace, and fired a burst from his machine-pistol at the lights. With that he looked around and, seeing Tom, grabbed him, the gun at his head. 'Barton disappears. His *family* disappears,' he snarled at him, his hands frisking him for weapons. 'Then all this. It ain't hard to figure what's happened here. A set-up. Well, I tell you this. If your CIA or whatever friends out there don't let me get to my plane, then I'm going to put a clip right up that smart ass of yours.' He looked down at the radio he had found in Tom's pocket.

'Hey, pretty boy. Call up your heroes out there on this thing. Tell them to call off this turkey shoot long enough for me to fly the hell out. Do it!' Pulling Tom's hair back, he shot a burst of automatic fire around his feet, clipping his right ankle, drawing blood, and then shoved the blisteringly hot barrel hard into his ass, carefully keeping Tom's body between him and the wall of light.

'Message!' Tom blurted. 'Bates. I've been taken. Being threatened. Advise. He wants free passage to his plane.'

'We see you clearly, Bates. Tell him we're considering. I'll get back.'

'They're thinking about it,' Tom yelled at Dino.

Another burst of fire, this time deliberately hitting his foot. Tom screamed in pain, staggering, but Dino held him up. 'Not good enough. There's nothing to think about. They do it, or you die. Tell them again. Last time!'

'Bates. He's going to kill me! I'm shot in the foot. Advise!'

'Stay calm and still, Bates. Which foot?'

'Left.'

'OK. In ten seconds, I'll say "go". When I do, throw yourself to your left. Hard. Do you understand?'

'Oh shit!'

'Do you *understand*?'

Tom closed his eyes. He knew what they were going to try, and he did not like it one bit. 'OK,' he heard himself say, and started counting. One – and, two – and, three – and . . .

The SAS's preferred sniper rifle is the 7.62 Accuracy International PM, but its safe distance for pin-point success is only some 500 metres. Tom Bates and the Mexican were 800 metres away, calling for the formidable American-made Barrett Light 50. Its twenty-two pounds means that the bipod stand is vital for this degree of accuracy, and the SAS marksman already had Dino in his 10X telescopic sights. The recoil pad was sitting snugly in his right shoulder, ready to absorb the sharp kick. The Barrett, a favourite with the US Marines, has an eleven-round magazine, firing massive half-inch calibre rounds four times the weight of a standard rifle bullet.

'GO!' The order was heard in the man's headset simultaneously with Tom, who flung himself to the side.

With a muzzle velocity of almost 2,000 miles an hour, the single bullet ripped a hole the size of a plate in Dino's chest, throwing him back a yard. His machine-pistol fell by Tom's bloody feet. Grabbing it, he saw one of the Mexican's bodyguards taking in what had happened and turning his gun slowly towards him. Firing instinctively, Tom sprayed bullets at the man's legs, and got in an unintended head shot, killing him.

Something new was now happening. Still disoriented, their heads and ears aching, the remaining Alliance men tried to come to terms with the strange, new sensation. A thunderous roaring noise grew louder and louder. Fierce winds were throwing papers, glasses and then even chairs around, like a small hurricane. Tom, still on the ground, partly covered his eyes, wondering what more could happen.

And then suddenly, from the swirling mists of the flares, grenades and reeking cordite, she descended from the black night sky. An experience at once awesome, and somehow mystical. The Harrier had its four nozzles down, hovering like a huge, magnificent angry hornet, the after-glow of its single Rolls-Royce Pegasus turbofan engine picked out, partly silhouetted against the searing white Dragon lights.

All resistance was immediately rendered pointless. Any vague plan of a flight to safety was dashed by the dramatic appearance of the RAF jet, her air-to-surface rocket pods sitting menacingly on the outside of her wings. This, in SAS parlance, was the sickener.

After two minutes of this, the major radioed the Harrier to withdraw so he could make himself heard again.

The pilot acknowledged, speaking into the UHF radio mictel plugged in under the chin strap of his bone-dome flying helmet. With his green pigskin-gloved hand, he pushed on the throttle to his left, nozzles partly aft, and accelerated. Almost immediately he rerotated the nozzles down to a pre-set fifty degrees and the 48-foot plane rose rapidly on a combination of wing lift and engine thrust, vibrating like a pig, before disappearing into the night. Its mission accomplished.

This time, when the major ordered them forward, they came like lambs. Any thought of air escape or armed resistance was now futile.

Tom meantime had somehow got to his feet, and was limping painfully back to the ranch to find Lydia. A couple of SAS men caught up, helping carry him. 'Barton. Where's Barton?' they demanded.

Of course. This thing was not yet over. They still had to arrest the key man. 'I locked him in the wine cellar. Help me, and I'll show you.'

They carried him down the stairs and readied themselves to burst in to the cellar. One nodded with great deliberateness to the other, and as the first man stood by the open door, the second ran in, fanning an arc with his H&K, as his partner followed through, covering another arc.

Once inside, however, even they froze momentarily at the carnage confronting them. Tom, following behind, cried out, 'Lydie!'

She looked up slowly, nursing Maddie's head in her arms like some grotesque, bloody baby. 'Sssh!' she chided. 'She's sleeping. Don't wake her. She's fine. Just sleeping . . .'

Maddie's glazed open eyes, however, told a different story.

Allan Calder poured Mitchell a couple of fingers of single malt. His man had just come over from the ops centre to make a preliminary verbal report. 'This place is supposed to be dry up here. So . . . medicinal.'

'Not far off the truth. I need something after that lot.' Mitchell added some still water and took a deep draught, feeling it gently burn his throat and slide down deep inside him.

'If I've forgotten to say it, well done. Both Oeiras and Belize went pretty well copy book.'

It was true. He had been able to have the SAS and SBS officers sign control of the two operations back to the local police exactly on schedule. The Portuguese lab had been incinerated, with no damage to life or property, the boffins having already taken all the bacterial samples they needed. In San Ignacio, in addition to James Barton, Madeleine and the Mexican leader, Dino, five guards had been killed, three of them from friendly fire. 'You know how these things are,' Mitchell replied. 'It may have gone well, but that was down to the special forces. Not me. Besides, it's not over. The Scud. The attack Barton paid for. We still have to wait and watch for that.'

Calder pushed a sheet of paper over to him. 'A Scud, sea-launched off Cyprus, struck Tel Aviv an hour ago. It hit a large parking lot, and there were no deaths. Some injuries from glass, but nothing worse.'

Mitchell skim-read the report. 'But the biological warhead? The bio-ethnic cleansing?'

Calder smiled. 'Blacher was a lapsed, but a good Jew. The Israeli scientists have found nothing lethal in the fall-out to the attack. Just some kind of advanced fertiliser. We have to assume he got to switch the containers before they were married with the weaponisation agents to make the warhead. That was his area of expertise, remember. He must have made the switch before hanging himself. A real hero, as soon as he realised what he had got involved in.'

'And the Israelis are happy to keep this quiet?'

'They'll publicly blame the Scud on Hizbollah or Syria, I expect. The last thing any of us want is to give this any publicity. Bio-ethnic cleansing . . . the threat of that particular nightmare hasn't gone away. But thanks to Barton, we now know a lot more about it. As a postscript, it won't surprise you that when the Portuguese went to arrest Rybinski at his Lisbon flat, he'd been assassinated. A single, silenced, low velocity bullet in his head.'

'Another George Bull?'

Calder shrugged his shoulders and frowned at his tired-looking old friend. 'Get some shut-eye, Perry. The written report can wait.'

Mitchell stood up to go. 'Thanks. I think I will. Goodnight.'

He was at the door when Calder called over, his glass in the air. 'To the next time, "Mr Recruiter". You chose well again.'

Mitchell thought of what he had done to Tom Bates. The American had come through brilliantly, but at what cost? He was not proud of himself for having forced him through it. 'The next time? Maybe. Only maybe . . .' he replied wearily, and left.

Epilogue

'**T**his is the *kepala*,' Banto said proudly.

Lydia did not know whether to shake his hand, curtsy, or what ... 'Pleased to meet you, sir,' she finally replied.

The old man was decked in his tribal finery, bird-of-paradise feathers in his head-band, his face and body oiled and painted. His intelligent eyes seemed to see into her soul as he spoke slowly and deliberately to Banto.

Translating, Banto smiled. 'He says tomorrow we honour you with a pig feast, and *sing-sing*. Big celebration. You get best part of pig. And also the tail.'

She somehow managed a smile back. There would, she knew, be no way out of this. 'Tell the *kepala* I am honoured. Thank you.'

Once more Banto translated and waited for his chief's reaction. The broad smile said it all, however, and the two men walked away together, leaving her alone by her lodge.

At her insistence, Banto had been released from charges for his killings. Including her father's. She argued that he had been abducted from his natural hunter-gatherer habitat, tortured and treated like a laboratory baboon. Dr Penny had supported her, telling the Belize police everything, after he was himself arrested for deportation back to the USA. Following frantic Foreign Office wheeling and dealing there had finally been a tacit agreement that Banto could be quietly returned home. That had then thrown up the next problem. Where exactly was his home? Which tribe was he? He certainly did not know in any terms that made sense to Western minds. But finally, an anthropologist in Port Moresby was able to pin-point his language and his description of his local highlands, river and forests. After that it was easy and, having travelled with him back to PNG, they then flew on together to the landing strip used by Chancey. From there he had joyfully marched her straight to his village.

The diversion, planned to take a couple of weeks, was proving a useful break for her as she somehow tried to come to terms with everything that had happened. Tom was recovering back in London, waiting for her, seemingly as keen as ever for them to move in together. Poor Maddie had been buried in the family crypt at the Manor's church, alongside James. The money – and there were still millions from her father's legitimate biotechnic business activities – would be split in his will between Lydia and the orphaned twins, now also very much to be her responsibility. As was the Manor and Chester Street.

And yet . . . what of her old life at the agency? Oliver? Her angry, passionate, campaigning work with the AFW? What of all that – now she had become a millionairess, with grand homes and a handsome, sexy husband there for the taking. And the twins – a ready-made family . . . Was this *her*? Was it what she really wanted? Or was it her father yet again imposing his life, his values on her from the grave? She had threatened once to give all his money away to her charities. But, now, would she . . .? The swirling contradictions of twenty-first century life, with all its gee-gaw material trappings crowded in on her, as she walked alone in the beautiful forest. Lost in thought, and drowning in doubt.

'What *is* the danger from the outside?' the *kepala* asked him, looking back to see that the woman was far away. 'What must we do to prepare?'

Banto looked to the ground. 'We have nothing to fear. They are weak, cowardly warriors.'

They walked on for several minutes in silence.

'And what have you learned? What can they teach us, these outsiders?' his chief finally asked.

'I have learned nothing. But maybe my spirit has. I must wait for it,' Banto replied simply. 'It is far behind, searching for me.'

The old man nodded, understanding. 'This – woman.' There was distaste in his voice. 'She owes you?'

'No, *kepala*. I had Payback.'

Again the old man nodded, the effect amplified by the tall feathers of his head-dress. Satisfied, he walked proudly away.

They never spoke of it again.